THE

TARGET

DEFENDANT

THE TARGET DEFENDANT

David Crump

QP BOOKS

New Orleans, Louisiana

Published in 2014 by QP Books.

ISBN 978-1-61027-234-6 (pbk)
ISBN 978-1-61027-233-9 (ePUB)

QP BOOKS
Quid Pro, LLC
5860 Citrus Blvd., suite D-101
New Orleans, Louisiana 70123
www.qpbooks.com

This is a work of fiction. The characters, names, events, dialogue and circumstances are imaginary or are used fictionally. Any resemblance to real persons or actual events is purely coincidental, fictitious or imaginary.

qp

Cataloging-in-Publication Data

Crump, David.
　　The Target Defendant / David Crump.
　　　　p. cm.
　　ISBN 978-1-61027-234-6 (pbk)

1. Trials—United States—Fiction. 2. Law Firms—United States—Fiction. I. Title.

PS3549.R3834C1 2014 832' .21.4—dc21
2014041390
CIP

Author's Preface

Most novels about lawyers are not about lawyers. They distort the picture. This story is different, because the main character is the American system of justice, the way it really is. The plot in a novel should grow out of the characters and their conflicts, and this one grows out of the character of American justice, which pulsates and shakes with internal conflicts.

But every story requires concessions to the demands of fiction. Real-life courtroom dramas are built on tedious work, and so a good courtroom novel requires what writers call "dramatic compression." This story is no exception.

Still, this is a story that shows reality. The critics have picked up on this, in describing my other novels. The word is, those stories show courtrooms the way they really are. And so does this novel, the one that you're reading. I've added a Postscript at the end, to describe the compromises that the conventions of fiction have required.

But now, it's time to go to court. If you turn the page, you can follow a lawyer named Robert Herrick, who is struggling to prevent the biggest case of his career from being dismissed.

THE

TARGET

DEFENDANT

1

THE MOTION TO DISMISS

Judge Marvin Raines frowned. "So, Mr. Herrick . . . why shouldn't this court dismiss your lawsuit? I mean, throw it out?"

Judge Raines glared at the plaintiff's lawyer. "The Bank is your target defendant," he growled. "The Velnikov Bank. But your claim against the Velnikov Bank doesn't involve any of the actual killers, and the Bank just did what banks always do. It took in deposits, and it lent money. . . .

"So, why shouldn't I grant the Bank's Motion to Dismiss?"

Robert Herrick's shirt was soaked with sweat. He visualized that gory building that the press had come to call "The Death House." He imagined the dead children, and he could see the blood on the walls.

The Velnikov Bank was responsible. The bank managers' stamp was on this crime just as much as the hired killers'. And the judge was about to throw out his clients' only chance for justice.

The Bank was going to get away with it.

He kept his voice even. "Judge, the Velnikov Bank took in money from depositors who actually had nothing. And then parceled it out to layers of fake borrowers that were controlled from inside Mexico. The Bank laundered money for the Balamarcas Drug Cartel."

Robert stretched his six-foot-two height upward to face the judge. Women jurors always found themselves attracted to Robert when he denounced a negligent company, with his striking blue eyes and with the shock of dark hair over his forehead. The men were impressed with his ability to speak without notes at the end of a long case and to admit the weakness in his evidence, without showing weakness.

His pinstriped suit was charcoal gray: the lawyer's uniform. His dotted tie was of the quality that symbolized success, worn by a man rich beyond imagination. But none of this mattered, because the bloody scene from six months ago flooded his mind.

"Judge, what this Bank did was essential to the operations of the Bala-marcas Drug Cartel."

"But did the Bank know that? How could the Bank have known?" The judge's head was bald and shiny, and his eyes were deep brown, almost black. Above the black knot of the tie that tucked into his black robe, his mouth was set. Judge Raines was tough on lawyers, and right now, he looked downright scary.

Jimmy Coleman was Robert's arch rival. He stood up on the opposite side of the courtroom, representing the Bank. "That's right, Judge. Nothing's unusual about a bank having depositors that it also lends to! That's the normal banking relationship."

Jimmy slapped his hand on the table. "Judge, this is the most deserving Motion to Dismiss that you're ever going to see!"

Jimmy Coleman was the head of the trial section at the mega-firm of Booker and Bayne, where an army of associates cranked out briefs to justify every harassing tactic he thought of. Normally, a dismissal was a long shot, but this Motion was supported by a dozen complicated arguments, conjured up by Jimmy's legions. Now, Jimmy's dirty grin was a mocking insult.

"Judge Raines, what this Bank did is not the normal banking relationship." Robert made himself speak confidently. "The Bank received millions of dollars from fake depositors who had no net worth, no personal fortunes. And they shifted the money through layers and layers of shadowy, empty-shell businesses. And these were the same fake businesses that helped the Cartel—the Balamarcas Cartel—get its drug money back to Mexico. The Velnikov Bank laundered money for drug dealers."

"It *laundered money?*" The judge looked at Robert with a mixture of curiosity and rejection. "But the Bank's not responsible if its people didn't know! Again, how can you say that the bank knew?"

Robert struggled to get his point across. "The Bank immediately turned around and lent the money to another group of people and businesses, and federal regulations forced it to collect their financial statements." He pointed at the Bank's officers. "These managers knew they were lending to fake borrowers, just like the fake depositors, and they used layer upon layer of empty-shell businesses to funnel the money to the Balamarcas Cartel. It's money laundering."

"Now that . . . that's just Mr. Herrick's speculation!" Jimmy sounded like sandpaper on concrete.

"Right away, the money made its way back to the Balamarcas drug lords."

"Without any action by this Bank!"

Robert shook his head. "Judge, we—the plaintiffs—have an accountant who will testify. And he will trace the money trail. It could not have happened by accident. Our accountant will show how the Bank worked together with the Balamarcas Cartel."

"An accountant can't salvage this lawsuit!" Jimmy's voice grated like hailstones in a canebrake. "This is the kind of speculation that the Motion to Dismiss was designed for."

Four other lawyers from Booker and Bayne sat behind Jimmy, each billing hundreds of dollars per hour. These black suits were overkill, because Jimmy was the only one who spoke. But the Booker and Bayne associates all smiled and nodded, now, to let everyone know how silly Robert's lawsuit was.

"Well, I understand your arguments." Judge Raines touched his laptop, and the ceiling lights reflected from his mirror-like scalp. "I'll let you know my ruling soon."

He hesitated. "But I can see that I'm in for a hindsighter in the court of appeals no matter what I decide." The judge let a tight smile show. "Oh, well. Those appellate judges can overturn my decision, but they can't make me read their order."

The lawyers both laughed politely at the judge's witticism, and they sat down.

* * *

After the judge left the bench, there were rustling sounds, as lawyers stuffed too-thick documents into too-small satchels and scrambled toward the door.

The Bank President stood up along with Jimmy Coleman. His name was Chola Velnikov: the Founder of the Velnikov Bank. He wore a purple suit with pinstripes, a purple shirt, and a purple tie—together with orange shoes. Purple and orange were his trademark. His white hair was cropped in a kind of burr cut, and his eyebrows grew together.

The purple-suited man had beamed like a lighthouse upon hearing the judge criticize the plaintiffs' case. He was still smiling.

Robert looked at his partner Tom Kennedy, the lawyer he worked with most often. Tom's voice was reassuring. "I have a good feeling. The judge can't grant the Motion to Dismiss if he follows the law, and Judge Raines is smart enough to know it."

Jimmy Coleman waddled by them. He carried a map of his life on his face, punctured by eyes so pale and dead that witnesses turned away when he cross-examined them. "Herrick, I almost hope the judge lets this piece-of-shit case of yours go ahead, because I'd like to try it in front of a jury. They'll dump you right out onto the street."

The black suits all giggled, and one of them said, "But the judge is going to be merciful and dismiss this worthless suit."

Booker and Bayne had offices in Washington, New York, London, Frankfurt, Moscow, and Tokyo, as well as Houston, and the associates were famous for heaping scorn on their opponents. Especially opponents who had sensitivities, like buttons that could be pushed.

Robert waited while the black suits passed by. Then: "Tom, I hope you're right about having a good feeling. Because I don't feel good at all."

And both of them thought back to the day when this lawsuit had begun, six months earlier. They thought about the bloody house, the death house, and the mayor's press conference. And they both thought, "How could this have happened?"

It was Tom Kennedy who finally broke the silence. "How could these murders have been committed in a civilized country? How could something happen, like what happened six months ago?"

2
SIX MONTHS EARLIER

The mayor trudged down three steps toward eager members of the press. The circle of microphones looked like the claws of predators in the blinding sunlight of August. Everywhere, cameras clicked. The building that the press had already begun to label "The Death House" was a black hulk behind the mayor.

Robert Herrick followed quietly. His face was pale and tight.

Dozens of shouted questions rang out, all at the same time. "How many bodies, Mr. Mayor?" ... "Who did this?"... "Is it one family or more?"

Feedback sang in one of the microphones, and then it was quiet, and the mayor spoke. "I'll make a short statement, and I'll take a few questions. There's a lot we don't know yet. This is going to be a long investigation. I know you understand: we just do not want to speculate at this early time."

There was a murmur from the circle of reporters. It told the mayor that on the contrary, the press wanted to hear some speculation.

"First, let me say that our hearts go out to the families of these unfortunate people who were taken from us. One of them, as you know, was a distinguished journalist, and we are all grateful for his excellent work. That's Rafael Castillo, the newspaper reporter. Our thoughts and prayers are with him and his family. We will not rest until this horrendous crime is solved."

The mayor raised his voice. "There are eight deceased persons inside this house. They include two children whose ages we do not know, but one is a toddler. There are three men and three women. Frankly, this is the ugliest crime scene I've ever seen. . . .

"The homicide division is inside now, investigating. Their work will include everything from photographs and videos to collecting blood and vacuuming for hairs and fibers. They will leave no stone unturned. And you can be sure of this: we will find the person or persons who did this and bring them to justice."

The mayor looked up at the sky and paused.

"At this time, our fine police department is keeping an open mind about this event. Every potential scenario is on the table, even the possibility of a murder-suicide situation. We do not know whether it is a crime committed by many individuals, or just one. We do not know whether it is a revenge killing, or carried out for some other criminal purpose. We do not know yet what weapon was used, or whether there were multiple kinds of weapons.

"And that is as much as I can tell you, now. We don't want to speculate, and I can take your questions, but I have to warn you: I probably won't be able to answer some of them."

The mayor was sweating more than the weather should have required. His eyes were wet. Even the reporters, who were not accustomed to feeling sympathy for politicians, could understand his stress.

The first question came from Channel 2. "Mr. Mayor, from what you're saying, it sounds drug-related. Is that one of the possibilities that the Police Department is considering? That this is a drug crime?"

"I can't confirm that. The investigation will go where it goes, and there are many possibilities." But the mayor's contorted face told the assembled reporters that the answer was . . . Yes, the mayor did think that this was a drug crime.

Channel 13 spoke next. "Do you have an explanation, then, that seems like the most likely motive for this event, yourself?"

"Well, I suppose I have theories within my own mind, yes, just as anyone would have."

There was a pause. The press waited, expecting the mayor to tell the world what his "theories" might be.

"But I cannot tell you anything about any theories!" The mayor's voice carried a hint of exasperation. "Remember, we aren't going to speculate at the earliest stage of this critical investigation. We aren't going to speculate."

Again, there was a pause. The reporters seemed to hope that the mayor would slip, somehow, and say something speculative, in spite of his determination.

And they hoped it would be quotable.

Finally the Chronicle broke the silence. "Mr. Mayor, can you tell us what this crime scene is like? I mean, you said it was the most brutal you've ever seen. Can you describe it and tell us why you'd say that?"

The mayor looked up, and the lines in his face grew deeper. He was a skillful politician, but he floundered, unable to describe this sight. The silence lasted, and then, there were murmurs from the crowd of journalists.

Robert Herrick whispered an answer. "There is blood. And more blood. There is blood on the walls and even on the ceiling." He was trying to help the mayor verbalize it.

The mayor reflected for a moment before deciding that he could say this. And that it would not be unwise to say it.

"There is blood. A lot of blood. There is blood on the walls and even on the ceiling."

The mayor's face tightened again. "The individuals standing behind me, ladies and gentlemen, are of course our excellent police chief and also Mr. Robert Herrick. Some of you may know Mr. Herrick as the well-known Lawyer for the Little Guy, and he has also been one of my trusted outside advisers. I am grateful to Robert Herrick for answering the call and consulting with me about this horrific crime."

Under the circumstances, Robert was surprised about being mentioned, particularly as a "trusted adviser." He mouthed the words, "I'll always be here, Mr. Mayor," and he added, ". . . whenever you call."

Meanwhile, it seemed that the detail about the blood on the ceiling had done the trick. It was the kind of lip-smacking shocker that the press wanted.

"I will leave it to the police chief to give you further information." The mayor turned and walked, at least figuratively, "offstage," and the reporters turned their attention to the police chief. Robert Herrick silently followed the mayor's lead. The mayor flopped onto the back seat of his long black car, and Robert joined him.

It was nine o'clock in the morning, and already it seemed like a long day.

* * *

Later that same day, Robert sat motionless in his office, with an unseeing stare.

Tom Kennedy, Robert's most trusted partner, was having trouble getting the boss's attention. "Robert, you need to work on your argument against this Request for Summary Judgment in the *Molinari* case. It's set for tomorrow. You know, the Summary Judgment the defendants want the judge to grant against us, in our lawsuit about that truck accident. The *Molinari* case."

He waited. Then: "Robert, I know you were called by the mayor this morning, and you walked with him through that crime scene. But this *Molinari* case is a completely different thing, and it's important too. It's set for tomorrow."

Robert Herrick's office was at the top of the Chase Tower. The tallest building in town. The floor-to-ceiling windows were built in a greenhouse style, and today was a beautiful sunny day. To the south, the downtown buildings rose up in spires of brown, gray, and white. To the west, Memorial Drive wound busily alongside the bayou. Its greensward pointed toward Memorial Park and then disappeared into the haze of the horizon.

"You need to work on your argument in that truck accident case," Tom repeated. "The *Molinari* case. To keep our lawsuit alive." He sat in front of Robert's big mahogany desk, in one of the three desk chairs.

The office was spacious. The furniture was spare but elegant. The dark parquet floor was covered by the most beautiful oriental carpet Kennedy had ever seen, with squares, crescents, circles, and diamonds in every color. Below the windows, a hundred geraniums bloomed in shades of red, pink, and white. But neither Robert nor Tom saw any of it right now.

"I'm . . . just not up to working on another case, after what I saw this morning." Robert's anguish was as though he had known all of the victims personally. "Eight innocent people, once living, . . . now dead. I realize, sometimes I identify with the people too much. But when it comes to thinking about a completely different case, even one that's set for tomorrow . . . I'm not up to it."

"I know you're not up to it. And I understand why. But our clients in the *Molinari* case are counting on you."

"I know. . . . Hey, Tom, how about this? Do you think you could argue this *Molinari* case tomorrow? . . . Instead of me?"

Tom had to crane his neck around a two-foot-high stack of accordion files on Robert's desk. Suddenly, he realized that all of this paper was from one single case: a pro bono suit for a small corporation that had been left bankrupt after a much bigger corporation had breached its contract. The whole office had spent hundreds of hours on this case, even though it was a likely loser, because Robert thought the client was right.

"Me, argue the *Molinari* case?" Tom's voice signaled his incredulity. "Normally, yes, but in this case, no. And you know why. It involves all kinds of engineering details about the truck, and I don't know anything about it. I'm just your coach."

"I know." Robert gazed idly toward the wall, where paintings by Mondrian, Picasso, and Wyeth hung in a row. The success of the law firm of Robert Herrick and Associates had been phenomenal. Once a one-lawyer operation, it had more than twenty attorneys now, all working for injured plaintiffs and small businesses.

There was a pause. Kennedy started to say something urgent about the clients in the *Molinari* case but thought better of it. "I realize that the death house scene this morning is affecting you, Robert. The mayor is lucky to have an outside advisor like you. An advisor who gives him straight advice."

"Tom . . . do you think . . . we could do something about the murders I saw this morning? To help that Castillo family's relatives, and to stop this kind of killing from happening?"

Kennedy sat bolt upright. "Robert! Come down to earth. We're civil lawyers. We can't do anything, not in a million years. The murderers may never get caught, and if they do get caught, they won't have any money to pay a judgment with, even if we sue the pants off of them."

"Well, that's right. I was just thinking. . . . And . . . Well, you're right. I need to focus."

Robert's weakness, Tom Kennedy always said, was thinking too much about what might be ideal. Thinking too much about right and wrong, unconnected from practicalities—and not thinking enough about finances. Still, he had to admit that the growth of Robert's practice had been amazing. Robert Herrick and Associates had more than a hundred employees, including an audio-visual studio that made exhibits and videos for use in court. And all of it had been built by Robert himself, after he had graduated from law school with nothing but debts. He had refused the big salaries offered by every big firm in town, because he'd wanted to go it alone.

Now, his firm handled large and small commercial cases along with large and small personal injury cases, almost always on the sides of individuals or mom-and-pop companies. The big-firm lawyers treated him with respect, especially when they agreed to settlements in the millions of dollars. His clients loved him, because he felt about their injuries the way they felt. He never left it to the bloodless pages of the law books.

"You're . . . right, Tom. Let's get to work on that *Molinari* case."

Several hours later, with plenty of commands from Tom to stay on the subject, Robert Herrick finally pronounced himself ready to defend against the Summary Judgment tomorrow. He poured two fingers of very good scotch from the bar in the corner of his office. And drank it too quickly. Then:

"I realize it doesn't have anything to do with the *Molinari* case, but Tom . . . do you think . . . there is any prospect that we could do anything about this massacre at the Castillo home? And about stopping all the drug murders that will probably come in the future?"

Tom shook his head. He always wanted the firm to represent more banks and insurance companies, the kind of clients who could pay the bills, but he never succeeded in persuading his senior partner.

"We can't do anything about the crime scene you saw this morning, Robert. Not in a million years."

3

EL JEFE

El Jefe, the Boss, looked out over the Sierra Madre Mountains and felt a warm, flowing spread of contentment.

There were three parts of his job that were tricky. But this event in Houston, these eight killings, helped move two of them past a cloudy uncertainty. It was nice to have Rafael Castillo dead, and all of his family.

El Jefe's "job" was to be the invisible hand behind a huge drug empire, the Balamarcas Cartel. One of the difficulties he faced, of course, was getting his sales inventory into the United States—his cocaine and heroin. But that was only his most obvious problem. The second issue, over and over again, was getting his money back from the United States. It had to be laundered first and consolidated into new cash, and then it usually had to be driven by trucks into Mexico in large bills, hidden in shipments of machines and computers. Electronic transfers were too likely to get intercepted by the DEA—the Drug Enforcement Agency. Old-fashioned vehicles were slower, but safer.

The other tricky part of his business was getting some kinds of murders done. Murders were an important part of the business. And the hardest ones to manage were the killings that were a long way away, especially in the United States, with hit men he didn't know. It wasn't that El Jefe felt anything about the people he ordered killed. It was a matter of getting it done right, with pride. El Jefe knew that when it came to his management of people, his image was as important as his business ability or his innovations in cruelty.

"*Bueno*," said El Jefe to his First Lieutenant, a man named José Luis Leyva. "Good. We've got those *gusanos*, those maggots, finally dead. Those *gusanos* from the newspaper."

"The *gusanos* in North America?" Sometimes it wasn't easy for José Luis to keep up with all of the groups that were candidates for execution.

"The *gusanos* that were in the way, yes. Disrupting our operation. Cutting into our money."

El Jefe was a man of cultured tastes, and he knew how to live well. This palace, balanced on a leveled space at the top of Colina del Pescador, his hill, let him see for a hundred miles. He lived in a ten-thousand-square foot space that had an indoor pool, an indoor shooting range, and a multi-million-dollar view. This was one of El Jefe's five houses, which were spread across Mexico, Costa Rica, and Argentina.

"Don't ever forget, José Luis, that people who spread lies about us are bigger enemies than the other Cartels, even the Marietas Cartel or the Escondidas Cartel. Journalists like Rafael Castillo are more dangerous than our competition. He was one of those news hacks who call us names and try to get the army on our backs. Rafael Castillo wrote a lot of ugly stories about the Balamarcas Cartel, and these killings were all about that. We've finally shut him down."

"Well, *Jefe,* the publicity you have put out across Mexico about the charitable operations of our Balamarcas group, our band of soldiers in this state, has been a gift from God. That's one reason our governor, our friend, visits us here at Colina del Pescador, your home."

"That, and the money, and the women. The governor likes it all." El Jefe smiled with his teeth, and he laughed.

El Jefe's black hair was slicked straight back on both sides of his broad flat face. He favored military fatigues, but they were always elegantly tailored and crisply starched. Here in his own drawing room, he wore a dress shirt with small brown camouflage spots and a green camouflage jacket with bigger spots. His trousers, sharply creased, matched the jacket. His feet were adorned with elegant brown loafers with unusual shapes, because they were made by Gucci and sold for hundreds of dollars.

El Jefe was what everyone called him in public, but his given name was Alejandro Carlos Gonzales-Huerta. Some people used his nickname: *El Más Loco,* or "The Craziest One," but rarely to his face. On the wall behind him, as he sat looking through the enormous plate glass windows in his drawing room, he kept his display pistols: relics and historical weapons. Even a gun formerly owned by Emiliano Zapata. There were two pistols that were gold-plated, and assorted other rarities. Each one rested on an elaborate individual shelf so that El Jefe could take it down, hold it, and feel it.

He favored classical music, and right now the smooth strings of Beethoven's Sixth Symphony began to weave their magic. El Jefe, or *El Más*

Loco, threw his head back and enjoyed it. Maybe he was The Craziest One, but he knew music.

"The greatest composition ever written for an orchestra!" Alejandro-The-Craziest-One told José Luis. "I'm sure you know, José Luis, that this Beethoven symphony is the one they call *The Pastorale*, with bass lines that are supposed to sound at first like sun on the meadow. And then, they blend into musical thunderstorms."

"Of course." José Luis did not know, or care, about this masterpiece, but he knew enough to go along with *El Más Loco*.

El-Jefe-The-Craziest-One listened, just listened, to the symphony for a full minute before he moved. Then, he stood up and stretched his legs. For the thousandth time, he spotted the famous words that were painted in big letters over the door to this luxurious room. He read them aloud, in the original Latin:

"*ODERINT UT METUANT.*"

And with that, for want of a wider audience, El Jefe turned to his lieutenant so that he could show off his knowledge of history, language, and culture. "José Luis, it is said that this was the motto of the Roman emperor Caligula. *'Oderint ut Metuant.'* And it means: *'Let everyone hate me, so long as they fear me.'* That's the translation."

El Jefe stretched his arms, now. "Today, they describe Caligula as the most brutal Roman who ever lived. Here's an example. Emperor Caligula once ordered his soldiers to push a whole section of spectators sitting in the Roman Colosseum onto the performance floor to be torn apart by lions, because there were no prisoners available for the purpose."

José Luis had heard it before, but he wisely pretended to be interested.

"Actually," El Jefe went on, "Caligula was a most capable manager. He knew how to lead people, and they did what he wanted. And do you know what, José Luis? His motto fits us, too. So I say it, right along with Caligula: *Let everyone hate me, so long as they fear me.*"

El-Jefe-The-Craziest-One smiled with satisfaction. He listened in silence to Beethoven before he spoke again. About business.

"José Luis, be sure that our partners who killed Rafael Castillo and his family are compensated beyond whatever the contract is. They have served our Balamarcas Group well, by getting rid of these *cucarachas*."

El Más Loco was nothing if not generous.

* * *

"I've never seen anything like those murders in that house." Robert Herrick sat with his wife in his living room, where the sunlight filtered through plantation shutters. "Not even in Viet Nam."

"It sounds unbelievable," agreed Maria Melendes, who was an assistant district attorney. "I've seen murder cases, but this sounds like one that tops them."

"The worst to see was the baby. Probably two years old." Robert looked toward Maria. For the thousandth time, he thought about how beautiful she was, with her huge almond eyes below her ringlets of red Hispanic hair. And with the pale, almost translucent skin, that showed her Cuban heritage.

Maria closed her eyes. "It had to be a drug deal gone bad. They're the only ones who do this kind of thing. I mean, killing everybody in the place, whoever happens to be there, at random, including babies who can't talk. It's a way of making their point by killing everyone."

"It had to be several people who did it, all organized, because the folks who lived there were armed. They were heavily armed. And the killers must have used guns to subdue all of them. But the murders—they were done with cutting instruments. Maybe a machete. That's what it looked like."

"Look there." Suddenly, she pointed at the television.

The screen had filled with pictures of the local news anchors, plus the weatherman and sportscaster, all wearing toothy smiles. Quickly, the camera focused on the man in the center. "Good evening, friends! I'm John Moreno, and This . . . Is . . . Action News!"

The anchor dropped his smile. Obviously there was unpleasant news to come. "The city's police force is investigating a multiple homicide on the southwest side."

Maria sat up. "Robert, this is about what we were . . . just discussing. The horrifying scene that you and the mayor saw."

John Moreno's voice rose. "For the first time, we are learning about the victims. One of them was Rafael Castillo. He was a twenty-year news reporter who did major service to this region. He broke the city hall scandal of two years ago, and he uncovered corruption in Enron Corporation before that. His most recent work was a series of articles on drug gangs from Mexico, such as the Balamarcas Cartel. About how they operate north of the border. He showed us all that the drug lords have their fingers here, in our city, much more than most people think."

The pictures shifted slightly as John Moreno smoothly turned to another camera. "This city is a major drug transshipment point, kind of a drug-gang clearinghouse for the entire country."

"So . . . the reason this entire family was killed was drugs? To shut a news reporter up?" Maria said it firmly.

"Wait. We don't know for sure, yet."

"I know." She was shaking her head in disgust.

The news anchor continued his explanation. "But Rafael Castillo was not the only victim. The dead include his wife and his children. And there were also his parents. The father and mother of Rafael Castillo. Neighbors say the parents did not live there. They just visited often."

"Yes, and they were in the wrong place at the wrong time," Maria whispered.

This was going to be one of the longer television news stories. A so-called "two-minute epic." Two minutes sounds like a short time, but it becomes a long time on the screen. Veteran newspeople will tell you that it takes a number of scene changes—actual footage of an event, or interviews, or the like—to keep viewers watching for two minutes without pushing the button on the remote.

"The Police Department has provided video of the scene at the death house," John Moreno announced breathlessly. "We warn you that these are graphic images, not suitable for all of our viewers."

The scene shifted to a hallway leading into the home. The camera panned downward from the top of a two-story entrance. Then it turned left, to show the body of a man. Part of the image had been blocked. Even with John Moreno's warning, and even with its taste for guts and gore, the television station had qualms about showing this footage. The path of the camera continued, and then it centered on the body of a woman, also edited.

"Rafael Castillo and his family." John Moreno's voice was somber. He kept up a running narrative during the rest of the camera's trip through the house, but at times he just let the video speak for itself. He was silent, for example, when the camera briefly showed the body of the murdered toddler.

"It's sensational, but I'm actually glad they're doing this," Maria said. "I see this kind of thing at the DA's office. Only a few jurors ever see it. But the entire public ought to witness how ugly murders are, without the editing, so that in this fine democracy, they can vote intelligently. Such as voting for more people who are concerned about crime."

Robert nodded. "A lot of people think of murder as a clean thing, like what Agatha Christie writes about."

"That's right. They do. But instead, it's dirty."

Maria Melendes knew what she was talking about. She lived it on a daily basis. She was an assistant district attorney, and she had an unusual job. When a convict received a death sentence, it was her responsibility to follow up. The death sentence meant nothing by itself; it always would be followed by a long chain of appeals and petitions for habeas corpus. In fact, there would be multiple loops through the habeas process. Maria's gut-wrenching task was to represent the state in pursuing the execution of the death sentence, often through more than a decade, and sometimes more than two decades, of hearings, briefs, motions, arguments, and rehearings, until the end.

Sometimes, there would be eleventh-hour claims of innocence—or of recently developed mental retardation, because the Supreme Court has told us that it is unconstitutional to execute the mentally retarded. Then, it was Maria's responsibility to evaluate these claims quickly, and sometimes, to agree with them. Or to oppose them, vigorously, as incorrect. It was a job that required more judgment than was ever comfortable.

Her responsibilities earned Maria an informal title. Everyone called her "The DA's Official Killer." She carried a Prada purse; she loved stuffed animals; and she traveled back and forth to the Walls Unit of the Texas Prison system, to see that executions were carried out.

Now, on television, John Moreno was ready to wrap up the Death House story. "Funeral arrangements will be made on the coming Monday for Rafael Castillo and his wife." And there was a sterner part of his finish. "One angle that the investigators are pursuing, we're told, is the possibility that this set of killings was an effort to silence Rafael Castillo." The anchor's voice was angry, now. "This has mobilized the police force, because it is a short distance from murders that silence the truth to the breakdown of democracy."

It was an unaccustomed lapse of editorial comment during a hard news broadcast, but perhaps forgivable.

4

THE CLIENTS

As soon as Robert Herrick stepped into the foyer of his law firm, the associates wanted to know the result of the hearing he'd just finished.

"Boss, how did the *Molinari* case go? That case about the truck collision?"

"Robert, did it come out right?"

His answer to each one was the same. "The judge didn't decide. He'll let us know soon. I can't see how he can throw out our case, but I can't make predictions."

Eventually, he made it back to his corner office. Donna DeCarlo stopped him.

"Robert, you have clients. The mayor sent them."

"What?" And then he realized. These probably were the clients he had wished for when he had talked to Tom Kennedy. Probably, they were relatives of the murdered journalist, Rafael Castillo. But at the same time, he dreaded meeting them, because he knew he couldn't help them.

He opened the door. A man and a woman, both elegantly dressed, were standing there. "Hi. I'm Robert Herrick."

"Mr. Herrick, I'm Patrick Castillo. I'm Rafael Castillo's brother."

"And I'm Anna Castillo Carter. Rafael's sister. Mr. Herrick, you were with the mayor when you went . . . to my brother's home." She hesitated. "We appreciate your . . . visit to . . . the place where he died."

"I'm so sorry for your loss. More so than anyone can imagine."

Patrick Castillo was fumbling for words. "I, I appreciate your visit too, Mr. Herrick."

"How can I help you folks? What can I do?"

Patrick shook his head. "We're not exactly sure. But we don't want to sit on our hands. We'd like to . . . do something. Something that the law will let us do."

Robert was sympathetic, but he had to tell them. "Well . . . we're all civil lawyers here. We don't know how to get someone arrested or prosecuted. The police department is pulling out all the stops to solve this case. To catch whoever did it. And I'm sure the DA's office will have the same attitude when the perpetrators get caught."

"We know about that, yes. We're here because we want to use the civil law. We'd like to sue the people behind it. The drug lords . . . who hired the killers."

"Come, sit down, please." But the reason Robert said it was that he needed to sit down himself.

"Suing a drug lord who's probably in another country? And connecting him to the murders? That's . . . beyond anything I know how to do. Even assuming you could persuade a court in this country to exercise jurisdiction over a drug lord who's in a foreign country."

Robert thought for a minute. "Let me ask you. Is there a security company that patrols that area? We could look into whether there was a lapse in the security. And possibly sue the security provider. But I doubt it would be a good lawsuit, and this firm does not file lawsuits that don't have evidence behind them."

"We know your reputation." Patrick Castillo's voice was quiet. It was also full of pain. "But we know there must have been people or companies here in the United States that helped the drug dealers. And we'd like to do something about that."

"People or companies . . . Like . . . Who?"

"We . . . don't know yet. We hoped that you . . . you could find out."

Robert knew the answer to that. A lawyer can try, and he can hope, but trying to find a shadow defendant to sue is not what a lawyer is good at.

"Well, maybe we can . . . put an investigator on it." Robert knew he sounded doubtful.

I ought to just say no, he told himself. *It would mean less heartbreak in the end, for both the lawyer and the clients.*

"We . . . would appreciate that." Anna Castillo Carter was the one who said it. "Thank you. Thank you."

She sounded as though she thought that this nice lawyer, Robert Herrick, was going to hurry to file a lawsuit that would stop drug violence for all time. At that, Robert felt an even heavier dread.

* * *

At the top of his mountain, Colina del Pescador, El Jefe spoke with a restrained kind of anger. "The governor called me. The *Federales* came to pay him a visit. You and I can do fine, if we have to deal with *Los Federales*. But the governor can't."

"Yes, that's a problem for the governor," José Luis answered softly.

El Jefe wore his usual uniform: a starched camouflage shirt under a green camouflage suit, with shiny Gucci shoes. He looked like a guerilla ready to conduct jungle warfare, except that it was all perfectly pressed.

"The governor depends on the Federal Government in Mexico City. If it were us, if we were having to deal with the *Federales*, we would give them what we call *la mordida*: a little morsel of a bribe. And the *Federales* would go away. But it's harder for the governor."

"What seems to be the reason for the *Federales'* visit, *Jefe?*"

"A bunch of unimportant people got killed in a bar near *la playa*, the beach." El Jefe frowned. "These dead people were nobody. Nothing."

Since the victims were unimportant, it annoyed El Jefe to have to think about this incident. Or to have the *Federales* nosing around. Why would they do that? For dead people who weren't important?

José Luis turned a strange color. He flinched. El Jefe noticed, and José Luis saw that he noticed.

El Jefe's voice changed. "One of the people who got killed was a young woman from Durango. The daughter of someone, I don't know who yet, in that Cartel. Our enemies, or at least our competitors, that particular Cartel. It amounts to a big pile of nada, a bunch of nothing, as far as I'm concerned, but the *drogistas* in that part of Durango are mad at us about it. They're really angry."

"And so . . . ."

"And so, the *Federales* want to try to convince the Durangans that it wasn't us who killed those people. Now, I know how these things are, when you're celebrating. It's hard to celebrate without killing a few people, especially women."

"That's right, and a few days ago . . . it was Fifteenth of Septiembre." José Luis brightened. El Jefe would understand, even if he was also known as *El Más Loco*.

September 15 is the night before Independence Day in Mexico. The celebration starts then. It begins with *El Grito*, or The Outcry, by the President of Mexico, who rings a bell and breaks out with a loud yell. The assembled multitude erupts with praise for heroes—*Viva Zapata! . . . Viva La Virgine de Guadalupe!*—and also, the people shout their condemnation of the bad guys, especially Spaniards, of course, because the Spanish were the villains from whom independence was won. The official Day of

Independence is September 16, but for the most determined revelers, the night before is the proper time for drunkenness and violence.

El Jefe smiled. "Well, okay . . . so everyone was out celebrating Independence Day. Not just our people, but the whole city. Anybody could have killed those people in Hemosillo. I guess that's what you're trying to tell me, José Luis?"

"*Exactamente*. It . . . it wasn't us." José Luis's voice wavered, ever so slightly. "We didn't do it."

"This isn't a time to lie to me." El Jefe turned away, toward his red and black billiard table, with its marble-and-gold billiard balls.

The subject was closed. José Luis knew it. Uncomfortably, he backed out of the room.

5

THE OIL PATCH

The judge has refused to throw us out in the *Molinari* case." The relief showed on Robert's face. "He's denied the Summary Judgment that the defendants asked for."

"He sure did make us feel like it was a cliffhanger." Tom Kennedy sat across the desk on a mahogany chair.

The rows of geraniums in Robert's big office bloomed as they always did, in red, pink and white. Far below the greenhouse-shaped windows, hundreds of cars moved like ants along the freeway. It was another too-hot-but-beautiful day.

"Now the real lawsuit begins in our *Molinari* case." Robert shook his head. "We get ready for trial. But there's one more thing that the judge's decision has accomplished."

"What's that?"

"The defense lawyers called me and made an offer. As they put it, 'The judge will lower the boom on us if we don't put some money on the table.' But it's a low-ball offer. These completely negligent defendants say they'll pay a hundred thousand dollars."

"A hundred thousand? For two guys with paraplegic injuries and one with the loss of an arm? It's ridiculous."

"Of course it is. But you know what happens. I talked to our plaintiffs and went back with a counteroffer. I told them the plaintiffs will take fifty million dollars to settle the case."

"And the dance begins." Kennedy nodded. "It's like a game of charades. Everybody comes closer. But they won't settle it for a realistic amount until the trial is a few days off."

"Right. But still, I'm glad they've offered this puny hundred thousand, because now the negotiations can start. And later, they'll come up with something a whole lot better for our injured guys."

The big-firm lawyers who settled multimillion-dollar cases with Robert had a nickname for him: "The Baby-Faced Assassin." He looked at least ten years younger than his age, and he beat them in trial like an assassin. Now, like two polished spheres of sapphire, his eyes flashed with determination. He would make sure that the *Molinari* lawsuit turned out right.

A moment later, he looked out the window toward the descending sun. "By the way, Tom," he said finally, "on a completely different subject, you remember the *Castillo* case? That horror of a case where someone—somebody who's not been caught yet—murdered those eight people?"

Tom looked startled. "Of course I remember it."

"Well . . . I finally put one of the investigators onto it. I sent Chipmunk to go find out what he can about who's behind those murders."

They both knew that this particular investigator had earned his nickname as a teenager, because of his big, puffy cheeks. Now, years later, he still was known as "Chipmunk." "I don't even know his real name," Robert mused.

"Come on, Robert. We'll never get anywhere with that Castillo case. You'd do better volunteering us all for the police force."

"Chipmunk came to us after a long career at the DEA. The Drug Enforcement Agency. If anybody can find anything, it's Chipmunk."

"What on earth is he going to do?" Kennedy's face was cloudy. "We should have told Patrick Castillo and his sister Anna the truth. We should have said, we can't do anything."

"I tried telling them that. But in answer to your question, Chipmunk left this afternoon for the Rio Grande Valley. He flew to Laredo, and he ought to be getting to his destination in the oil patch right about now."

"Laredo? Why?"

Robert smiled. "To meet with an old buddy of his from work."

* * *

At this exact moment, five hundred miles to the south, the man with the bulging cheeks was nosing his rented Ford pickup along a gravel road, located thirty miles from the City of Cotulla, Texas.

Cotulla, he knew, was ground zero in the shale oil revolution. It was the center of the famous Eagle Ford Formation, where well fracking technology had freed reserves of oil and gas that had been unimaginable a few years earlier. Cotulla shook with the continuous grinding noise from eighteen-wheelers carrying drill pipe, drilling mud, and oilfield machinery, but it was the sound of new and exploding wealth. The oil boom had built a dozen hotels in a couple of years and brought a continuous crowd of contractor pickups to every freshly minted restaurant, at every lunchtime.

Suddenly the gravel road ended, and Chipmunk eased onto a rocky drilling pad. He jammed the gearshift into park. The oil exploration rig rose in front of him. Around him, the hollowed-out square of ugly earth that surrounded the rig looked like a red-and-white moonscape, plopped into the scrub-oak-and-mesquite vegetation of the Rio Grande Valley just north of Laredo, Texas.

"Hi. I'm Chipmunk. Where's the boss man? You know, the guy who's called the 'toolpusher' on an oil rig? The boss. The toolpusher."

The man he asked was the first man he'd approached. The man was wearing a red hard hat, a dirty T-shirt from the Hard Rock Café in Las Vegas, and a wooly mass of facial hair that was difficult to distinguish as either a beard or mustache but was probably both. "The boss man? He's mad about what happened today to the drill bit. The bit just flat broke off. He's so mad, in fact, that he's sitting in his pickup, so he can turn up the air conditioning."

The bearded man's grin was missing an incisor or two. "So, my beloved boss, the toolpusher, is over there." And he pointed.

The drilling rig towered above the blanket of mesquite scrub. Way up on the top deck, roughnecks struggled with the dangerous job of pulling the pipe. Chipmunk looked up and saw the tedious work that the broken bit had made necessary. Drilling mud was all over the metal surfaces of the pipe, so that it alternately gleamed and blackened. Down below, more of the crew struggled to crane the pipe out. Along the crisscrossed rails of the derrick, a row of mud chains hung like fringe on a western coat.

Chipmunk found the tool pusher sleeping soundly in an enormous maroon pickup: a Dodge Ram with what seemed like acres of chrome trim.

"Tar Man! Tar Man!" There was no difficulty in guessing where this tool pusher, formally called George Pitts but now known to all as "Tar Pitts," had gotten his nickname. "Hey, Tar Pitts. Tar Pitts! I'm here, you lazy bastard!"

Tar Pitts shifted, then opened one eye. He sat up a little. "Screw you, Chipmunk." But George-Pitts-the-Tar-Man smiled when he said it. "I'm the tool pusher on this rig. That means, I'm the boss. Show some respect."

Chipmunk shook his head, "Remember when we worked for the DEA? You look about as wide awake as when we wasted the whole night chasing that buy-burn case in the slums underneath Chicago."

And both of them thought back to the long series of stakeouts they'd done for the Drug Enforcement Agency on a littered street lined with cardboard-and-plywood hovels, smack in the middle of the South Side, trying to catch a glimpse of whoever had shot and almost killed a fellow DEA agent. The bad guy's motive was to pull off a buy-burn, which meant that he wanted to rip off both the money and the five pound block of heroin that the money was supposed to buy. The guy, whoever he was, had succeeded in getting both, and then he had gotten away.

"I left that life." Tar Pitts stretched. "It's been more'n two years since my time at the DEA. The only kinda guys they had working there was sorry-ass crackers born in trailer parks and raised by half-naked pork mamas. Like you, Chipmunk."

The man with the puffy cheeks slung his big frame into the passenger's seat. He closed the door fast, to seal out the Texas heat. "What's going on here with this rig? It's not making any money. You pulling the pipe?"

"Yeah. The bit got busted off. This is a dumbass company I'm working for. It bought us this real cheap pipe and a burned-out bit. I mean, this bit's got most of the diamond wore off, anyway. We're gonna have to fish the thing out. We'll lose the big part of a week, jacking around to shoehorn that blasted bit out."

"Sorry."

"Yeah." Tar Pitts yawned. He sounded weary. "So Chipmunk, I hear you got a new case. Not a DEA case, but maybe involving some a them there controlled substances that the underground folks love so much."

"That's right."

"Only it's a case where your guys can make a cool hundred million in a civil court. Right?"

"I wish." Chipmunk laughed. Then he was serious. "Anyway, Tar Pitts, You've had some time to think about the situation I told you about. They've got eight people knocked out, all from the same family, including babies. I saw the pictures, and it's a cruel scene. Got to be dopers who did it."

"I thought about what you called me about. For about two minutes, and then I realized I'm not a DEA station chief in any more. I'm off duty." Tar Pitts acted like he was going to clam up. "I'm ... whaddaya call it? Incognito. Incommunicado."

Chipmunk just waited.

"So, in that two minutes I spent thinking about your case, . . . yeah, I guess I had a few ideas about who mighta helped on this side of the border, and about who on the other side mighta told 'em to get it done."

Tar Pitts looked at his watch. "The sun's going down. Nothing I can do here that's any good. Let's glide into that big metropolis of Cotulla, where they got this beer joint that respects us oil field trash. Place called Yokohama Mama's—yeah, I know, it oughta be named after Luisa Martinez or Yolanda Soledad in this part of the country, but that's what it's called, Yokohama Mama's—and I'll give you a coupla loose suggestions. While we work together at gettin' blotto, like old times."

6

DIFFICULTIES IN SIERRA MADRE

José Luis, things are happening that displease me." El Jefe, Alejandro-The-Boss, also known as The Craziest One, did indeed look very displeased.

"I know, *Jefe*. But tell me what's wrong."

"There was this *aeronave,* this airplane, that we had stolen to bring home our hard-earned money. It crashed, right near here, in Hidalgo. With all of our money on board."

El Jefe wore his favorite outfit, his camouflage jacket and tailored trousers over his starched camouflage shirt, and a shining pair of Guccis. Behind him on the wall, his priceless collection of novelty weapons and historic pistols gleamed. In front of him, through the plate glass window, he could see the Sierra Madre Mountains for a hundred miles.

"I know, *Jefe*." José Luis was hesitant. "That aircraft had more than five million dollars."

"And what happened, is that the villagers all went out to the aircraft, before we knew about it. They ignored the dead bodies, of course. They looted the aircraft. They stole our money, which is ours. I want it back."

"How do we get it back?"

"Think, José Luis! Go to the village. Tell everyone you see that El Jefe is unhappy with what these maggots did. The Jefe wants the money back. All of it. Or else, El Jefe wants their blood. Everybody's blood in the whole town."

"*Sí, Jefe.*" José Luis was relieved, because he knew how to do this. "It will be done."

"But that is not all."

"What else, *Jefe?*"

"The police in *Norteamerica* have arrested two police officers. Police officers! And that goofy police department arrested them instead of just asking for a cut of the money, the way any civilized police department would do."

"This is news to me. What was the cause for the arrest?"

"These police officers—our police officers—were escorting a mixed bag of *drogas* across the city. It was a good operation. The heroin and cocaine were in the trunk of a 1980 Chevrolet, which was being towed by our driver, who was in a tow truck. At least, we thought he was our driver."

José Luis waited while El Jefe shook his head.

"The problem is, it turns out that the tow truck driver was not our driver. He turns out to have been an undercover officer himself. He gave the officers, our officers, a thousand dollars to divide between themselves. He called in on a secure cell phone, and the police department comes in and arrests our officers. They are indicted, now, for bribery."

Again, José Luis waited.

"So, we lose the thousand dollars. Our money . . . money that we earned by hard work. And the worst thing is, we lose thousands of dollars' worth of *drogas* too."

José Luis had an idea. "Do you want to take out the undercover policeman who turned them in, my *Jefe?* There will be no evidence of the bribes, then."

"No, José Luis, of course not. Kill a police officer in the United States? That way, we bring down the entire United States legal system to look for revenge against us."

José Luis was silent. El Jefe might be crazy, and he might even qualify as The Craziest One, but he wasn't stupid.

A porter in a white coat brought in an encrypted telephone. "*Jefe,* it is Chola Velnikov calling you. The Bank President, from *Norteamerica.*"

"Yes?" El Jefe spoke in perfectly accented English. ". . . All right, Velnikov. This shipment of money, in the airplane that crashed, is it insured? . . . Yes? . . . But only partly, with a huge deductible, you say? . . . Well, let's collect on it."

If he could get the insurance money and also get the cash back from the villagers, as he expected, El Jefe would be twice as rich from this disaster. El Jefe was a businessman.

"Oh, well, Velnikov, you've done a great job. Whether we get the insurance or not, we've got that maggot Castillo out of the way. He's as dead as a ghost, and that's a good thing. . . . I know, I know, Velnikov, you have to keep distant from killing Castillo, but it's just you and I who are talking here, and of course we both know you were into killing Castillo, all the way, back then. . . . You've graduated into as much a stone assassin as I am. All right. . . . All right. . . . So, get to work on it and collect the insurance for me. . . . So long. *Hasta luego.*"

El Jefe turned to José Luis. "The one good thing," he said contentedly, "is the operation where we took out that newspaper reporter. The maggot who was writing those lies about us."

* * *

Inside Robert Herrick's office, Tom Kennedy shook his head. "Chipmunk hasn't come up with very much."

"I know."

It was a beautiful day, with puffy clouds, and the sun illuminated the entire green stripe of Buffalo Bayou outside the greenhouse windows. Inside, the huge oriental carpet shone in a riot of colors, and the geraniums bloomed.

"There's these two police officers who took bribes to escort that shipment of heroin," Kennedy went on. "But we can't tie that incident to the eight Castillo murders. We also can't tie it back to any particular drug cartel. Best candidate is the Balamarcas Cartel, but we don't have any evidence."

"I know."

"Chipmunk's information is based on what the DEA thinks, and according to the DEA, this one particular Bank—a Bank called the Velnikov Bank—is laundering money for the Balamarcas Cartel. For the head of the Cartel, some guy named Alejandro, but everyone calls him El Jefe because he's 'The Chief' of the Balamarcas Cartel. But there's not much evidence about the Bank doing anything wrong, either. Still, the DEA is pretty sure the Bank is laundering money for the Cartel, and maybe you could even say they '*know*' the Bank is doing it, but proving it—that's a whole different thing. And they can't prove it."

"I know."

"Robert, we need to do what we should have done in the first place. We should have told Patrick Castillo and his sister the truth. There's nothing we can do about these drug murders. The police department is pursuing it as hard as they can, and the prosecutors are ready to push it too, but we're civil lawyers."

"Well, I tend to agree. . . . But there is this one long shot, this Velnikov Bank, and it's like what you said. The DEA thinks the Velnikov Bank is working with the Balamarcas Cartel. And laundering the Cartel's drug money."

Kennedy frowned. "But Robert, don't you remember all those conspiracy cases from law school? Providing services to a criminal isn't a crime, even if you think he's using it to commit crimes. Being a bank and having a criminal deposit money with you and take out loans isn't illegal. Remember that famous case in criminal law class where the defendant sold sugar to a moonshiner? And it was so much sugar that the courts all agreed, the defendant must have known that the moonshiner was using it for, well, exactly what he was using it for, namely, making illegal whiskey. And the courts all said, no crime. Selling a lawful, legal commodity or service isn't normally a crime, even if you know it's going to be used in a crime."

"Well, you're probably right. It's a long shot. But then, if this Bank was laundering money for the Cartel . . . if . . . if . . . and if we can tie it to the Cartel, and if we can show it was an essential part of the Cartel's operation, that they couldn't do without . . . if . . . if . . . then maybe . . . maybe . . . ."

"Too many ifs," Kennedy said flatly. "This Bank—what's it called? 'VEL-nee-koff' Bank—isn't a very good defendant to target in a case like this."

"You're probably right. But . . . I've already sent Chipmunk over to the VEL-nee-koff Bank to nose around a little bit. So. . . . Maybe, maybe."

Kennedy stared at him. He remembered: Robert had asked, again and again, "Isn't there some way we can do something about these drug murders?" And now, he was trying to do something, even though there wasn't anything there. "Not in a million years," said Kennedy softly. With resignation.

As if to emphasize that point, Donna DeCarlo's voice came over the intercom. "Robert, there's a telephone call for you. It's that guy you'd rather not talk to. It's Jimmy Coleman, with the law firm of Booker and Bayne. Sorry."

"Great. Jimmy Coleman." Robert switched on the telephone and tried to sound cordial. "Hello, Jimmy. Tom Kennedy and I are here and you're on speaker. What can we do for you? How can we help?"

"You can get your crazy investigator to stay the hell away from the Velnikov Bank, that's how!" The gravelly voice was unnaturally loud. "This guy you sent, he interrupted everybody's work at the Bank. Turned the whole place into a madhouse by asking a million crazy questions. He's cut into the profit of my good client."

Robert knew what Jimmy meant by referring to his "good client." It didn't have anything to do with the Bank's being a model corporate citizen. It meant that the Bank paid millions of dollars a year to Booker and

Bayne, always paid it on time, and never questioned the bill. And in return, Booker and Bayne bailed the Bank out of the legal consequences that came from the Bank's shady deals.

"Jimmy, that's not the reaction I'd expect. All my investigator did was to ask questions. You and I are both in the business of asking questions."

Jimmy answered with an unprintable expression. Then: "He made it clear, this investigator did, that he was asking questions to prepare for a potential lawsuit."

"That's what we usually do in this office." Robert's voice was steady. "We don't hide what we're doing. We think it's fair to the people we question, to let them know the purpose."

"I'll tell you what, Herrick. If you file a lawsuit against this fine Bank on some phony ground like this investigator was suggesting, something off-brand like laundering drug money, which this Bank isn't even close to doing, you'll get dumped out of court so fast you won't even have time to read the Motion to Dismiss. And then, you'll get a Motion for Sanctions, and the court will collect a fine from you personally for filing a frivolous suit!"

An explosive click from the other end of the line told them that the conversation was over.

"Charming," was Robert's reaction, after he got over his surprise.

"Well, Jimmy Coleman's not into courtesy. I'll grant you that."

"No, he's not."

"But he's right." Kennedy's jaw was set as he stared out the window. "This lawsuit you're thinking about isn't just a long shot, Robert. It's a shot that doesn't have a chance." Kennedy shook his head. "Not in a million years."

7

THE TURNCOAT WITNESS

José Luis knew that something was up. He was not surprised when he got the call that he dreaded. It wasn't easy, being El Jefe's right hand man.

"Ola, Hermano!" It was Rico. His friend from so long ago that neither one of them could remember. "I have bad news, and I am calling to warn you."

"What?" José Luis felt his pulse race.

"El Jefe does not know that we go way back, you and I. He cannot know."

"Yes. My father and mother took your entire family in when you and I were children."

"And I owe you. But we both work for El Jefe. I am risking it all, to tell you."

"What is it?" All of José Luis's breath left his body.

"El Jefe has to take action. He has to. He has to do it. The Escondidas Cartel demands a piece of blood. The Escondidas *capitan*—you know, their Jefe—well, that guy's brother's daughter got killed in Hermosillo. And the rumor is, our guys did it."

"That is a pretty good rumor," José Luis whispered.

"The rumor also is . . . also is, José Luis, you were there."

José Luis was silent. He tried to speak but he couldn't.

"The Escondidas capitan, he demands a piece of blood. Or else he will take it—he will take a piece of blood. El Jefe is able to respond if that happens, of course, by taking his own piece of blood from the Escondidas Cartel. But that would interfere with business. Neither side wants to go to war."

José Luis just waited.

"And . . . and . . ."—this was difficult, obviously, for Rico to tell him—"And El Jefe, who does not know about my history with you . . . has told me . . . . He has told me to 'visit' with you, José Luis."

"To . . . to . . . ."

"To kill you, José Luis. But I cannot."

There was a long silence.

"Listen, Hermano, my brother. I can see only one thing for you to do."

José Luis tried to say, "What is it?" But he made a croaking sound instead.

"You will have to turn yourself in to the *Policía*."

"To the *Federales?*" José Luis was dumfounded at the suggestion.

"No, no, Hermano! That would be suicide, to talk to the Federal Police here. Worse than suicide; El Jefe would make sure that you got chopped, and spindled, and burned. No, no. Not the *Federales!* You must contact the DEA, the Drug Enforcement Agency, in the United States."

"What?! That's crazy," José Luis mumbled.

"It is not crazy. It is the sanest thing you can do! Hermano, por favor!"

"And I suppose you are going to tell me to do it quickly. In case someone else finishes the job, my Rico, that you do not finish."

"Yes. Yes! You had better not even visit your hacienda. And one reason why you should do it now—this minute—go to the airport, now, and fly away, Hermano—one reason why that is so, is that otherwise, the dead man is me, Rico."

* * *

Three days later, Robert Herrick sat at his big mahogany desk, overlooking the greenhouse windows and the green, green view to the west.

"Chipmunk says we might get a break. We might turn out to have something to say against the Velnikov Bank after all."

"Oh, yeah?" Tom Kennedy was intrigued, but his skepticism was showing.

"Chipmunk went over there, and nosed around like I asked him to, and the guys at the Bank are nervous."

Kennedy frowned. "And from that, he thinks there's a case?"

"No, no. The Bank security man stonewalled him. And he asked to see the President, and the President wouldn't meet him. It was some sort of Vice President he met with. They have a dozen Vice Presidents, and this was somebody who worked in Human Relations, about as far from the Bank's finances as you could get. He was nervous, too."

"Well, that and a dime won't even get you a cup of coffee these days."

"I know. It's not what Chipmunk found at the Bank."

Kennedy's eyebrow snaked into a question mark. "Okay, I give up. What is it, then?"

"There is some sort of turncoat witness that the DEA has found. Somebody inside the Balamarcas Cartel. Someone who can spill the beans, and not just spill some of the beans. Chipmunk says the DEA thinks this guy can spill all of the beans. His name is José-Luis-Something."

Kennedy shook his head. "Well, it's a wonder. . . ."

"That we found out about this witness?"

"No." Kennedy shook his head again. "It's a wonder that this alleged witness who can spill all the beans is alive. If he is. And it will be a wonder if he says that way."

* * *

Even if there was big news in the Castillo Death House case, even as big as gaining a new witness who could prove the entire case, that fact didn't excuse Robert Herrick from family traditions. At least once a month, the entire Herrick clan gathered. Tonight, everyone was here.

And Robert cooked. Just as he was doing now. "It's Truit aus Amandes et Creme," he explained. And he mugged a little, to make himself sound bilingual.

"I guess that means trout with almond and cream." Maria laughed at him. "If you can speak French."

"It means trout with almonds and cream even if you can't speak French."

"I don't suppose you had many occasions to make prepare fancy trout back in Viet Nam, when you were a cook in the army?"

"You'd be surprised. Not for the enlisted men, but the officers' mess." He smiled. "But not very often. Remember, I was infantry until I got shot near the DMZ, way up north. Commander of Alpha Company, in Eye Corps."

"Shot? You got scratched," she teased.

"Good enough for a Purple Heart, and it sure did hurt at the time."

A voice came from the living room. "We're hungry!" And another voice said, "What's for dinner? Anything?"

"All right! Everybody sit down."

And now, the clan descended on the table. First, there was Pepper Herrick—you'd better not call her by her given name, Cynthia—and she sat by custom next to her father and next to her new husband, Jonathan. Rosalie, Robert's mother, was at the other side of the table, next to the high chair for little grandson Robert III, known as Robert Three, and beside him, there was Robert's son Robert Jr., who was called Robbie to minimize the confusion. Maria sat at the end opposite from Big Robert, as he was known.

"So, Robert, you had some good fortune today. A witness?"

"That's right. We don't know yet what he's going to say, but we hope it's helpful."

"Rosalie, you just never know." Maria was the voice of caution.

Maria Melendez had made it from Cuba to Miami at the age of twelve, unable to speak a word of English. Her father had been the respected Director-General of the hospital at Miramar, until he got crosswise of the communist health care administration. As soon as he was able to bribe his way out of Castro's jails, he hustled his family out of Cuba on a raft that was little more than an inner-tube contraption.

She smiled. Robert looked at her. She was beautiful, with ringlets of red hair and alabaster Hispanic skin. Now, she was serious, as she said, "But you know, I've always found that it's best to approach a witness with optimism rather than skepticism. Not with 'Tell me whatever it is you think you know,' but with the attitude, 'I know you can tell us something important about this, because you know it well.'"

Maria's father, when she was a child, had settled into a small bungalow in Hialeah, near Miami, and her mother had changed from a proud society lady to a domestic servant at a hotel. From there, Maria had followed a strange path to her job today as an assistant district attorney, because her first permanent position had been as a showgirl in Las Vegas.

Robert loved to tease her about that. He kept a picture from a newspaper feature story that showed Maria in a blue bustier, tiny skirt, blue feathers, blue eye shadow, blue eye liner, blue lashes, unidentifiable other blue eye makeup, blue heels, and a mountain of hair, which fortunately was her normal red color. The caption read, "The showgirl turned prosecutor: Assistant District Attorney Maria Melendes."

"No, Robert," she would say to him, "we were not exotic dancers, as you love to pretend. It was a family show! We were like the Rockettes." And both of them would laugh.

Today, she handled witnesses of all types, from forensic firearms experts to frightened teenagers, from survivors of unthinkable crimes to turncoat hit men, and Robert always listened when she had something to say about the subject.

Like now.

"The best opening with a witness you meet for the first time," Maria went on, "is to give lots of compliments. And to project confidence." She nodded as she said it. "You've got to stay skeptical in the back of your mind, of course. The witness is almost certain to tell you something that's wrong, or even lie about it. But . . . the best approach is optimism."

Robert stared at her. She was right, he realized—this advice was not always correct, but what she was saying was more likely to work in more situations than any other approach, even if he wouldn't have been able to verbalize it himself.

Okay, so that's how he needed to approach this new witness, José Luis. He would naturally disbelieve a witness so immersed in a culture of violence and deception, but . . . he would start with optimism. He would discipline himself.

"I know, this case isn't just a lawsuit for you, Robert." Her tone was skeptical. "This is a quest. An adventure worthy of Don Quixote, and it'll absorb all of your energy, all of your breath, so that I'll only see you when you're worn out. And since you'd never listen to me about the disadvantages, I can only say, 'Here we go again.' And so, here . . . we . . . go . . . again."

"Well, I'll keep my life within reason." He realized how lame he sounded. "I'll always have time for what's important, especially . . . you."

And he stared at her, wearing jeans and a T-shirt instead of a blue bustier, with little heels instead of shoe-biz tall ones, and he discovered for the hundredth time how beautiful she was. She saw him looking, and she smiled with full lips and perfect teeth. He felt that familiar puddle in his stomach, the way he always did.

8
THE SUBSTITUTE

Nobody wanted to tell El Jefe about José Luis and his quick departure. A dozen men went to the top of the mountain to see the Boss, all in a group, so that the responsibility could be shared. And maybe diluted.

"*Jefe*," one of them began. And then he hesitated, looking down at the floor.

Then, another man spoke. "There is bad news."

This method of telling the story, by a kind of message chain, had not been arranged. It just sort of happened.

El Jefe looked up sharply. He saw the group, all twelve or so in a line. And he said, quietly, "Tell me."

No one spoke.

"What is it?" El Jefe's voice was still quiet, but now, it was impatient. "You big strong men! You look like *NorteAmericanos*. A bunch of wimps. Are you guys here to ask for a raise or something?"

As timid as they were, the wimps all laughed at that. Nervously.

"It is about José Luis." Another man spoke, who had not spoken yet.

"Tragic," said El Jefe, who expected to be told the news that poor José Luis was dead. "Tragic," he repeated. "Poor José Luis."

"José Luis is gone." A fourth voice from the crowd.

"Gone? Yes, I imagine he is gone." El Jefe nodded.

"As best we can determine, yes, he is gone, because he left by Aeronaves de Mexico. The big Mexican domestic airline."

It took a minute for El Jefe to process this unwelcome news.

"What?"

Another voice. "Jefe, there is a rumor that he has . . . defected."

"Gone to *NorteAmerica*."

"And to the DEA." Yet another voice.

Now, El Jefe's attention was focused. This was dangerous. Very, very dangerous. It would be difficult to trace José Luis, and more difficult to kill him. The DEA was not like the *Federales*. Not nearly so civilized. They would have José Luis hidden, and they did not take bribes, not usually.

El Jefe snapped to his senses. He couldn't look weak, not in front of all of these men. He shifted his concern.

"You two, come here." He pointed to a couple of men, who tried to blend into the woodwork but were unsuccessful at looking inconspicuous. "The rest of you can go. You've told me what you needed to tell me. But you two—yes, you two—come here."

After ten men shuffled out, with just the two designated followers in the room, El Jefe turned to some unpleasant business. "The most immediate problem I see is that José Luis's body was supposed to be turned over to the Escondidas as a peace offering for his involvement in the murder of that woman. So . . . you two will carry out what needs to be done."

"Yes, . . . *Jefe*."

"We will have to have a substitute. It will require a public display, in downtown Hermosillo, not just a disappearance. You will need to . . . 'visit' . . . with another one of our group here, to show the Escondidas that we are peaceful."

"Yes, *Jefe*. And who is it that we must . . . visit?"

El Jefe did not have to think about it. The substitute peace offering would be the man who was designated to kill José Luis, but who didn't get the job done. "Rico," said El Jefe. Calmly. "Rico."

The two men shifted uncomfortably. They knew Rico and had known him for years. But duty was calling, and they did not argue.

"Oh, and make it look like a big party," El Jefe added. The two men nodded, awkwardly. They knew what that meant.

* * *

Back in the United States, Robert Herrick drove his antique Duesenberg toward downtown. This was a stretch of Highway 59 that the locals called The Southwest Freeway.

Maria sat next to him. "I always feel like Cruella De Vil riding in this car, your old Duesenberg. You know, the evil, evil villain in *One Hundred and One Dalmatians*. Cruella wants to make the Dalmatians into fur coats. And she has a burgundy-colored car just like this, with open seats and with exhaust pipes sticking out along the sides."

"They're my one indulgence, these old cars." Robert looked with satisfaction over the bulging, curved hood of the Duesenberg. Underneath it, twelve cylinders stroked in perfect synchronization. It was expensive to keep this car tuned right, but when it was, the twelve cylinders sounded so much better than six. They blended in a purr that was louder and yet lower-pitched, and to Robert more satisfying, than any of his nineteen other cars, from the Testarossa to the '38 Packard.

"Your *one* indulgence?" She laughed at him. "There's also the vineyard. And the winery, up in Brenham. And your collection of first editions in the library at home. And, well, the chamber orchestra that you set up last year. And your sponsorship of Big Brothers Big Sisters, and the Women's Center, and. . . ."

"All right. All right. I probably should have called the cars my 'biggest' indulgence."

He grinned. His 1931 Stutz Bearcat had a fold-down windshield and a rumble seat. The 1930 Bentley was the favorite of James Bond at one time, Agent 007, and Robert had one that was dark green. His 1930 Cadillac had an incredible total of sixteen cylinders that warbled like a bird but got eight miles to the gallon.

Actually, he sometimes was reluctant to spend money for these luxuries because he didn't want to act like the rich and powerful people he disliked. But these beautiful old cars were something else. He had added onto his garage three times. "And it's got better temperature and humidity controls than you'd have in a wine cellar," he mused.

"I guess my favorite, believe it or not, is my 1963 Lincoln Continental. I don't drive it a lot, but what's fun is to watch the convertible top go up and down."

She just laughed at him.

"Anyway," he went on, "you've seen it. But to me, it's magic. First, this flap comes out, and these two screws stick up and start twirling, and they push out the ragtop, and they retract, and. . . ."

Her iPhone rang and startled both of them. It seemed unnaturally loud.

"I've got to take this." She pursed her lips and waited. "Yes, Mr. District Attorney." She waited some more.

"Yes," she said finally, with a mixture of excitement and dread. "I'll be right there."

She turned to Robert. "We've caught at least one of the killers. The ones who killed those eight people in the so-called 'Death House.' They've arrested a Mexican national named Baldassaro, who is here illegally. That was the District Attorney. I've got to go to Riesner Street. To the Cop Shop."

He stared at her. It wasn't ever boring, having an assistant district attorney as his wife.

"It started with a tip," she continued. "There were literally thousands of tips, but this one hit pay dirt. With a search warrant, some detective from the homicide division went to this guy's apartment. They used Luminol on all his clothes—you know, that stuff that detects blood, and it turned up blood . . . yes. For sure. All over."

She looked at him, with wonder about how it had been done. "Then, the homicide cops got those particular clothes washed out with solvent and collected DNA. There was blood, and not of the suspect. It was the blood of Rafael Castillo. You know, the news reporter who got killed. One of the victims."

"So. . . ."

"So, that's right. The District Attorney wants me to go write the indictment. Not much to some parts of it, in a way; the process is automated, with forms that are tried and tested. But there will be some judgment calls, which are important. And it's certainly a case where he wants someone who's got experience. Who's been around the block. And so . . . I get the call."

"Who is . . . who is this? . . . I mean, what sort of individual did it?"

"It's a guy who was in Mexico until recently. Not surprising: they import someone to do a job like that. Guy name of Baldassaro, is all I know. I don't remember whether the District Attorney even told me Baldassaro's first name."

"Baldassaro . . . . So, what about the concert we're going to? The one we've planned for, and that we're driving to right now?"

"Oh, you can still go, Robert."

"But it's called Mostly Mozart. And Maria, you really should go to this concert. Mostly Mozart."

"Well, you've listened to everything Mozart ever did. And you've made sure that I listened to everything he ever did. And the answer is, duty calls me, and I can't go to a concert tonight."

"Yes, but tonight . . . the Jupiter Symphony, that's what they're doing . . . we shouldn't miss it."

She smiled, in spite of herself. "You can still go, Robert. Just head this Cruella De Vil car, your fancy fire-breathing Duesenberg hot rod, over to Riesner Street, first. To the Cop Shop. And drop me off there."

* * *

As soon as she arrived at the Police Station, Maria found an officer waiting for her. "Ma'am, before you go to intake the case and write the indictments, they want you in the Homicide Division."

She stepped into the ancient elevator, with her escort. "This city really needs a new police building."

"Tell me about it."

"What's up? I mean, why are we going to the Homicide Division first?"

"Your two favorite homicide cops are waiting to meet with you. Derrigan Slaughter and Donnie Cashdollar." At that, Maria smiled. She liked these two detectives: a true odd couple.

The officer went on: "They have one of the suspects with them, who has confessed to these eight murders in the Death House. They think he's only minimally involved, and there may be plans to have him testify against the other two perpetrators."

The Homicide Division was like the rest of the Police Station, only more dilapidated, if that was possible. The floor was linoleum of a design long abandoned everywhere else, with green and yellow flecks. The walls were white, with nothing but a couple of official notices stuck on it—and strangely, a poster showing Harrison Ford in Star Wars, affixed with tape to one wall. The desks were metal with plastic tops. And in the middle of the room, Derrigan Slaughter and Donnie Cashdollar stood together with a much smaller individual, who was unkempt and dirty.

"World's champion cops!" Maria knew these two detectives from enough past cases so that she couldn't remember how many.

"Hello, Mizz Melendes," they said in unison. And smiled, in spite of the seriousness of the situation.

The detectives were dressed in their usual fashion, which was actually unusual, but which was well known here. Derrigan Slaughter was a big African-American officer. He wore a navy pinstriped suit with a silver tie, and every part of it signaled elegance. Donnie Cashdollar was as sloppy as his partner was neat. His ill-coordinated outfit consisted of green trousers, a blue jacket, a pink shirt, and a red tie that had a pattern of misshapen stars on it.

Detective Cashdollar touched the smaller man. "We got this gentleman, this one here, whose name is Jorge Baron Baldassaro. He admits that he drove the car for the two guys who went into the Death House and killed the Castillo family. He's given us an oral confession and a written confession, and he wants to testify against the two other killers."

"I don't have authority to make that kind of deal. But I think it will go through. I'll recommend it."

Derrigan Slaughter spoke next. "Okay, Jorge Baron Baldassaro, you done got the floor now. You need to tell yo' story to this nice lady. She is an assistant district attorney."

Maria was aware that a camera, not particularly noticeable but always there, was recording everything.

"We . . . went to this Bank." Jorge Baron Baldassaro spoke slowly and with an accent. "I can't know the name of that Bank. I go inside to the Bank, with the other two guys. They go up to the little cage where the person with the money stands."

"The teller's window?"

"Yeah. . . . And the people there give them money. A thousand dollars. This was first payment for the job of killing. Another payment later."

"If you don't know the name of the Bank, can you at least describe it?"

"I guess so. Black building. Made with little black rocks. Downtown. Inside, big room with green floor. Green carpet."

"Then what happened?"

"Not very much. I drive them to this house where they tell me to go. I got the word, later, that it was Castillo's house. Other two guys go in. They have guns and they have machetes, too. I stay outside. I hear a lot of noise. And a lot of . . . screaming: screaming, like death. And the two guys come running out and yell at me, *"Drive!,"* and I drive. I go up to maybe a hundred miles an hour when we get to the freeway. I was scared."

"This is unbelievable," Maria said to the officers. She looked sharply at Jorge Baron Baldassaro. "But . . . it's probably true."

She said to the prisoner, "We will listen to you. We've got to know, for sure, that you're telling the truth, and it's always hard to know that. But if it checks out, and if you testify truthfully, I'll recommend that we give you a break. A break of some kind, that is." And with that, she said a quick goodbye to Detectives Slaughter and Cashdollar and turned to go.

"What happens now?" The prisoner wanted to know.

"I will go downstairs to prepare indictments against all three of the defendants. Including you. I'll have to see, but it probably will be all for the same crimes. We don't have a plea bargain completed yet with you. There are no deals yet, but we will talk again to you. And right now, you'll go back to the lockup, or wherever these two gentlemen need to put you. These two detectives are your charming hosts."

And again, she turned to go. Her next stop would be the cramped quarters that the assistant D.A.'s called "Intake."

9
THE INDICTMENT

The prosecutor on duty at the Intake Station was new, but he was trying to act as though he knew more about criminal law than that superficial course in law school had taught him. "We have to write a lot more in this indictment than in the usual murder case, of course," he said wisely.

"Not every murder case is a capital murder. Not every murder qualifies for the death penalty," he added.

"Last time I looked, only about five percent of murders qualify for the death penalty," Maria agreed. "And yes, we have some work to do to prepare this indictment."

She had read all of the police reports, with increasing disgust. And the lab reports. And the defendant's confession. And the autopsy reports. And she had looked at the crime scene photographs, which were much worse than the television pictures she had seen.

Murders of eight people, with machetes. It was unthinkable—but here were the pictures. Now, it was time to consider the language that should go into the indictment. This was a crucial step. Leaving something out could ruin the case.

"We've got at least three ways I can see, that this case is a capital murder," Maria said finally. She looked at the Penal Code section that defines capital murder. Section 19.03. She read the key language out loud. "First, the law says it's a death penalty case if the defendant causes the murder, quote, *'of more than one person in the same criminal transaction,'* unquote."

She noticed with satisfaction that the new prosecutor had tamed his I-know-it act and was paying attention. "Well, I guess that applies here," he said quietly. "Eight murders."

"Yes. And second, it's a murder for hire, and that's a capital case too. Actually, it's a murder, quote, *'for remuneration,'* unquote, in the language of the statute. The defendant's confession tells how he and the two other killers got paid. Ten thousand dollars."

"Remuneration?"

"It's an old-fashioned way of saying, they did it to get paid. Remuneration. It means, 'for compensation.' Usually, money. But 'remuneration' is what the death penalty law says, and so . . . our indictment has to say that too."

"Okay. So that fits."

"I see here where this Baldassaro confessed, and he says he got paid. He says the money came to him in cash that he picked up at a Bank called the Velnikov Bank, all in a bank bag, in wrapped hundred-dollar bills. Kind of weird."

"Weird, and suspicious about that particular Bank, too."

"Well, but we've got to find out whether this Bank paid for murder, before we go after the Bank. It happens every day, that people get cash from banks."

"That's right, of course." The new prosecutor had been caught, again, trying too eagerly to reach a conclusion that lay beyond what could be proved.

"All right. So, second, is that he did it for 'remuneration.' Let's go on to the third kind of capital murder here. And the third kind is, the death penalty statute covers the murder of a child, or actually, of, quote, *'an individual less than six years of age,'* unquote."

They both were somber at that, even more than they had been before. "That's . . . the murder of the little one. Little Jonathan Castillo. Two years old." This obviously was a heavier case than the beginner prosecutor had seen, until now.

"So. Here's the standard form for a capital murder indictment based on more than one victim in the same criminal transaction." Maria knew the words conceptually, but she studied the form to be sure about getting it right. "Now: Here's a question for you. Should we list all eight victims as the 'more than one' person killed? Or only one additional person?"

"Well . . . if we charge him for the murders of all eight, and the killer didn't intend to kill one of them, we might get a dismissal of the death penalty language," said the new prosecutor. "We might have to prove all eight or else have our proof fail, and we'd be increasing the burden of what we have to prove."

"Very good thought," Maria answered. "But I don't think so." She looked at the research she had done. "Here's a case decided by the Texas

Court of Criminal Appeals: *Rabbani v. State.* It says, no, that's not a problem, charging murders that don't get proved. Just because you can't prove it all, doesn't mean you throw out all the rest. Here's the language in the case. '*When the charge authorizes the jury to convict on several different theories, the verdict will be upheld if the evidence is sufficient on any of the theories.*'"

"So . . . even if proof of one of the eight murders fails, it's good enough if any two get proved. Wow."

"Right. And here's another case: *Medrano v. State.* The indictment charged four murders, and the court said that any two would be enough. So the answer is: we include all eight murders, here."

It sounded too clinical and unemotional, debating whether to write the names of two or eight murdered human beings in the indictment. It sounded bloodless and cold, when the photographs of the crime scene screamed murder in front of them. And yes, it was clinical and unemotional. But that was necessary, because that was the way this work had to be done.

"So," Maria continued. Which one of the eight do we put first?"

"I'd say . . . Little Jonathan Castillo. The most tragic case. Two years old."

"Right." And using the form, she filled in the name of Jonathan Castillo first, and then all of the other seven. And she added the other requirements. When she finished, the first paragraphs of the indictment looked like this, with the standard form language in regular type, and the particulars of the case in bold:

> **"In the Name and by Authority of the State of Texas:**
> **"The Grand Jury, duly organized at the term of court of the 208th District Court of Harris County, Texas, charges that, anterior to this date, in Harris County, Texas, Jorge Baron Baldassaro, hereinafter styled the defendant, did then and there unlawfully:**
> **"intentionally and knowingly cause the deaths of Jonathan Castillo, Rafael Castillo, Silvia Castillo, Paula Castillo, Donna Castillo, Ruben Castillo, Riley Castillo, and Margherita Castillo, hereinafter styled the complainants,**
> **"by cutting and stabbing them with a machete, and by a manner and means to the grand jury unknown.**
> **"Against the Peace and Dignity of the State."**

And at the bottom, there was a blank for the Presiding Juror to sign, once the Grand Jury had determined whether to vote for the indictment.

"Good grief!" The new prosecutor's voice was anguished. "These defendants took out an entire family."

"Three generations." Maria's voice was quiet.

"What's this stuff about *'manner and means to the grand jury unknown'* in there for?"

"Well, imagine that one of the killers used another weapon. A weapon that wasn't a machete. A knife, say. Then, the indictment couldn't be proved as to that victim, because it says 'a machete.' This way, if some of it was with one weapon and some of it was with an unknown weapon, we still can prove our case."

An hour later, they had added two more sets of paragraphs to the indictment, charging Jorge Baron Baldassaro with murder for remuneration and with murder of a child under six.

About two o'clock in the morning, Maria called Robert. "Come get me. It's been a long night."

* * *

On top of the Colina del Pescador, looking at pictures from the town of Hermosillo, Mexico, El Jefe looked satisfied.

One of the compensations of being a drug lord was that sometimes you could see the results of your orders on television. Staring at an enormous flat screen, El Jefe saw a mass of bodies.

He turned to his companions. "Those two gentlemen did it right. Look here. That's Rico. Our substitute. Our sacrificed companion. Bloody, bloody, and dead. The Escondidas Cartel will be happy. And around Rico, look at all of this."

The camera panned over a sign that said, "El Bar del Rincon." The Corner Bar. The concrete floor was littered with bodies. Next to the unfortunate Rico, who was the essential target, was the body of a middle-aged woman. It looked like a pincushion, with red oozing out of all of the holes. There was a man next to her, and another man, and another woman, and yet more people, and an occasional child.

El Jefe turned the sound up. An off-screen announcer said, ". . . twenty-seven dead. We do not know what they did to earn this fate. We do not know why they are all dead. Is it only for show?"

"Yes. For show." El Jefe bellowed it back to the television, as a response to the announcer. "I told my guys to make it a big party. The extra attendance at the party, in addition to Rico, is to show the Escondidas Cartel that we mean business. Just killing Rico would have been enough, maybe, but this will tell the Escondidas of our sincerity. And what is more, it will also tell them that we know how to use an assault rifle from the

United States, on either our neighbors or our enemies. It's always a good thing if other people who might be rivals can be told that."

"From what appears," the announcer went on, "it's random. It's just a killing of all the people who happened to be here at The Corner Bar. There are at least two survivors. Injured, but alive. We understand that they cannot identify anyone who committed these acts. They cannot identify the killers. The killers did not wear masks, but the survivors cannot identify them."

El Jefe frowned. "They'd better not identify anyone," was all he said.

* * *

Maria worried more every day. Not about herself, but about Robert, because his lawsuit was going to mix him up with a drug gang. She knew a lot about his case. And finally, she decided to get some advice.

Being from Cuba, she was used to talking to the saints. More than that, she was used to consulting the spirits. She sometimes sought the guidance of those undefined, supernatural forces out there somewhere, which were mysterious—but real.

And that was why, at this moment, she was here in this strange place. Consulting a medium of the occult, one she hoped she could believe in.

The psychic circled her hand over the crystals and stones that would help her to read the future. "Now, dear, you know that the messages we receive will depend upon you. You've got to complete the suggestions that the spirits send me. Will you help?"

It was straight from the psychics' handbooks. From the beginning, the books advise, the fortune-teller should make the mark feel responsible for her own success.

"I know I've got to work at it, Mother Serena," said Maria Melendes immediately. "I'll try hard."

"Good. Now: you've got to give me some idea why you came here. What part of the future do you need to uncover?" Mother Serena smiled confidently.

The psychic was dressed in a grayish-blue robe. It shimmered in the subdued light with dots that might be stars, which were randomly distributed over her ample frame. Her face was lined from the effort of reading thousands of fortunes, and her hair was grayish-white and full of wisdom.

Mother Serena and Maria sat on opposite sides of a hexagonal table in a triangular room with one corner cut off by a curtain marked by mystery shapes. Strangely, the two humans were surrounded by seven cats—no, eight dark-coated cats, Maria realized—which sat on ledges like sentinels, or like knowledgeable consultants who might be there to help the psychic.

Maria hesitated. "I . . . want to know about my husband. He is known as 'The Trial Lawyer for the Little Guy.' He's just filed a major lawsuit that worries me. Will it involve him in danger? Or . . . will it mean that our whole family is in danger? What . . . What will happen to him?"

The psychic changed the subject, intending to collect more information. "I'm sensing that you may have thought about visiting a psychic before this. Or, at least, you've thought about it, and maybe you've even gone to see a psychic before. Is that true, dear?"

This question too was from taken straight from the psychic handbooks. It was a so-called "Barnum question," named after the circus magnate P.T. Barnum. A question like this can fool the mark into believing the fortune-teller, because it sounds clairvoyant. But the remark is contrived so that it applies to most people. Mother Serena knew that almost everyone has at least "thought about" visiting a psychic, if only for fun.

Maria brightened. "How did you know? . . . Well . . . I guess that's why you can do what you do, and figure out the future. Yes, I consulted someone else. Another psychic. But she didn't seem to know very much."

"I understand, dear. Now, I'm getting a message from the spirits. It tells me that your husband's lawsuit is about a person hurt very badly . . . or . . . even someone who was killed, but I see . . . that your husband . . . also does business-type cases."

This was what the psychic handbooks call a "Rainbow Statement," because it contains multiple options that are polar opposites. Personal injury suits are half of the lawyering world, and business lawsuits cover the rest, so the statement was likely true. But if the mark wanted to believe, it appeared to show that the psychic had unnatural powers.

"That's right!" Maria's eyes bulged. "His lawsuit is that one that's made the newspapers. Eight people killed. You know, that journalist and all of his family. It's a terrible scene of death, just horrifying, but I wish Robert would leave it to the police."

Now the psychic had all the information necessary to make some amazing predictions. She passed her hand over the crystals again. "You are worried because there are powerful, dangerous people on the other side of the lawsuit. Is that right?"

"Yes!" This psychic, it seemed, could really consult the spirits.

"You are correct . . . in your worries." Mother Serena spoke slowly, as she prepared to shift into the future. Into fortune-telling.

Paradoxically, the easiest statements for a psychic are those that foresee the future. Predictions can be shaped to fit the information that the psychic has already fished out of from the mark, and as of now—in the present—they cannot be disproved. If they fail to come true, the mark can choose to believe that she has changed outcomes by following the medium's advice.

"Your husband is in danger." Mother Serena's voice carried a hint of fear. "He should get himself out of this situation."

"But he is determined to win this lawsuit. He has poured his soul into it."

"Well, yes. That is the way he is. But the lawsuit will be lost. He will get nothing from this lawsuit, nothing but danger and heartache. He is risking everything for nothing, because he will lose this case and get nothing. He should get out of this lawsuit."

"And so I've got to try hard to get him out of it."

"Well, but . . . No. No, and here's why. I get a message saying that you should not do anything, and you should act normal, . . . even enthusiastic. It won't work if you pressure him."

This advice allowed the medium to have it both ways. If Maria did nothing, whatever happened would fit. And so, Mother Serena repeated herself. "You should act normally about this lawsuit. You should even be enthusiastic. You must not push him."

"How can I do that? You're saying, I'm supposed to . . . just sit by and not try to stop him?"

The medium said nothing. She just nodded.

Fifteen minutes later, Maria left the psychic's odd-shaped building. She suddenly realized that she had heard nothing in the last half of the session. The clang of the early words reverberated in her ears. "Your husband is in danger . . . He should get himself out . . . He will lose this case . . . He will get nothing . . . ."

Could Mother Serena be right? . . . Yes, she was right. Maria knew that she was right. But she remembered more advice: "You should not do anything." And she was determined, finally, to support her husband in handling this lawsuit against the Bank, no matter how much she wanted him out of it.

10

YES . . . BUT WHAT ABOUT THOSE TECHNICALITIES?

O kay. Thanks, Chipmunk. What you've discovered is helpful." Robert Herrick sat at the big mahogany desk in front of the greenhouse windows.

"It's not evidence." Chipmunk was pleased, but he wanted to wave a cautionary red flag.

"I know. But it will give us a road map for questioning this witness, this . . . José Luis, when we get the opportunity to question him before trial. To find out what he's going to say."

"José Luis Leyva." Tom Kennedy said helpfully. "The defector from the Balamarcas Cartel."

Robert nodded. "And before that, we'll file suit. It's much easier to question this kind of witness after you file the suit papers."

Then: "Let's think it through," he said. "Chipmunk, you're telling us your sources say this Bank, the Velnikov Bank, is laundering money. It takes in huge deposits from people who have nothing. It makes huge loans to the same people who have nothing."

"And the money makes its way back to Mexico, back to the drug lords, to pay for the heroin and cocaine they've sold," said Kennedy.

"Of course, that's not enough."

Chipmunk said, "That's where this turncoat witness, José Luis Leyva, comes in. He ties it together. By explaining how the Cartel coordinates with the Bank, and how the money gets back to Mexico, and how often this guy called El Jefe communicates with the Velnikov Bank, and what they talk about. But you've got to have José Luis."

"Well . . . we do have him, right?"

"I don't know." Chipmunk looked down at the floor. "I think so. Again, what I've heard is conversations in confidence from DEA agents, and it's not evidence. What you've read is just my report. It's just the stuff I've learned from talking to the DEA guys. Let's not get too confident."

It was a wet, rainy day. The sky outside was all mist: all cloudy and uncertain. The swath of land around Buffalo Bayou was greener than green, all covered in a cloak of airborne water.

"You know what worries me?" Tom Kennedy tapped a pencil. "So, we tie the Bank to the Cartel. The Bank is laundering money. How do we tie the Cartel to these eight murders? And what's more, how do we tie the Bank, the blessed Velnikov Bank, to the murders? You've got to have proximate causation to have a lawsuit."

Robert and Tom both found themselves transported back to law school. Negligence isn't enough. Intent isn't enough. Even a criminal act isn't enough. The wrongdoing has to be connected to the injury and the damages. It has to be what lawyers call a "proximate cause" of the injury and damages. It's got to be connected to the result, in a natural sequence, with results that come about in a foreseeable way for the defendant—here, the Bank.

"The Bank was part of a drug cartel," Tom Kennedy began.

Robert filled in the thought. "And it knew what a drug cartel does, or it could know. And should know. Everybody knows that if you help a drug cartel from Mexico to do its business, there are going to be murders as a result."

"Well, but . . . murders on this side of the border?"

"I don't know. Proximate cause, or tying the wrongful act to the result, is a mysterious thing, I'll admit, but I doubt it makes distinctions quite that fine and abstract." Robert had decided. "Draw up the suit papers, Tom. We'll include the three killers who actually did the deed, even though we're not going to get anything from them because they're sure to be penniless. And let's include the cartel. Call it *'The Balamarcas Cartel, an Enterprise.'* And then, there's the real defendant, the target defendant, the one we actually hope we can successfully execute a judgment against. The Velnikov Bank."

"Yes. But what about those technicalities? The legalistic requirements? Like proximate cause?"

"It's gonna be an interesting lawsuit." Chipmunk had been silently waiting, but with this, he had the last word.

* * *

The secretarial bays at the law firm of Booker and Bayne were made of white birch. They stretched down the hall as far as the eye could see. The firm had harvested all of the matched veneers for its ten floors of offices from a single growth of this prized wood in Vermont.

Booker and Bayne was founded by Colonel Henry Anderson Booker more than a century ago, in 1897. Colonel Booker was a confidant of governors and presidents. He kept a spittoon in his office and wore striped suspenders. "The Colonel" had put together the financing to build that rich subdivision called River Oaks; he had qualified the bonds that dredged the Ship Channel; and he even had represented the city council when the Astrodome was built. Every time a client wanted to do a shady deal, The Colonel was famous for asking the question: "Yes, but is it fair?"

And after that, Colonel Booker always found a perfectly legal way to do whatever it was that his clients wanted to do, whether it was fair or not.

Today, Booker and Bayne prospered as never before, even though Colonel Booker had passed on to that great courtroom in the sky from which there is no appeal. The firm represented General Brands, First Texas Bank, American Petroleum, Habushita, The Spinelli Corporation, and a thousand more of the world's biggest clients. It had seven hundred and thirty-eight lawyers, and in addition to the original office here, it had lawyers across the world. The firm had long since stopped handling personal injury cases, unless they were massive. You couldn't make money by charging those piddling little fees, like a mere three hundred dollars an hour.

But the basic philosophy of the firm had never changed. It still lived by the Colonel's original formula for success: "Find out what the client wants, and then do whatever it takes!"

If there was any successor at Booker and Bayne to the legend of Colonel Henry Anderson Booker, it was Jimmy Coleman. Jimmy had led the team of lawyers that won the biggest judgment in history—over eleven billion dollars—on behalf of Emperor Corporation, in the Emperor–Newcorp litigation. The lawyers sometimes got confused in that case and accidentally said "million" when they meant "billion." But not Jimmy Coleman. It seemed easy for him to take billions of dollars from the other side.

Now, as Jimmy Coleman strolled through the glass doors that posted the gold-lettered name "Booker and Bayne," he looked down the long rows of white birch and smiled. He felt increasing satisfaction as he heard the familiar sounds of Booker and Bayne lawyers at work.

At the door of Bentley Carelli, he heard his deep-voiced partner shout a few four-letter words into the telephone. The listener was an attorney who wanted his client to keep using a patented product. Unfortunately for him, the product happened to be an iPhone add-on for electronic games, invented by Bentley's client. "... Of course your client infringed our patent! Haven't you heard of the doctrine of equivalents? Your printed circuit is functionally identical to the one claimed in our patent, and it's obviously equivalent! If you don't settle this, you'll need an electronic add-on to figure out the damages you'll pay!"

No one inside the firm would have been able to tell whether Bentley Carelli believed what he was saying about the "doctrine of equivalents." But it made Jimmy smile.

The next office was Martha Peters. The head of the oil and gas group, and the first woman to become a partner here. "... No, sir, you don't get it," she was yelling at an attorney on the other end of the line. "We have no intention of plugging that well, because it's still producing. And look: that entire property is held under the lease, because of production from this well. If you poke another well into this land, my client is gonna own every barrel you pump!"

Jimmy laughed. What was fun about listening to Martha was remembering that her bite was much worse than her bark.

Then, there was Brady McLaughlin's office. A bankruptcy lawyer known for pushing around his opponents. Jimmy heard Brady's voice: "... My client is on the creditors' committee in this case, and if you don't play ball with us, you're going to get crammed down so bad, your butt's gonna come over your head!"

Jimmy loved the stab-your-brother-in-the-back lawsuits that developed from bankruptcy cases. He smiled again.

Finally, at the end of the corridor, he waddled to the last secretarial bay. "Hello, Lisa. I'm here."

Lisa stood up, all six feet of her. "Hello, Jimmy!" She towered over him as she threw her arms around his neck.

His partners constantly kidded Jimmy for hiring Lisa Marshall as his secretary. It wasn't because he liked women taller than he was, although he did. Instead, it was because Lisa could type ten error-free pages quickly, juggle all his telephone calls, and keep her cool when Jimmy started a new crooked deal.

Jimmy Coleman wasn't tall. He stood just five foot eight. "But he sure seems taller, especially with that straight-back mane of white hair," one of his partners said. "He looks the way a Mafia godfather would look, if a Mafia godfather ever became a lawyer."

Eyes like a dead fish, cold and gray. A voice like tractor tires on gravel. A pear-shaped body, with half a dozen chins. And then, there were the qualities that made Jimmy a charismatic leader in the firm: his brain-power, his long hours, his give-no-quarter litigation skills, and his plain old-fashioned nastiness when it was needed.

Lisa smiled. "I know you want to meet with Jennifer Lowenstein about that lawsuit Robert Herrick's filed against the Velnikov Bank."

"That's right. Find her."

Jimmy waded into his big corner office. It was piled a foot deep with mail, but you could still see the exquisite handwork in Jimmy's Italian intarsiato desk, with its white trees, green vines, and brown flowers carved into the honey-colored wood. The desk and armchair had been custom made by craftsmen in Venice to match his favorite piece of furniture—the seventeenth century armoire that was inlaid with the same flowering vines, winding around its glittering gold hardware. Two sides of the office were floor-to-ceiling windows that looked over the Southwest Freeway, where hundreds of cars inched like insects toward downtown.

Jimmy tossed the mail aside and found Robert Herrick's lawsuit. The complaint that had started the case. It was detailed and specific. But his practiced eye quickly spotted a dozen conclusionary words that could be attacked under the vagaries of the Supreme Court's decisions. And then he saw the attached memorandum from Jennifer Lowenstein. "Ripe for a Motion to Dismiss," was the headline. The memorandum went on to list a dozen cases dealing with Motions to Dismiss, cases that found plaintiffs' lawsuits to be inadequate.

Jennifer had always had an instinct for the jugular, Jimmy thought with satisfaction. Now, she arrived at his door, out of breath from running up four floors. "Get your ass in here!" Jimmy told her, affectionately.

"Yes, sir." She smiled, because every associate wanted to work for Jimmy. Your work would be completely billed, and at top dollar. You'd get to see how a master did it. And for all his ruthlessness, Jimmy was known as a marvelous teacher.

"You got it right, little girl," he told Jennifer, now. "It may not be granted, but a Motion to Dismiss will get Robert Herrick's law firm to run around and do a ton of work, without costing us anything."

"And the way things are with the law today, it might even get granted."

"Right. The case got docketed with Judge Marvin Raines. He is a stickler."

"Jimmy, is there any danger of our client getting sanctioned for filing this Motion to Dismiss, when the complaint is so detailed?" Jennifer smiled again. She knew the answer, but she wanted to be seen as thinking it through. "The complaint really does tell us everything we'd need to know to file an answer."

"No problem." Jimmy seemed excited about this lawsuit. "The way the Supreme Court has messed up this area of the law, you can never tell whether a complaint is good enough. You can always attack the plaintiff's papers, and nobody can say that you don't have an argument."

"Right. I can see that."

"Sometimes I think those Supreme Court Justices can't possibly have read the nonsense they write. When it comes to Motions to Dismiss, they really have their heads up their ass."

Jennifer laughed. If you worked for Jimmy, your chances of making partner went up, and you'd make outrageous amounts of money just as an associate. He earned his five-million-a-year draw by being a ferocious trial lawyer, an eighty-hour-a-week worker, and a consummate field general. He took care of his people. He fought within the firm to favor the associates who worked for him. And it was always fun to listen to him.

"Anyway," Jimmy's voice dropped, and it sounded like sandpaper on balsa wood. "Listen, Jennifer, because I want you to write this Motion to Dismiss. And an accompanying brief. You need to keep repeating that the Bank just did what banks always do. It took in deposits and lent money. Over and over again, you'll say that Herrick's complaint just shows that the Bank took in deposits and lent money. And here's how I want you to write it. . . ."

11

THE LISTENING POSTS

ust outside Brenham, Texas, northwest of Houston, Robert Herrick's Duesenberg cruised to a stop in front of the rustic portico of his country villa. The huge burgundy hood stopped purring, and the exhaust pipes that ran along each side were silent. Robert looked off to his left, where row after row of grapevines marched across the gently rolling landscape. He went immediately in that direction.

Maria was disgusted. "You can't even come into the house before running off to your precious vines?"

"Julio is here. His time is valuable." And Robert turned to his partner. "Hello, Julio, my friend."

Maria shook her head. It wasn't that Julio's time was valuable. It was that Robert wanted to get into the field.

But it was nice, she thought, that her husband wasn't thinking about his big lawsuit. Maybe there was hope: a possibility, perhaps, that he might get out of it. "He is in danger. . . . He will lose." . . . The psychic's warnings were all over her mind.

Julio's usual good cheer was displaced by a trace of concern. He sounded a little less robust than usual when he answered, "Yo, Robert!"

"What's . . . what's the matter?"

"They're behind schedule." Already, the two men were walking the manicured, short-mowed aisles between the vines. Beneath the greenery, a line of hoses snaked from one stalk to the next, to carry water to the thirsty leaves. Above that, another hose line glistened, black and slick in the sunlight.

"How much behind?" Suddenly Robert was concerned too.

"I don't know. At least several weeks." Julio held up a shining wet mass of tiny green spheres. "They're harder than they ought to be. No sugar in them. Not enough juice."

"They need to be twice that size before we can even think about harvesting them," Robert agreed. "So . . . we can forget about our contract labor schedule. We're going to need our pickers later than we thought."

Robert looked along the line of grape stems sticking out of the earth and saw the carefully trimmed leaves. And he was contented.

He brightened as he spoke again. "Listen, Julio, it will be all right. Up the water in the hoses. Increase it just a little. And delay the harvest. That will be all right."

"I'm afraid we'll miss the market. But . . . maybe not."

Maria's voice interrupted them. "Robert, telephone. It's Tom Kennedy. He says it's important. And he says he's got to talk to you now."

Robert mumbled under his breath. But he took the telephone.

Tom's voice was weary. "Robert, a week ago, we filed the suit against the Velnikov Bank and the other defendants. The eight-murder case, you remember, on behalf of the Castillos. And now, we have a Motion to Dismiss from the other side."

Robert's mumbling grew louder. "Who's filed this blessed Motion to Dismiss? Who represents the Bank?" This kind of procedure was not usual in response to a suit of this kind.

"You're not going to like it. Jimmy Coleman."

Now, Robert's mumbling was loud enough to be called something more than mumbling. His mind conjured up a picture of the street fighter who was head of litigation at the enormous firm of Booker and Bayne. Short, fat, rumpled, slovenly, hot-voiced Jimmy Coleman, who never went anywhere without a long trail of expensive, black-suited associates behind him. Jimmy could always justify unorthodox tactics, like this Motion to Dismiss, by having long, intricate briefing done by his minions. They could dress up any delaying tactic as righteous law, at God-knows-what cost to the clients.

"Coleman has asked for an emergency hearing." Tom Kennedy sounded disgusted. "He's added all this rhetoric about how the Velnikov Bank has to report to the regulators next month and has an unblemished record except for this 'frivolous suit' filed by that opportunist law firm, namely us. And so, our lawsuit against poor little Velnikov Bank, which actually is a huge operation, will cause so-called 'irreparable harm' to this innocent little Bank, unless Jimmy's Motion to Dismiss is granted."

The description of Jimmy Coleman as a street fighter was literally true. He had grown up as a gang member in South Los Angeles. It was rumored that he'd been involved in at least one murder, but there wasn't enough evidence to tie him to it, although three of his compadres had gone to prison. No one knew how this primitive child had gotten into law school at UCLA, or how he had managed to graduate.

"Okay, Tom." Robert tried to stay calm. "Respond that we need at least two months to put together our evidence, and then we need time to amend the pleadings."

He looked across the green, green field, with its straight rows and neat watering stations. "I'm at the vineyard," he added, "and I'll think about Jimmy Coleman tomorrow."

Tom was agreeable. "Well, it'll give us another fun opportunity to see all those strange lawyers who are Jimmy's associates in their uniforms. I've never seen so many black suits since grandma's cat died back in Tennesee."

Robert loosened up a little and laughed, at that. But he was determined to put Jimmy Coleman and his associates out of his mind. And to tend to his grapes.

* * *

At about the same time, many miles to the south, El Jefe called his new First Lieutenant, and he gave him orders from his magnificent villa at the top of La Colina del Pescador. The-Craziest-One-known-as-El-Jefe was tired of hearing about the *Federales* visting the governor, especially after he had been so nice about the complaints of the Escondidas. He had thought the mass killing he'd ordered at *El Bar del Rincon*, The Corner Bar, would satisfy everyone, especially since it included a fine Cartel soldier as a pre-eminent corpse. The unfortunate Rico had been offered as a sacrifice, and the other murders surrounding Rico's had been an exclamation point, an extra message of conciliation.

What more did the Escondidas Cartel want from this sovereign organization, the Balamarcas Cartel, as a revenge payment for an incidental killing of a mere woman, an unimportant woman? Wasn't this peace offering enough, even if she did happen to be somebody's daughter?

El Jefe's telephones were encrypted, of course. But not very well. In fact, when it came to encryption, he had a stone-age system. With really, really, old transformations. It used what mathematicians called a "tiny key." And that tiny key meant that the code had fewer pieces for an enemy to recognize, and it was easy to crack.

El Jefe did not know how poorly he was protected. He wasn't much of a technician, of course. Back when he'd first thought about protecting his communications, he had just told his then-Lieutenant to get an encryption system. "José Luis, go out and buy one." And then he had considered himself pretty well protected, because he had installed an expensive, commercially-bought coding machine.

Other men in the Cartel didn't need encryption, because they could buy prepaid phones and get rid of them after a few days, which worked fine for them. But that wouldn't work for El Jefe, because his signal came from a fixed source, at the top of Colina del Pescador, and the enemy—specifically, the National Security Agency of the United States, or the "NSA"—could identify El Jefe by location. And so he solved the problem by buying a privacy system that he thought was the market standard. Surely, that would be enough to keep out the snooping ears of the United States.

And so it was that now, El Jefe used his old style encrypted telephone to tell his First Lieutenant about a simple plan to protect the local governor from the investigating *Federales*. And it was a very simple plan: namely, to kill all the *Federales* in the area. The station here was tiny, and after all, El Jefe had a private army that was capable of overwhelming the Federal police encampment. Other drug lords had wiped out companies of the Mexican national police force in the past. It could be done without leaving evidence traceable to El Jefe's stronghold at the top of La Colina del Pescador.

Everyone would suspect El Jefe as the source of an assault like this, of course; but no one would know for sure, and no one could prove it. Most importantly, everyone would look for an excuse to avoid disturbing the Cartel. El Jefe was confident. After all, confidence about the use of violence was one of his qualifications for his job. Besides, it was not without reason that he was known as The Craziest One.

But on this rare occasion, he was wrong about his confidence. His coded communication was about to give him away. Now, as El Jefe gave orders to his main Lieutenant, the National Security Agency of the United States was online. In fact, the NSA had not one, and not two, but three listening posts tuned to Colina del Pescardor.

The three NSA listening posts worked together now, as they recorded what el Jefe was saying. One was a huge American aircraft called an "RC-135," which in reality was a flying computer. It patrolled the Bay of California in international waters, between the Mexican State of Sonora and Baja California. And the second listening post caught the signal from twenty thousand feet below the circling airplane. This was a light cruiser that directed an antenna toward the mountain where El Jefe was headquartered.

And there was a third ear, too. At 22,000 miles up in airless space, a geostationary satellite, programmed so that its orbit kept it sitting above the same earthly spot, also heard what El Jefe said. And it relayed its message to a place where the NSA used a battery of satellite receivers: a place known as the Roaring Creek Station, near the little village of Catawissa, Pennsylvania. Just one more unfamiliar, nearly nameless station maintained by the NSA in rural America.

The airplane, the ship, and the satellite all recorded El Jefe's angry words. "That's Right! Kill them all! I don't care if they're Federal Police! Kill them all!"

The three listening posts talked to each other, of course. Not in English or any human language, but in bursts of electrons, and they quickly confirmed that they had found the signal from Colina del Pescador. The three electronic ears could "triangulate"—meaning that they could zero in on a single, unique patch of earth, and locate it within a few feet, just by each one's figuring the direction from which the signal originated and drawing imaginary lines toward it.

But acquiring the signal, even with three different listening posts, was only the beginning. Next came the code-cracking part of the interception. The signal went to the National Security Agency's "High Performance Computing Center"—an enormous array of buildings, antennas, and assorted strange structures, known as "Site M," near Fort Meade, Maryland. The Computing Center acquired the triple signal from El Jefe. And it went to work.

El Jefe's words were in Spanish, but very clear. ". . . Kill them all! I don't care if they're Federal Police! Kill them all!"

The task of Site M was to decode the message. But that was quickly done in this case. Instead of quintillions of calculations, all the NSA needed was a measly few quadrillion. Just a set of computations numbered by 1 with 15 zeroes after it. A quadrillion-calculation task is small, by NSA standards, and this time, the computers did not need even that much, because they had decoded similar messages from El Jefe before. The job was slightly more complicated because the words were in Spanish, but only slightly more. And within moments of its utterance by The Craziest One, the NSA had received, relayed, decoded, and translated everything El Jefe had said about attacking the Mexican national police station.

The technical work at Site M was over, now. But the most sensitive step was yet to come. Most Americans do not know that a warrant is required for listening to some kinds of signals. The so-called "FISA court," or the Foreign Intelligence Surveillance Court, which is a top-secret court set up by the Foreign Intelligence Surveillance Act, has to issue a warrant before humans can look inside a domestic communication that the NSA's computers have found. In this case, José Luis Leyva had supplied the necessary information to get the necessary court order. The NSA already had its warrant from the judges who made up the super-secret FISA court.

And now, after so many complicated tasks that actually took only seconds each, the process was over. It would have taken longer to describe it than to accomplish it. And now, a systems analyst working for the NSA at Site M retrieved the message, all decrypted and translated into English. He whistled when he saw what El Jefe had said. Immediately, he contacted the "Ninth Floor," the top management of the NSA, and he sent The Craziest One's words to the NSA's Deputy Director.

"I don't care if they're Federal Police! Kill them all!"

The Deputy Director of the National Security Agency sits at the top of a black, nine-story building in northern Maryland, at a site chosen to be close to the nation's capital but distant enough so that a nuclear attack on Washington, D.C. will not incapacitate it. There, reading this message in his office among the offices of the other Ninth-Floor brass, the Deputy Director whistled too. Without hesitating, he sent El Jefe's words to the Latin America liaison at the State Department.

Within less than an hour, the President of Mexico read El Jefe's message. And with shock, he read it again. This message sent by El Jefe was nothing less than a declaration of war by the Cartel against the National Government of Mexico. "Kill them all!"

Immediately, the President's jaw was set. If Mexico ever was, in fact, the *Land of Manana*, it wasn't any more, at least not when it came to fighting drug violence. *El Presidente* did not hesitate as he gave the orders that would deploy a massive operation by the Mexican Army, in response to what El Jefe had said.

12

GOOD NEWS, BAD NEWS

Robert, I've got some good news and some bad news." Chipmunk's enormous cheeks wobbled as he shook his head.

They sat, together with Tom Kennedy, around the big mahogany desk in Robert's office. Outside the high windows, puffy clouds drifted through another hot, gorgeous day. Along Allen Parkway, vehicles more than seventy floors down crept westward, and traffic on Interstate 45 crossed over them. Right beside these major roadways, Buffalo Bayou stretched toward the afternoon sun.

"Okay, Chipmunk." Robert was philosophical. "Hit me with the bad news first."

"The bad news, is that all information from José Luis Leyva is entirely cut off. You know, the insider from the Balamarcas Cartel who left his life of crime because he was about to become a crime victim himself. The DEA has him hidden and has cut off all communication. They won't let anyone talk to José Luis."

"What? . . . Why is that?"

"He's hidden away in some kind of witness protection program. That's what I understand from my sources. In fact, they won't even say that much. They won't say whether they have him or what he might say, or even whether they have a witness protection program."

"They won't say where he is?"

"Worse than that. The DEA's position is, quote, 'The Drug Enforcement Administration can neither confirm nor deny the existence of any program for the protection of witnesses, and it does not provide public information about whether it has, or the contents provided by, any confidential sources of information.' "

"Translated into English, this means. . . ."

"The translation, unfortunately, is that no one in the DEA will say any-thing about José Luis Leyva. They won't even say whether there is anyone known as José Luis Leyva."

Kennedy looked at the floor. "Great. We've got this wonderful witness who was going to give us everything we needed to prove our case, and suddenly, he vanishes. Maybe he exists—or at least we think he exists—but he might as well not exist."

Robert laughed, along with Kennedy, at that, not because it was funny, but because all they could do was laugh. "But . . . Chipmunk, you said something about how there was some . . . some good news . . . ahhh . . . some good news, somewhere? Right?"

"The good news is that the State of Texas is hopping mad, and pretty much exquisitely angry, you might say, over this kind of garbage from the DEA." Chipmunk wore a look of annoyed exhaustion, probably because of long experience with this kind of bureaucratic wrangling. "Our District Attorney's office, right here, has a pretty serious murder case on file, of course. Eight victims. With three defendants, all charged with death-penalty killings."

"Of course," said Robert somberly.

"And this same José Luis," Chipmunk went on, "well, he's pretty im-portant to the State of Texas, too. The District Attorney's office can make the case without José Luis, because there's sufficient evidence against these three guys, but there's only just enough. And they have to have proof beyond a reasonable doubt in that criminal case, not just the least amount of proof you can get by with. And so, for their eight-victim-three-defendant death-penalty murder case, they really need this witness, this José Luis Leyva, to explain the whys and wherefores. To tell about the motive, and to tie it all to organized drug gangs."

"And so. . . ."

"And so, the feds don't have any criminal cases on file. I think with José Luis in their custody, they'll be able to make some federal cases, maybe, eventually. But meanwhile, the State, through our District Attor-ney's office, has a really strong need for José Luis. An immediate need."

"And so. . . ."

"And so, in my experience, whenever there's been this kind of conflict, things usually work out. I mean, when one government agency really needs a witness and another one holds that witness, the guys who really need their witness usually get their witness. And what that means is, I think the District Attorney's office and the State are going to get to use José Luis as a witness."

"That's ... good," Robert said. "That's very nice, for the State. But look, Chipmunk. I was assuming, when you said there was good news, that you meant there was good news for our suit against the Velnikov Bank. Because we need José Luis Leyva even more than the District Attorney's office does."

"Well ... our getting the witness, I'll admit, is a whole 'nother step. What I hope is that when the District Attorney's office and the State of Texas get José Luis Leyva, if they do, we may be able to get a shot at taking his deposition at the same time, for our case."

Chipmunk smiled an unhappy smile. "And I'm afraid, that's ... as good as the good news gets."

* * *

El Jefe got advance word of the orders given by the President of Mexico. He knew that the *Ejercito Mexicano*, the National Army, was coming. It was inevitable that El Jefe would know, of course, because he had informants everywhere.

He didn't know that the NSA had listened to his plans to "Kill them all." He didn't know that the President of Mexico had ordered an overwhelming force to attack him. He did know that the national army was coming. But he did not fear the Mexican army, because drug cartels had beaten the army in the past.

"I understand the reason for the orders by the President," he told his new *Lugarteniente*, the man who had replaced José Luis. "I know why he is sending the army."

His Lieutenant nodded. "Our plans to discipline the Federal Police personnel are more serious than visits to civilians, and more serious, even, than killings of state police officers."

"That's right. The President's orders come from own actions. We have already begun our selective assassinations of Federal Police commanders, which ought to remove the threat implied by the *Federales'* repeated visits to the governor. And regrettably, it has taken a mass of messages to many individuals to organize our planned operation."

El Jefe paused before confiding his next thought. "I don't know whether intercepted telephone messages, or a turncoat within this cartel, or something else has tipped off the Mexican President. I suspect that it might be those bungling *NorteAmericanos* in the United States, such as the CIA, or DIA, or NSA, or whatever it's called—one of those tyrannical groups that listen to private thoughts that they have no business to hear."

"I know, Jefe. If it is someone inside of us, a pretended friend, we will find out. But meanwhile, the *Ejercito is* coming—the Mexican army."

For most of history, the Mexican *Ejercito* had been a force against hostile foreign nations. But that had changed abruptly on December 11, 2006, when the New Mexican President, Felipe Calderon, had sent thousands of troops to Michoacan State to end drug violence there. Mexico soon had more than 50,000 soldiers combatting drug crime, along with *La Policía,* the state police, and the *Federales*, or national police. Unhappily, El Jefe knew all of this.

And he knew what he had to do. A Cartel like his always has a formidable army, itself. El Jefe could pull together as many as five thousand men.

"They will all be ready to fight, because they are well acquainted with fighting. We must prepare for the coming invasion, and we must call them all to come here. And I expect our fighters to prevail, because they will have the advantage of location. An invading force will have to come up the mountain, up Colina del Pescador, and the approaches are few and narrow."

* * *

Maria went to see Mother Serena three more times in rapid succession. The psychic learned more and more about Robert's lawsuit. This, of course, meant that she could make more amazing predictions.

"It will seem that he's winning. But he won't, in the end." . . .

"Maybe he can overcome the danger. But that's what's bad about danger. Maybe he can escape it, but . . . maybe not." . . .

"He will recognize the size of this danger, at some point in time. He will take more steps to protect himself." . . .

I have *got* to do something, Maria thought to herself. To get him out of it.

But Mother Serena was good at reading Maria, by now. "No. Don't do it. My dear, it's best if you don't even think about it."

13

INVASION

Okay, so, there's got to be a way we can get the court to tell the DEA to let us question this guy, this José Luis." Robert tapped a pencil on the desk.

"Well, I've looked into it. A procedure does exist to ask a court to produce someone to testify. It's a 'Request to Hand Over the Witness to Testify'—in other words, a request to get him to us, to testify. But formally it's called by a weird name. It's got a complicated name, if you want to be exact." Tom Kennedy looked baffled, even as he said it. "I never heard of it before."

"Okay. You've got me as puzzled as a porcupine. What's this weird Motion called? What's its weird name?"

"It's called a 'Petition for Writ of Habeas Corpus, ad Testificandum.' Weird, but that's what it's called."

"It's called a . . . what?"

"Well, it's . . . Latin. It's got a Latin name, like lots of stuff in the law. But hey, . . . just call it A 'Request for an Order to Hand Over the Witness to Testify.'"

"They never taught me that kind of Latin in law school, I'm embarrassed to say."

"They never taught anyone here about that . . . in anybody's law school."

"What does it mean?"

"Well, the words 'habeas corpus' don't mean what you might think they mean. 'Habeas corpus,' . . . literally . . . it's Latin for 'Hand Over the Person.' In this case, 'Hand Him Over to Testify.' And that's enough of translating Latin, Robert."

"You sound like a visiting professor, Tom."

"Yes. So listen carefully, student. I did a lot of reading to understand this stuff. Just think of it as a 'Request to the Court to Order Them to Hand Over the Witness to Testify.' We'll use that Latin name when we file it with the court, just to be correct, but as far as we're concerned here, it's only a 'Request to the Court to Order Them to Hand Over the Witness to Testify.'"

"So: I guess it's simple. It just has a fancy name. Right?"

Tom laughed. "Right. Robert, you're a good student."

"Usually, we'd just get a subpoena. But since the witness is being held by the DEA and we don't know where, we have to go through all of this rigmarole, instead. With all the Latin."

"We can't use a subpoena on José Luis Leyva because we don't know where he is. We have to deal with the DEA. They have him. And we've got to get the court to order the DEA to 'Hand Over José Luis to Testify.' If the court will do it, that is."

"Okay. Okay. So, we file our . . . Application for Writ of . . . well, never mind. It's our 'Request for an Order to Get Them to Hand Over the Witness.'"

"Right."

Robert laughed at the complexity of it all, at how tangled the law could be. How difficult it could make the simplest things.

Tom Kennedy still wasn't through. "But there's a real down side to all of this. A major problem."

"Oh, heck. Just when I was getting so comfortable with understanding it. Including the Latin."

"Here's the problem. We're in a state court, as of now. Courteous judges. Laws that aren't always completely right, but at least predictable. But then, which government is the DEA a part of? It's part of the Federal Government. That means that the Department of Justice will come into the case representing the DEA, and the Department of Justice will remove the entire case to Federal Court. We'll end up in front of a Federal Judge. Exactly where we don't want to be."

Robert groaned. "Federal judges! They're appointed for life. They have fewer rules. We'll get a judge who doesn't have to get elected and who may think he doesn't need to be fair or courteous. And the Feds at the Department of Justice will invade our case and cause all kinds of trouble."

"And yes . . . we'll get a Federal Judge who'll be in charge of our entire case. That's what it means."

"But we've got to have José Luis Leyva as a witness. We don't have any choice. So, we're going to get a Federal Judge, and we'll be in a Federal Court, but we can't avoid that." Robert sighed and looked out the window.

"It's like what my friend Lynne Liberato always says. You know her: she was president of the Bar Association, the State Bar Association. When things get sticky and disaster is near, her analysis is three words long: 'Nothing's ever easy.' It's short and clear."

"I know. That's exactly what Lynne would say: ... 'Nothing's ever easy.' And it sure applies to this case."

* * *

A day and a half later, on top of Colina del Pescador, it happened just as El Jefe had predicted. A small splinter of the Mexican Army came to his mountain. El Jefe knew about it beforehand. As he said to everyone within earshot, "I even know the precise day when their attack will start, from my informants. I do not know precisely what time it will begin, or what the Army will do, but I can find out."

He smiled. "And we are ready."

The most important shortcoming of El Jefe's forces, he knew, was that like all soldiers in drug cartels, they were trained to traffic in drugs, not to fight military battles. They were not familiar with the tactics or strategies of war. "But we have advantages," he mused. "Our men are tested in their loyalty. They are used to violent encounters, and we occupy the higher ground since we are on the top of our mountain."

His Lieutenant agreed. "La Colina del Pescador is chosen by you, *Jefe*, to resist attacks, and this hacienda is designed to be impregnable."

El Jefe was all business, now. He was still The Craziest One, but he did not seem like it. "Let us concentrate our forces along the two ridges that make up Colina del Pescador, near the point where the two ridges meet and crest."

The Lieutenant relayed the message. And there, at the ridge line, the forces of the Cartel waited.

Unfortunately for him, El Jefe did not know how to deploy his forces to mitigate the effect of an air attack, or how to tell them to dig in. At dawn on the appointed day, without warning, a rain of Tomahawk missiles exploded along the ridge tops, right among El Jefe's troops. The missiles had been launched from the Bay of California from a heavy destroyer built in the United States, but owned by the Mexican Navy.

It was a bad start, losing so many Cartel soldiers. But really, El Jefe knew, it was only a temporary setback.

A moment later, small arms fire came up the mountain from a short battalion of a few hundred Mexican Army soldiers, dressed in the wood-land camouflage that had replaced their old-fashioned uniforms of dark green. El Jefe was delighted to see that it was a puny force, but the uniforms impressed him. "We must get camouflage uniforms too, for our men to wear on ceremonial occasions, after this battle is over."

Meanwhile, the Cartel's soldiers were only slightly shell-shocked, the ones whom the missiles had left standing, and they returned fire almost immediately. They advanced with determination down the mountain toward the enemy—toward the soldiers of the National Defense Army, as the *Ejercito Mexicano* is known. El Jefe had heard, days ago, that the attack would involve only a battalion of soldiers, and the news had cheered him; perhaps the national government was not so very determined, and it had decided to send a force that he could overcome. "Maybe my government knows that I am a good citizen, a productive employer, and a builder of the modern Mexico," he had said proudly.

But unfortunately for El Jefe's forces, the much-criticized *Ejercito* had studied the terrain, and the Mexican commanders had found it perfect for a classic but simple strategy. A "flanking maneuver," as it is called. Too late, the cartel soldiers discovered that the tiny force from the Mexican Army below them was only there to gain their attention. In military terminology, it was a "fixing force," designed to distract their attention. And while it was true that the infantrymen coming up the mountain were only a battalion, the main contingent of Mexican Army soldiers, ferried first by American-made Blackhawk helicopters and then arriving in a mass on foot, had gained the top of the mountain and were bearing down on the Cartel forces.

El Jefe's soldiers suddenly were caught in the middle. The Mexican Army, true to El Jefe's information, had sent a small force up the front slope of the mountain, but it had sent a much larger force to attack from the side—the flank. A force large enough so that it was much more than adequate to handle the Cartel, especially with the element of surprise that the flanking maneuver had gained them.

Meanwhile, a company of Mexican Army soldiers turned to El Jefe's hacienda and quickly overwhelmed the palace guard. Within seconds, they found Alejandro Carlos Gonzales-Huerta, the man known as El Jefe, also called *El Más Loco*, The Craziest One, who was one of the most powerful leaders in the country and one of the richest men in the world. El Jefe stood meekly in his study, with his hands in the air.

"*A tierra!*" barked the Colonel who led the soldiers. "Get on the ground with your hands in back." He pointed down with his *Xiuhcoatl* assault rifle—a weapon made in Mexico, which the Colonel used instead of the American M-4 as a matter of national pride.

"Sí, señor." And with those words, El Jefe complied with the order.

14

INADMISSIBLE EVIDENCE

You could play a pretty good-sized touch football game in Judge
Marvin Raines's courtroom, if you moved all the tables and the
jury box. This huge space, on the eighth floor of Houston's Federal Building, symbolizes all of the prestige and power of the United States
of America. The bench where the judge sits is wide, and an enormous
granite backdrop rises up high behind it, to let everyone know that a
federal judge, in this government, is the most powerful official that there
is.

And today, this big courtroom would be needed, because Judge Raines
would hear the Request for an Order to Hand Over José Luis Leyva to
Testify, filed by Robert Herrick and Associates. The document had been
filed with its proper Latin name, but it explained itself, by saying, in effect,
"What we want is to question the witness." Judge Raines also would have
to consider the opposition to that Request by the United States Attorney
and the Department of Justice, which was written in vigorous terminology. It was full of predictions of disaster for the witness if even his existence
were to become known, as well as warnings about catastrophes in the War
on Terror.

Hours before the appointed time, the courtroom began to fill.

Officially, the lawsuit was called *Castillo v. The Velnikov Bank,* but
this controversy was not between those parties. It was between the plaintiffs and the United States of America. A sideshow had taken over the
circus, so to speak. Patrick Castillo sat in one of the front rows, and Anna
Castillo Carter was there too. The news reporters were there in force,
because not only was this hearing part of the case of the eight murders in
the Death House, but also, it involved two powerful parties. "It's a battle
between Titans of the Law," said one courtroom watcher.

Jimmy Coleman probably wouldn't have much of a role in this case, but he got there early. If nothing else, he could use the occasion to make snide remarks to Robert Herrick.

Jimmy favored Robert with a dirty grin. "Thanks, Herrick, for filing this silly Request for whatever it is. And getting this loser case of yours removed to federal court, where you've just bought yourself nothing but a harder time in front of a federal judge."

Robert looked at him and realized, of course, that the insult was not a casual act. It was a part of Jimmy's strategy, aimed at undermining Robert's confidence in the case. And the best counter-strategy was to smile and give it back.

"Jimmy, I always enjoy trying a case against you. I learn something about unconventional tactics every time. And I'll say this for you, Jimmy. You've got the talking part of the game mastered."

Jimmy didn't get it. "A Request for . . . this Latin term? *'Habeas Corpus Ad Testificandum?'* It sounds like someone saying, *'get me out of jail so I can talk!'* "

Behind Jimmy, there were the inevitable four Booker and Bayne associates, billing ungodly fees to the Velnikov Bank. One of them just couldn't resist joining Jimmy in the fun, and this young lawyer spoke up with his own kind of insult. *"Habeas Corpus Ad Testifi-*condom? What kind of 'condom' is that?"

Jimmy laughed. So did the four associates. "Well, next week we've got the Motion to Dismiss in this case scheduled for argument. That will make it all go away."

"We'll be ready." Robert grinned back. He acted more certain than he really was, but as he told himself: That's the best way to deal with Jimmy.

"Yep. The Motion to Dismiss will put this silly case of yours out of its misery." Jimmy was nothing if not persistent. Beside him sat the Bank President, Chola Velnikov, the man with the strange name and the trademark purple-suit-purple-shirt-orange-shoes combination. Chola Velnikov let out a guffaw, and his tied-together eyebrows bobbed.

Suddenly, four loud knocks shot across the courtroom, originating in the door to the judge's chambers. A law clerk opened it and shouted, "Hear ye, hear ye, hear ye, hear ye! Order in the court! Everyone rise, please!"

And now, everyone watched as Judge Marvin Raines walked briskly up the stairs to the magnificent bench. The ceiling lights glinted like sparks from his too-bald head, and his dark brown, almost black eyes were set. As was his custom, Judge Raines wore a black knot of a tie that tucked into his black robe. There was no doubt about it: Judge Raines preferred a very formal courtroom.

The law clerk continued: "The United States District Court for the Southern District of Texas is now open, pursuant to law, the Honorable Judge Marvin Raines presiding. All ye having business before this court, draw nigh, and ye shall be heard."

Judge Raines sat down, with everyone else standing, as the law clerk finished by saying, "God save the United States and this honorable court!"

"Be seated, please," said the judge pleasantly. And there was a rustling sound as the assembled multitude all sat.

The judge got right down to business. *"Castillo versus The Velnikov Bank.* This is a motion asking me to order the United States to produce a witness named José Luis Leyva for deposition." He turned toward Robert. "Mr. Herrick, you represent the plaintiffs. Do I have it right, what you're asking for?"

Robert stood and nodded. "Yes, your honor."

"And I see Mr. Taylor Underwood, the United States Attorney for the Southern District of Texas. You will represent the United States?"

"Yes, your honor." It was not customary for the United States Attorney himself to appear in court. His assistants had thousands of cases and more than a dozen courtrooms to cover. But the United States evidently considered this a crucial case. Several other lawyers sat with Taylor Underwood, all trying to look busy.

"Your honor," the United States Attorney began, "Let me introduce James Mendoza, from the Department of Justice in Washington D.C.—which we call 'Main Justice.' Mr. Mendoza is an expert in the law of government privilege. He will join me in representing the Government."

"Thank you." The judge turned again toward the plaintiffs' side of the courtroom. "Mr. Herrick, it's your Application. Tell me: Why should the court grant it?"

"Your honor, the court should grant it because government secrecy in this area is narrow. And there's that old saying: 'the law is entitled to everyone's evidence,' and it fits, here. The law assumes that the witness is available to testify. The Government has to disprove that assumption, and they can't.

"But most importantly, our case involves a serious issue, with eight hired murders. It has been described by our mayor as 'one of the ugliest crime scenes I've ever seen.' As our affidavits show, Mr. José Luis Leyva is a crucial witness. This witness is an insider who can testify from first-hand knowledge about the role of the Bank in supporting the murderous operations of the Cartel."

"Your honor." It was James Mendoza, from Main Justice, who spoke. "The cases are clear, and they say that none of that is relevant. If the government secrets privilege applies, it stops Mr. Herrick from getting to the source of information. Period."

"Your honor, that is generally correct," Robert agreed. "But there are situations in which the court has to balance the plaintiffs' need for the information against the government's need for secrecy. And this is one of those situations."

"How so?" The judge's skepticism was written on his face. "I've read your briefs, both sides' briefs, and it seems to me that Mr. Mendoza has a point. The question isn't whether you have a strong case or a weak case against the Bank. The question is whether the government has a right to keep its secrets."

"Your honor, normally, so. But here, the Government has shared the secret, so that it is no longer a secret. As our papers point out, the Government has made this witness, José Luis Leyva, available to the local District Attorney here. Also, Mr. Leyva has testified in front of the Grand Jury. In connection with that, Mr. Leyva was interviewed by newspaper reporters outside the Grand Jury room. He has been made available to the government of Mexico and two other foreign countries. In addition to having told his full story to the DEA."

Robert's voice rose. "In this situation, your honor, the United States cannot hide behind a pretense of secrecy, because it has not kept its secrecy. The government is simply denying justice to its citizens. In this situation, the government secrets privilege does not exist, and the government's argument changes to a simple balancing question: balancing the government's desire for secrecy against the citizen's need for the information."

James Mendoza sounded outraged. "The cases Mr. Herrick cites for that are completely different! Allowing a witness who is protected to testify in front of a Grand Jury is not like publishing the information to the world, and the Government has preserved its secret!"

His voice lowered. "In fact, the position of the Drug Enforcement Agency and of the United States is the same as it always has been. Namely, we do not confirm, nor do we deny, the existence of any person in a witness protection plan, and that applies here. We cannot confirm even the existence of a person named José Luis Leyva."

The judge held a telephone to his ear. There had been no sound; apparently he had had it on silent and had felt it vibrate. "I've got to take this one," he announced to the lawyers. There was a murmur from the audience. Most citizens are surprised the first time they see a judge talking on the telephone from the bench to someone outside the courtroom, although it is amazing how many judges do it.

The silence, then, was awkward, because those close to the bench could hear the judge's end of the conversation. "John . . . did . . . what? . . . Sweetheart, I'm in the middle of a hearing. . . . Lots of lawyers. . . . Well, I'll see what I can do. . . . I'll get over there as quickly as I can."

Suddenly, Judge Marvin Raines was ready to rule. "I've studied all the papers. They cover all of the issues we've talked about here. It's obvious to me that Mr. Mendoza is right. The Government can't operate if it can't keep secrets. The Application for Writ of Habeas Corpus Ad Testificandum is denied."

"Thank you, your honor." The United States Attorney spoke quietly. And across the courtroom, Jimmy Coleman's grin spread across his face like a rising sun seen through a discolored lens.

Robert sat down, heavily. Tom Kennedy was the only one who spoke. "There goes our case. Unless . . . let me get back to the office and write up a Notice of Appeal. Our chances are poor, but we can always . . . hope."

* * *

El Jefe thought it was unfortunate that he wasn't treated in prison the way some big shots he knew about were treated.

After the Mexican army had taken over his home, he had been hustled, roughly, into an armored car. And driven quickly to Mexico City. And then put here, behind bars.

"Well, but . . . those well-treated guys mostly surrendered, *Jefe,* and they bargained with the *Federales,*" one of the guards told him sympathetically. "Too bad. You didn't know you were going to be captured, because then you could have had a big ceremony to give yourself up."

El Jefe answered with an unprintable expression.

So, El Jefe didn't get to pass the time in a fake kind of house arrest, and he didn't get a hacienda full of flowers and beautiful women. But that didn't mean that he was an ordinary prisoner. Far from it. He had three cells, all linked together, with mahogany furniture, wall hangings, and privacy curtains. And servants, recruited from among the other inmates. Power has a way of following the man, and anyone with any sense still avoided offending El Jefe. Anyone with sense knew he'd better stay afraid of the man.

Still, El Jefe thought he deserved better.

"You have a visitor!" One of the guards announced. *"Su Abogado, Jefe!* Your lawyer!"

"Oh. Great." El Jefe wasn't very interested in conferring with his lawyer. The man seemed pretty useless. This lawyer wasn't helpful, for instance, in locating José Luis Leyva so that he could be assassinated. Which is what ought to happen in a rational world, according to El Jefe. The lawyer couldn't even get him that hoped-for hacienda outside the prison system where El Jefe could pretend to be under house arrest.

"These are papers in a civil lawsuit, *Jefe*." The lawyer said it deferentially, because lawyers for cartel members in Mexico know that they aren't any more immune to disappearing violently than anyone else. "These are papers from a suit filed in the United States. It is called *Castillo versus The Velnikov Bank*, and below the name of the first defendant, Velnikov Bank, you are named as a defendant too."

"So what?" El Jefe recognized the name Castillo. That cockroach journalist in Houston had been named Castillo. But he was sure that nobody from Houston could get to this great man, El Jefe, here in Mexico.

"The papers are legal. They were served on you according to international treaties. The lawsuit will result in a judgment in the United States. Here in Mexico, *Jefe*, you still have millions of dollars in cash and property. But if they get a judgment against you, even in the United States, the possibility exists that they can enforce the judgment here by having your money seized."

"In Mexico? Give me a break."

Again, the lawyer was deferential. And philosophical. "What do you want to do about it, *Jefe?*" This client was not likely to follow any lawyer's advice. For the lawyer, it was not a problem. The lawyer's fee had already been paid, and it was substantial. That is what puts a spring in a lawyer's step.

"Nothing. Leave it alone. Throw away these lawsuit papers from the Gringos. If you have to bother me with the law, do it for something important. Such as getting me out of here."

"Yes. . . . Yes, *Jefe*."

15
THE MOTION TO DISMISS

The day had finally arrived. The court had set the Motion to Dismiss to be heard today. The plaintiffs' lawyers felt the day almost as a condemned prisoner feels his execution date. The defense lawyers felt the opposite; they were excited and happy.

In Jimmy Coleman's office, the priceless Italian intarsiato chest sparkled. Its gold hardware glistened, next to the custom-made desk that matched its inlaid green-and-gold flowers. Toward the south, the sun was rising, and dozens of floors below, traffic crept along Travis Street toward town.

Jimmy sat behind the desk, and his favorite associate, Jennifer Lowenstein, sat at one of the desk chairs. Several other Booker and Bayne associates looked on from behind. They all wanted to be here, because whatever else he might be, Jimmy was a marvelous teacher. And he liked an audience. Besides, you were sure to get all of your time billed whether it was needed or not when you worked for Jimmy, and that helps an associate who is trying to make partner.

"Today's the day," Jimmy exulted. His grin was an ugly mixture of brown and off-beige. "We finally get to argue our Motion to Dismiss against Robert Herrick's lawsuit." His grin grew bigger. "I like arguing a Motion to Dismiss because it's hard for the plaintiff to do much to hurt you, and you can hurt him. Real bad."

The associates, all wearing black suits, all giggled.

"Why's it taken so long, Jimmy?" Jennifer was used to seeing Jimmy Coleman get his hearings set on whatever dates he wanted.

"It's strange, especially since we've already had hearings about the evidence in this case. Unusual. All I can say is, the court coordinator in this court who schedules everything, is brand new. She's a bumblepuppy.

Doesn't matter much. We're ahead, given what's happened with that witness, the guy named Leyva. Given that Herrick can't get to the witness he needs."

"And I know you're ready for this Motion to Dismiss, Jimmy."

"Yes. More than ready. We've written an excellent brief. Judge Raines is good about reading the briefs."

"What happens if we don't get it dismissed? Getting a Motion to Dismiss granted is unusual, we all know. If we have to try it, is our client innocent? The Bank is clean, right?"

Jimmy frowned. "Let's put it this way. We'll defend the case vigorously. But the truth is, our good client, The Velnikov Bank, does have some expo-o-o-sure. In fact, a lot of expo-o-o-sure."

Jennifer knew what this verbiage meant. Calling the Bank a "good client" meant that the Bank paid Booker and Bayne millions a year. And saying that the Bank had "some expo-o-o-sure, and in fact a lot of expo-o-o-sure," meant that the Bank was likely to get hammered by a jury, if things got that far. It meant that there was a lot of ev-i-dence that created the expo-o-o-sure.

Actually, it might mean that the Bank was as guilty as sin. But Booker and Bayne would use every rule or procedure or piece of evidence to make it impossible, or at least difficult, to prove its guilt.

Remembering the pictures she had seen—the photographs that were part of the evidence, showing the massacre in the Death House—Jennifer shivered in spite of herself. Being a big-time lawyer meant representing some very bad clients and using the law to cover up what they had done, all legally. She wasn't quite used to it.

"Okay, Buckaroos!" Jimmy grinned again, as he addressed his foot soldiers. "Time to go. Let's head over to the Federal Courthouse and kick those bad guys' asses . . . for suing our good client."

* * *

Judge Marvin Raines ascended to the bench. It took some climbing, because the judge's magnificent roost in this courtroom is elevated. The huge granite wall symbolizes the power of a federal court. "Be seated, please," said the judge to the lawyers and audience, all standing.

"I don't quite understand this," the judge began. "Today, we're hearing the Motion to Dismiss in *Castillo v. The Velnikov Bank*. But we've already had hearings in this case, which would have been unnecessary if the Motion to Dismiss were granted. We had that hearing about the witness, that José Luis Leyva. How did that happen?"

"Judge, I don't know." Jimmy Coleman stood, across the courtroom. He sounded like nails scraping on a blackboard. "We moved for an early hearing, and this was the earliest date the court coordinator could give us."

"Oh, well, it happens." The judge grinned. "We screw up, and it makes more work. So, let's get on with it and get the work done."

He held up a fistful of documents. "I've read the Complaint filed by Mr. Herrick for the Castillo plaintiffs, of course, and I've read the Motion to Dismiss filed by Mr. Coleman for the Bank. And both of you have written some way-too long briefs"—he held up a bigger fistful—". . . why can't any of these briefs be shorter? . . . But I've read them."

And now, Judge Raines shook his head and frowned. It was obvious that he thought there was something wrong with this case. "So, Mr. Herrick . . . why shouldn't this court dismiss your lawsuit? I mean, throw it out?"

He glared at the plaintiff's lawyer. "The Bank is your target defendant. The Velnikov Bank. But your claim against the Velnikov Bank doesn't involve any of the actual killers, and the Bank just did what banks always do. It took in deposits and it lent money."

He frowned again. "So, why shouldn't I grant the Bank's Motion to Dismiss?"

Robert Herrick's eyes tightened. As if it were yesterday, he visualized that gory building that the press had come to call "The Death House." And now, he thought, the judge is about to throw out my clients' only chance for justice. The Bank is going to get away with it.

He kept his voice even. "Well, judge, the Velnikov Bank took in money from depositors who had nothing. . . . This Bank laundered money for drug gangs."

"But did the Bank know that? How could the Bank have known?" The judge stared at Robert with eyes that were narrowed to slits.

"That's right, Judge." Jimmy Coleman's dirty grin seemed out of place, almost surreal. "Nothing's unusual about a bank having depositors that it also lends to! That's the usual banking relationship."

"I'm inclined to think so, too," agreed the judge.

The Bank President with the strange name, Chola Velnikov, nodded so hard at the judge's words it almost seemed that his neck would break.

Jimmy Coleman was just getting warmed up. "Judge, there is at least one benefit to that hearing we had earlier. The one about the absent witness, José Luis Leyva. Your honor denied Mr. Herrick's request to question that witness. Mr. Leyva is off limits to Mr. Herrick, and the plaintiffs don't have any direct evidence, or any prospect of getting any."

"Exactly." The judge nodded.

Robert didn't remember much of the hearing after that. He remembered telling the judge that the Bank had used multiple layers of penniless borrowers—fake borrowers—and that these funds had found their way back to the Cartel. He vaguely recalled telling the judge that the money from which the lending was funded had come from the same straw borrowers, as depositors—a telltale sign of money laundering. He remembered detailing for the judge the testimony he planned to offer from his expert witness, an accountant, who would trace the path of the money.

"The transfers of money could not have happened without the full knowledge and cooperation of this Bank," he remembered saying. "And without that kind of money laundering, the Cartel could not have operated, and the horrifying massacre of the Castillo family in the Death House could not have happened. And we plan to show that the Bank's highest managers knew that this drug trade involved murders—many murders."

Dimly, he remembered Jimmy's anger as he denounced these arguments. "That's just Mr. Herrick's speculation!"

And nothing Robert could say seemed to impress the judge.

And after the hearing, he remembered what Jimmy had said as he walked out of the courtroom. "Herrick, I almost hope the judge lets this piece-of-shit case of yours go ahead, 'cause I look forward to trying it in front of a jury."

The usual unnecessary gaggle of four Booker and Bayne associates had followed Jimmy out of the courtroom, all in black suits. They had all laughed, and one of them had said, "But the judge is going to be merciful and dismiss this worthless suit. To minimize the pain."

16

THE FIFTH AMENDMENT

Tom Kennedy sat across from Robert at the big mahogany desk. "If we lose the Motion to Dismiss, and the Bank gets released from the lawsuit, do we have any other recourse? Is there another defendant we can recover anything from?"

"I don't think so. The three local defendants, the actual killers, have ignored our lawsuit."

Tom shook his head. "I'm not surprised, of course. We can take a default judgment, if we even want to bother with it."

"It's a waste of time, of course." Robert looked out the greenhouse windows toward the south, and saw the city towers in grey, brown, and white. "The reason those particular defendants ignored everything is because they don't have anything to pay a judgment with."

"Should we even bother?"

"Well, yes. When any defendant fails to answer any lawsuit, I always think you should take a default judgment against that defendant. You never know. One of these guys might have a rich uncle with no other relatives."

Kennedy laughed under his breath, at that. But then, he said: "What's going to be interesting is that guy in Mexico we've also sued. Alejandro Carlos Gonzales-Huerta. The big guy who heads up the Cartel—the one they call El Jefe. It looks like he's going to default, too, because the deadline's coming, and he hasn't answered the suit either."

"But there's a problem there too." Robert looked out the window toward an unidentified something, far away.

"What?" Kennedy looked surprised. "Something with the international papers? We were careful with those. It took hours and hours just to translate everything into Spanish, the way the treaties require."

"That's not the problem. It's worse for us than that."

"What?"

"Well, I put Chipmunk onto finding out what assets there are in that Cartel. And yes, El Jefe owns a lot of stuff. But Chipmunk's sources, and they're pretty reliable in this instance, tell us that the Mexican government is going to lighten El Jefe's pockets."

"What do you mean?"

"I mean they're going to lighten El Jefe's pockets to zero. I mean that the Mexican National Government has put a hold on everything El Jefe owns, and they are in the process of forfeiting everything."

"Oh." Kennedy looked shell-shocked. ". . . Oh, well."

"It's going to go to the people of Mexico. All of it."

"Oh. I see."

"It makes a certain amount of sense, even if it's not good for us. Mexico and the Mexican citizens have suffered a lot more pain, loss, and damage than anyone in the United States. The Mexican Government will have the first shot at everything El Jefe has. So, yes, Tom; take a default judgment, because you never know. But don't start counting the money. The judgment against El Jefe is going to wind up being about as valuable as a blank piece of paper."

Now, Kennedy looked at an unknown spot outside the window. "It's like what we were saying the other day. 'Nothing's ever easy.'"

"And our only solvent defendant, now, is that Velnikov Bank. Those white collar crooks over there are into this Cartel's crimes up to their eyeballs, of course. The Bank was as necessary to these killings as the hands-on killers were. But nothing's going to be easy about proving it."

He brought his wandering eyes back to the room. "So, we need to get to the Bank. And for that, we need that witness. José Luis Leyva. The guy the DEA is hiding; the guy they won't admit even exists."

* * *

Two hours later, an excited Tom Kennedy burst into Robert's office again. "Look here. We won in the court of appeals! At least, we won a small victory, or part of a small victory. . . . Well, let me put it this way. . . . We've won a *tiny* part of a *small* victory."

"Okay, I give up. What have we won?" The tall windows behind Robert's desk showed a dreary day, with visibility of only half the greenery that usually sparkled alongside the meanders of Buffalo Bayou.

"We got the right result from the court of appeals about José Luis Leyva. Our hoped-for witness. About the Request for an Order to the DEA to Hand Over the Witness—you know, that thing with the Latin name. It's a strong opinion in our favor, from the court of appeals."

"Is that so???"

"Yes, indeed. Let me read you just an excerpt. It's pretty short:

". . . The United States has made the witness, José Luis Leyva, available both to the State's District Attorney and to newspaper reporters. The witness's testimony has been made known public-ly.

"Therefore, the usual government secrets privilege does not ap-ply. All that remains is the Government's claim that it will be harmed if the witness testifies. The court must balance the plain-tiffs' interest in obtaining the witness's information against the potential harm to the Government.

"The plaintiffs can question the witness at a secure location to be chosen by the Drug Enforcement Agency. The harm to the Gov-ernment is minimal. But the plaintiffs have an important need for the witness, and they have eight claims for wrongful death.

"The balance tilts so heavily in favor of the witness testifying that we must REVERSE the decision of the trial judge and order the United States to make the witness available."

Robert was listening intently, and he started to smile. "Well, I'll be darned. Sometimes things do work out for the best."

"We'd better get started on arranging with the DEA to question José Luis Leyva and preserve his testimony. I mean, we need to move on this right away."

"It's nice to have a battle that we win, occasionally."

* * *

Two hours later, Kennedy was back again in Robert's office. "I have an outline of questions to ask José Luis Leyva. And I've written the notice that's required, so we can get the arrangements under way."

Donna DeCarlo's voice came over the intercom. "Robert, the investiga-tor is here. You know, Chipmunk. He has something to tell you about the *Castillo* case—you know, the case where we've filed suit against that Bank. He says it's important."

"Tell him to come in." Robert was in a good mood. "Chipmunk must have gotten through to the DEA. I don't understand why they've given us so much trouble in the first place."

But as the man with the big cheeks walked into the room, he didn't seem to share Robert's enthusiasm. "I can see that you're excited about the court of appeals decision. Well, don't get too excited."

"Why?" Suddenly, Robert was cautious, and his enthusiasm faded.

"My guy at the DEA tells me that José Luis Leyva won't testify. The agent in charge really, really doesn't want him to testify."

Robert frowned, at that. "Well, give the agent in charge a medal. But it doesn't matter what the DEA agent in charge thinks. The court says for the DEA to produce him to testify."

Chipmunk shook his head, and his cheeks wiggled. "Get this. Now, the DEA says that José Luis Leyva will take the Fifth Amendment. That's what my guys there tell me, straight from the agent in charge. José Luis will refuse to testify in our case on the ground that it would tend to incriminate him."

"I don't understand."

"The DEA will produce the witness, they tell me, and you can ask José Luis questions, but José Luis won't answer any of them. That's what I hear. Any question you ask, José Luis will just say, 'I'll take the Fifth Amendment on that.'"

"What . . . ? I still don't understand."

"Well, José Luis Leyva is . . . well, he's a criminal, of course. He was a high-up assistant to the man they called El Jefe. He was a big player in the Cartel at the time the murders we're suing about went down, and he was certain to have been involved in them. He's claiming the right against self-incrimination, just like any street criminal."

Robert flopped his head down. "That's crazy."

Kennedy was just as dumfounded. "The DEA must be orchestrating this. I can't believe this witness, this José Luis, thought this up on his own. Especially in terms of saying he'll testify in two other cases, the DEA case and the state murder prosecution, but not in our civil lawsuit."

He paused. "What do we do now?"

Robert's answer came slowly. "We . . . we go back to the district court again. And we try to get an order requiring the witness to testify and ordering the DEA not to tell him not to."

"Well, I don't know." Kennedy's good humor, by now, was completely gone. "I wish us good luck in trying to do that, but our chances sound like there are only two of them. Namely: . . . Slim . . . and . . . None."

"And Slim?" Robert stared out the window. "Well, Slim just left town." He stared at another spot in the gray, wet mist. "Slim and None—and Slim's disappeared. But . . . we'll give it a try. We need that witness."

"Why does this happen to us? We're nice people."

"Why is our Government treating us this way? That's what I'd like to know. Anyway, without José Luis, we'll have a totally uphill battle in this lawsuit against the Bank, even if we know the Bank is guilty as sin."

17
THE DRIVE-BY

Jimmy Coleman laughed out loud when he saw the report saying that José Luis was taking the Fifth Amendment.

Jennifer Lowenstein sat in front of Jimmy's ornate intarsiato desk. The honey-colored wood was crisscrossed with inlaid brown, green, and white, and the priceless matching armoire glittered with its gold fixtures. The floor-to-ceiling windows looked down at cars swarming over the Southwest Freeway in the darkening dusk, as rush hour traffic started to build.

"That Drug Enforcement Administration, they're doing the right thing," Jimmy exulted.

"It's almost like they're on our side," Jennifer agreed.

"Oh, they are on our side. I've been in touch with them throughout all of this. We've done everything we could to support the DEA."

"I didn't know that."

"In my first year practicing law, a criminal defense lawyer told me something I've always remembered." Jimmy showed his dirty teeth. "He said, 'It's nice to win, of course, but that's not the biggest thrill. The biggest thrill, and there's nothing that measures up to it, is getting somebody off who you know, for sure, is guilty of a really bad crime.'"

This time, it was Jennifer's turn to laugh.

"We're going to kick a little tail in this case." Jimmy turned a little more serious. "But we'll need the DEA to keep this guy quiet, this José Luis."

"Why . . . why is that?"

"Jennifer, I think we might have a chance in this case to have that big thrill that the criminal lawyer told me about in my first year."

"You mean our client, the Velnikov Bank, is . . . guilty?"

"They're into it up to their ass. Guilty as sin. The Bank president looks all shifty-eyed when I ask him about it. He tells me stuff about the Bank's loans in this case that is the most obvious kind of science fiction. And I think this José Luis—this witness that the DEA is hiding—I think he can tell about all of it."

Jimmy Coleman was a street fighter, and everyone knew it. Literally. He had grown up in a gang as a teenager in South Los Angeles, where the meanest streets in America teemed with hopeless young men who made themselves a bare living by petty extortion, robbery, and occasional kidnappings. That community, if community is the right word, had been his family. No one understood how this primitive child had pulled himself up to graduate from law school, much less how he had managed to get hired at a silk-stocking law firm like Booker and Bayne. But here he was, at the top of his profession.

"Jimmy ... when you were back in Los Angeles, what do you remember most?" Jennifer knew only the broadest background, but she knew that Jimmy was a good storyteller. It was rumored that sometimes you could get him to talk, and if you could, he'd astound you.

"Jennifer, believe me. You don't want to know."

"Of course I do! Everyone wants to know the boss, the one they work for."

Jimmy's forehead darkened. "I can see a picture of it today. Still. We did a drive-by at a place on Sepulveda, supposed to be where one of the Guardians stayed. A rival gang, those Guardians, and they were vicious. We planned on just leaving a calling card, you know, because the Guardians had tried to shake down the liquor stores on one of our blocks, where we already had them under, you know, contract. They'd already paid it to us, to keep them safe, or actually to keep us from starting a fire on the premises, and it wouldn't do if another team like the Guardians were going to cut in."

Jennifer was silent. She stared at Jimmy.

"One of our guys, a guy named Cochise, was riding shotgun. The front passenger seat. And he was literally riding shotgun, with a shotgun. We went by, I guess, in a pretty quick pass—you've got to be quick or you'll get blasted back at, but we went too fast—and Cochise missed. Sort of. That's the only name I knew him by, Cochise. And Cochise hit the apartment next door, just past this guy who was a member of the Guardians.

"And that evening, on television, they showed what had happened. There was a ten-year-old girl who lived there, and she was there, and Cochise hit her. The TV had a picture of her head, where she got hit. Our guys laughed about it afterward. This girl had nothing to do with it, and in fact she was located at a whole different address, but Cochise had shot at that address by mistake, and she was dead, dead, dead. And in an indirect way, that was good for us. It helped us, which was one reason the guys laughed."

"Why . . . why would that help anyone? Why would murdering the wrong person, a completely uninvolved person, help your gang?"

"The meaner you are, the bigger the rep."

"I don't understand."

"The world will fear you if you're crazy about being violent. And this showed that we were violent, and crazy too. And the police swarmed all over everyone, but they never got to Cochise. I heard he died in a shootout a few years later, but I wasn't there."

Jennifer just looked at him.

"Anyway, in this Velnikov Bank case, we need to keep encouraging the DEA. And we need to get the Motion to Dismiss granted before Herrick can get anything from José Luis."

* * *

"The law says José Luis Leyva doesn't have the right to claim the Fifth Amendment." Tom Kennedy sounded disgusted.

"I agree. You've done a good job with this Motion to Compel Testimony." Robert smiled. "If I were the judge, I'd grant it."

"Well, you're . . . biased. But yes, I think it's pretty clear: we're right. The law doesn't let a witness be selective about who he's going to tell his story to."

"That's our argument. He's given up the right to claim the Fifth Amendment, because he's already told his story."

"Right. All of the cases say that. If you tell your story, or even part of it, you've given up the right to claim the Fifth. In technical language, you've *'waived'* the right to remain silent."

"And in this case, José Luis has obviously told his story to the DEA. And we know he blabbed to a couple of news reporters early on, because the DEA let him."

"He must have been in the custody of a pretty inexperienced DEA agent."

"A newbie to the DEA, I guess, to let him talk to the press."

"A bumblepuppy?"

"Yes. Or maybe a guy who was a real hamburger, but a hamburger without much meat."

"Not the brightest bulb in the chandelier."

"A couple of bottles short of a six-pack, maybe."

"Or, maybe, a few sandwiches less than a picnic. Anyway, Robert, this drive-by DEA agent wasn't too smart, and he let José Luis talk to the press. And old José Luis, he told those news guys enough to get all over TV, the internet, and the newspapers. . . ."

". . . And we can hope, at least, that Judge Raines will see it our way."

The two plaintiffs' lawyers looked at each other and nodded, but with expressions that were not entirely confident. "We can hope," they both said, simultaneously.

18
José Luis Appears

El Jefe was angry. He paced back and forth across his three prison cells. His black hair was carefully combed straight back, and his brown-spotted camouflage shirt was starched and pressed. His jailers weren't sure how he managed to maintain this kind of costume inside a prison, but he did it. His broad, small-eyed face was red, now, with annoyance.

"This so-called 'investigator,' he's stepped into something he doesn't know how to handle," said The Craziest One to no listener in particular. "It's dangerous. That Velnikov Bank is the key to our financial success."

"What has happened, *Jefe*?" The jailer was sympathetic. His official assignment was to keep inmates such as The Craziest One securely imprisoned, but his informal assignment was to help El Jefe continue to manage his drug cartel from here, behind bars. "What is dangerous?"

"The Bank is a choke point in our operation. We cannot operate without it. That's the way we get the money that we earn: through the Velnikov Bank. If this investigator interferes, he will cost us money."

"Can he do it, *Jefe*? Can he really interfere?"

"I don't know. But this investigator is a man who worked before for the DEA, the Drug Enforcement Agency."

"I see. That is a problem, yes."

El Jefe thought for a moment, but just for a moment. Quick judgment had been essential in his rise to power within the Cartel.

"We need to take him out. I mean, I'd like to make this pipsqueak investigator into *guiso*, stew, to send a message to others who might interfere, but we're a long distance away, here, and it's another country. Just killing him will have to do, in the best way possible."

"I will convey your orders, *Jefe*."

The guard who was The Craziest One's messenger stepped out. At the unit station, he met his sergeant, who usually kidded him about his function as El Jefe's servant. "What did he want? Did he order you to wash the windows?"

"He wants this particular guy killed in the United States. The way of killing him doesn't matter, so long as it's done. He said that's all we can do, but if he could, he'd make the guy into stew." El Jefe's personal guard looked puzzled. "I can only guess what that means."

"El Jefe is known for killing his most detested enemies in a particular way." The sergeant had a strange expression. "He has the guy stuffed into a 55-gallon steel drum. And then. . . ."

"Never mind! I get the idea." El Jefe's guard wore an even stranger expression, pale and wide-eyed.

"This Jefe is the most sadistic guy in his business. That's part of his success. It's why he still has his entire enterprise working for him, even from inside this prison. Everybody is afraid to disobey him. With good reason. Including us. You and me."

The sergeant shook his head. "There is a special place reserved for this Jefe in the inner circle of Hell, in the place for the worst and the lowest, the place for the greatest evil. And you can be sure of it." He shivered, involuntarily, and blessed himself with the sign of the cross, before adding, "Unless, that is, the Devil himself is afraid of El Jefe."

* * *

Back in the United States, Judge Marvin Raines ascended to the bench and surveyed his courtroom. "Mr. James Mendoza? You're here again from Main Justice in Washington, to represent the DEA? This hearing is about whether José Luis Leyva can claim the right to remain silent."

"Yes, your honor. From the Department of Justice. And as this court ordered us to do, we have brought José Luis Leyva in person. He is present in court, right next to me."

The witness who had been El Jefe's second in command at the Cartel was uncomfortably dressed in a blue suit with a blue tie. His dark hair was parted neatly. His eyes looked nervously left and right from his narrow face. José Luis Leyva looked like a hunted animal instead of the second-in-command of one of the most violent cartels in the world.

The judge nodded. "We need Mr. Leyva here because of his claim of the Fifth Amendment, since Mr. Herrick has filed a Motion to Compel his testimony. It's Mr. Leyva's personal privilege, of course, if the privilege exists—the privilege against self-incrimination. He has to be present."

"Of course, your honor. There is no question that Mr. Leyva's evidence would involve crimes. His testimony would involve his participation in the Cartel in ways that suggest criminal activity. Just based on that, he has the right to take the Fifth Amendment."

"No one disputes that," said the judge flatly. "But Mr. Herrick points out that the privilege may have disappeared. Am I reading you right, Mr. Herrick?"

Robert stood to address the court. "Entirely right, your honor. If the witness has made statements to other people about the same subject, then the privilege disappears. In the terminology of the Supreme Court, the privilege is waived. And Mr. Leyva has made a lot of statements."

"That's why he's here. To find out whether he has. Mr. Leyva? Mr. Leyva, you should stand when addressing the court. Please stand."

Through an interpreter, José Luis responded. "Sí, señor."

"Mr. Leyva, you claim the right to remain silent. I have been advised by counsel for the Government that you claim that right."

"Yes, sir."

"Normally, Mr. Leyva, you are entitled to that right. But I need to ask you some questions to determine whether the privilege still exists in this case. Mr. Leyva, have you made statements to the U.S. Government about your activities in Mexico with the so-called Cartel?"

José Luis looked nervously at the Government attorneys who surrounded him. Then: "No, sir." But the witness was looking straight down at the floor as he spoke. His eyes blinked. Even the DEA lawyers shook their heads at the man's transparent lie.

The judge reacted with surprise. "You haven't discussed your experiences and your possible testimony with the Government lawyers?"

Suddenly there was consternation at the Government counsel table. The DEA firmly wanted this witness not to testify. But no one could get away with this kind of perjury. After a long period of whispering back and forth with Mr. Mendoza, José Luis Leyva looked up.

"My many apologies, my judge," he said through the interpreter. "I maybe misunderstood. The correct answer is, yes, I have talked over my experiences in Mexico with Mr. Mendoza."

The judge stared at him. "And I have been furnished with a copy of a newspaper article that purports to quote you. Does it?"

More whispering, this time with the interpreter. And finally: "Your honor, Mr. Leyva does not understand the word 'purports,' even as I have tried to translate it."

"Serves me right for using fancy lawyer-talk," the judge muttered. "Let me try again. Mr. Leyva, look at this newspaper article that I hold in my hand. Is it a story about you, telling the story that you told to the newspaper reporter?"

". . . Yes, sir."

The judge turned to the other side of the courtroom. "Mr. Coleman, you're here representing the Bank. It's not really your business, I guess, because it's the Government that is trying to keep the witness from having to testify, but in the interest of completeness, do you have anything to add?"

Jimmy stood. "We agree with the Government, your honor. And I would add that the Supreme Court cases, such as *Byers v. California*, say that the Fifth Amendment is supposed to be 'balanced' against community security. And in this case, the Government's interest in prosecuting crimes committed by an entire drug cartel outweighs a private lawsuit."

By now, the judge was annoyed. "Mr. Mendoza, it's obvious that Mr. Herrick is right. The Fifth Amendment doesn't apply. A witness can't decide to blab his story to one listener, or in this instance several listeners, and then refuse to provide it to the court in another case."

The judge looked at the Government lawyer in frustration. "Mr. Mendoza, why on earth are you trying to keep Mr. Leyva from testifying in this case, which involves a claim about eight murders?"

James Mendoza shifted nervously on his feet. "Whenever a witness testifies, we must give that testimony to any defendant that he testifies against later. And it gives away strategies, and defendants try to shape their stories around it. And the testimony is going to vary a little bit, over months or years, and those variations will be used to impeach the witness. To show contradictions."

"But there are instances where a witness testifies in many cases, one after another. That happens all the time." The judge was irritated.

"Yes, your honor."

Now, the judge was ready to rule. "There is no Fifth Amendment privilege here. The witness is required to testify at a regular deposition, in response to Mr. Herrick's questions. Mr. Herrick, prepare me an order to sign."

The judge left the bench briskly. And then there was the usual hubbub, as the herd of attorneys stuffed papers into briefcases and left the courtroom.

"Congratulations, Robert." Tom Kennedy was elated. "We won. You may have found a way to make this case against the Bank actually work out."

"Well. . . ." Robert was cautious. "We haven't gotten his answers yet. You saw how he testified, denying that he told Mendoza anything until

Mendoza told him to admit it. He'll say anything." Robert shook his head. "I won't be surprised if he denies knowing anything we ask about, and if we get absolutely nothing from taking his deposition."

19

BAIL FOR EL JEFE?

Nearly a thousand miles to the south, the *abogado del estado*, the prosecutor who was the attorney for the Mexican Government, was aghast. "Your honor, you're saying that we must prosecute this case against the man known as El Jefe in a Mexican *state* court? Not a court of the Mexican Federal Government?"

"That's right." The judge representing the Mexican Federal Government was impassive.

"But . . . your honor . . . the charges include the fact that this defendant was waging war against the Mexican Federal Army!"

"The evidence you have submitted does not begin to support that charge. It is a matter of jurisdiction. And the truth is, I have no jurisdiction, except to dismiss this attempted prosecution." The judge looked down at the prosecutor with complete indifference.

"Waging war against the Federal Army is not a federal crime? The statutes say. . . ."

"I know what the statutes say." The judge began to get angry. "The answer is, the man you call El Jefe did not 'wage war against the Federal Army.' Instead, the Federal Army came to him. The Federal Army used its utmost technology, first, with missiles launched from a heavy destroyer. There is no evidence that this defendant, El Jefe, even knew what was happening until afterward, except that he knew he needed to defend his home."

The defense lawyer for El Jefe was a former Minister of Justice for Mexico. With barely concealed outrage, he said, "Your honor, that's exactly right. The Army turned the area around this man's home into a smoking, burned-out battlefield. And I might add, they didn't have a warrant. At least, not the right kind of warrant."

"That is another issue." The judge nodded. "But I don't have jurisdiction, so I can't decide that."

"Your honor," said the defense attorney, "my client should be admitted to bail. There is no case against him. There is not even a charge against him since this court lacks jurisdiction, owing to the bungling done by the Mexican prosecutor."

"I'm inclined to agree. Mr. Prosecutor, you are entitled to be heard concerning the amount of bail."

The prosecutor stood, dumfounded, unable to think of a proper "amount of bail."

"Just to be on the safe side, make it a high bail," suggested the defense lawyer. "Say, five hundred thousand pesos, maybe."

The prosecutor recovered, finally. "Your honor, this man is a flight risk. More than a flight risk. He is guaranteed to disappear. He should not be admitted to bail."

"Your honor, there are no pending charges. He must be admitted to bail."

The prosecutor had another thought, now. "Your honor, assuming that the Government files charges, next, in a state court, there is no reason to assume that the state court judge will agree with your honor's order of dismissal, here. And if he does, there is no reason to assume that the court of appeals will agree that it is a state court case. We may end up years from now with the case bouncing out of the state courts, and at that time, it will be completely impossible to find this defendant. He will disappear."

"Bail of five hundred thousand pesos," the judge announced. "That is for the pending federal charges in this court during the national government's appeal and not for the charges that I assume you will file, or may file, in a proper state court. The cause is dismissed. The court is adjourned."

The judge stepped down from the bench. The attorneys stood and began to pack their papers.

To his assistant, the prosecutor confided, "This defendant has been running his enterprise, his Cartel, from the inside. Everyone is afraid of him." Before expressing his next thought, the prosecutor paused. "Even the courts are afraid of El Jefe. Even the judges. Even justice itself, even that magnificent ideal called justice, shivers in fear before a defendant like this man."

* * *

Hundreds of miles to the north, Robert and Tom were on a mission that also involved being inside a lockup. They were on their way to interview a murderer. As they left the free world and entered the county jail, each of them shivered with a creepy feeling, even though they had an official escort. Detectives Derrigan Slaughter and Donnie Cashdollar walked beside them.

"I've never seen a jail I liked," Robert admitted. "This one included. But we've got to be here, because we need to interview Jorge Baron Baldassaro. The driver for the killers."

The county jail is right next to the county courthouses, but it's like another country. For reasons of security, it's a dull-looking building, with tiny windows and not many design features, unless you look at it through the eyes of a prison architect. Robert and Tom, walking beside Detectives Slaughter and Cashdollar, were on their way up to the fourth floor, where they would meet the getaway driver for the murderers.

The detectives laughed. Then: "You not in this here jail for real and permanent," Derrigan Slaughter said. "You gonna get back out. But I know how it feel. You can't he'p thinkin, maybe they make a mistake, and somehow they keep me in here."

As usual, the detectives sported contrasting outfits. Detective Slaughter, an African-American officer whose style was always simple but elegant, wore a pearl gray suit cut perfectly for his size, with a brown tie. His partner, Donnie Cashdollar, featured a big selection of colors: a green shirt, an orange tie, a blue jacket, and brown trousers. As always, they were an odd couple.

"I guess you had to fight through some red tape, getting this interview with Baldassaro." Cashdollar grinned. "When you called us, we understood. This is the guy who has confessed about the murders of the Castillo family. He's the least culpable one, just the driver, and he'll testify in the criminal cases against the other two characters. And he's also important to your civil case against the Bank, and you'll need to have him testify too."

"Right. But I wish we could have arranged to meet with him in one of those not-so-fancy attorney interview rooms."

Again the Detectives laughed, because the meeting with Baldassaro was going to be a standup conversation inside the jail. "Well, we cut some of the red tape. But you ain't his lawyer—you don't represent Baldassaro—"

"Thank goodness," said Tom.

More laughter from the detectives. "—and so they wasn't gonna give you no interview room. But we'll get him to tell you how it went down. He's our prisoner, and we're buddies with him by now, us two detectives."

They arrived at the fourth floor. The hallway was narrow, but the dayroom was enormous. Groups of prisoners in jail-white shirts and baggy white trousers sat or stood, and the feeling was oppressive. There were too many prisoners for the dayroom, but that is a standard condition in a lot of jails.

"Baldassaro!" Derrigan Slaughter shouted it. This was the old-fashioned communication method, often used inside jails. "Baldassaro! Come up front! Yo' second family is here."

A small man with wispy hair and a mustache too big for his size came slowly out of the crowd. His brown eyes pushed wide open. He had a tattoo of some unrecognizable species of animal on his face. Detective Slaughter introduced the two lawyers. "Don't hold back, Jorge. Tell 'em what you know." Baldassaro held onto two bars, floor-to-ceiling bars in a dull gray color, stained from being held onto frequently this way.

"I drive the car. That's all I did. I not see anything." The little man was hesitant, and his accent was thick.

"Please tell us the whole story." Robert tried to hide his disgust. "You drove the other two men to the home of the Castillo family, as I understand it?"

"We park in parking lot of a business of . . . what you call it, . . . a dry laundry. . . . Near the place they wanted to go. Castillo house. These two guys get out and I see them go to the Castillo house. I not know then it is Castillo house, but I now know. They kick at the door and go in. Fast. I hear screaming. Seemed very long time, the noises. Then they run out and tell me, 'drive!' That is all I know."

"And before that, you went to . . . a bank?"

"Yes. Before, we go to a bank downtown. We all three go inside. Go to a window thing. The waiter there—"

"The teller?

"—Yes. The . . . teller . . . he give us thousand dollars. Supposed to be first payment, and there be more payment when job is done. But I not know the name of the bank. Or which bank it was."

"Can you tell us what the bank looked like?"

"The room inside had very high . . . a high . . . top. High . . . ceiling. Big room. Green floor. Green carpet on floor. But where the wall was, that the . . . tellers stood behind, the wall beneath them was red. And outside, the building was made of those little rocks, and the rocks were black. Little square rocks. I forget what you call them."

"Bricks? Black bricks?"

"Yes. Black . . . bricks. And a big sign in orange letters, or gold."

"The Velnikov Bank. Only one like that." Tom seemed satisfied with the information. "So, it's true. The Velnikov Bank actually paid the murderers. Amazing."

Thirty minutes later, they walked away and started the long process of getting out of the jail. The duty officer took a long time examining their driver's licenses, comparing the pictures to each lawyer's appearance, and checking them against his computer. He looked over the officers' badges carefully. Too carefully, according to the lawyers, who were nervous about getting out.

"It's a lot easier, I guess, to get into a jail," said Tom, "than it is to get out of jail."

*　*　*

Chipmunk, the investigator, lived in the Meyerland subdivision of the city. After years of Government service, he finally earned a solid salary at the law firm known as Robert Herrick and Associates. His habit, developed through long exposure to criminals of extraordinary ruthlessness, was to look first to security before any other consideration about his home. The Drug Enforcement Administration dealt with outlaws that were more desperate, more reckless, and more determined even than members of terrorist groups or traditional organized crime families. And even though Chipmunk had left the DEA, he still had reason to worry.

A few days after El Jefe issued his order to "kill the investigator," two men dressed in black scaled the ten-foot fence that surrounded all of Chipmunk's home. The top of the fence cap bristled with steel cylinders that stood up like nails, and these slowed the hired killers' effort. A motion detector found them, and immediately, klieg lights flooded the yard and a siren sounded.

Chipmunk picked up his daughter and handed her to his wife. "Get into the safe room." Just as quickly, he picked up his Glock 41 and his AR-15 assault rifle. He bounded down a half of the stairs, and then, where they turned, took the rest of the stairs one at a time, but fast.

In the light, he spotted the two figures. Just as he saw them, the closest one opened fire, rapid fire, semi-automatic fire, and Chipmunk fell to one knee, because a bullet had creased the fat part of his calf. From that position, he returned fire. The two figures raced to the side of the house and vaulted the fence in the opposite direction this time, and faster than they had entered.

Chipmunk struggled to stand. He ripped his pajama shirt and bound his calf. Then he retrieved the telephone and hit two numbers that dialed his contact at the DEA. "They came for me," was all he said. The next call was to the police department, which was likely to get there first, and the next call was to 911 for an ambulance. By this time, he had the bleeding stopped.

"No, I can't identify them," he found himself saying to the two officers who responded first. A DEA agent was not far behind. "No, I can't identify them," he repeated.

"They will be back," said the DEA agent, to no one but Chipmunk.

"Chipmunk!" His wife hadn't heard that comment, but she had enough experience to figure things out. "Please take some time off. And get yourself out of this case!"

20

THE DEPOSITION

Finally, the day arrived for the questioning of José Luis Leyva. In the big conference room of Robert Herrick and Associates, Robert explained to his clients, the Castillos, what was about to happen.

"This afternoon, we will be taking the deposition of José Luis Leyva. The witness who defected. The guy who left the Cartel."

"What is a . . . 'deposition'?" Patrick Castillo asked. The obvious question.

Robert smiled. "A 'deposition' is nothing but a fancy term for questions we ask a witness before trial, and answers by that witness. It's the best way of finding out what the witnesses are going to say. In this case, I'll be asking Mr. Leyva questions. He'll be required to answer those questions under oath, just as though we were in court. Our objective is to find out what Mr. Leyva knows and how he's going to testify."

"So you'll have more evidence, after this afternoon."

"That's what we hope."

"That's what we hope, *fervently*," Tom Kennedy added.

Robert laughed at that, in spite of the tension. "What Tom means is that you can have the strongest kinds of hopes, but you never know what you're going to get when you take a deposition. The witness may give you lots of valuable information: testimony that includes true confessions. Or, the witness may tell you a fantasy story, one that isn't true at all. Or, the witness may be so confused, in some cases, that he can't narrate a coherent story.

"And it's even possible that the witness may refuse to testify, just as this witness has refused to testify in the past. We don't think he can do that now, given the judge's orders. But it's possible."

"And it's also possible that we'll get a mixture of all four of those responses." Kennedy shook his head. "Some truth, some falsehood, some confusion, and some refusals to answer."

"With this witness, anything is possible," Robert agreed.

And with that, they waited. Soon, the conference room filled, and the witness was there.

* * *

"Would you state your full name for the court reporter, please, Mr. Leyva?"

The interpreter translated, then received the witness's answer: "José Luis Leyva."

"Do you understand what a deposition is, Mr. Leyva?"

Again, there was a delay produced by the interpreter, and then, the witness answered, "Yes. The Government lawyers told me that I have to answer questions."

"Then you also know that the answers you give are sworn to, under oath, and they carry the same penalties of perjury as testimony in court?"

". . . If the judge says so."

The conference room was uncharacteristically crowded. The Government lawyer from Main Justice in Washington was decked out in a dark gray suit and a red-and-blue striped tie: the perfect Government uniform. He was accompanied by three other Government lawyers, an FBI agent, and a high-level DEA operative.

Jimmy Coleman was there too, in a light blue suit and dark blue tie, with his white hair unkempt and his big nose even redder than usual. Beside him sat the inevitable entourage of Booker and Bayne associates, all eagerly taking notes, all billing the client an unreasonable amount of money.

Robert and Tom Kennedy were outnumbered, as they sat next to the court reporter and across from the witness.

"Mr. Leyva," Robert began, "Please tell us your main professional activity or employment before coming to the United States and contacting the DEA."

"Objection to the form of the question," said Jimmy Coleman in a ragged, gravelly voice. "It's compound and hypothetical, and it assumes facts not in evidence, such as that the witness actually had some sort of employment."

Robert and Tom were used to this objection, which they had referred to in the past as "that sleazy Coleman tactic." They had predicted that

Jimmy would object this way to most questions. Not because they actually would be objectionable, but to confuse and delay the process.

"You may answer," Robert told the witness.

After a series of translations, the interpreter relayed the witness's answer. "... I worked for a man named Alejandro Carlos Gonzales-Huerta. Known to me as 'El Jefe.' In Mexico."

"And what were your duties?"

"Not much. Call people, relay his requests."

"Objection." Jimmy's voice sounded as though it were scraped against the wall. "That's irrelevant, immaterial, and incompetent."

"Did your job sometimes include passing on directions from El Jefe that involved killing people?"

"... No! Certainly not. Only if it was legal to kill them."

Immediately, the Government lawyers descended on the witness, and there was a lot of whispering. And a long pause. Robert just waited.

"Well, I guess the answer is yes," José Luis Leyva corrected, finally.

In this twisted manner, while frequently contradicting himself, the witness answered Robert's questions, with descriptions of his history, his education (not much), his skills (not many), and his experience with the Cartel (which the witness minimized). Jimmy's objections dragged out the process, and so did confusion from translations by the interpreter. But the biggest delays resulted from conferences with the Government lawyers, who had to get José Luis Leyva to change his answers dozens of times.

After several hours, Robert said, "The court reporter needs to have a break." The lawyers and agents stretched and milled about in the hallways.

"Now, that is a bad witness," said Tom Kennedy to Robert. "I hope he drove an automatic transmission in Mexico, because I don't think he could handle the extra pedal for a clutch. I hope his dinner table has nothing but a fork beside the plate, because the usual knife and spoon probably would be too complicated for him to handle. And I hope he has shoes without strings, because I can't picture him tying them."

"Careful," said Robert. "Believe it or not, ... he's *our* witness. José Luis Leyva is a big part of *our* case. For better or for worse."

"I know." Kennedy shook his head. "I know that, only too well."

* * *

When the deposition started again, Robert began asking the more difficult questions. He was ready to ask José Luis Leyva about the Velnikov Bank, about money laundering, and about the massacre of the Castillo family at the Death House.

"Mr. Leyva, do you know about a Bank called 'The Velnikov Bank'?"

Jimmy Coleman weighed in with a long-winded objection. Robert ignored it. Fortunately, the witness was learning to ignore Jimmy too.

". . . Well, yes, approximately. Sort of."

Robert resisted the temptation to ask how someone could "approximately" know about a particular Bank. "And when did you first hear about the Velnikov Bank?"

Another long objection from Jimmy.

"Years ago. I am not exactly sure which year."

"And how did you first hear of it?"

"I don't know. It could even have been in the newspapers or something."

"Did your work with El Jefe ever involve the Velnikov Bank?"

A long objection, in Jimmy Coleman's cement-mixer voice.

"Yes. Of course."

"Please tell us about how your work involved the Velnikov Bank."

Another objection.

"Mr. Alejandro Carlos Gonzales-Huerta, who is known as El Jefe, was on the telephone with the President of the Bank and his assistant almost every day, and sometimes he had me call them."

"What did you call the Bank about, yourself?"

"I don't know."

Sometimes, when you get an absurd answer, the best thing to do is to ask the same question, again. So Robert did. "What did you call the Bank about, yourself?"

"I called when El Jefe told me to. And the usual message was to tell the Bank President, 'Where is our money? Hurry up with our money'!"

"Was this the same thing that El Jefe called about?"

"No. Maybe sometimes. I'm not sure."

This answer, again, produced a lot of whispering with the Government lawyers. Then, the witness added: "El Jefe always wanted them to hurry up with our money."

"What did that mean to you? Why was the Bank supposed to hurry up with El Jefe's money?"

Jimmy said, with his teeth grinding, "Objection. It calls for speculation and an opinion that the witness is not qualified to give."

The witness shifted uncomfortably. "I never understood how it all worked, or how the Bank got us our money. I just understood that we sent merchandise north into America, and the money came back through the Bank. If you called the Bank and yelled at the President, like El Jefe did, it helped the money to get speeded up."

"Did you see that happen, that it got speeded up?"

"Yes. I think so. I'm not sure, but maybe."

"Mr. Leyva, did you have any contact with anyone about Rafael Castillo and his family, about them being killed in Houston?"

Jimmy's objection to this question was long enough to fill a whole page of transcript.

"Yes. I think so."

"Who was it, that you had contact with, about killing Rafael Castillo?"

"El Jefe himself, several times. After it happened, he was happy, and he talked about it. Before it happened, he was working hard to get it to happen."

Robert paused, then took a shot in the dark. "Mr. Leyva, do you know whether El Jefe had any contact with the Velnikov Bank about killing Rafael Castillo and his family?"

The objection from Jimmy, here, sounded like a bulldozer scraping on rocks.

"Yes. I remember hearing him talking to the Bank President about it. Before it happened. I think it was the President. Maybe his assistant. But he mentioned the Bank in the same conversation, and I think he said that he would do something so that Castillo would not write any more stories about the Bank and about the drug trade."

Jimmy Coleman should have been shocked. He just sat impassively. As for Robert, he was disgusted, himself, but this was proof of his case. And the evidence that is crucial is always unpleasant.

After this, Robert asked just a few more questions. Only a few, because he was afraid of getting the witness to contradict himself. Finally, he said. "That's all. I pass the witness."

"I have no questions," said Jimmy Coleman, surprising everyone. Maybe Jimmy was afraid of the same thing; whatever he asked was as likely to get answers hurtful to him, from this loose-cannon witness, as it was to get helpful ones.

But Jimmy wasn't about to admit that.

"This witness," Jimmy thundered, "is so self-contradictory, and so full of fantasy, that his testimony ought to be completely suppressed. Thrown out, entirely. That doesn't happen much, these days, no matter how untruthful the witness is. But this testimony amounts to *nothing!* We will maintain our Motion to Dismiss, on the ground that this witness cannot add anything to the evidence because he cannot be believed about anything, and we will join it with a Motion for Summary Judgment."

On that cheerful note, the deposition adjourned.

21

THE COURT'S RULING

'm mad as hell, and I don't mind saying so." In fact, El Jefe was so angry that he was jumping up and down. He bounced around in his jail cell like grease splattered from a fry-pan, and he yelled at the guard. ". . . I don't understand. That judge down in Mexico City dismissed my case and set bond. They released me. So . . . why am I back behind bars?"

He found himself in a local jail, in Northern Mexico, to his disgust. The guards here were completely different from the ones he'd seen in Mexico City. This particular guard was not sympathetic—not at all. "Look," he said. It's simple. When you got released by the Mexican Federal court, you were still able to be prosecuted in a Mexican State court. The President knew this.

"He ordered the *Federales* to arrest you as soon as you left the jail in Mexico City," the guard said flatly. "And you got transported here, to the State jail, on charges that the President got filed immediately in the State courts."

"But since I'm back in my home State, surely I can bribe my way out. Or threaten to kill somebody. I ought to be able to get out."

"Not likely, Mr. *Jefe*. The President is not stupid, and he has figured things out. Right now, we are surrounded. There is a cordon of Mexican army soldiers circling this State prison, and they have orders not to depart until your case is finished."

"Well, but then, there's still the judge. The state judge who has my case. I can reach the judge."

"*El Presidente* thought of that, too. I'm sorry, Mr. *Jefe*. The judge is a substitute judge, a replacement, because the law allows for that, when local conditions require it. And they require it in your case, exactly because you want to bribe or threaten the judge, and everyone knows it, because you've done it before. And so, to take care of that, the President has appointed a judge well known to be clean. And tough. And the President has the Army following the judge everywhere, to guard him."

El Jefe was so angry that he looked as though he had just swallowed a handful of jalapenos, piled on top of a plate of habaneros.

"The same with the prosecutor." The guard spoke bluntly. "The President has appointed an assistant attorney general who is known to avoid corruption, and the Army is protecting him, too."

El Jefe didn't like this prison, the State prison. Instead of the comfortable three-cell operation he had had in Mexico City, he now had only two cells. The guards weren't helpful. They wouldn't relay his orders to the outside. No doubt the President of Mexico had tampered with the guards, too. The President was interfering with things that a politician had no business interfering with.

"And I should tell you this additional fact." The guard was impassive. "The Mexican National Prosecutors have appealed the dismissal by that judge in Mexico City. They say the odds are that the court of appeals will reverse that dismissal and order you to be prosecuted in the Federal courts. You'll be back where you started, but without the elegant accommodations in your prison."

El Jefe cursed. The only method he had, now, to relay his orders to his soldiers of the Cartel, was his lawyer. He met secretly with the lawyer, of course, and the lawyer was still afraid of him. His lawyer didn't have army protection, and El Jefe could still get the lawyer to tell his *Lugarteniente* to have someone killed, or how to move a shipment of heroin. The lawyer was a lifeline, still.

But it was a clumsy method of communication. The lawyer was not schooled in the ways of the Balamarcas Cartel, and he didn't always understand what he was doing. Besides, the lawyer couldn't be there all the time to take orders, the way the guards in Mexico City had.

El Jefe cursed again, this time more violently. "I'd like to make stew out of all of them," he said under his breath, referring to the judge, the prosecutor, and the soldiers who surrounded him. And, for that matter, the President of Mexico. But under these conditions, it became much, much harder to kill all of these people. To El Jefe, it was disorienting. This wasn't the way the world was supposed to be.

* * *

Several hundred miles to the north, a horde of lawyers congregated in the federal courtroom where the case of *Castillo v. The Velnikov Bank* was to be heard. They stood, together with the audience, when the judge was announced.

In front of that magnificent granite backdrop, Judge Raines ascended to the bench. "Be seated, please."

Judge Raines was known as a no-nonsense judge, and now, he lived up to that reputation. "First thing, let me announce: the Motion to Dismiss is denied. I've entered an order today, denying a dismissal."

An audible sound, a combination of a gasp and a sigh, rose up from the crowd of lawyers and audience.

"Mr. Herrick's suit paper, his complaint, is adequate now," Judge Raines continued. "In fact, there's no question it's adequate. Of course, having an adequate complaint is one thing. And proving it is another. And I don't mind saying, Mr. Herrick, that you will have a hard case to prove. You will have a big hill to climb, at trial. Going to trial with a theory that a Bank's loans and deposits caused a set of eight murders? It sounds preposterous.

"But Mr. Coleman, the complaint that Mr. Herrick has filed quotes the testimony of José Luis Leyva. That testimony, if a jury believes it, establishes that The Velnikov Bank was deeply involved in the business of the Cartel, and there is sufficient evidence that its actions proximately caused the murders in this case. I don't say that José Luis Leyva is a good witness or a bad witness, but if he's believed, there is enough so that this court can't throw out this case."

Jimmy Coleman was red-faced. "Judge, that witness is worthless! José Luis Leyva contradicted himself on almost every page. The testimony in his deposition is as full of perjury as grandma's homemade jam is lumpy with persimmons. This witness can't be believed at all, and he can't support any of Mr. Herrick's allegations." Jimmy sounded like an eighteen-wheeler shifting into gear: a highway truck, roaring its engine.

"Well, you can argue about the persimmons to the jury. It will be up to the jury to believe José Luis Leyva—or not to believe him. I can see that it's quite likely that a jury will disregard everything José Luis Leyva might say. In any event, I will issue a full opinion of the court very soon, explaining this decision to deny the Motion to Dismiss."

The judge looked up, sharply. "But it's best to announce my ruling to you now, with the lawyers all assembled together here. The reason is, I expect to try this case within two months. Listen carefully to this order of the court: . . . within *two months*." The judge's nearly-black eyes flashed with determination.

"Judge, I object to that schedule." Now, Jimmy Coleman's voice was like scratchy honey. "We have dozens of witnesses to question in dozens of pretrial depositions. We still are hunting for documents that Mr. Herrick has demanded. We can't find most of them, frankly. And Mr. Herrick hasn't produced the documents we've demanded."

"That's another reason I asked everyone to appear here today. We need to plan how to get it all done. We need to schedule all of that discovery."

"Your honor." Robert stood up. "I don't object to the court's schedule, on behalf of the plaintiffs. We want to try this case."

"That's good. But remember what the court has said. You will have an uphill battle, and there is no guarantee that you'll even have enough evidence to make out a case that the jury can decide. This court will not hesitate to throw your claim out during trial, if the evidence is insufficient. This court will order a judgment as a matter of law in favor of the defendant."

"Of course, judge. That's understood. But what I was going to ask, is this. Would your honor please enter an order requiring Mr. Coleman to produce the documents that we have requested, within a week? These are not obscure documents. In fact, they're the bank's own records. Our expert accountant needs these documents to complete his consideration of our claim that the Bank laundered money. Not hard stuff to find, and we're asking for it within a week, to be ready for the trial your honor has ordered."

"Mr. Coleman?"

Jimmy had no option but to agree. "Yes, your honor. We will produce what we have within a week."

Then, Jimmy's voice grated on. "But we will need to get discovery from Mr. Herrick immediately, too. We need to take the testimony of the plaintiffs' accountant, Mr. Martin Blankford. That's essential, and we think it should be done right after he gets the Bank's records of deposits and loans. Also, we have more than a dozen other witnesses that we need to take testimony from, all within a short time, if we are even going to have an outside chance to meet your honor's schedule."

"Mr. Herrick?"

Now, it was Robert who had to give in. "Judge, we have no problem with that. We will produce Mr. Martin Blankford, our expert accountant, to answer Mr. Coleman's questions within a week after we receive all of the documents we've requested from the Bank. Within a month after Mr. Coleman provides us with a list, we will produce all of the witnesses within our control, to give deposition testimony."

"And you need discovery too, Mr. Herrick. Right?"

"Yes, your honor. For example, we need to get testimony from Mr. Chola Velnikov, the Bank President. And his assistant. We will provide a list to Mr. Coleman, and we ask that he produce all of the witnesses he controls within a month—on the same schedule that I have to follow."

The judge turned to the court reporter. "Type up this conversation. This exchange between me and the lawyers. From your transcript." And then, he turned back to the lawyers. "I will have an order written and issued by tomorrow, including all of the scheduling matters covered here, together with the other orders that I usually issue before trial."

He looked, again, at Robert Herrick. "And so, you will have your chance, Mr. Herrick. To prove it all, at a trial. But I don't envy you. All that this court has done today is to deny the Motion to Dismiss and to plan discovery, so that we can try this case. In the meantime, let me say this to you, Mr. Herrick, and to your clients. *You ought to settle this case.* For whatever you can get from Mr. Coleman, at his most generous. I've never seen a case in which a bank has been found guilty for allegedly subsidizing murders. Frankly, it's a pretty far-out claim."

The judge shook his head. "Mr. Herrick, you ought to settle this case for whatever you can get."

* * *

But it was Maria who had the last word. She said it that evening, after Robert had given her the day's news.

"Robert, I always support you. I want you to handle this case successfully. And that means: you ought to listen to the judge. The judge is telling you the way it really is. You should settle it. Otherwise, he's saying, you are going to lose."

It was not only the judge who was worth listening to, Maria thought to herself. The psychic also knew.

But Maria followed the advice of the spirits and didn't push.

22

THE OTHER DEFENDANTS

Robert," said Donna DeCarlo's voice over the intercom, "You have a visitor. One we know. Francel Williams is here."

At that, Robert smiled, because Francel Williams always made him smile. Behind him, the greenhouse windows showed off another beautiful day, with puffy clouds and plenty of blue. Beside him, a hundred geraniums bloomed in shades of pink, red and white.

"Hello, Robert, my friend!" You always knew that Francel had thirty-two teeth. He showed all of them when he smiled, which was most of the time.

"Hello, Francel." Robert grinned almost as widely.

"You know that the court has appointed me," said Francel, "to represent the defendants who haven't answered your suit. The ones who haven't answered the suit; the ones who've defaulted. So now, I represent all of those defendants, all the other defendants. Other than the Velnikov Bank."

Francel's gleaming smile turned into a beaming smile. "And I'm so-o-o-o-o pleased to be involved in this case against you, Robert! But we don't have to be against each other if we can work just a few things out."

Francel stretched the word "so-o-o-o-o" to about five seconds long, and he made it descend all the way from treble to bass in pitch. "But if we are against each other, and if I lose, at least I'll know I had the finest lawyer in the world against me!"

Robert laughed out loud, in spite of himself. Francel Williams was six-foot-three, balding on top, and full of power and confidence. He was the best-known African-American lawyer in town, and he was a leader not just in the black community, but in the city as a whole. In fact, Francel had once been a judge. He had resigned, though, because he enjoyed practicing law too much.

Francel always wore a dark pinstriped suit and a silver tie, almost like a trademark. His real identifier, though, was his optimism. He always was jolly, no matter what happened.

"This is a won-der-ful-l-l-l case to be a part of!" Francel boomed, as he dropped his accordion file folder on Robert's desk. "I mean, it's a terrible tragedy, brought about by the fact that there's evil in the world. Evil like that awful Velnikov Bank. But Robert, you've got it under control."

"I'm not so sure about that."

"Oh, but you've got the goods on the Bank. And you're going to do a wonderful-l-l-l job trying the case, the way you always do."

"Wait just a minute, Francel. Tell me this. How can you represent all of the defaulting defendants? Baldassaro and the other hands-on murderers, and also Alejandro Carlos Gonzales-Huerta, the one they call El Jefe, and the Cartel? They have opposing interests, don't they?"

"Well, ask Judge Raines that question if you want to!" Francel smiled. "I know what you're talking about. But when a judge tells me to do something, it's my job to do it."

"I . . . guess so." Robert was trying to think through the implications for the conflict-of-interest rules that lawyers have to follow. Each of Francel's clients could blame the others.

"So, my solution is to treat them all as innocent." Francel smiled again.

"But in the face of the evidence, you really can't do that. Can you?"

"Yes. The way I see it, these defendants whom I represent, they are innocent, but the evidence against them is overwhelming. The evidence shows that they are guilty, even if I assume they aren't." Francel smiled even wider.

It was just like Francel, Robert thought. Thinking back, he remembered the trial of another, unrelated lawsuit, which had been interrupted in mid-testimony so that the bailiff could tell Francel Williams his uncle had died. "Uncle George was the one who raised me after my Daddy passed away!" Francel had said, with a stricken look on his face. "How did it happen?"

The bailiff had quietly answered, "Your uncle had a heart attack while he was teaching his class at Huston-Tilltson College." And that explanation had made Francel grin as wide as the courtroom. "What a wonderful thing to happen to Uncle George!" he had said, in a booming voice. "He always wanted to go that way."

That was Francel Williams. And now, Robert realized, this same Francel Williams was going to use his optimism, as well as his other lawyering skills, to do what he had been appointed to do. To try to walk these guilty-as-sin defendants who hadn't even answered the suit right out of the courtroom without a judgment against them, if he could. Or more likely, to get them the best outcome he could.

"You see, Robert, all of the conflict disappears, if you and I can come up with a joint strategy." Francel beamed again.

"How's that?" But Robert was smiling too.

"Well, Robert, you want the jury to put most of the fault, or all of the fault, on the Velnikov Bank. The law is pretty complicated, but what it means is that if the jury finds that most of the fault is to be blamed on Baldassaro and the other two who did the act, and on this El Jefe gentleman, the law says that it reduces what you can recover from the Velnikov Bank. Since you can't recover anything from Baldassaro and El Jefe, you want the jury to put the fault on The Velnikov Bank, or most of the fault."

"That's . . . right."

"That's the way the law is written. It's comparative fault. If the jury finds my clients, Baldassaro and El Jefe and the others, to be the only really guilty parties, and the Bank is only a little bit guilty, then you recover only whatever perecentage of the blame the jury puts on the Bank. So, just to take some figures, imagine that the jury says 50 percent of the negligence is El Jefe's, and 40 percent of it belongs to Baldassaro and the other two who were there. And the Bank is only ten percent at fault. Then, you only get 10 percent of your damages. El Jefe can't pay, even assuming you could get at any assets in Mexico. Baldassaro surely can't pay. So, Robert, you want the jury to put as little fault on my clients as possible."

"Francel, you sound almost like a visiting professor."

"So, Robert." Francel's smile grew. "You want the jury to put most of the fault on The Velnikov Bank. And guess what? I want the jury to put most of the fault on the Velnikov Bank, too."

"Well. . . ."

"And so, we can come to an agreement. What the law calls a 'joint defense agreement.'"

"But Fancel, your clients can't get off scot free. Not with all of this evidence. And with the horror of what they did."

"Oh, no, no, no!" Francel shook his head and kept his smile. "I'm not trying to get a zero-liability for these clients of mine, not with all of this evidence, even if I assume that they're innocent. I want to limit the liability."

Robert had always understood this point, of course. It was an ironic situation. In fact, it was crazy. The law creates crazy situations. One of the difficulties of the case against the Bank was that the head of the Cartel, El Jefe, was the most guilty party. But the plaintiffs probably would never recover anything from him. If the jury put most of the fault on El Jefe, Robert's clients would get a judgment that would be smaller against the Bank. The same reasoning applied to the hands-on murderers, Baldassaro and the others. If the jury put most of the negligence on these other defendants, the Bank would end up owing next to nothing, perhaps. It was a strange result, but one caused by the law.

He and Tom Kennedy had spent hours planning how to try the case to accomplish their goal. They couldn't deny the liability of El Jefe or the other murderers, even assuming they wanted to, which they didn't. But they needed to get the jury not only to find the Bank negligent, but also to decide that the percentage fault of the Bank was as large as possible. Which meant persuading the jury that it should put less of the fault on the other defendants than it otherwise might. Even though those other defendants had done the murders more directly. Tom and Robert had never come to a very good solution, because it was a hard problem to solve.

Now, Francel Williams was offering a way to help get it done.

"What do you propose, Francel?"

"Well, first, a joint defense agreement. And during the trial, you and I will cooperate. As allies. I will tell the jury that there isn't enough evidence to find a lot of fault against my defendants. But I will tell the jury, just as firmly, that the Bank is heavily at fault. 90 percent at fault. 95 percent. Without the Bank paying these alleged killers, and also laundering the Cartel's money, it never would have happened. And Robert"—Francel beamed—"you'll be saying the same thing to the jury."

"I don't like it."

"Of course not." Francel's smile never wavered. "The law makes us do strange things."

"Assuming we do this, will it work?"

"No guarantees." Francel looked a little more serious. "But with a defense lawyer, like me, saying that the plaintiff's damages are huge and they're caused by this awful Bank, and the plaintiff's lawyer, namely Robert Herrick, telling them the same thing, it's got a good chance of working."

"I don't . . . like it. . . ."

"Robert, it's your best chance to get justice for your clients. And to help stop money laundering, which will help stop the drug lords."

A pause. Then: "Assuming we make a joint defense agreement, what's next?"

"Well, I'm glad you asked." Francel was still smiling, because he almost always smiled. But he sounded serious. "To agree to this, I'd have to have you put an absolute limit on what you could recover from my defendants. It won't affect what the jury does or what you recover from the Bank, but I need a limit. My defendants have to be provided with something."

"A limit? Francel, that's hard. What did you have in mind?"

"No matter what percentage of fault the jury puts on my clients, the judgment against them cannot exceed a certain amount. . . . Say . . . ten thousand dollars, and we agree. Your clients, the plaintiffs, agree."

"I can't do that. It's got to be more."

"A hundred thousand dollars."

"Well . . . more." This is a strange negotiation, he thought to himself.

"Five hundred thousand dollars. Bear in mind, it's what I call ghost dollars. Because you're certain never to get them."

A pause. Robert shook his head and was no longer smiling. Finally: "All right, Francel. You've got me. This is a crazy solution, but the law creates a crazy problem. I'll never get anything from El Jefe, and I'll never get anything from Baldassaro. So it doesn't do any harm to limit the judgment to five hundred thousand from them, even for this horrifying case, since it's really limited to zero anyway."

Francel's smile had faded. These two lawyers had been dealing with a case involving pure evil, from opposite sides, and they had come to a mutual understanding. At the same time, it wasn't a bloodless process. Both lawyers knew the tragedy they were dealing with.

"Of course, we'll have to disclose this settlement to the court right away. The rules say so." Robert was thinking to himself, it's always a pleasure to have a case with Francel, even if I don't get everything I want.

"I knew we could work it out." Francel's grin was as bright as a floodlight. "We just needed to reason together. You see what I mean, Robert? This is a won-der-ful-l-l-l case!"

* * *

Before leaving, Francel had gushed, "When an agreement solves this big a problem, it's always best to paper it up right away!"

And so, after Francel had left, Robert sat in his office, studying an eighteen-page document that Francel had given him, called "Joint Defense and Trial Agreement." Its message was simple, in spite of all the "provides," "herewiths," and "notwithstandings." The defense would take the position before the jury that the most guilty party was the Bank. And if the jury found against Francel's clients, even if it found a large percentage of negligence against them, the judgment against Francel's clients could not be greater than $500,000.

So, in spite of partially settling the case, Francel would stay in the case, but he and Robert would have the same interests. They both would be trying the case against the Bank. The judge would disclose the settlement terms, and if it fit his strategy, Jimmy could tell the jury about it. Everything would be open and above board.

Robert smiled to himself. Francel had whipped this document out of his file as soon as he and Robert had pronounced an agreement. "I just happen to have it all written up. You won't have to do any more work on our deal, Robert." It was mildly upsetting, after what Robert had thought were equal negotiations, to find out that his opponent had written out the result beforehand. But Francel was fun to have as an opponent.

He looked out the window, and his mind drifted.

And quickly, he realized: there was that other lawyer, the one named Jimmy Coleman. Jimmy was extraordinarily effective in front of a jury. Jimmy would be fighting Robert and Francel every step of the way. Jimmy's Bank was guilty, and there was a lot of evidence that said so. But Jimmy would find ways to exclude a lot of the evidence, to cross-examine and undermine it, and to belittle Robert's arguments.

And Jimmy had something else to work with: the issue of percentage fault. Jimmy would be saying to the jury that all of these murders had been caused by the Cartel, and by El Jefe, and by Baldassaro, and by the other killers. And Jimmy would have a persuasive argument. El Jefe had been the instigator, and the others had done the killings. This meeting with Francel had been a pleasant interlude, but Robert's stomach tightened when he thought about what was about to happen.

He was not looking forward to this trial. In fact, he realized, . . . "I'm expecting a bad outcome."

23

THE CARTEL EXPERT

We're going to land at Kennedy Airport from the west," said Robert. "That's good, as far as airplanes sightseeing goes."

"Why's it good for sightseeing?" Maria wanted to know.

Beside them, the clouds flew by, as they skipped along the east coast in Robert's G-2 aircraft. It had been the finest available craft back when he had bought it, and although there were newer models, Robert wasn't one to throw away a perfectly good airplane for one that merely was newer. They had strayed farther east than the route from Texas to New York would usually have taken them, just to be tourists and see the coastline. Now, the green swells of Virginia and Maryland zigzagged along the line made by the ocean to the east.

"Well, as we come in from the west, we'll be flying toward the east side of New York City. To the northwest, on the side of the aircraft where you're sitting, Maria, you'll be able to see the outline of Manhattan in the distance. We won't be close enough for you to see the Empire State Building, but if you watch closely, you may see the Statue of Liberty. We'll fly over Queens, which is one of the five boroughs of New York—Manhattan is another of the five—but before we get there, we'll see the barrier shoals that lie south of Long Island, and we'll cross over Jamaica Bay, which is spectacular. Right about when you can see Manhattan, we'll turn eastward toward the airport, and we'll travel above a whole bunch of crowded New York Freeways. It's an airplane sightseeing tour."

"Cool." Maria smiled. "Except for the crowded freeway part of it."

"We're going to fly over them, is the good news."

Tom Kennedy laughed. "Until we land, that is. Then, we're going to be prisoners of local traffic, just like every New Yorker."

"I guess so. But it's really not that far, where we're going."

"Speaking of which, what I'd like to know," Tom went on, "is why we're traveling to the State University of New York."

"The State University of New York at Stony Brook, to be precise. Stony Brook is right here on Long Island, not too far away."

"So we're going to the State University of New York at Stony Brook because it's not far away from the airport?" Maria laughed.

"No." Robert laughed too. "You always make me have fun, mostly by just plain silliness. It takes a really smart person to be that silly."

"Thank you!"

"Well, so . . . the reason we are going to the State University of New York at Stony Brook is that they have a professor there named Julian Cuevas. And Professor Cuevas is the world's expert on drug organizations and the drug trade in Mexico."

"Do we really need an expert witness on that subject?" Tom wanted to know. "Don't people on juries know about the drug trade? And where it comes from? And that our case has all the indications of having been done as part of the drug trade?"

"Well, yes, but it's the details in our situation that matter. For instance, the need for a drug cartel like the one in this case to launder the money. The difficulty of getting it back across the border, and the way it's typically done. Then, people on a jury may know that the drug trade kills people, but they may not know just how casual drug lords like this El Jefe are about killing people who get in their way. It dovetails with the effect that El Jefe wanted to kill Rafael Castillo badly enough to get it done, even north of the border."

"Why's the world's expert on that kind of stuff at a place called Stony Brook, in New York?"

"He's in the Government Department there, Professor Cuevas is. His Ph.D. thesis is about the Government of Mexico and the effect of political parties there. He edged over from that to become an expert on how Mexico has been affected by drug dealers, and then he got interested in the drug cartels. Which are a kind of government unto themselves. And there's one other thing. Professor Cuevas has been a witness before, and he's been consulted by the United States Department of Justice. I'm hoping he'll know how to talk to a jury."

"Okay." Tom nodded. "So, I can see that this Professor . . . Cuevas? . . . could help our case, maybe. But will the judge let him testify? Is a judge going to think that this kind of evidence is relevant, and will this sort of expert fit within the rules about what's admissible in front of a jury?"

"That's a good question. I expect Jimmy Coleman to go wild with objections. But my instinct is that the judge will probably allow Professor

Cuevas to tell the jury at least some of what he knows. And guess what, Tom. That's one of the questions of law that you and your team can research and write a brief to the court about."

"I had already figured that out."

"Well, I'll see you guys at night, when you have your meeting with this professor all done." Maria laughed. "I'm going to the City, to Fifth Avenue—to Bloomingdales, to Saks—to spend some of your money, Robert my love."

* * *

Professor Cuevas looked like a professor. He had a brown herringbone jacket with patches on the elbows. His eyeglasses were rimless and his face was round, so that he had a jolly sort of expression. His shirt was off-white, and his tie was brown with undistinguishable squarish patterns on it. Brown tassel loafers completed the outfit. He smiled and nodded frequently. Good, Robert thought. Juries like that.

". . . This kind of invasion and blanket killing is typical of what drug cartels do," the professor said. "What happened to the Castillos is almost a calling card. It's not necessary to kill everyone, but the cartels do. The baby in this case was not a potential witness. It's a warning to other people who might get in the way. A kind of statement that 'We don't fool around.'"

"Would the weapons used in this case be typical of a drug cartel's operations?"

"I would say, no. From the information you supplied, it looks like the killers were recently in this country. It looks like they used machetes, instead of those AR-15's that the United States gun authorities allowed to be smuggled illegally into Mexico." The Professor shook his head. "They thought they had a sting operation going, where they would recover the guns and make arrests, but all they did was to give these killers their favorite weapons inside Mexico. But here, instead of using easy-to-get AR-15's, these killers used machetes. Tragic."

"Why do you think they did that?"

"It's likely . . . because they wanted a bloody crime scene. A gruesome scene. It sends a stronger message. It's like a bigger billboard.

Robert shivered, at that. But he had a job to do, and more questions to ask.

"Now, professor, I want to ask you some questions about the money trail. The path of the money that a drug cartel would use in buying drugs in the first place, sending them across the border, selling them in the

United States, and getting the money back to the drug lords in the United States."

For three more hours, Robert and Tom asked questions and listened to the answers. Tom had produced almost a legal pad full of notes when Robert finally said, "Well, I guess that's all of our questions, except about this head of the Cartel. This Alejandro Carlos Gonzales-Huerta, the one they call El Jefe, or the one they also call *El Más Loco*. What's he like, and why do they call him The Craziest One?"

"The world has never seen people like these drug lords," Professor Cuevas responded. "This guy, El Jefe, marks a kind of cruelty that we haven't seen since some of the Roman Emperors. I think about the Emperor called Caligula, for example. He's the one who pioneered the idea of putting captives and prisoners into the Colosseum together with lions, so that people could watch the spectacle."

The professor frowned. "Caligula's motto was 'Who cares if they hate me, so long as they fear me?' Well, the Emperor Caligula's motto is printed in Latin on a wall in Alejandro Carlos Gonzales-Huerta's home. It's his motto too."

Robert shivered again. The professor was familiar with this subject matter, but no one could discuss it coldly.

"This cartel head, El Jefe, or The Craziest One, delights in inflicting torture and pain," Professor Cuevas went on. "He has studied how to kill his enemies in the most spectacular and cruel ways. It's part of his business plan. He wants to have a reputation for arbitrary violence. The more random the cruelty, in fact, the better. The case you've got, Mr. Herrick, is an example of the mindset that's involved in drug cartels, but as far as the manner of killing the victims is concerned, I'm afraid it's one of the milder examples."

24
THE SHADOW JURY

At the office of Booker and Bayne, hundreds of lawyers were thinking about the upcoming trial. Inside these white birch corridors,
the Velnikov Bank case was all that anyone talked about. Some of
the lawyers even made bets, after spirited arguments about how long the
trial would take and what the exact outcome might be.

Now, in Jimmy Coleman's office, a half dozen lawyers sat on elegant
chairs with their eyes all glued to a television screen. It was show-and-tell
time. It was time, that is, for Dr. Randolph Murphy to give his report. Dr.
Murphy was a psychologist from Litigation Consultants, Inc., and Booker
and Bayne lawyers asked him to study their strategies before every trial.

This is the age of consultants. Everyone appreciated that. If a Booker
and Bayne lawyer was preparing for the defense of a drug manufacturer
whose product had killed a few hundred people, consultants could tell him
whether ambidextrous architects would be better as jurors for the defense
than left-handed longshoremen, almost like modern fortune-tellers. Or
whether Republican dentists would exonerate Booker and Bayne's client
in a big contract case. Dr. Murphy was good at predictions. He could tell
you these things and much more.

Dr. Murphy's firm, Litigation Consultants, specialized in using what
were called "focus groups" to forecast what juries would do. Focus groups
could tell you how a jury might react to a given witness, help you to figure
out the most devastating cross-examination of the witness, or show you
what arguments to use at the end of the case. A focus group could function
as a kind of substitute jury, but a jury that talked back and would tell you
what worked and what didn't. Right now, most of the lawyers defending
the Velnikov Bank were clustered near the priceless Italian chest in Jimmy

Coleman's office, to hear how a focus group led by Dr. Murphy had reacted to the evidence in the Death House case.

Dr. Murphy's image appeared on the monitor screen. "We assembled a typical focus group," his image explained. "We had a mixture of occupations, ages, and ethnicities. There were two housewives, a college instructor, a retired geologist, a substitute teacher, and a freelance writer. We try our best to get working people, but it's difficult, so we use retired people sometimes. We had six people in all, which is what we aim for."

The camera panned to Jimmy Coleman, who was sitting alongside the psychologist. "Doctor, please explain why you use six-member groups. Some people might think you need more. Or for that matter, fewer."

"We want feedback, and with a lot more members in the group, people's willingness to open up and talk gets stifled. With fewer, we don't get the kind of diversity of opinion that we want."

Dr. Murphy readied his pointer, and he went on. "We showed the focus group the video of the murder victims inside the Death House, but we did that at the end." He showed a still picture of the House and pointed at it. "A curious thing happened. If you show the video after giving all the other evidence, including a verbal description of the murders, the belief of the focus group in the guilt of the Bank actually goes down, not up. It's a paradox. The video inside the Death House helps the Bank, not the plaintiffs."

On the screen, the image of Jimmy seemed to be alerted by this information. "Doctor, why do you think this happened?"

"The best we could tell from what the focus group members said, was that it seemed less and less like something a Bank would have done." He pointed at the screen, which showed the interior of the focus group room, which was accessible to the experimenters through a one-way mirror. On the screen, the retired geologist was talking. "This video is gruesome. It just doesn't look like a crime that would be committed by a Bank."

The substitute teacher spoke next. "Well, the evidence does show that the Bank was in touch with the Cartel, and the evidence from the accountant shows that the Bank laundered money."

"Yes," said the writer.

"I know." The geologist nodded. "It's done bad things, the Bank. All I'm saying is that it doesn't seem that the evidence ties the Bank to these gruesome murders. They just don't seem like something a bank would do."

Jimmy paused the television, and the image of Dr. Murphy stopped moving. Jimmy was excited. "So! This is useful! One of our tactics will be to find some way to set things up so that Mr. Herrick shows this video late in the trial, rather than early."

Jennifer Lowenstein smiled. "Jimmy, it's rare to see this kind of reaction from you. This kind of excitement. I love it. But I get the message. We'll start working on how to object to the predicate evidence for this Death-House video. We'll find several different ways to object, to string it out."

Jimmy nodded. "And that way, we can use different objections at different places, to delay the admissibility of the video, so that it gets shown as late in Mr. Herrick's evidence as we can make it. Good, Jennifer, you've got the idea."

Another lawyer spoke next. "It just may happen that Herrick puts on the Death House video last, anyway."

"Sure. But this way, we'll be prepared in case we need to delay it." Jimmy smiled.

There was silence for a moment. Then, Jimmy said, "There are a lot of other interesting things that came out of this focus group. One of the best tactics is to blame the whole thing on the Cartel, and El Jefe, and the hands-on murderers. We'll be constantly saying to the jury, 'Where are the real defendants'?"

"We'll use the old 'empty chair trick.'" Jennifer laughed.

"Right," said the lawyer sitting next to her. "Jimmy, you'll pull out a chair. You'll push it toward the jury. You'll point with a heavy finger and say, 'This chair is *empty!*' And you'll say to the jury, 'This chair ought to be occupied by members of the Cartel. By the killer known as El Jefe. And there are other empty chairs that ought to be occupied by the Death House killers, the ones who committed this crime. Where are the real defendants?'"

"Right." Jimmy Coleman was having a good time. "Now, watch the rest of Dr. Murphy's report, because he'll show you how to use the empty chair. And how to do a whole lot of other things."

* * *

But the defendants weren't the only ones who used jury consultants. So did the plaintiffs' lawyers. Right now, at the top of the Chase Bank Tower, the lawyers for the plaintiffs—the lawyers for the Castillo family— were doing just that.

Robert Herrick was holding a report in his hands: a report from a consulting firm named "Calkins Jurimetrics." Professor Alistair Calkins was a member of the Department of Sociology at Rice University, but he made most of his income preparing reports like this one. The cover of the report had a big title saying, "Jury Pool Study for the Trial of the Velnikov Bank Case: A Survey and Analysis."

"It doesn't make any sense!" Tom Kennedy blurted out. "This Survey and Analysis of the potential jury pool . . . it doesn't make any sense."

"Watch out, Tom." Robert smiled. "I've always found Professor Calkins to be pretty knowledgeable. I'd pay attention to what he says."

"Well, but it doesn't make any sense," Kennedy said again. He held up his own copy of the Study. "Professor Calkins says here that black jurors are good for us. Good for the plaintiff. Okay. But so are white jurors, at least Anglo ones. Anglos are about the same as black people, favoring the plaintiff. But Mexican Americans and Hispanics, he says, are 'much worse for the plaintiff.' And there are sure to be many, many Hispanics on the jury panel, in this city."

Next, Kennedy read the words Professor Calkins had written. " 'And other recent-immigrant ethic groups, such as Asian-Americans, favored the Bank by a substantial margin.' This stuff looks like he just threw some darts at a board that had various races written on it."

"Of course, it's against the law to use these kinds of discriminants," said Robert. "It's against the law to pick a jury by racial factors. And we won't do it on a racial basis. But you can bet that Jimmy Coleman will. For instance, he'll strike all the black jurors off the jury. He'll assume that they're pro-plaintiff. And if he does, this study from Professor Calkins will help us to fight back. Unless he's done the same kind of study, Mr. Coleman won't know that white jurors are pro-plaintiff too."

Robert smiled. "That would be ironic . . . if Coleman were to illegally strike all the black jurors and keep all the white ones, when it won't do him any good, because Professor Calkins tells us that white jurors will favor the plaintiff, just like black jurors."

"But look, Robert. Think about it. We've got a really appealing victim, this little boy who was two years old and who was murdered in the Death House. And he's Mexican-American. We've got a famous Mexican-American journalist as a victim, and an entire Mexican-American family. You know that Hispanics and Mexican-Americans on the jury would identify with them."

"I suppose. But still, that doesn't mean that Professor Calkins is wrong. He and his team did over five hundred telephone interviews. They gave every interviewee a scenario, then asked them questions. And they didn't tell the people they interviewed which side they were on. It's a scientific poll. That's what Professor Calkins has done."

"But . . . but he didn't show videos of the victims, like we will. And he didn't include expert witnesses."

"No. All the interviewers did was to find out about initial attitudes. The attitudes that different kinds of people would come into the courtroom with. But I'll tell you what. Give Jimmy Coleman a jury of twelve people whose initial attitudes favor his side from the beginning, and ... well, he'll win the case every time. Beginning attitudes are important, and this Study tells us about that."

Kennedy read from another part of the report. "Professor Calkins says, 'Wealthier and highly-educated respondents favored the plaintiff. Less educated persons, and those with lower incomes, tended to side with the Bank.'"

He looked up and shook his head. "Robert ... this is nonsense. Usually, less educated and lower-income people favor the plaintiff, because they don't trust those big, evil corporations. It's the opposite from what Calkins's Study is telling us. Lower-income, less-educated people usually side with the plaintiff, because they don't like big defendants."

"True. But Tom, this case is ... just *different* from the average personal injury case. And that's why it makes sense, what Professor Calkins found. Lower-income people are likely to say to themselves, 'Banks just don't need to do this kind of thing because they're already rolling in money.' Wealthy, better-educated people will know that bankers have lots of temptations to break the law. And that they'll engage in money laundering, if the temptation is strong enough. I have a friend who says to me, 'You know what, Robert? Bankers are even sleazier than lawyers!'"

Tom laughed. Then he frowned, and he said, "But Robert, this stuff from Professor Calkins is pure voodoo. Listen to this, from page 16. 'The major religious groups differed in preference, too. Catholics and fundamentalist Protestants were less favorable to the plaintiff than Baptists, Methodists, Jews, and Presbyterians.' How could that possibly be true?"

"I don't know. And I imagine that Professor Calkins doesn't know, either. He'd probably have to speculate as to why there are these religious differences in attitudes. It's much harder to know the Why—why these attitudes exist, or where they come from—than it is to know which groups are for us and which groups are against. Dr. Calkins wasn't doing basic research. He just wanted to find out exactly what he did find out. And that's what we want, too."

"Look here." Kennedy read again from the study. "Retired persons and middle managers are good for the plaintiffs. That's what Professor Calkins says. In every other case we've ever tried, Robert, you know that ... middle managers have been *terrible* jurors for the injured plaintiff. And Professor Calkins says, 'Occupational data show that groups like medical personnel and college professors are bad for the plaintiffs. So are people in traditionally female occupations such as secretaries, clerks, and beauticians.' But the problem is, those are always our *best* jurors, whereas this Calkins Study is saying that they're the worst!"

"Well, I'll promise you this," Robert answered. "We'll take it all with a grain of salt when we actually pick the jury. We'll also consider what the people do and say when we question them. But this study"—he held up the Calkins Jurimetrics report—"this study is a good starting point for our efforts to keep Jimmy Coleman honest."

"Wonderful," said Kennedy. "Marvelous. So the ideal juror for us, allegedly, is a middle manager in a big company, who is wealthy and highly educated, not in a traditionally female occupation such as a secretary or beautician. And the ideal juror is either white or black, and not Catholic or fundamentalist, but mainstream Protestant like Baptist or Methodist. It's the opposite from every other case we've ever tried. Wonderful."

"Well, according to Professor Calkins, that's right."

"Robert, why don't we just throw out the whole jury and use an opinion poll to give us a verdict, without any evidence?"

Robert laughed. "Don't worry. We'll talk to the potential jurors and get a feel for them. One thing you're thinking, Tom, is absolutely right. A lawyer can do a much better job of picking a jury than a sociologist."

"And so, what we want is assistant vice presidents of big companies, who are middle managers, but who have the souls of poets."

"Right." Robert smiled. "Oh, and Tom. There's one more characteristic that well educated, wealthier people have, that we want. It's at page twenty-three of Professor Calkins's Study."

"What's that?"

"Reasonable amounts of damages. You see, when educated, wealthier people become persuaded that the plaintiffs are right, they award higher damages than lower-income people. They might award damages that can really begin to compensate the plaintiffs."

"Oh. Yes," Kennedy admitted. "That certainly is a characteristic that we want in our jurors."

25

THE EDGE OF TRIAL

Three weeks had passed since the hearing in which Judge Raines had ordered a trial within two months. "It's all been a blur," Tom Kennedy said.

"It sure has," Robert agreed. "But there's an advantage to doing it now, at the edge of trial. We know what we're going to use these witnesses for. And these documents. We don't have to wait months, or even years, to see the payoff. Months and years make you lose your place."

"Speaking of losing your place . . . tell me who it is that we are going to question today. I've forgotten."

"It's Chola Velnikov. The President of the Bank. And in fact, they're all in the conference room, together with our friend Jimmy Coleman."

It took another fifteen minutes for them to take their seats in the big conference room, listen to the court reporter swear the witness to tell the truth, and hear some bluster from Jimmy Coleman. "This is going to be a short depostion," he informed them.

"Mr. Velnikov," Robert began after he had covered the preliminaries, "please tell us your full name."

"Chola Velnikov." The witness wore his customary purple shirt under a purple pinstriped suit together with his customary orange shoes. His grown-together eyebrows shook.

Robert found it difficult to look at this witness. "And what is your business or profession, Mr. Velnikov?"

The witness looked at Jimmy Coleman. Who nodded.

"I decline to answer that question, and I assert the Fifth Amendment." The witness smiled maliciously as he said it.

Robert thought he hadn't heard it right. "Let me ask again in a different way, Mr. Velnikov. Are you the President of the Velnikov Bank?"

"I decline to answer that question, and I assert the Fifth Amendment."

"You're not even going to tell us whether you're the President of the Bank?"

By now, Jimmy Coleman was smiling too. "Objection. Privileged. The witness is asserting a privilege."

"Off the record," Robert said to the court reporter, signaling that this discussion should not be recorded in the reporter's notes. He was angry, but he suppressed his emotion as he turned to Jimmy. "Am I to understand that the witness will not answer anything about this lawsuit?"

"That's correct."

"Well . . . I'll need to go back on the record to have him tell me that."

"Suit yourself." Jimmy's voice grated, and his smile communicated his indifference to Robert's surprise.

"Mr. Velnikov, is it your intention not to answer any questions about the subject of this lawsuit?" Again, the man in the purple suit smiled.

"I decline to answer that question, and I assert the Fifth Amendment."

"Will you give me that answer to any question I ask about this lawsuit?"

"I decline to answer that question, and I assert the Fifth Amendment."

Robert hesitated, thinking, but only for a minute. "That's all the questions I have at this particular time. But I agree only to adjourning the witness's testimony, on a temporary basis, pending the judge's ruling."

"Suit yourself," said Jimmy again, with his best dirty smile.

"Stay on the record, please," said Robert to the court reporter. "Please record this discussion. Mr. Coleman," Robert turned to his opponent, "can you assure us that Mr. Velnikov will not be a witness at trial, or that he will claim the Fifth Amendment and refuse to testify?"

"I don't have to tell you that." Still, the dirty smile.

"Well, here's why I ask. The judge is not going to allow the witness to testify at trial, and spring a lot of surprises on the plaintiffs, after refusing to give any pretrial testimony, by which we might be able to get proper discovery of what he's going to say."

"I don't have to tell you anything."

"Mr. Velnikov, will you be present for trial?"

"I decline to answer that question, and I assert the Fifth Amendment."

"Do you expect to testify at trial?"

"I decline to answer that question, and I assert the Fifth Amendment."

"Mr. Coleman, we have produced every witness on your list that we have any control over. We're not trying to spring any surprises, and the plaintiffs have complied with our duties about discovery. Once again, will this witness, Mr. Velnikov, testify at trial, or is it possible that he might testify?"

"And once again, I don't have to tell you that."

On that note, everyone rose to leave the conference room. When he was alone with Tom Kennedy, Robert made no effort to hide his disgust.

"Can we tell the jury that he's claimed the privilege against self-incrimination? Or call him as a witness, and make him claim the privilege in front of the jury?"

"No," Robert answered. "Not usually. Not unless it's an improper claim of the privilege, which this probably isn't. This Bank is deep into committing crimes. And that means this Mr. Velnikov is a solid suspect to be deep into those same crimes. He probably has the right to claim the privilege against self-incrimination."

"Okay. But I'll look into it. What an awful individual, and what an awful Bank. I want to be sure that we can't tell the jury."

"Well, if Jimmy doesn't call him as a witness, we can point out to the jury that Jimmy didn't call him, without saying anything about the Fifth Amendment. The courts allow us to do that. But this isn't my biggest concern."

"What's . . . your biggest concern?

"Jimmy will know our case, backward and forward. The rules of procedure require us to let him know. The rules of discovery require us to produce our witnesses. But we won't know what Mr. Velnikov knows. In other words, one of the biggest witnesses on the other side is unknown to us."

"But if Mr. Velnikov doesn't testify, that's okay."

"Ah, yes . . . but what if Jimmy decides to call him to the witness stand, anyway, in the middle of the case?"

"Oh, I see. He might do that. . . ."

"Knowing Jimmy Coleman, it's a likely thing for him to do. We'll give him all our information, because we play by the rules. But he'll be able to withhold one of his most important witnesses, because he doesn't follow the rules. Then, in the last part of the trial, Jimmy may call Mr. Velnikov.

"At that point, we will have already given our opening statement, called all our witnesses, and told the jury what we think of the case. Jimmy can sandbag us, by having Velnikov testify then, as a surprise— Whoops! The evidence now forces me to call this witness—and Velnikov testifies to facts that aren't true, but we can't disprove them, because we didn't know to expect them."

"So . . . what do we do?"

"Only thing I can think of is to file a Motion with the court asking Judge Raines to order Jimmy not to create this kind of surprise witness. A Motion asking the judge to order Jimmy to put up or shut up. Either to say he isn't going to call this witness, or to present him for questioning, now."

"Will the judge grant that kind of order, do you think?"

"That's the problem. I don't know. But I do know this: Jimmy will do his best to sandbag us, so that he can pull off the biggest surprise possible."

* * *

The expert accountant, Martin Blankford, was in the conference room next, that afternoon. But this time, it was Jimmy Coleman who was asking the questions.

Within the first fifteen minutes, Jimmy had asked the witness, "Mr. Blankford, isn't it true that you went to a fourth-rate business school?" And also, "You've never testified in a criminal case about money laundering, have you?" and "You've been paid a princely sum of $350 per hour to give opinions that are agreeable to Mr. Herrick, isn't that right?"

Questions like these are not unexpected during questioning, when it is done for the purpose of discovering the opponent's evidence. They can be proper questions. But Jimmy's ghostly eyes, his ugly delivery of accusations, and his hammering voice, were often unnerving to witnesses. With Martin Blankford, who was a gentlemanly sort, Jimmy's manner was all too effective. "Yes, I guess so," was his answer to the question whether he'd had a fourth-rate education, and he also said, "No, I've never testified in a case quite like this," and "Yes, I've earned a big fee from this case."

It wasn't that Martin Blankford lacked credentials. He just was an agreeable sort. But then, Robert relaxed a little, because Blankford had solid answers to the questions about his opinions on the case. "No, there's no question. This is a classic pattern of money laundering." And as Blankford explained, "The loans that the Bank made were covered by inadequate reserves, were not properly secured, and were accompanied by nonconforming documentation. And the layering of loans through different empty-shell companies, all in a row, is an indicator of money laundering."

Robert made a mental note: I've got to prepare this witness to testify in front of the jury. Terminology like "inadequate reserves" will put every juror to sleep. So will assertions about whether the loans were "properly secured," or whether the documentation was "nonconforming." It would take hours of work to get this language translated into testimony for a jury.

But for now, that was fine. The witness answered the questions Jimmy asked. If the testimony at trial turned out to be clearer . . . well, that was what trial preparation was for.

26
EL JEFE'S ORDERS

efe, I want to retire," said the lawyer. "It isn't a question of money. But I'm 65 years old, and every lawyer I grew up with has retired. I had planned to retire by now, even before saying this."

"Well, I want you to keep on with it." Inside his jail cells, El Jefe wore his customary camouflage shirt and camouflage jacket and trousers, and he sported his usual Gucci shoes. He must be the only prisoner wearing clothes other than prison-issue, the lawyer thought. That is, if "prisoner" was the right term for this privileged guest of the state.

"But *Jefe*, . . . I have served you well, . . . and I'm tired. I'm too old for this." What the lawyer did not say was that any lawyer would get tired quickly of being summoned to a Mexican jail for the sole purpose of carrying a drug lord's illegal orders to a cartel.

"And my answer is no." El Jefe was becoming irritated. "You'd better keep on doing what you're doing."

". . . As . . . as you wish, Jefe." Obviously, one reason was that The Boss did not want to recruit and train another messenger.

"That's my wish. Now, listen." Suddenly, El Jefe was angry. "I gave orders weeks ago that this investigator in Texas who was bothering my Bank was supposed to die. It didn't happen."

"Yes, *Jefe*."

"You know that I dislike incompetence. I dislike people who can't carry out orders. It undermines discipline in my organization. I can't have this kind of thing."

"Yes, *Jefe*."

"Carry this message. It is to be done. It had better be done. It had better be done right this time."

"Yes, *Jefe*." Suddenly the lawyer realized that there was urgency to these orders. El Jefe was not a warm and kind person, and he was not above killing the messenger. The lawyer shivered. He had no desire to have happen to him what he knew could happen to him, from a single short order given by this client of his.

"Now, *Señor Abogado*, Mister Lawyer, you said that you had something to tell me about business. What sort of business? What was it that you had to tell me about business?"

"Not exactly . . . 'business,' *Jefe*." The lawyer hesitated, and his voice shook. "I, I . . . am afraid . . . that the United States has begun proceedings to . . . extradite . . . you to the United States. . . ."

"What?" El Jefe looked up sharply.

"The *Norteamericanos* want our Government in Mexico to send you to the United States. It means that a grand jury there has issued an indictment against you. It probably is a sealed indictment. Secret. The United States wants you . . . extradited . . . to the United States."

"When did you find this out?" The lawyer had never seen El Jefe shaken before. He actually seemed frightened. "That's not acceptable. The President of Mexico has always been prejudiced and is not going to be fair about this. And the *NorteAmericanos* will not be reasonable at all. They will pretend to hold a trial, but it won't really be a trial. They'll railroad me. And *El Presidente* does not care about that."

"Unfortunately, . . . you are right about that, . . . *Jefe*."

"Get to work. No, you can't retire. You aren't going to quit on me. This . . . extradition . . . will not happen."

* * *

"Ladies and gentlemen," Judge Marvin Raines told the assembled lawyers in his courtroom, "we've got two days until the trial begins in this case of *Castillo v. The Velnikov Bank*. Just two days."

It was unnecessary to tell the lawyers this, except perhaps as a means of letting them know that the judge was serious.

Jimmy Coleman and Robert Herrick both stood. "Yes, your honor," each of them said.

"Is your discovery finished? All the documents produced that have to be produced, and all the depositions taken?"

"Well, not exactly, your honor," Robert said. "We have two depositions to cram in for my clients the plaintiffs, this very afternoon. And two more tomorrow."

"All right. Get it done." The judge's voice was firm. "We're going to trial, day after tomorrow."

"And also, your honor, I'm afraid that I must tell you that we have moved to compel answers to questions from several of Mr. Coleman's witnesses. We disagree with his decisions to tell those witnesses not to answer these particular questions."

"But you will be ready, day after tomorrow, right?" It wasn't a question.

"Judge, on behalf of the plaintiffs, we want to try this case. It's time. But we believe the court will agree with us that Mr. Coleman's refusal to have these witnesses answer is wrong."

"All right. We'll consider that motion later in this hearing. I want to clear the decks."

"Yes, your honor." Again, each lawyer answered. When a judge is as determined as this one was, there's little to be gained from arguing.

"Our first Motion," Jimmy Coleman said hoarsely, "is a Motion to Exclude Evidence. Improper evidence, but evidence that Mr. Herrick has been trumpeting throughout this case. Evidence that the jury is not permitted to hear. That's the Motion we call our 'Motion in Limine,' or Motion to Exclude Evidence, and it's on top of the stack."

"I've seen it." The judge nodded. "You want Mr. Herrick and all of the plaintiff's witnesses to be forbidden to refer to 'the Balamarcas Cartel' by name. Or to use the words 'El Jefe,' 'El Más Loco,' or 'the Craziest One.' And you've got about a dozen other pieces of terminology that you want Mr. Herrick and his witnesses to be prohibited from saying in front of the jury."

"Exactly, your honor. These terms are prejudicial. And there's no reason for the plaintiffs to use them. Even if they have a case, which we don't think they do, these words are unnecessary, and they can tell their story without them."

"All right. Mr. Herrick? Response?"

"Your honor, it will be extraordinarily difficult to have the witnesses tell what they know without using the terminology that every one of them is familiar with. These are the people with whom The Velnikov Bank and Mr. Velnikov did business. In some instances, they will testify about conversations with others, including personnel of the Bank, in which these words were used. Mr. Coleman's Motion amounts to a request to hide the truth from the jury."

"Can't you refer to something called 'the group in Mexico' instead of the Balamarcas Cartel, and 'the head of the group' instead of El Más Loco?" The judge was impassive, even though the suggestion he was offering was nonsense.

"What if a conversation refers to one of them by name, your honor? You are saying I should tell the witnesses not to say so?"

The judge was becoming impatient. "Yes. That's what I'm saying. Mr. Coleman's Motion to Exclude Evidence is granted, at least in part. You may not use the words 'The Balamarcas Cartel,' or 'El Más Loco,' or 'The Craziest One.' The phrases 'The Cartel' and 'El Jefe' are permissible. Mr. Herrick, if at some point in the trial, you believe that it has become important to use these words, you still cannot use them, until and unless you obtain a hearing before the court outside the presence of the jury, at which the court permits you to do so."

The judge glared at the plaintiff's lawyer.

"Yes, your honor." This was the only response that Robert could give.

Four hours later, the judge and the parties had plowed through more than twenty pretrial motions filed by Jimmy Coleman on behalf of the Bank, and through five motions filed by Robert for the plaintiffs. The judge's rulings on some of these motions seemed irrational to Robert. But the judge was ruling rapidly—as fast as possible—to preserve the trial setting two days away. Robert felt his evidence slipping away, his case becoming strained, and his chances for justice virtually bleeding to death.

Eventually, the hearing was finished. The judge had ruled on the last motion.

But then, the judge looked up sharply. "One more thing. This is a case that ought to be settled. Mr. Coleman! Have you made an offer to Mr. Herrick to settle the case? Have you given him your best shot?"

"Yes, your honor. Yes, of course." Jimmy smiled. He had indeed offered to settle the case. The day before this hearing, he had told Robert, "We'll pay you ten thousand dollars to settle this case. To avoid the nuisance of going to trial. This $10,000 is what we consider the 'nuisance value of your case.'"

This charade had allowed Jimmy to tell the judge he had given it his "best shot." Jimmy had even said, at the time, that he was making the offer because "the judge is likely to ask us and to hold it against whoever doesn't make an effort to settle."

"What about you, Mr. Herrick? Remember what I told you. You've got an uphill battle at trial. You ought to take what you can get. Have you given Mr. Coleman your best shot?"

"Yes, your honor." Robert said it unenthusiastically. He had met with his clients a week ago. Patrick and Anna had not wanted to accept any amount to settle. After a painful hour, in which they had expressed the belief more than once that their lawyer seemed to be taking the opposite side, they had agreed to accept a hundred million dollars to settle the case. Robert had conveyed the offer to Jimmy Coleman. Jimmy had scoffed.

"Keep at it, lawyers," said the judge in a voice that brooked no nonsense. "This is the kind of case that can be settled. We're scheduled for trial day after tomorrow, but there's still time . . . to . . . settle . . . it!"

The lawyers started to pack up to leave. But then, suddenly, the judge shouted, "*Wait!* Wait a minute." And everyone looked up at the bench. "I have an idea."

And at that, every lawyer was surprised, and then apprehensive. No one can tell what is going to happen when a judge shocks everyone with a new "idea."

"I haven't ordered you ladies and gentlemen to go to mediation yet, on this case!" The judge's eyes flashed, blacker than ever. "Who knows? A day in mediation is nothing but assisted settlement, with a mediator who talks to you, without having any power to impose a solution—just trying to get you to settle. It can't do any harm if I order you to go to mediation."

All of the lawyers groaned. They were ready to start trial, and they hated the thought of delaying the inevitable. Especially for a meeting with a mediator, who would harangue and cajole and push for settlement, using arguments everyone had already heard. But the lawyers kept their groaning quiet, so as not to annoy the judge.

"I've got just the right man to appoint as a mediator," said Judge Raines. "He's a former judge himself. I'm entering an order appointing him, and I'll get him there tomorrow, no matter what else he has on his plate. Ladies and gentlemen, use this opportunity at mediation to . . . *settle* . . . this . . . case!"

27
THE MEDIATOR

A judge has power to order the parties to mediate. To try to settle the case. And so the attorneys and the parties were all there, early the next day. The mediator spoke with a loud, clear voice.

"As your mediator, it's my job to get you to settle this case. And we will settle it. We *will*. My name is Judge Harry Cotton, and I'm a former judge, not a judge any more because I retired, but I've been around the block a lot of times, and I know we can settle this case."

The mediator, former Judge Harry Cotton, wasn't very impressive looking. A wispy mustache. Scraggly hair on top of his head. Impossibly clunky glasses, with coke-bottle lenses and heavy black plastic frames. A grayish jacket, and beneath it, trousers in a different gray that didn't go with the jacket. A green tie with coffee stains. The mediator looked like a wimp.

Former Judge Cotton didn't seem like the kind of guy who could persuade lawyers to settling anything, much less a big case.

But Robert knew this mediator. Before coming to the meeting, he had told Tom, "Don't underestimate how pushy this mediator is. When he was a judge, Cotton was good at getting people who came to his court to settle. A judge is different when he's trying to push people to settle—different from the courtroom, that is. This Judge Cotton is retired as a judge, now, and he's making a lot of money as a mediator."

"That's good, in a way," Tom had said. "He might be able to get Jimmy Coleman to be serious about this case and offer a realistic amount to settle it."

"Maybe so," Robert had said, rubbing his chin. "But I'm afraid it won't work out well. What will happen, I think, is that Jimmy will offer something . . . something small . . . a low-ball offer. And he won't raise it much after that. And the mediator—that is, Judge Cotton—he will have talked to Judge Raines, and Judge Raines will want us to settle for whatever we can get, and Judge Cotton, as the mediator, will pressure us to settle it for Jimmy's low-ball offer.

"What I mean is, Judge Cotton, as mediator, will put us in an awkward position if he can, and he'll threaten to tell Judge Raines we were obstructionists, and there's not a lot we can do about that."

"Well, most mediations don't work out to be quite that bad."

"As a former judge, Harry Cotton knows that judges like Judge Raines really want the parties to settle. And Cotton wants to keep getting appointed to be a mediator, because it pays well. He'll make several thousand for a day's work, with no expenses. And so, he'll be trying to get us to settle it, without caring whether it's fair."

By now, inside the main conference room, the mediator had launched into his prepared introduction. The same speech that mediators always give. Everybody could talk freely, he announced, without fear of anything being used in the lawsuit against them, because mediation was a privileged environment. So, talk freely. That helps get things settled. Vent your emotions.

The two sides would negotiate, and he would just help them reach agreement, without having any power to decide anything. But at the same time that he was denying that he would be forceful, the mediator, Judge Cotton, dropped a lot of hints about forcing the two sides to reach agreement. "Judge Raines expects both parties to negotiate seriously . . . Judge Raines would like to know that everyone tried to reach agreement . . . and if you do that, you can settle this case. . . . We can settle it and let Judge Raines know that we have a peaceful resolution of the case. . . ."

Translation: *If either side is unreasonable, if either side doesn't work hard toward settling . . . then I, Harry Cotton, am going to have a conversation with Judge Raines about how you screwed up, and he's likely to make every possible ruling against you in front of the jury at your trial.* That was what this mediator actually meant, however he sounded, and every lawyer understood it.

Finally, Judge-Cotton-the-Mediator stopped speaking, and he turned to Robert Herrick. "You get to make a statement first. Your client and you: both of you can make statements." It was the usual mediator treatment, even if this case was far from usual.

By prearrangement, Robert said, "Mr. Castillo?" and he turned to Patrick. He and his client had carefully worked out the few sentences his client would speak.

"This Bank hurt me very badly," said Patrick, with his eyes quietly misting. "This Bank launders money for the drug lords. The evidence is going to show that the Bank even paid the hired murderers. They hurt me . . . very . . . badly."

Patrick was looking straight at two Bank vice presidents who were here to represent the Bank. Chola Velnikov wasn't here, and not surprisingly, he had sent two of his underlings.

"This was an obscene act, an act of murder by the Bank," Patrick Castillo said in a commanding voice. "And you people, inside the Bank, were in this up to your eyeballs." The two Bank vice presidents looked away.

"That's true," Robert said. "We will have testimony from one of the hired killers, who will tell the jury how he and his accomplices were paid. By this Bank, which he will describe, and his description fits the Velnikov Bank exactly, even though he can't recall the name of the Bank. We will have evidence from the second-in-command of the Cartel, that's José Luis Leyva, and he will tell how deeply involved this Bank was with the Cartel. We will have accountants, respected accountants, who will trace the money flow through the Velnikov Bank, and he will explain that the Bank was a deliberate, willing accomplice, too."

This was a rented conference room, to which the mediator had summoned them. It had green-and white striped walls with elegant furnishings and a long table, filled on one side by Jimmy Coleman and his inevitable entourage of four associates—and the two bank vice presidents, who looked miserable. On each side of the conference room, there were two smaller rooms. Breakout rooms. After the first session, the mediator would put the two sides in different rooms and shuttle back and forth, cajoling each side, huffing, and puffing, in an effort to get them to reach agreement. Now, he turned to Robert with a face drained of emotion.

"Your demand for settlement, Mr. Herrick?" The mediator wanted the bottom line.

"One hundred million dollars," said Robert evenly. He had discussed the figure with Patrick Castillo. They had also talked about fallback positions—lesser amounts that might be acceptable—if the alternative amounts might settle the case.

"Mr. Coleman?" The mediator was as impassive as Jimmy was.

"Judge, in view of the settlement demand, we have very little to say." Jimmy's voice sounded like a scrap-metal grinder. "This is a fine Bank. The witnesses from the Bank will deny having had any contact with any Cartel. All that the Velnikov Bank did was to lend money and take in deposits, just like any Bank."

"The alleged 'witness' that Mr. Herrick talks about, who is one of the murderers, . . . he can't tell you which Bank he got his alleged payment from, and even if it sounds like this Bank, all that the Bank did was to pay out a deposit, whichever bank it was. There's no evidence justifying anything like a hundred million dollars. That's imaginary."

"Your settlement offer, Mr. Coleman?" Again, the mediator was impassive. "You want to work at settling this case, don't you, so that I can tell Judge Raines that both sides cooperated?"

"Sure," said Jimmy indifferently. "We'd like to settle, and we'd pay a token amount just to get rid of the case. But given Mr. Herrick's stratospheric demand, we can only offer to pay one hundred thousand dollars, not one hundred million. We've got no responsibility for these killings. But the Bank will generously pay that amount to avoid the expense of a trial."

"All right," said the mediator. "We can settle this case. I want to tell Judge Raines that both sides tried hard. Let's break into two groups, and I'll meet with the defense lawyers and the Bank representatives first." He looked at Jimmy. "Be thinking about a bigger number, please."

* * *

Inside his Mexican jail cell, El Jefe was getting a little stir-crazy. He had asked to see his lawyer.

"How come you haven't got me out yet?"

"*Jefe*, it is impossible. The jail is surrounded by the national army, and the army takes orders from the President."

"Carry the message to my *Lugarteniente*, my First Lientenant, that I want him to make sure the judge gets the word—I want out, and I will make stew out of him if I don't get out."

"*Jefe*, he cannot get to the judge. The judge is a substitute judge, appointed by the President. And the army is surrounding the judge, just as it is surrounding this jail. The prosecutor, the *abogado del estado*, is not the usual local guy, either. This prosecutor is appointed by the President too, and he has a big group of soldiers around him."

El Jefe cursed. He looked around, wildly.

"Well," he said finally, "what about that investigator in America that was harassing the Bank? Is he dead yet?"

"No, *Jefe*. I carried your message to your brothers in the Cartel, and they have tried. I understand that their assassins in America are no longer available."

"No longer available?" El Jefe sputtered. "What does that mean?"

"They got arrested on some separate charges for separate crimes, is my best information. But *Jefe*, the investigator has not bothered the Bank any more. The Bank is at peace now, except for the lawsuit against it. But listen: there is something else that you might do."

"What is that?"

"You can go after the lawyer in that case against the Bank. The lawyer who is suing the Bank."

"Ah." El Jefe was beginning to appreciate his own lawyer a little, because this was a good suggestion. "Get with the *Lugarteniente*. Tell him to get some new assassins. That lawyer is responsible for starting all of the problems. I'm a businessman and a patriot, and I don't need this kind of trouble from some silly lawyer."

"*Jefe*, I will do it. The lawyer is the source of the problem. This lawyer named . . . Hec-reek. I mean, *Herrick*."

* * *

Back at the green-and-white conference room, the mediation was approaching its eighth hour. Each side was in one of the smaller rooms.

"It looks as though the mediator has had some success with Jimmy Coleman," said Tom Kennedy. "Jimmy's come a long way from where he was. Five million dollars. Five million? I wonder why he's offered that?"

"Jimmy's pretty coarse, but he's not stupid. He'd like to make this case go away if he can. He sees that we've got some evidence, even though he croaks and blusters as if we didn't."

By now, the mediator had shuttled back and forth more than a dozen times, pushing the two sides, criticizing their assumptions, and getting concessions from both parties, a little at a time.

"And I guess this mediator's done well with us, too, since we're down to a demand of only fifty million. Five million to fifty million."

Patrick Castillo shifted uneasily in his seat.

"I know, Patrick. It's not just a piece of commerce, this lawsuit. We won't settle without your being satisfied."

At that, the mediator called them into the conference room. "Sometimes an all-parties meeting helps. We are going to settle this case. Mr. Coleman, I expect you to give us a much bigger number. Mr. Herrick, I expect you to come down to a more modest number. You know we can do this. . . . We can settle it. . . ."

Nine o'clock came and went. Jimmy Coleman had offered eight million. Robert had offered to accept forty-five million.

And before anyone knew it, the time was two o'clock in the morning. They had been at it for fourteen hours. The mediator called them into the green-and-white conference room again.

"No," said Patrick Castillo. "I will not go lower." Robert's last settlement offer had been forty million dollars. Down from a hundred million. But the plaintiffs had not budged for three hours.

"Forty million is it," said Robert.

Jimmy Coleman shook his head. "In that case, Judge Cotton, all I can do is repeat our last offer of ten million dollars." Jimmy had not budged for hours, either. "And that's all my Bank will do. It's already too much."

The mediator saw that it was over. But he tried once more, with everyone present. "Come up just a little bit to get us moving again."

"No, Judge, we're at top dollar."

"Come down just a little bit to get us moving again."

"Judge, we can't. Our client has said absolutely not. We have eight people who were murdered."

"Impasse," said Judge Cotton finally. "I'm declaring an impasse." He brightened, in spite of the hour, and said, "But I will be in touch with each of you tomorrow morning. Sleep on it." He was a hard-working mediator, however drab and dull he might look. There was always the possibility of a settlement on the day after mediation. It happens.

It was Jimmy Coleman who had the last word, while everyone was packing up to go home. "We'll be occupied tomorrow morning, Judge. We'll start the trial. We'll be there to give Mr. Herrick a good ass-kicking. The Bank is right, and we'll try this case and win it."

28
THE JURY PANEL

The next day was the day of trial. The judge had been definite about
that.

The Federal Building was a square, boxy structure. Light-
colored, like a crackerbox. It had small, square windows—small, probably,
for security reasons. The window frames were red, probably in an effort to
make the building look less institutional, even though anyone would have
said, "That looks like a federal building."

The plaza in front was called Tranquility Park, and it was open and
spacious. Surprisingly, the appearance of all of it was fresh and modern,
although federal courthouses elsewhere were not always that way. It was a
big building for a federal courthouse, because in an urban center there is a
great deal of crime, and there also are a lot of lawsuits, and federal judges
hear both kinds of cases.

It was early morning when Robert and Tom walked through Tranquility Park on their way to the Federal Building. The sky was clear and
the temperature was perfect, just as it is during many months of the year
in this city. In fact, hundreds of robin redbreasts strutted comfortably on
grassy patches in the Park, stopping on their way north. The two lawyers
paused for a moment to watch them, in spite of their singular concentra-
tion on their case.

"The closer we get to the courthouse," said Tom slowly, "the more I
wish we had settled the case yesterday."

"Well, me too, of course." Robert's laugh was nervous. "Everyone
wants to settle if you get fair settlement value. And if the clients agree. But
I'm more optimistic. We've got some serious evidence."

He said it in spite of the gremlins he felt inside his stomach, turning his insides around. He always wished he could avoid being so nervous—not just nervous, but *scared!*—before every trial. He was scared of being blindsided. Scared of doing something dumb.

But he worked at maintaining his optimism.

Tom was the naysayer. "Remember what the judge said. We have a hill to climb. A hard job to do, proving this case. And the judge is right. We should try one more time to get Patrick and Anna to settle. Jimmy Coleman isn't a nice guy, but given the difficulty of the case, Jimmy's settlement offer is equal to fair settlement value."

"Maybe. We'll see." Robert's intestines twisted and bubbled.

When they reached the courthouse door, they walked among a knot of other people and their discussion of the case stopped. They walked silently through the metal detector and into the elevator. Robert punched the button for the eighth floor.

* * *

Patrick and Anna—their clients—were already in the courtroom when Robert and Tom walked in. By now, they were accustomed to this cavernous, sterile courtroom. Judge Raines was at the bench, hearing motions in other cases.

"We want to get the counsel table closest to the jury," said Robert. They nodded to Patrick and Anna, walked past the bar, and placed some of their files at the best table, to "claim the spot." That was one reason for being here early.

Another reason was to watch Judge Raines and guess what his mood was today. The first case they saw involved a motion in an enormous breach-of-contract suit. The judge had already begun hearing arguments. The defense lawyer was asking the judge to order the plaintiff to find and turn over thousands of electronic records—maybe records in the millions; no one knew. "Judge, these are emails between employees of the plaintiff, discussing the product that the plaintiff claims is defective," said the lawyer. "We've got to have these, to prepare our defense."

By now, Robert was queasy enough to consider going to the men's room and losing his breakfast.

"Judge, our electronic expert estimates that it will cost over a hundred thousand dollars to produce this stuff," answered the plaintiff hotly. "Most of it has nothing to do with anything. And even those that do have to do with it, . . . those are from an earlier time, when nobody knew about the defects. More than a hundred thousand, for records that are useless!"

The judge listened for a little less than ten minutes, and he asked a few questions. Then, he ordered the plaintiff to find and produce the records.

The next case was a product liability suit involving a jet ski. Ten minutes, and a then a very firm order—issued with an edge to the judge's voice. Next, a criminal case—a securities fraud case, with more than a dozen defendants. The trial was supposed to start next month. The judge took just over fifteen minutes to decide a blizzard of issues involving ten different motions, some by the defendants and some by the United States Attorney, and he verbally decided them in crisp sentences.

"Each prevailing side, write me an order. And listen, ladies and gentlemen. I want these orders to be faithful to what I've said here, or you will not like the consequences." The gaggle of men and women representing the defendants all nodded.

Jimmy Coleman stepped into the courtroom, followed by his train of associates and his bank-vice-president clients, who looked shell-shocked by the space they surveyed. Jimmy sat at the other counsel table as Robert and Tom claimed their table. They motioned to Patrick and Anna to join them.

"Good morning, ladies and gentlemen." Judge Marvin Raines was already weary, but he smiled tightly. Robert thought to himself, the judge is calm, but the tension is just under the surface, and he might blow up.

"I see that the mediation hasn't settled the case . . . *yet*," said Judge Raines. ". . . But that doesn't mean that you can't settle it . . . *now*. We will bring in the jury panel in thirty minutes. Talk to each other. And try again to settle this case."

The courtroom was beginning to fill with spectators. News reporters, attorneys, and just-plain-curious lawsuit fans. They stood as Judge Raines walked out. Robert felt the sweat running down his back.

* * *

Exactly thirty minutes later to the minute, Judge Raines ascended to the bench, in front of the huge granite backdrop that made this space look like a throne room. "Be seated, please."

And then, "All right, Mr. Bailiff. Bring them in!"

Led by court officers, a throng of citizens marched into the courtroom in single file. The lawyers craned their necks to see. Robert was still battling his nerves. His hands shook, and he stuffed them into his pocket.

"Right there." The bailiff pointed at a row of churchlike pews. "First eight of you, there. Next, . . . there. No, just nine through sixteen. Row three, seventeen through twenty-four. . . ."

There were plenty of potential jurors, because in a case like this with publicity overflowing from the media, there would be jurors who couldn't serve.

The bailiff handed sets of photocopied papers to Robert and to Jimmy. The jury forms. The potential jurors' answers to standard questions. To experienced lawyers, these are a gold mine of information about which citizens would be favorable and which not.

The judge smiled at the jury panel. "Good morning, ladies and gentlemen. My name is Judge Marvin Raines. The case on trial here is called *Castillo v. The Velnikov Bank*. This is a civil case that will be tried in front of a jury. . . ."

The lawyers were barely listening. Mostly, they were looking at the jury forms, at the jury panel, and back at the forms, while trying to do it surreptitiously so that the jurors wouldn't think they were spying on them. Tom Kennedy frowned. "This is a terrible panel!"

"Shhhh." Robert stared at the forms. But Tom was right. The first potential juror was exactly the kind that their Jury Study had warned them against. A secretary for a church; the wrong age, the wrong everything. The second was bad, too: a shoe saleslady for Penney's Department store, also the wrong age and the wrong everything else. The Jury Study said that people in "traditional female occupations" were bad for the plaintiffs. Robert felt his stomach bubbling again.

The judge was still talking, with a standard opening. "Do any of you know any of the attorneys? Do any of you know the parties?" Then, Judge Raines launched into a short discussion of the issues: what the plaintiff claimed and what the defendant claimed. Robert cringed, as he always did when a judge undertook to define the case. It always sounded radically different from what he would have said.

The third potential juror was a man who worked at the Methodist Hospital as a nurse's aide. Health-care professionals were bad for the plaintiffs, according to the Jury Study. Robert's sweat was falling in rivers. He heard the judge talking to the jury panel, but only vaguely, as if from a long distance.

"This is not a criminal case," the judge went on. "It's a civil case. In a criminal case, the prosecutor has to prove the case beyond a reasonable doubt—an overwhelming proof—but not here, because this is a civil case. The plaintiff only has to prove the case by what we call the *'preponderance of the evidence.'* That's just a fancy way of saying, 'the greater weight of the evidence.' If the plaintiff has just a tiny amount of weight on its side—just the weight of a feather—then the plaintiff wins."

Robert liked that description. But the jury panel was awful.

And after that, it seemed that the judge went off the rails. "It all traces back to King John and The Great Charter. *Magna Charta*. That's where our idea of 'due process of law' comes from: *Magna Charta*. It all happened at a place called *"Rooney-o-meade,"* which is a little town in England."

"Runnymede," Robert's brain silently corrected. But the judge went on. Evidently, he loved giving a history lesson, even though it had nothing to do with the case.

Finally, the judge said, "The attorneys will now proceed to examine you concerning your qualifications as jurors. Do not evade their questions or give incorrect answers. They aren't trying to pry. They're just trying to select fair and impartial jurors."

That's standard rhetoric, Robert thought, but inaccurate. Both sides were trying to get jurors who were biased and prejudiced, but biased and prejudiced in their own favor.

"Mr. Herrick? You may begin your examination."

Robert stood up and smiled a small smile. He struggled to control his nerves. To control his . . . fear.

29

SELECTING A JURY

I t seemed to Robert that it took forever from the time the judge stopped talking until he faced the jury panel himself. He still had the same tight smile as he stood and turned toward the thirty citizens. His adrenalin was rising. But that meant that his fear was disappearing.

"Good morning, ladies and gentlemen of the jury panel."

And the members of the panel murmured or spoke, "Good morning," in return. That was good. Lawyers like jurors who talk back. It's easier to get to know them.

"The judge introduced me, and he said my name is Robert Herrick, and it is. And he said I represent these two fine people seated next to me, Patrick and Anna, and I do."

For some strange reason, he had found that this silly way of putting it, in a courtroom, tended to break the ice. It sounded funny. And in a courtroom, to potential jurors who have been herded around and who are skeptical of lawyers anyway, anything even vaguely funny is welcome. A widespread splatter of laughter from the crowd greeted Robert. Also good.

"I want to make sure of one question. No one knows Mr. Coleman, or his clients, or any of his associates? . . . I didn't think so. Thank you."

He stepped toward the opposite end of the jurors' seats, just to emphasize the next point. "Mr. Kennedy and I, with the help of Patrick and Anna, will show you three themes. Our three essential points."

He held up one finger. "First, that The Velnikov Bank and its officers were just as much of a participant in these murders as the killers who physically went into the Castillo home. In fact, more so."

Now, two fingers. "Second, that the Bank and its officers were the essential ingredient, the most important player, in these murders. You will hear Mr. Coleman pointing fingers at other people, but that's just a diversion. The Bank and its officers were the biggest cause."

Three fingers. "Third, that the damages exceed a hundred million dollars. And the jury should find punitive damages of twice that amount."

The jurors looked up sharply, at that. A hundred million dollars?

"Ms. Anderson." Robert looked to the first panel member and smiled. She smiled back. Still another good sign.

"Ms. Anderson, you're the first member of the jury panel, and it's customary to ask you some key questions. Sometimes, not-too-clever lawyers refer to the first person as 'the guinea pig juror.' Because you get the questions, to answer for everyone. He paused. Then: "Ahhh . . . it's supposed to be . . . a compliment."

Laughter. Good, again.

"Ms. Anderson, a hundred million dollars may sound like a huge amount. A gargantuan amount. But it's not. There are eight people deliberately killed, with ages from a toddler to grandparents. Ms. Anderson, my question is, if the evidence shows it, could you write a hundred million dollars as the verdict?"

Ms. Anderson was nervous. "I haven't heard the evidence yet. I can't say."

This was why the Jury Study had warned about people like Ms. Anderson. Decisions were not part of the daily routine for a secretary in a church. She was uncertain. And deciding to award damages was, well . . . above her pay grade.

"Oh, of course!" Robert was understanding. "That's why I said, please assume that the evidence supports it. Please assume that the evidence supports a hundred million dollars as the real damages. Look at it this way. If the evidence shows that the plaintiffs had a loss of hundred million dollars, it would be wrong not to say that the loss was a hundred million dollars. Wouldn't it?"

"Oh. Ohhhh." Ms. Anderson was slow, but she got it, finally. "I guess so, when you put it that way."

He turned to the second potential juror. "Ms. Cortelli, would you say the same thing?"

"Of course!"

This lady was also in a not-so-favorable profession, but she was better at making a decision. Good. "Then, let me ask you, Ms. Cortelli, about the other themes. Can you accept evidence that bank officers may have been essential participants in these murders?"

"It sounds strange for a bank."

"Yes, it does. And it's not the usual way to operate, for a bank. But if the evidence shows that this bank did it, could you accept that evidence?"

"Of course! If the evidence did show it." Ms. Cortelli smiled, incongruously, and then laughed. "I've known some bankers. And their wives tell me that they can do some sleazy things."

Laughter from the panel. Good.

Robert went through all thirty of the panel members, asking similar questions. About how much they knew about drug cartels in Mexico, and the answer seemed to be, they knew a great deal. About whether they knew what "money laundering" meant. Yes. About whether they knew about the need for drug cartels to launder money. Somewhat . . . not completely . . . but yes, it made sense to them that drug cartels needed to launder money. Good, because this meant that the jurors would be able to follow the path of the money back to Mexico when the experts talked about it. And they could understand how deeply this Bank was involved.

And there were more questions: about the kinds of evidence that the jurors would hear, about the defense arguments and their ability to reject them if the evidence didn't support them, and about the damages.

Could the jury panel accept evidence from Patrick and Anna? "Please stand up, Patrick and Anna. Members of the jury, please look at them. Is there anything about them that makes you think badly of them? Is there anything that tells you, in the back of your mind, that our side will be starting this race from ten yards back?" This question never got any response, because jurors all think that they are fair, but the point was to get an implied promise.

"Can you assure Patrick and Anna that you will listen to the evidence of their loss and make a finding of the amount it truly is, if it is more than a hundred million dollars?

Robert took just over an hour to talk to the potential jurors. Then: "In a moment, I'll sit down, and Mr. Coleman will talk to you. I may disagree with what he says. But even if it's wrong, I can't correct it. I don't get to talk again until later. If he says something that's wrong, I trust you to correct it, and say it's wrong. . . .

"So: Thank you, ladies and gentlemen. I know it's a sacrifice to be here, but you are performing a service that only free people can perform. I thank you, and Patrick and Anna thank you."

Robert stood at his full height, and his blue eyes shone, and he smiled, this time a genuine smile, and he nodded to the jurors. The sweat was still rolling down his back when, at last, he sat down.

But it was sweat, now, from effort, not from fear.

* * *

Francel Williams was still in this case too, and now he stood to talk to the jurors. His time speaking was short. But it also was effective. He had agreed to help the plaintiffs, and he did.

"Ladies and gentleman of the jury panel, I represent what you might call the 'absent' defendants. The Cartel. And the head of the Cartel, Alejandro Carlos Gonzales-Huerta. And the three defendants who are accused of the murders."

"First, let me say that we agree with the plaintiffs about their damages. The plaintiffs' damages are huge. A hundred million dollars is right. Does anybody have a bias against that, if proved? . . . I didn't think so."

"Second, we agree that this Bank is responsible, and the Bank is the biggest cause of this tragedy. I assume there's no one who would disagree, if it's proved? . . . Again, I didn't think so."

With that, Francel thanked the potential jurors and sat down. The panel members murmured in surprise. A defense lawyer, who agreed with the plaintiffs' claims?

But Francel had helped his own clients, the absent defendants, by helping the plaintiffs.

The judge spoke, next. "I'm reminded that it's lunchtime. Ladies and gentlemen of the jury, you have an hour and a half. Please return promptly."

* * *

And so, an hour and a half later, Jimmy Coleman stood before the jury panel. Judge Raines was nothing if not efficient about time.

"I'm Jimmy Coleman, my friends. I represent The Velnikov Bank. It is a fine Bank and it is innocent of any of the reckless charges Mr. Herrick has made. I believe so with all my heart, or else I wouldn't represent them."

Robert started to stand up and object, because it is unethical for a lawyer to express a personal opinion, other than one based on the evidence. But he held himself back. This prohibition on swearing personally to the innocence of the client was one of the hardest ethical rules to enforce. If he objected, it might draw only a mild ruling from the judge, if even that, and the net effect would only be to sharpen the jurors' memory of these improper remarks. And so, with effort, Robert stayed where he sat.

Jimmy had spoken only four sentences in this trial, and he had already violated the rules. But Jimmy's ethical lapse was the perfect crime, committed by a master at doing things the wrong way. Robert knew that this first time would not be the last.

"Mr. Herrick's so-called three themes are hogwash," Jimmy went on. "The Bank did not participate in any cartel, much less being involved in any criminal acts. It certainly was not the biggest cause of any murders, because it wasn't a cause at all. And a hundred million dollars? Even for a large loss, it's a ridiculous figure."

Jimmy zeroed in on a particular panel member who happened to be an accountant. "Mr. Zelikov," he said, "you are a man who understands figures. Imagine that someone were to invest a hundred million dollars in municipal bonds. There would be many million dollars of income per year, wouldn't there?

"Many millions. That's right." Mr. Zelikov smiled and nodded.

"And all of it would be tax-free." Jimmy smiled. Then laughed. "Mr. Herrick has named a figure that would let you live in a mansion, own a yacht, and play table limits in Las Vegas, tax free, just from the income!"

The jurors smiled at that. Some of them snickered.

"It's ridiculous, but it's not funny in the end, because it's just Mr. Herrick trying to profit from a tragedy. And I'll tell you what else. The rest of his so-called themes are just as ridiculous. They are imaginary. They are exaggerated. And they are based on so-called evidence that doesn't stand up."

Through Robert's eyes, this was painful to watch. It was also dishonest. But it probably was having an effect. Jimmy Coleman might be a sleazebag, but there was no denying his ability to sway jurors.

Jimmy addressed more members of the panel, individually. His voice rasped, but it oozed like honey when he talked to the potential jurors. From the church secretary, Ms. Anderson, he extracted a promise to disbelieve any witness who told lies, and he tied that characterization securely to José Luis Leyva. *My key witness*, Robert thought miserably. From the medical assistant, Ms. Cortelli, he got an agreement to the point that if a getaway car driver like Jorge Baron Baldassaro was a participant in a crime, his testimony wasn't worth anything. From many of the potential jurors, he obtained commitments to see the Bank as a normal Bank, and to presume it innocent, because Banks usually didn't commit murders. And everybody was entitled to be presumed innocent, especially when sued in a made-up lawsuit.

Jimmy said funny things, and made serious accusations, and promised the destruction of "Mister Herrick's falsehoods." And he seemed to have the entire jury panel laughing when he wanted them to, and frowning when he wanted them to.

"As for that man, Mister Francel Williams," Jimmy went on, "his words are bought and paid for. He has made a deal—an agreement with

Mister Herrick—to help the plaintiff and blame the Bank. We will show you the agreement when we present evidence. You can't believe a word that Francel Williams says."

When Jimmy finally thanked the jurors in a scratchy but sincere-sounding voice, Robert felt the same squeezing pangs in his stomach that he had brought into the courtroom.

Now, Judge Raines spoke. "Ladies and gentlemen of the jury panel, I'm going to excuse you for the day. The lawyers will have to complete the process of selecting this jury."

And while the judge warned the jurors against talking to anyone about the case or watching the news, Robert thought, Oh, great. And with his stomach bubbling, he said to himself, "It's a disaster. Jimmy Coleman has just gutted my case the way a fisherman guts a brook trout, and the jurors will have all night to digest the unfair stuff my opponent has told them."

But he didn't have time to think about that, because now was the time to choose the jurors.

* * *

People usually think that a jury has to have exactly twelve people, but in reality, the number varies. The Supreme Court has said that there must be at least six members. Federal judges like to use the minimum number, because judges want to lighten their caseloads, and six-member juries take less time. And so in civil cases, six-member juries are typical.

But in Judge Marvin Raines's court, the number was eight jurors, because the judge usually added two more, as alternates, in case one of the six original members got sick or became unable to serve for some other reason. If there were alternates, it wasn't necessary to start the trial over again from the beginning.

And so, when Robert and Tom huddled with their clients to pick this jury, they were looking for a final number of eight. But no one really "picks" a jury. It is a process of elimination. The plaintiff has the right to "strike" three people, and so does the defendant.

"We've got to strike that first panel member," said Tom immediately.

"I liked that woman!" protested Anna Castillo Carter. "She seemed like a thoughtful person. She didn't answer right away. She was honest."

"Well, Anna, Tom is right." Robert said immediately. But he thought to himself, "I wish I didn't always have to argue with my own client to avoid a jury that's bad for my client." Then he explained: "That lady fits the profile of a juror who is unfavorable to us—a very bad juror for us." And he explained the advice in the jury psychologist's report.

"Second panel member is okay." Tom tapped on the table with a pencil. "She looks bad on paper, but her answers to the questions show that she'll be for us, or at least not automatically against us."

"Well, we've probably got to leave her on the jury." Robert frowned. "We've got two other strikes, and there are other people who are worse."

Tom turned to Anna and Patrick. "By the way, don't get too optimistic. Jimmy Coleman's doing the same thing we are, but he's trying to strike the ones we'd most like to have."

Patrick Castillo shook his head. "It's a strange system. It seems unfair."

Tom nodded. "Welcome to the seamy side of American justice."

Fifteen minutes later they were finished, because Robert and Tom knew which jurors were worst for them, and also, because the judge would not have allowed them to take very long. Robert crossed out the names of three potential jurors and handed the list to the clerk.

Jimmy Coleman did the same.

Robert was not surprised to see that Jimmy had done what his strategy called for. The remaining eight people—the ones who didn't get struck and who would decide the case—were mostly people about whom the jury psychologist had warned Robert and Tom. The only hope, he told himself, was that the two members who fit the description of jurors favorable to the plaintiff could persuade the other six. He felt a stab of dread as he walked to counsel table, and he thought: "This is another reason we're going to lose this case."

30

THE ATTACK

The opening statements took up most of the next afternoon.

Robert had written out his opening statement long beforehand. He didn't read it to the jury, of course, or even refer to it, but it was with him, in his head. Ironically, the opening statements by both lawyers seemed anti-climactic, because the lawyers had covered the same issues during jury selection. That was not surprising. Opening statements carry less drama if there is a thorough jury selection beforehand.

Robert started, once again, with his three themes. First, the Bank was involved in the crimes; second, the Bank was the most important guilty party; and third, the damages were more than a hundred million dollars. And then, methodically, he previewed the evidence. He told the jury what José Luis Leyva was going to say, and he read from José Luis's deposition—from the parts, that is, that didn't have contradictions. He referred to José Luis as "The Insider" in the Cartel. And he told the jury what the getaway car driver, Jorge Baron Baldassaro, was going to say. And the cartel expert, Professor Cuevas. And the accountant, the plaintiffs, the officers who first entered the Death House, and numerous other witnesses. . . .

And also, the witnesses who supported the damages. Here, Robert actually worked up some fire in his voice. But for the most part, the opening statement was mechanical. Essential, functional, useful, but ... less exciting than the evidence was going to be.

Jimmy Coleman worked up some fire, too. Instead of the factual parts of José Luis Leyva's deposition, he read the parts that showed that José Luis obviously lied and had to be corrected by the Government lawyers. And he pointed out that Jorge Baron Baldassaro didn't know which bank he had been to or what had happened inside the Death House. But Jimmy's hoarse voice turned into a roar when he talked about the fact that both of these witnesses were turncoats, testifying about their own crimes against the accomplices with whom they earlier had conspired, and—according to Jimmy—both were worthless as witnesses.

"Both of these so-called 'witnesses' are pieces of human wreckage, and they're selling their testimony!" Jimmy thundered. "They've got every possible motive to lie. Every motive to say whatever Mr. Herrick wants them to, whether it's true or not! José Luis Leyva is bargaining for freedom after a life of drug smuggling and contract killings. Jorge Baron Baldassaro is bargaining for leniency after participating in eight murders. Either one of them will say anything—*anything*—to save his own worthless skin!"

"I've got a hearing on another case," Judge Raines announced, then. It seemed to Robert that Judge Raines was going to cut off the proceedings whenever Jimmy left something with the jurors that would flood their minds. "Everyone be here at two o'clock. We'll start again, then."

* * *

Robert had arranged to have some shadow jurors in the courtroom. Three of them.

The shadow jurors did not know which side had hired them. The jury consultant, Professor Calkins, had stationed them in different parts of the audience. Their instructions were to avoid contact with each other, to listen and observe, and to communicate their impressions to Professor Calkins.

Now, the jury consultant met with Robert just outside the courtroom. He seemed worried. "All three shadow jurors believed Jimmy Coleman when he attacked the credibility of the witnesses."

"What do you think that means?"

"Hard to tell. Jurors usually think that deals with witnesses are improper. They don't like them. Sometimes, during a trial, they begin to realize that it is the only way to get some crucial kinds of information. But sometimes, they just resent it throughout the trial. We'll know later."

"What kind of overall impression do they have?"

"Well, . . . they say they can't tell anything. That it's like a tie. Two of them say that, and one seems to side with the defense."

"That's bad." Robert was accustomed to hearing observers pronounce the plaintiff as the winner of the opening statements. If it was a tie . . . or if the defendant was ahead at this point . . . well, that was very, very bad.

"Maybe not," said Professor Calkins. "But it could be better. And the testimony . . . we hope that when they hear it from the witness stand. . . ."

"Well, yes. I hope so too. But it's not a good start."

Both of them knew what all of the jury studies by psychologists showed. The jurors form a framework of what the case is about very early in the case, and they rarely vary from it. They usually know "what this case is about," or what they think it is about, before the evidence begins. They get clues from the jury selection and from the opening statements. They filter out what their experience tells them to discard.

It isn't that they have the case decided, or that they know who they think should win. It is only a framework. But the framework stays with them, and it is the screen through which they look at all of the evidence.

If Robert's "three themes" were what the jurors thought the case was about, that would be a good thing. But if Jimmy's argument that the witnesses were worthless was the framework, then the plaintiffs were likely to lose.

And it sounded as though it was Jimmy's version that the jurors were going to use to guide them.

* * *

Later that evening, Robert sat with Maria in the living room. The sun was just going down. Its red-orange-yellow flares licked at the big plantation shutters.

"I don't really believe it," Maria said. "I don't believe that the shadow jurors have swallowed Jimmy Coleman's theories about your case. Or the real jurors, for that matter."

The sky was darkening quickly.

"Why do you say that?"

"I haven't used shadow jurors very much, obviously. There's no money in the D.A.'s office to pay people just to sit there. But there have been occasions when I've had other people from the office who weren't lawyers—investigators, secretaries, that sort of non-lawyers—sit in and listen to something, and then tell me what they think. And do you know what they do? They always try to cut it down the middle. To say that it's a tie between the two sides."

"Really? That's your experience?"

"They'll always try to tell you that you're doing a great job, but that it's a tie. The two sides are even. But it may not be true. What they're really saying is that . . . as of now, they don't know the final verdict. They don't want to predict who's going to win. That's not what they usually get asked, of course, but that's how they hear the question. You ask them, what do you think? And they answer as if you had asked them, 'Who's going to win'?"

The sun always seems to move faster, the closer it gets to sunset. And by now it was far enough down to make everything dark.

"Okay . . . but how do you learn anything from these courtroom observers? Why would you even ask their opinion, if it's so useless?"

"I didn't say it's useless. It's a matter of asking different questions. It's better to ask them what they think probably happened, rather than who they believe. For example, if they say, 'the defendant broadsided the plaintiff's car, and the question is whether the defendant ran a red light like the plaintiff says,' then the plaintiff probably is ahead."

"Well, what you're saying is good news. Professor Calkins told me that two of the jurors said they wanted to see whether the Bank was really deeply involved in the Cartel."

"There you go. They do accept your way of thinking."

Then she caught herself, remembering Mother Serena. "But Robert! Come to your senses and settle this case. Right now is probably a good time."

Robert was silent for a moment. The moon was hiding tonight, and there wasn't much illumination outside. By now, the sky was black. And suddenly, it was dark inside the room, too. He walked across the carpet to turn on another light.

And at that moment, the night exploded.

"Get down!" he yelled at Maria. He himself was already down. From her chair, it took her a moment more. The chatter from the assault rifle continued.

"It's automatic fire. I'd say an AK-47. Meaning that we have very, very bad guys outside. It's a good thing we heard from Chipmunk about this threat. I told the detectives—you know, Derrigan Slaughter and Donnie Cashdollar—"

The windows shattered, and the plantation shutters broke into slats and toothpicks.

"You told me. And they told me too. And Slaughter and Cashdollar made sure that there were two guys outside."

Robert was crawling into the hallway to get his own AR-15. Not automatic, so that it was still legal. And suddenly, the gunfire seemed to come from several different directions.

And then there was silence.

A knock at the door. "Police! Is everyone safe and uninjured?"

"Yes! Yes." Robert looked, then opened the door.

The uniformed officer held his gun, still. "It looked like two guys. One driving, one shooting. They took off. My partner's in pursuit."

Right behind him, almost immediately, Chipmunk was there too. With a DEA agent, who was armed with a weapon Robert couldn't even recognize.

The uniformed officer paused. "It looks like you've got some damage to these windows." And then he pointed. "And damage to the walls, too." There was a line of bullets across the opposite side of the sheetrock.

"It's the Cartel," Chipmunk said. "Same guys who were after me, and now they're mad at you about your lawsuit. It was probably ordered by El Jefe himself, from his jail cell."

"Well, Robert, I guess you must be getting to them," Maria said. "You're doing a lot better with your case than I even thought."

The psychic's words banged in her head. "He's in danger. . . . He will lose." And she blurted out what she was thinking. "Robert! Settle this case and let's get out of this."

Then she remembered Mother Serena's other warning. "Do not try to pressure him." And so, incongruously, she forced herself to laugh. "It's a good thing the house is insured, isn't it? But I bet our deductible is high enough so that it won't do any good."

31
ARYAN BROTHERHOOD

Robert was there at the courthouse early the next day, in spite of what had happened. "If we give up on our usual activities, the bad guys win," he told Tom.

But the judge wore a troubled look. "Robert, take a day. And let us know if you need more. Make sure you're safe. Nobody wants to see something like this happen."

Even Jimmy Coleman had a look of concern. "Sure, Robert. We'll take up this trial in a day or so."

The judge called the jurors into the courtroom. "We have some outside issues that I have to deal with, together with the attorneys. They are not issues that concern the evidence before you. As before, do not discuss this case with anyone, including your wife or husband, and do not speculate about what the court and the lawyers are discussing."

The judge paused. "For one thing, if you speculated, you'd be likely to be wrong in your speculation, so don't speculate!"

Some of the jurors smiled at that. This kind of court order is impossible for jurors to obey. Speculation is just what jurors do. If for no other reason, they speculate because being told not to speculate makes them want to speculate.

Outside the courtroom, Robert said, "I was surprised by that show of graciousness from Jimmy Coleman. I guess he doesn't approve of assassinations, at least not publicly."

Tom was even more cynical. "Or: at least not by people shooting automatic rifles who are co-conspirators of his client."

* * *

Later that day, Robert, Tom, and Chipmunk met with the detectives. It was a serious, heavy-duty meeting. The division chief of the police department was there, and he apologized for the absence of the police chief himself, who was out of town. "We are really concerned about this."

"We gonna IN-crease that security detail," added Derrigan Slaughter.

"And I've contacted the security company that provides our security guards at the office," added Chipmunk. "We'll have a private army at Robert's house."

"I've sent the kids away, to stay with their grandmother." Robert's voice was sober. "Maria won't move. Suddenly, she's the original stay-at-home wife. She wants to stay with me."

"By the way, we've got an idea who's behind the attack on your home." Detective Cashdollar frowned.

"Who's that?"

"Lately, the drug cartels have been making deals with the Aryan Brotherhood. We think, from just a glimpse that our guys got of the car they were in, that that's who this was. The Aryan Brotherhood. He saw one of the two guys in the car."

"The . . . Aryan Brotherhood?"

"In a way, it's not surprising. The Brotherhood will do anything. This is a way to make some money, working with drug cartels. A lot of money, without a lot of effort."

"But . . . the Aryan Brotherhood? I thought they were a prison gang."

"They are. But if you join, you join for life. And it's a tight organization. You get an order in the Aryan Brotherhood, you're bound to carry it out."

Derrigan Slaughter nodded. "'Cause if you don't carry it out, the next order gonna be about you. And recently, there been a bunch of killings of Brotherhood members, and no clear reason, 'cept for the possibility they done disobeyed orders."

"So . . . do you know who it is? I mean, which Aryan guy it was who . . . paid me a visit?"

"Remember, we ain't really sure. But our best guess is it's a guy named Billy Ray Boner. They call him 'Billy Ray Bonebreaker.' He's a bad actor. Got a burr haircut, which a lot of them Aryans, they be sportin this kind of head-shave. Always wears just a white T-shirt, even in freezing weather. Got a big eagle tattoo splashed across his chest with them splayed-out wings, and a gang sign on his shoulder, and on his arm, it says, '*My Momma tried, but it didn't work.*'"

"Standard-issue uniform, for these Aryan Brotherhood guys." Donnie Cashdollar was matter-of-fact about the description.

"But . . . back up." Robert was puzzled. "I thought this Aryan group was a prison gang."

"It is. It is a counterpart to other gangs defined by race, such as the Mexican Mafia. A lot of Caucasians who enter prison, and who join the Aryans, do it for protection. The gang is weaker in the more open prisons, where there are nonviolent offenders and minor criminals. It's more serious in the hard-core prisons. Like the Walls Unit, in Huntsville."

Detective Slaughter took it from there. "But see, when you get released outta prison, you still gonna be a member a' them Aryans. Some guys manage to retire, but it's hard. And if you a criminal anyway and you stick to bein' a criminal, it's gonna be a natural for you to stay with the Aryans who, after all, they be like yo' brothers. They be family."

Robert paused for a moment. Then: "So . . . what do I do, based on this?"

"First, we gonna keep at it with intelligence about this group. We can find out things. It ain't perfect, 'cause they ain't no intelligence that's perfect, but we gonna double the effort. And then, they's several things that you gotta do."

"Transportation," said Donnie Cashdollar. "Whenever you go anywhere, always remember that transportation points are where a lot of crime goes down. You need some armor."

"And since we been worryin about you and your transportation," said Derrigan Slaughter, we done got you a surprise. Some protection for when you drivin around." And then, he laughed out loud. "Let's go out to the courtyard, and we gonna DIS-play some armor for you."

* * *

"It's called a M-R-A-P." Donnie Cashdollar was laughing too, when they got outside. "That's pronounced 'M-Rap.' Which stands for 'Mine-Resistant, Ambush-Protected Vehicle.' "

"Wow." Robert found himself staring at an eighteen-ton fighting machine. A desert-colored monster of a vehicle.

"See?" Slaughter pointed. "This thing was the answer to them roadside bombs during the Eye-rack War."

"Now, it's a tool for law enforcement." Cashdollar grinned. "Just a little something we got outta the military surplus program. They drove them in the Iraqi desert, at a half million a pop, but there's no military use for them anymore."

"So our PO-leece Department got a few of 'em." Slaughter grinned too. "See the gun turrets on top? And these vents on the sides are there because of an internal air circulation system. There's real thick armor everywhere, in case you stumbles on some kinda explodin mine, and that's all bullet-resistant glass, of course."

"It's armored. It's heavy. It's intimidating. And it was free. . . . Problem is, it gets about five miles to the gallon, and it can't go over a bridge unless it's reinforced."

"But it's gonna do fine, takin you downtown to the courthouse. Most other places too. And you really gonna impress folks when you drive up to 'em in yo' M-Rap."

Robert was still staring. This vehicle, if vehicle was the right word, was topped with grappling hooks and levers. A forest of searchlights festooned the hood. There were four steps on each side for climbing up to the passenger compartment.

"Maria is going to love this," he said finally. "I can just hear her saying, 'Let's take it for a spin! I need to go to Saks Fifth Avenue.'"

"Only thing is," Slaughter said slowly, "You gotta run when you get out. Between this thing and the courthouse—or between this thing and Saks Fifth Avenue—you don't have no armor. Ain't nothing but air."

"I gotta run? This is starting to sound like a war."

Donnie Cashdollar nodded. "That's what it is."

* * *

He made it home later than usual. In complete darkness.

"Go to sleep early tonight," said Maria, after expressing a lot of excitement over the M-Rap. He thought she was happy about it. But in fact, Maria remembered the psychic's predictions of danger. And the psychic's prediction that Robert would finally recognize the danger and "protect himself." Maria was sure of it: Mother Serena had foreseen, correctly, that Robert would wind up tooling around in an armored car just like this. Mother Serena was a genius.

But she knew she couldn't push him. "Go to sleep. Tomorrow, you go back to trial. In your armored car, you go to the courthouse and back to trial. Please . . . be. . . careful."

"Early. Yes. Like now." He found that he was exhausted.

"Come here. Hug me. Give me a kiss."

"O-o-o-kay."

"A little more energy about it. And while you're kissing me, put your hand on my breast."

She laughed at him. "No, not that one. The other breast. Are you trying to be a contortionist?"

"Well . . . no. I guess this is okay, with you being my wife and all. But tell me. Tired as I am, why am I doing this?"

She laughed at him, again. "Because I like it."

"Okay, sweetheart, love of my life. I'm going to bed."

She sighed. "I'm worried about you. Please, please: settle this case. It's too much. I wish it were over."

"You and me both."

32

THE MAYOR

Your honor, as our first witness, the plaintiffs call The Mayor of this city. Mayor Chalmers Neal." Robert was back in the court-room, after arriving in his armored car: his M-Rap.

The jury was in the box, early in the morning. The mayor began to make his way toward the witness stand. The real trial was beginning. And a buzz went up from the spectators and the jury alike. The mayor was going to testify? It must be an important trial.

"Mr. Mayor?" The judge suddenly was courtly. Every federal judge is a good politician, and this was one politician greeting another. "Good morn-ing, Mr. Mayor."

"Good morning, your honor. It is a privilege to appear in your court-room."

Just as suddenly, Jimmy Coleman was apoplectic. He jumped up to object. "Your honor, this witness can't add anything that won't be added by the movie of the Death House scene that Mr. Herrick plans to broad-cast to this jury! The Velnikov Bank vigorously objects to this charade. This man is just a politician. And it's just for politics!"

Jimmy was right about that, of course. But it didn't matter. The mayor was a witness, and a witness was a witness.

"Overruled," said the judge promptly. "Welcome, Mr. Mayor."

As the mayor smoothed his silver hair and stood to take the oath, everyone looked at him. Gold-rimmed glasses. Gray suit, a little baggy, probably to show that he was a man of the people.

Robert sat down and, as he prepared to ask his questions, reflected that Jimmy had made some points with his speech just now. His objection wasn't designed to keep the mayor off the witness stand. Jimmy would have known that it wouldn't work. Instead, it was a message to the jury, telling these citizens that Robert was opening with a show-business stunt. This is an improper reason for making an objection, but Jimmy had done it without getting caught. "Let's hope it backfires and makes the jury attach more importance to the mayor," Robert thought.

"Introduce yourself to the members of the jury, please, Mr. Mayor."

"Mayor Chalmers Neal." The witness smiled at the jury with all thirty-two teeth.

"And how are you employed, Mr. Neal?"

"As mayor of this city." The mayor looked as though he was trying to restrain himself from saying something. Then, he said it, with an even bigger smile. "I guess that makes me a . . . *politician*, at least according to one of the lawyers in this courtroom."

The jurors laughed. At Jimmy Coleman's expense, Robert was delighted to see.

"Were you elected to this position, Mr. Mayor?"

"Yes, six years ago. And then re-elected, two years ago."

"Are we taking you away from some important business of the city? Our apologies in advance."

"Yes. I'm working hard for the taxpayers these days. The City Council has competing plans in front of it, for refinancing the city's pension debt. You know, the debt and deficit for pensions of our employees."

He looked toward the jurors. "Our predecessor governments promised big pensions to firefighters, police, and everyone else. But they didn't pay the money. Didn't make the contributions needed for all those years. Now the time has come to pay the piper. It's what keeps me awake at night."

"The job of being mayor isn't just about parades and excitement, I guess?"

Another big smile. "Nossir."

"Mr. Mayor, let me direct your attention to the date in question. The date of your visit to the Castillo home. That awful day."

Instantly, the mayor was somber. Everyone else in the courtroom was too.

"Mr. Mayor, did you receive a telephone call from the police chief that morning?"

"Yes." By now, the mayor was pale. The smile was gone.

"What was it about?"

"I've never heard Chief Wiggins sound quite like this. He said, 'You'd better come.' He said, 'It's more than just a multiple homicide. It's a horrible scene, one of the worst I've ever seen. And it's a reporter and his family. It looks like revenge.' "

"Objection." Jimmy's response was real, this time. "Hearsay. And no foundation for the speculation."

"Sustained," said the judge. "Ladies and gentlemen of the jury, you will disregard that last sentence and consider it for no purpose."

Robert was undisturbed, because it was only background anyway, and the jurors would know what the purpose of the mayor's visit was, now.

"Mr. Mayor, were you driven to the Castillo home by police escort?"

"Yes."

"And . . . Did you enter the Castillo home?"

"I . . . did." The mayor was not acting like a politician now.

"Tell the ladies and gentlemen of the jury what you saw."

"Immediately upon stepping into the entrance, you could see a body to the left. This was the body of Rafael Castillo. I knew him to be a nationally famous journalist. He had reported on misconduct in our city, high-level misconduct, by administrations earlier than mine, and I considered Mr. Castillo to be a fine journalist."

Jimmy looked as though he was about to object, but then decided not to. A wise choice, Robert reflected.

"Mr. Mayor, what was the . . . appearance of Mr. Castillo at . . . this . . . time?"

"He was face down, unnatural looking, with his . . . arms to his side, where he had fallen without using his hands to break his fall. And he lay in a puddle—I mean, a . . . puddle of blood. Not a spot, but a puddle. The blood was as red as you can imagine. Unnaturally red."

"It was blood from. . . ."

"There was a wound in the back of his head, a pink area that was hollowed out with a chunk missing. The blood was blood that came from the head. From the brain. It was what they call heavily oxygenated blood, and unnaturally red, redder than red, because blood that comes from the brain is . . . like that."

Step by step, Robert took the mayor through the house, through what he had observed about every death. The mayor was marvelously expressive, able to describe what he had seen in a you-are-there style. The jurors stared at him throughout his testimony.

When he came to the part of the story that involved little Jonathan Castillo, the murdered toddler, his eyes misted. The wound was another head wound, and the blood, again, was a puddle rather than a spot. Moments later, there were jurors, too, with tears in their eyes.

Finally, Robert led the witness to the end of the story. "Mr. Mayor, were you accompanied by anyone as you went through this . . . scene?"

"Yes. By the Police Chief, Chief Wiggins. And also, by you, Mr. Herrick." The mayor paused. "Before I came to office, Mr. Herrick, you were one of my most trusted advisors. I knew that, in your profession, and after your service in the army, you would be able to advise me during this difficult visit. And I was grateful to have you drop everything you were doing and come with me, Mr. Herrick. So, yes, I had company. Chief Wiggins and . . . you, Mr. Herrick."

Robert paused. Then: "Thank you, Mr. Mayor. I pass the witness."

Francel Williams saw that Robert was winning with this witness. "No questions, your honor."

* * *

Jimmy Coleman's cross examination was short. But it was very effective.

"Mr. Mayor, while you were inside the Castillo home, you didn't see any indication of The Velnikov Bank being involved, did you?"

"Inside the. . . ? No, I didn't see anything about the Bank inside the home."

"Mr. Mayor, you've had bank presidents support you, haven't you?"

"Yes, of course. Many."

"You've never known of any of those bankers being involved in a multiple-homicide scene, have you?"

"No. No."

"It would be unusual, extremely unusual, to think of a bank being involved in these kinds of hired killings, wouldn't it?"

"Unusual . . . yes."

"In fact, as you went through the Castillo house, the thought of a bank being involved was about the farthest thing from your mind, wasn't it?"

"Yes. Absolutely."

"Mr. Mayor, do you know Mr. Chola Velnikov? You know him personally, don't you?"

"Yes. Not well, but yes."

"And you know Mr. Chola Velnikov's character for being peaceful and nonviolent, don't you?"

"I . . . I guess."

"And he has a good character for being peaceful and nonviolent, to your knowledge, doesn't he?"

"Objection," said Robert. "Character evidence is inadmissible in a civil case."

Jimmy stood, determined. "This is a homicide case, in which hired killers separate from this Bank did what they did."

"Overruled. I'll permit it."

"Mr. Mayor, you know that Mr. Velnikov has a good character for being peaceful. Isn't that correct?"

"Yes, I reckon so."

* * *

Robert asked for a short recess. He needed to think of something to ask, to get the testimony back on track.

"Let's get started again," said the judge after the fifteen minutes he had given Robert. "Bring in the jury."

"Mr. Mayor," Robert said when the jury returned, "Mr. Coleman asked you about the Bank president's *character*. Whenever character is admissible, reputation is admissible too. But reputation is different. It's about what you've *heard* about the defendant. Now, the 'reputation' of Mr. Velnikov is different from his character known to you, because you've heard from the police department, right?"

"That's right."

"Do you know the reputation of Mr. Velnikov in running a bank that was involved in violence?"

"I do."

"And what is that reputation?"

"It's bad. He was mixed up in this very case."

Jimmy was on his feet. "It's improper to use the particular incident on trial as the basis of character evidence."

"That's sustained." The judge looked angry. "The jury is instructed to disregard that last evidence and to consider it for no purpose whatsoever." He turned to Robert. "Mr. Herrick, that's improper. And that's your one bite at the apple. Don't do it again."

"I . . . pass the witness," said Robert.

"I certainly have no further questions!" Jimmy's voice was a scratchy roar.

"Let's take a break," said the judge, "so that the court reporter can recover."

As the jury filed out, Robert thought: What just happened? To Tom, he said, "That was supposed to be our best witness."

"I know," Tom replied unhappily. "Jimmy Coleman got to us."

33

THE EXPERT

During trial, a lawyer has to act a lot like a quarterback in a football game, when he gets sacked. He has to get back up every time he gets knocked down. He has to be able to forget the time he got hit, even if it was the last play, and concentrate on what is happening now. And he has to do it optimistically. Enthusiastically.

Professor Julian Cuevas was waiting in the back of the courtroom. "Our next witness," said Robert to Tom. "Our expert on drug cartels. From the State University of New York."

But as Robert called Professor Cuevas's name, Jimmy Coleman stood up. "Your honor, this is one of the witnesses we don't think is qualified, at least not to testify on the subjects he's being called for. Your honor has said that you would hold hearings on the witnesses during the trial, right before each one testifies. This witness will need a hearing, because we think he has a whole boatload of opinions that aren't proper."

Judge Raines looked weary. "Take the jury out, please."

Everyone stood while the jury exited. Then, Jimmy said, "Your honor, the defendant objects to the testimony of this witness on grounds of Federal Rules of Evidence 702 and 703."

"Mr. Herrick, you know what that means." The judge shook his head. "You'll have to narrate to this court what opinions this witness is going to testify to. And then, we'll examine whether these opinions can be heard by the jury, under the Supreme Court cases that interpret Rules 702 and 703."

This was not unexpected, and Robert was ready to do that. But he thought to himself, Jimmy has done it again. If the witness, by chance, were to be prevented from testifying, the jury might assume that there was a hole in his case. Jimmy had objected in front of the jury. If the witness then didn't testify, the jury would notice—and assume that something was wrong with Robert's case.

"Your honor, first I will get Professor Cuevas to tell about his qualifications, which are excellent. Then, he will describe how drug gangs operate to enforce discipline, protect their shipments, and convey drugs across the border. This testimony will show why the Cartel was interested in killing Rafael Castillo. He will also describe the method of selling the drugs in the United States, and he will testify to the need for money laundering to get the proceeds back to Mexico. He will tie these matters to the Cartel, which he has studied for many years. And he will tie them specifically to The Velnikov Bank."

"And we object to each of those opinions, your honor." Jimmy sounded like an overloaded concrete truck. "Especially to references about the Cartel and this Bank."

"You may begin, Mr. Herrick." The judge looked skeptical of both sides. "I will listen to this without the jury present."

"Please state your name, Professor Cuevas."

"Julian Cuevas, Professor of Government at the State University of New York."

Quickly, Robert led the professor through his college degree and his Ph.D.—his doctorate in Government. His thesis had been about the Government of Mexico and the effects of political parties there, and it had included a big chapter on the suppression of local Mexican parties by drug cartels. He had been an assistant, then an associate, and then a full professor of Government, progressing through three different universities before coming to the State University of New York. His scholarly publications were in the hundreds, and his books were in the dozens, including one that specifically covered the Balamarcas Cartel.

"Professor, you've heard my statement to the court of your intended testimony. Let me ask you some questions about those opinions. First, are those opinions 'falsifiable,' meaning, if they were wrong, could someone prove them wrong?" He paused. "I should add that, this is one of the issues the Supreme Court has emphasized about expert witnesses. So, what I'm asking is this. If you were wrong in these opinions, could someone else prove it?"

"Well, yes, I suppose they could." The professor rubbed his chin. "The other experts can look at the same kinds of evidence that I've studied, and they can consider whether I'm right."

"And another factor the Supreme Court emphasizes is whether there are a lot of scholarly publications about these same issues. Are there?"

"Yes, certainly."

"And are your books, including the one on this Cartel, considered generally accepted among experts on the drug trade? That's another factor the Supreme Court considers."

"I should certainly hope so!" The witness was adamant. Then, he caught himself. "I mean, yes."

"Your honor, the witness is qualified to express these opinions, and they meet the tests of the Federal Rules of Evidence."

"Mr. Coleman?" The judge turned to the other side of the courtroom.

"Just a few questions, your honor." Jimmy turned toward the witness with dead-fish eyes, so colorless that they looked spooky. The witness turned away.

Jimmy sensed his advantage. "Mister Cuevas"—Jimmy was clear in saying "Mister," instead of "Professor"—"Do you have any idea what the address of The Velnikov Bank is?"

"Well, no."

"Or what its main branch looks like?"

"No."

"Or whether it's a state bank or a federal bank?"

"Those questions haven't been relevant to my work."

"And you haven't written a single line in any of your articles, or in any of your books, that mentions The Velnikov Bank, have you?"

"Offhand . . . I couldn't say, but I can't recall any."

"It's absolutely fair to say that you don't have any expertise about The Velnikov Bank, Mr. Cuevas. Isn't that right?" Jimmy sounded like a jackhammer, now.

"I . . . suppose so."

"Your honor, this witness is not qualified to tell the jury anything about The Velnikov Bank." Jimmy's voice was respectful of the court, now, but firm. Definite.

Robert stood, immediately. "But your honor, he knows about The Velnikov Bank, and he would tell you that the Bank and the Cartel are closely related!"

But the judge had heard enough. "The witness may testify, but there will be no mention of this defendant, The Velnikov Bank." He looked at the clock. "We'll be in recess until one-thirty."

* * *

"No, Robert," said Tom. "We didn't lose the witness, and Jimmy didn't cut the heart out of his testimony. I know, I know; the key to this case is tying the Bank to the drug trade. But other witnesses can do that. They'll include José Luis Leyva, the fugitive from the Cartel. Jorge Baldassaro, the getaway car driver. And our accountant."

"I know. We'll have to rely on those. But the reason I called Professor Cuevas now was to set the entire stage."

"Well, we can call José Luis Leyva next. He can talk about the Bank."

Robert knew the answer to that. José Luis wasn't a credible witness. Jimmy would be able to show his lies and evasions. "Maybe we should call the accountant, next, after Professor Cuevas."

* * *

After the hearing before the judge about whether Professor Cuevas could testify at all, the testimony he gave in front of the jury seemed like an anticlimax. But Robert knew this feeling. It always felt that way when a major battle about the witness occurred with the judge before that witness testified. But the jurors were hearing the professor for the first time, and they were paying attention.

Once again, Robert covered the witness's qualifications, in greater detail this time. And then, he had Professor Cuevas tell the jurors about his articles and his book that covered this Cartel.

The witness described how the Cartel was organized under Alejandro Carlos Gonzales-Huerta, also known as "El Jefe," and also known as "The Craziest One." The second in command for many years was José Luis Leyva, who was going to be a witness in this very trial. Yes, José Luis would be an authoritative source about the Cartel, knowledgeable about El Jefe's most intimate thoughts and most horrific actions.

The witness testified about the methods of discipline that El Jefe used to keep the members of the Cartel in line. And the public. He described the killings at the Bar del Rincon, the Corner Bar, in which more than twenty people had been executed just to send a message. Robert was particularly sensitive about getting the witness to describe the method of killing those victims that El Jefe particularly hated. The method that El Jefe described as "stew." He made sure that Professor Cuevas got the point across but left a great deal to the imagination.

The witness described the many methods of getting the Cartel's product, its heroin and cocaine, across the border into the United States. "It takes ingenuity. Every time there is a successful pathway, the Cartel knows that it needs to change the pathway, so that it doesn't get discovered."

And then, there was the method of getting the money back into Mexico. "The drug proceeds have to be laundered, and then they have to be put into large bills." Why large bills? "Because they will be sent back into

Mexico physically, by smuggling, usually on trucks, hidden within cargoes of legitimate merchandise. If it were electronically transferred, it would get intercepted by the Drug Enforcement Administration. As it is, all that is necessary is to get past border security, which is much easier."

"Do you have an opinion about whether the murders at the Castillo home were committed under the orders of the Cartel?"

"Yes. I do. These murders were committed under orders of the Balamarcas Cartel."

"Why do you say that?"

"It fits the pattern exactly. Killing everyone, including a tiny child too young to do any harm to the Cartel. Just to send a message. It's characteristic of El Jefe's operations. And the fact that it was in this city. A major transshipment point for the Balamarcas Cartel. And because the target was Rafael Castillo. A journalist. El Jefe was famous for assassinating anyone who publicized his operations. And Rafael Castillo had just done an entire series of articles about the Balamarcas Cartel. It all fits."

The jurors seemed fascinated. "Pass the witness," said Robert with satisfaction.

* * *

Francel Williams asked just a few questions. "The Velnikov Bank acted secretly and stayed in the shadows. Is that right?"

"Yes. That's a good way of putting it. The Bank was a shadow defendant."

"And this shadow defendant was right here, in the same city as the murders?"

"Yes."

"And the Bank was essential to the Balamarcas Cartel's crimes?"

"Yes."

"And by paying the killers, it was even more directly involved than the Cartel?"

"I'd say so, yes."

With that, Francel had made his point. "I pass the witness."

* * *

This time, the judge didn't take a recess. "Mr. Coleman? Cross examination?"

Jimmy didn't waste any time. "Professor Cuevas, you had occasion just last month to retract an accusation you had made against a different cartel, didn't you?"

". . . Well, yes." The witness looked surprised at being asked this.

"You accused the wrong cartel of a particular mass murder, didn't you? Because another one claimed responsibility, different from the one you accused, and it was proved right."

"Yes. . . . You're right."

"And you were just as sure of that accusation as you are of your accusations here, weren't you?"

"I don't know how to answer that. I don't think so."

"You don't know anything about the three men who are accused of actually carrying out these murders at the Castillo home, do you?"

"Not really. It isn't relevant to my work."

"You're going to be paid a princely sum for your testimony here, aren't you?"

"I don't think it's at all 'princely.' It's the same amount I usually charge for this kind of work."

"How much are you paid, per hour?"

"Three hundred and fifty dollars an hour."

"Including all your traveling time? When you're waiting at an airport?"

"It's customary."

"And your pay as a professor is just a tiny fraction of what Mr. Herrick's paying you? You're getting about five or six times as much per hour, aren't you?"

"Maybe. I can't say exactly. I haven't done any of that math."

It was standard cross-examination, and it would have been much less impressive to lawyers than to lay people. But the jurors, of course, were not lawyers, and they looked up sharply at that last exchange. "You sure took the wind out of his sails," Robert heard one of the Booker and Bayne associates say to Jimmy, as they left the courtroom for the day.

34
CONTEMPT OF COURT

El Jefe was not a happy drug dealer these days. The only contact he could use to give orders was his lawyer. But his lawyer didn't understand much of anything, and he wasn't very good at getting things done. More than once, in angry moments, El Jefe had thought about having his lawyer killed. But that didn't make sense. His lawyer was the only human being he could meet without having guards present, and it didn't seem likely that it would work very well if he told his lawyer to instruct the cartel members to kill the lawyer, himself.

"When I told them to get rid of that journalist guy, Castillo, it got done right away!" El Jefe was close to jumping up and down in frustration. "Now, I tell you to tell them to kill that investigator, and it doesn't work, and I tell you to tell them to kill that lawyer … and nothing happens! What's the deal? What's wrong? What's the world coming to?"

"I am sorry, *Jefe*, but the organization is not the same."

"What do you mean, it isn't the same?"

"It just isn't the same. For one thing, some of those men who worked for you have gotten arrested, just like you got arrested yourself."

"Well, but that's always happened, here and there, and we got them out of it."

"Harder to do today." The lawyer nodded vigorously, to communicate that this was an understatement. "And it's dangerous."

"Dangerous? How?"

"They are facing long prison terms. They may decide to make deals."

"And if they do?"

"They might agree to testify against you, *Jefe*. Excuse me for saying so."

"Impossible."

174

"And then, some of the old guys are working for themselves, not for the Cartel. They have used the old routes, the old connections, the old methods, to do their own business. Their own drug trails, and they keep the money for themselves. They've made it into, like, a franchise operation."

"Impossible," said El Jefe again.

"*Jefe*, I am your lawyer. I am bound to tell you the truth. Please listen to me when I tell you. Unless I tell you, you won't know. And if I do tell you, maybe you can do something about it."

The Craziest One was silent, at that. It was true. If he succeeded in getting this lawyer killed, it might be hard to get another one, and as far as he was concerned, all lawyers were stupid anyway. If he did get another lawyer, there was no way to guarantee that the new guy would be any better, and he might be worse.

The lawyer sighed. "But *Jefe*, I haven't told you about the most serious problem."

"Yeah? What?"

"The *Norteamericanos* have been moving forward with their request to extradite you. To the United States."

This got El Jefe's attention. Extradition to the United States would be a living death. He would be among people who did not follow orders at all.

"The President's warrant from the United States has been received and filed with the national courts here," the lawyer continued. "Our Government will insist that the *Norteamericanos* remove the death penalty as an option, because Mexico never extradites anyone who is a possible subject of the death penalty, but the United States Justice Department is used to this, and they will agree to remove the death penalty."

The lawyer was afraid because it was risky to tell bad news to El Más Loco, but he had to go on.

"*Jefe*, we will oppose the warrant, and we will fight the proof that they will offer to support it, and we will put on a defense case, contrary to the extradition. We will have plenty of character witnesses, for example, to swear that you are not a violent person and could not possibly have committed the horrible crimes that supposedly support the warrant. It will take a long time for any extradition to be completed."

"A long time?"

"Shorter than it used to be, but a year or so, and then, if we lose, we will appeal. And if we lose that—"

The lawyer noticed that there was one issue that quieted El Jefe. Extradition.

"If we lose that, we still can appeal to the national government."

Which, they both knew, would be of no value whatsoever. The lawyer decided to change the subject. To quit while he was still ahead. And still alive.

"*Jefe*, I have brought you more of your camouflage uniforms. And a new pair of the shoes you like, from that designer ... ahhhh, Gucci? Is that it, Gucci? ..."

* * *

Several hundred miles to the north, the trial before Judge Raines resumed.

"Your honor, the plaintiffs call José Luis Leyva." Robert pointed to the entrance to the courtroom. "Your honor, this is the witness who is in DEA custody, who will testify to his former membership in the Cartel."

The witness came forward slowly. Or rather, a whole group of people came forward slowly. There was the witness in the center, wearing a conspicuous bulletproof vest. A half dozen official-looking men and women surrounded him, people who must be agents, also wearing bulletproof vests. Behind this parade, there were several lawyers, following at a safe distance. The lawyers looked like they wanted bulletproof vests.

The clerk stood. "Raise your right hand, please. Do you solemnly swear or affirm that you will tell the truth, the whole truth, and nothing but the truth?"

The interpreter had on a bulletproof vest too. He translated. And then he translated back, with José Luis Leyva's words. "He says, 'I'm not going to testify to anything and I won't swear anything.'"

There was silence.

Then, the judge sat bolt upright. "What was that? What was *that?* Tell him again to take the oath."

The interpreter wore a look of indifference as his translation of the judge's words reached the witness, and as the communication traveled back with the witness's answer.

"He says, 'I will not testify to anything.'"

The judge was angry. He looked at the witness. And he said, in a voice that one would think would allow no nonsense, "You are ordered to take the oath and to testify."

Translation, by the interpreter. Then, the reverse translation. And José Luis's words came through: "I won't do it and you can't make me."

The judge's near-black eyes were narrow. His brow was furrowed in a frown, and the court personnel all shared his surprise. The court reporter stared, the law clerks stared, and the bailiff stared.

Meanwhile, the lawyers were as stunned as everyone else. Robert's jaw dropped. Even Jimmy Coleman was frozen. But the lawyers had little to do or say. The jurors all stared too, in silence, but the jurors had no part in this. The judge was the one who carried this moment.

"If you fail and refuse to testify, you will be held in contempt of court."

Translation, by the interpreter. Then, reverse translation. "What can anyone do to me?"

Silence.

It probably occurred to every lawyer in the courtroom that the witness was right—no one could do anything meaningful to him—and this might be the perfect crime.

Finally, the judge tried again, a little less hopefully, and got the same answer.

More silence. And finally, the judge said, to no one in particular, "Take this witness—or rather, this individual—out of this courtroom."

He turned to the jury. "Ladies and gentlemen, in these circumstances, I have no choice but to say, we will be in recess. Until tomorrow morning."

* * *

"What do we do now?" asked Tom Kennedy, as they left the courtroom.

"I suppose there is only one thing we can do." Robert spoke slowly.

"Show the jury his deposition?"

"Yes. We'll show the jury the videotape of his deposition testimony. The Federal Rules of Civil Procedure will let us do that. The Rules say that one instance when you can show the deposition is when the witness is, quote, 'unavailable,' unquote. Well, this witness is unavailable—he refuses to testify, even after he's been threatened with contempt."

"It's just a shame. The deposition is cluttered with all kinds of evasions, falsehoods, and outright lies."

"And in addition to that, a deposition always makes less of an impression on a jury than testimony from the witness stand by a live witness. A deposition is boring. We'll have the jurors watching several hours of deposition testimony on little TV monitors. It's excruciatingly boring, and it's easy for people to miss the point that way."

"But what can we do? We can't make the deposition any more interesting."

"No, we can't do anything . . . about that. But we still have a lot of work to do. One of the questions we have to figure out, and fast, is whether we should play the deposition straight through, with all of those evasions, falsehoods, and outright lies, or whether we edit the deposition to show the parts that we want. The parts that help our case?"

"We're entitled to do that. To show the parts that we want to show, and to let Jimmy Coleman bring out the parts that he wants to show. After we do our thing with the parts we want."

"What a choice! One way, we end up showing several hours, much more time than the parts we want or need. That's if we show it straight through. And we end up with all kinds of interruptions, changes in direction, and arguments by lawyers, and we're guaranteed to lose the jurors. The other way, we end up having a sequence of testimony that the jury knows is edited, and we give Jimmy Coleman the opportunity to go back and show the jury the stuff we edited out. With the implication that we're hiding something. Jimmy will make it all sound as if we're dishonest."

* * *

Maria met them at the office. "I won't stay," she said. "I'd be in your way. But Robert, this is the only way I get to see you!"

"And you can give us some advice." Robert sketched the issue they faced, for her. "Do you think we ought to edit the videotape of the deposition, or play it straight through?"

"No question about it," was her instant answer. "Edit the deposition. In the first place, there's too much likelihood of the story getting lost, if there's a lot of Jimmy-Coleman-style argument and bickering and accusations and irrelevance throughout it. You need a clear story from your witness. That's going to be hard enough with this witness, even if the jury concentrates on the parts that matter. And in the second place, if Jimmy follows up and shows the parts you left out, it's going to be pure confusion. Often, when a witness gets attacked for telling different stories, the contradiction gets lost. The jury will come away with an impression that this guy is not a very good witness. That's true. But that's unavoidable, and they'd come away with that impression anyway."

She raised her voice. "And I'll tell you what else. Jimmy Coleman's personality is bound to come through to the jurors when he plays the videotape with the parts he wants. I bet, during this trial, he's acting really friendly in front of the jury. Polite. Dignified. Like a cuddly teddy bear. But I'm sure he wasn't that way during the deposition. And if the witness comes across as less than fully credible, Jimmy Coleman will come across even worse."

Robert and Tom looked at each other. And then, with the assistance of the firm's audio-visual director, they got to work. It was going to take them hours, until late in the night, to edit the videotape of the deposition.

35

THE TURNCOAT WITNESS

Call your next witness," said Judge Marvin Raines.

"The plaintiffs call José Luis Leyva." Robert stood to address the court. "Same witness as yesterday, but because of what happened yesterday, we will present Mr. Leyva by deposition instead."

"Yes, I see that you have set up television monitors throughout the courtroom." The judge turned to the jury. "Ladies and gentlemen, you will hear and see a 'deposition' from this witness, José Luis Leyva. The witness who did not testify, so you'll get his testimony by deposition.

"A deposition just means testimony taken before the trial. It is taken under the same oath as here in the courtroom. This deposition is to be considered by you as evidence, like other kinds of evidence, and you are the judges of the credibility of the evidence."

Jimmy Coleman was on his feet. "Objection, your honor. The rule says that the deposition cannot be used as evidence unless the witness is 'unavailable.' José Luis Leyva isn't unavailable. He was in this courtroom yesterday, and he can be made available by the DEA—the Drug Enforcement Administration. The deposition is improper."

Robert had prepared an answer for this. "But Rule 804 of the Federal Rules of Evidence says that a witness is considered unavailable if he 'persists' in refusing to testify when ordered by the court. That's the word in the Rule: the witness 'persists' in refusing. Mr. Leyva certainly persisted in refusing to testify."

But Jimmy had an answer too. A more complicated answer. "Rule 804 covers hearsay evidence of certain specified kinds. But that's not what this is. This is a deposition. And the cases don't support reading a deposition just because the witness refuses to testify."

Judge Raines pushed his glasses to the end of his nose and stared at Jimmy with a puzzled look.

"Your honor," Jimmy went on, "we've filed a brief this morning, showing why a deposition from José Luis Leyva would be inadmissible evidence. Here's a copy for Mr. Herrick. Our brief shows that the opinions of the courts do not allow the deposition in this situation."

Judge Raines looked weary. "Take the jury out. Ladies and gentlemen of the jury, I'll have to meet with the lawyers again. All right, Mr. Coleman. I'll look at your brief." He hefted a copy of Jimmy's arguments with two hands. "We'd better take a couple of hours, Mr. Bailiff, for me to resolve this issue."

* * *

An hour later, Robert and Tom found themselves in the county law library, looking at the cases Jimmy had cited.

"Here," said Tom. "Here's another misleading quotation. Page 6 of Jimmy's brief mentions a case that says, simply, that the defendant in that case argued that, quote, 'the deposition was improper.' Jimmy's brief quotes the words, 'the deposition was improper.' But then, the case that Jimmy has quoted goes on to say, 'The court rejects this argument.' In other words, Jimmy quotes the exact words correctly, but doesn't say that the court's decision went the opposite way."

"Okay, good." Robert made a note of the case name and the relevant quotations. The list of wrong quotations and misleading arguments in Jimmy's brief was getting longer.

"The truth is, there are a few case decisions that don't help us, that could be taken to imply that Jimmy is right. But there's nothing really on point that says what he's trying to make the cases sound like."

"And there are case decisions that squarely support our position." Robert looked at another list he was keeping, a list of authorities that contradicted Jimmy's arguments.

"We won't have time to write this up as a brief."

"No. We'll have to just make two lists of cases. Cases cited by the defendant's brief that do not support the defendant's argument. And ... cases that support us: the plaintiffs' position."

Fifteen minutes later, they had their two lists. Each case had a sentence following it, to say either why it did not support Jimmy Coleman's position or why it instead supported Robert and Tom. In other words, why it did not require the court to exclude José Luis Leyva's deposition, or why it instead justified the court in letting the jury hear the deposition.

* * *

Suddenly, Robert's telephone rang.

Donna DeCarlo knew how to get right to business when her boss was in trial. "Robert, you have a call from Detectives Derrigan Slaughter and Donnie Cashdollar. You know, the ones who are working the same case you are, the Castillo murders, in the criminal courts."

"Donna, do I need to return it right away?"

"I think so. They said something about a second man who's about to plead guilty. They said, they know you'll want to talk to this guy who is one of the murderers and they can tell you about him."

"Well, that's right. I'm not sure I . . . *want* to talk to him. But sure, I should."

He hung up and immediately called Derrigan Slaughter.

"This guy is gonna get life imprisonment without parole," the detective said. "He'll be testifyin against the third guy, who is the worst of the three. That guy will be tried for the death penalty. But here's what's important to you, Robert. This guy, who's about to plead guilty, remembers the bank real good. And he'll be available to testify.

"And they's one more thing. Miss Maria, yo' wife, has a message. She says, 'Settle this case.' And I always think that, too."

"Thanks." Robert had to laugh. He said goodbye, and he and Tom began walking back to the federal courthouse.

* * *

"The deposition is admissible in evidence," said Judge Raines finally. "I've read your brief, Mr. Coleman, and I've read your list of cases, Mr. Herrick. And the law is clear. The jury can hear this deposition."

He turned to the bailiff. "Bring the jury in."

Robert fiddled with the monitors and with his remote while the eight men and women filled their chairs. The audiovisual director of the firm was here in the courtroom, so there was little need for fiddling. But Robert had learned, years ago, that video evidence was good when handled well, but disastrous if the equipment malfunctioned, and he always worried about it.

"Ladies and gentlemen," said the judge, "remember what I told you earlier about the deposition you are about to see and hear. It is just like any other evidence in the case, and you are the sole judges of the credibility of the witness."

Robert switched the monitors all on simultaneously, using the remote. The scene, on two large screens in front of the jury, showed an uncomfortable witness, too thin to look healthy, too pale to look anything but scared.

"Would you state your full name for the reporter, please, Mr. Leyva?" Robert's voice came through the monitor, from behind the camera, unseen. The witness filled the screen.

The sound on the monitor followed the deposition as the interpreter translated, then received the witness's answer, exactly as the answer had been given weeks before, at the deposition. "José Luis Leyva."

"Do you understand what a deposition is, Mr. Leyva?"

"Yes. The Government lawyers told me that I have to answer questions."

According to the editing of the videotape that Robert and Tom had done, the questioning skipped forward. "Mr. Leyva, please tell us your main professional activity or employment before coming to the United States."

The screen played Jimmy Coleman's gravelly voice, next. "Objection to the form of the question. It's compound and hypothetical, and it assumes facts not in evidence, such as that the witness actually had some sort of employment."

Robert and Tom had left some of Jimmy's objections in the video, just to show his obstructionism.

The edited tape moved forward to the witness's answer. "I worked for a man named Alejandro Carlos Gonzales-Huerta, known to me as 'El Jefe.' In Mexico."

"Did your job sometimes include passing on directions from El Jefe that involved killing people?"

There was a jump, a dislocation, of the tape on the screen, to show another edit. "Well, I guess the answer is yes."

The jurors sat forward. They knew, now, that this was the man they had heard described as the "inside" witness. The "turncoat" witness. The one who was going to tell about the operations of the Cartel. The eight men and women paid close attention as the witness described how the Cartel did its business. And then:

"Mr. Leyva, do you know about a Bank called 'The Velnikov Bank'?"

A long-winded objection from Jimmy entertained the jurors, who laughed at it, this time.

"Well, yes, approximately. Sort of." This answer from the witness didn't make a lot of sense, but there it was on the screen, and nothing could be done about that.

"And when did you first hear about the Velnikov Bank?"

Jimmy's objection emerged from the monitor and grated across the courtroom.

This time the witness's answer made more sense. "Years ago. I am not exactly sure which year."

"Please tell us about how your work involved the Velnikov Bank."

Another objection.

"Mr. Alejandro Carlos Gonzales-Huerta, who is known as El Jefe, was on the telephone with the President of the Bank and his assistant almost every day, and sometimes he had me call them."

"What did you call the Bank about, yourself?"

"I called when El Jefe told me to. And the usual message was to tell the Bank President, 'Where is our money? Hurry up with our money!' "

The jury was staring at the monitors, Robert saw with satisfaction. Staring at them the way a jury stares at a witness who is at one and the same time both fascinating and repulsive. After several more questions about the Bank, the screen played back Robert's shot-in-the-dark question:

"Mr. Leyva, do you know whether El Jefe had any contact with the Velnikov Bank about killing Rafael Castillo and his family?"

Now, the jurors were bug-eyed. Not just staring, but gaping at the witness. Another grating objection by Jimmy sounded from the monitors.

"Yes, I remember hearing him talking to the President about it. Before it happened. I think it was the President. Maybe his assistant. But he mentioned the Bank in the same conversation, and I think he said that he would do something so that Castillo would not write any more stories about the drug trade."

The jury stayed alert during the last few questions, after which Robert's voice said, "That's all. I pass the witness."

Robert and Tom had kept Jimmy Coleman's response to that on the edited tape: "I have no questions."

Jimmy's refusal to question the witness probably was based on the expectation that the witness would testify live at the trial. In that event, Jimmy would not have wanted to give any more information to the plaintiffs. But in front of the jury, Jimmy's statement sounded as though he had approved of what the witness had said.

* * *

On the way back to the office, riding in Robert's armored M-Rap, Tom was elated. "We've got 'em! We've got 'em!," he kept saying. At one sidewalk corner, he got out and leapfrogged over a fire hydrant, but he missed slightly because he underestimated the height of the hydrant, and he almost tore his trousers.

Robert was not so sure, at all. "But now comes the part that is going to be hard for us to listen to."

"What's that?"

"Jimmy Coleman is going to play the parts of the deposition that show what a liar this witness can be. Or at best, how confused he is." Robert found, suddenly, that he had the same kind of sickness in his stomach that he'd felt throughout this trial. "Jimmy will be just as good at editing that tape as we've been."

"I don't think he can destroy this witness's credibility completely, after today."

"Frankly, I don't know. I worry that Jimmy may be able to make the witness look like such a complete liar that the jury shouldn't believe any of it. I hope you're right, Tom, and I hope Jimmy doesn't succeed at what he'll be trying to do, which is to destroy this witness's credibility.

"And ... I hate to say this.... I hope that what he shows the jury won't destroy *our* credibility completely, too."

36

NOT AS GOOD AS WE WOULD HAVE WANTED

The television monitors were still in place in front of the jury. But now it was Jimmy Coleman's turn to show the parts of the deposition that he wanted them to see. Robert and Tom were both on the edges of their seats. This witness had been full of contradictions, confusions, and outright falsehoods.

Jimmy touched the remote. A picture appeared on the screen, and it gradually resolved to show the witness, José Luis Leyva. From somewhere offscreen, a voice came through. It was Robert Herrick's voice from a time before the beginning of trial, asking a question.

". . . Then you also know that the answers you give are sworn to, and they carry the same penalties of perjury as testimony in court?"

". . . If the judge says so," said the image of the witness on the screen.

Jimmy stopped the recording for a brief moment and shook his head. Robert felt a mixture of disappointment and disgust at this witness. This repetition of the meaning of the oath was a prelude to a mass of lies. "And yet this is my witness," he whispered to himself.

Now, Jimmy was ready to establish the worthlessness of José Luis Leyva as a witness. He pressed the remote, and quickly, Robert's voice emerged from the monitor again.

"Did your job sometimes include passing on directions from El Jefe that involved killing people?"

". . . No! certainly not," answered the image of José Luis Leyva on the screen. "Only if it was legal to kill them."

Robert hated seeing it. Several jurors were squinting in disbelief, at that last statement.

Immediately, the screen showed that Government lawyers descended on the witness, and there was a lot of whispering. The monitor didn't make any of the whispering loud enough to hear. But the message was clear: the Government lawyers wanted José Luis to correct the lie he had just told.

"Well, . . . I guess the answer is yes," said the image on the screen, after a long pause.

Jimmy kept the monitor going for another forty-five minutes. The scenes he showed from the deposition were edited flawlessly to show only the question and the translated answer, and each time, the point was made in just a few sentences. But the experience seemed to go on forever for Robert.

Finally, Jimmy turned off the monitors. "Your honor, that concludes our use of José Luis Leyva's deposition." Jimmy spat out these words, to signal his disapproval.

"Thank you," said Judge Raines. "Now: this trial will be in recess until ten o'clock Monday morning." He gave the jury the usual warnings about not watching television or discussing the case with anyone. "Aside from that, ladies and gentlemen of the jury, enjoy your weekend."

As they left the courtroom, Tom whispered to Robert: "We can say goodbye to our main witness. The jury's going to throw out José Luis's entire story."

"It was . . . certainly . . . not as good as we might have wanted." Robert smiled weakly. "But you know, Tom, sometimes juries can find truth even in the testimony of the worst kinds of witnesses. And so . . . I hope they're more forgiving than you are. And for that matter, more forgiving than I feel right now."

But the flip-flops in his stomach told him that this sort of jury forgiveness wasn't likely.

* * *

Saturday morning. Instead of getting up at 6 and getting to the office at 7, Robert slept until 8. He put on a pair of jeans and a baseball shirt, and he headed downstairs to eat something quickly and leave for the office.

"Robert, it's Saturday." Maria Melendes was adamant. "It's a day for you to spend some quality time with your wife. Me."

"But next week is going to be crucial. We're going to call the accountant to the witness stand. To tell the jury how the Velnikov Bank worked together with the drug cartel."

"I know. And that's even aside from calling another murderer and a lot of detectives and suchlike. But you need to have a life, too. And in addition to your needing a life, I need a life. Me, your wife."

He flopped into a chair. "And what is it you want this quality time to consist of?"

"First, we go and have breakfast somewhere nice. Second, you take me to the Art Museum to see the exhibit I've been asking you for months to take me to."

"What's that? I've forgotten."

She sighed. "It's called 'The Surreal Artists.' It will include a lot of Dada art and cubism. But mostly surrealism. At the Menil Museum."

Now it was his turn to sigh. "Great. Dada art. I know what that is. It's full of combinations of objects that don't make any sense together."

She laughed at him. "That's why it's good art. It wouldn't be very good, if a guy like you could figure it out."

"All right. Going to breakfast and to the Art Museum in our armored M-Rap is just what I want to do this morning."

* * *

"The Treachery of Images," said the title on the sign beside the painting. The artist was listed as "René Magritte." The painting consisted of a polished, exacting image of a pipe, with its stem and bowl shining in burled wood, below which was written, "Ceci n'est pas une pipe."

"That means, *'This is not a pipe,'*" Maria said helpfully.

"I know," he said. "That much, I could read. And I could read the title, which is *The Treachery of Images.* Magritte was one of the earliest surrealists."

"Then you know what this painting means."

"Magritte denied the existence of art, really, even though it's what he did. Art was indistinguishable from objects, and objects disappeared into art. Here, what he's written on the painting is true, because it's certainly *not* a pipe. It's only a *painting* of a pipe. Images are treacherous. Life fools us, constantly, by showing us things we think we recognize, but we don't."

"I'm impressed," she said, while laughing to show that she was not really impressed at all.

"And that reminds me of my case on trial. We presented a witness by deposition, this guy named José Luis Leyva. His image was there, on a screen. He appeared to be testifying. In fact, he had testified, in front of a video camera, earlier. But he only appeared to be a witness. He only seemed to be testifying. His testimony got so thoroughly destroyed that he only appeared to be a real witness. He was only an image, instead. That's what images are like. It's *The Treachery of Images,* as René Magritte would have said it."

"You need to settle that case." But then, she caught herself: Don't push. And she asked, "Does everything you're going to say relate to your trial?"

"Just about."

"Well, let's try another painting to see whether we can get you away from it. Here's one called *The Human Condition.* It's also by Magritte, but it's different from the last one, because it doesn't have anything written on it."

Robert stared at the painting for a moment. It showed a window, from inside a room, looking out at a tree and a meadow. The room, window, and outdoor scene were shown precisely, in Magritte's usual style. But if you looked closely . . . and then, if you looked even more closely, you saw something unexpected: the three legs of an easel. The easel, in turn, held a painting. The painting was a picture of the same outdoor scene, and it was oriented to fit exactly into the scene, so that it looked as though you were looking at the scene, but actually you were looking at the scene and at the painting in the middle of it which fit into the scene and supplied part of the scene, but on second thought, it was the outdoor scene . . . but it was an illusion, because there was a painting of the selfsame outdoor scene in the middle of it.

"That's certainly surrealism," said Robert. "This painting is about illusion, and that's why it's called *The Human Condition.* Magritte is telling us that what we see seems real, and in a way it is, but at the same time, it's an illusion. And that reminds me of my case, again. . . . In our case on trial, we've had the illusion that we've been presenting witnesses. But all we've presented has been an illusion. We are experiencing *The Human Condition.* While we've been thinking that we were showing the jury the testimony of credible witnesses, the jury members all knew that we were just showing them something that wasn't really there. That's probably what René Magritte would say, if he were here today."

"See whether you can find a way to think about something other than your trial. Or better yet, settle the case," she pleaded.

Their next stop was in front of a strange sculpture. It was nothing but a bicycle wheel, upside down, mounted in the center of a stool.

"Dada was the forerunner of surrealism, and it was anti-art," said Maria. "This statue, if you can call it a statute, is by Marcel Duchamp. The Dada artists thought there was really no such thing as art, and instead, ordinary objects were the real thing, the thing that qualified as art."

"Right. And so this one is called *Bicycle Wheel.*"

"Art consists of something that transforms whatever it is that you're looking at," she said. "And this is art, because it does. The wheel is upside down, so it can't move a bicycle. It can only spin and be looked at. And it's combined with this stool that it's stuck into the middle of. The combination and the upside-down-ness transform these two objects and make them into . . . well, art."

"You could have fooled me, about whether it's art. But I get the message. The message from Marcel Duchamp is, there is no deeper message. And that reminds me of our case on trial. The testimony that we've been giving the jury in our trial is nothing deeper than words. It's not any more useful than an upside-down bicycle tire. In the end, when we try to get the jury to find something more profound in what we've shown them, the jury won't be able to see it because it isn't really there. And that means that our theory that the Bank is guilty of these horrible crimes is nothing but so much talk between lawyers and witnesses, and only the words are there."

She frowned at him. "I'm beginning to see a pattern in your reactions to all of these works of art."

"Really?" He tried to look innocent. "I guess I feel a powerful need to go to the office to prepare for next week."

With that, Robert stopped comparing the images of meaninglessness in the art works to his worries about his trial. He realized that if he didn't, Maria might do something he wouldn't like. And an hour later, after seeing Salvador Dali's painting called "The Persistence of Memory," which features clock faces so distorted that they look as though they are melting, and after that, seeing blobs of color by Joan Miró, emaciated figures by Dorothea Tanning, and weird mannequins by Man Ray . . . they came to the end of the exhibit.

"All right," Maria announced. "You've done your job, Robert, by bringing me here. That was nice. Take me to lunch, and then you can go to the office, where you've wanted to go all morning. And . . . figure out how to settle this case."

37

MONEY LAUNDERING

After working the rest of the weekend, Robert was still not quite ready for the blur of witnesses he planned to call on Monday, Tuesday, and Wednesday. As his spinning mind told him, that wasn't all, because there would be other days after that. It was all becoming a blur. He had known to expect that. After days of trial and nights of preparation, it always becomes a blur.

Monday morning came. The medical examiner was the first witness of the week: a medical doctor specializing in pathology, or the science of investigating injuries, diseases, and death.

"Doctor, can you tell us what the medical examiner does?," he asked.

"The office is called 'the coroner' in many locations. We investigate deaths, perform autopsies, and describe causes of death."

"Doctor, please let me refer you to the eight autopsies that you conducted in this case. Is there any similarity in the causes of death?"

"Yes. All eight autopsies showed that the cause of death was severance or other destruction of bodily organs by a cutting device, most likely a machete. Or multiple machetes."

"On what do you base the conclusion that machetes were the weapon that was used?"

"The remains, or the bodies, showed cutting, but very deep cutting, including cutting of bones in some instances. The wounds were of a type indicating that the killer administered blows and cuts with greater force than a knife could administer."

"I direct your attention to the autopsy of the youngest child, little Jonathan Castillo. Can you tell me the cause of death and the wounds?"

"The cause of death was bleeding from the blood vessels of the neck. The neck was parted by a cut that nearly severed the head. In addition, there were wounds to the arms, hands, and abdomen."

"Doctor, can you tell us what 'defensive wounds' are, and whether you found any defensive wounds on Jonathan Castillo?"

"Yes. Defensive wounds are caused when a weapon is swung or stabbed at a victim, and the still-living victim tries to defend against the attack by whatever is possible to use. Which is usually the victim's hands. The victim makes a vain attempt to shield himself or herself from the killing force by the pathetic act of extending his hands. In this instance, there were severe cuts or wounds to this baby's hands, when the baby attempted to raise them to ward off the blows and was unsuccessful."

"Even at such a young age, is the victim likely to try to defend, and to suffer defensive wounds, in this manner?"

"Yes. It is virtually universal and instinctive. I have seen even younger children with defensive wounds."

"Would this manner of death be painful, for whatever length of time it took for death to occur?"

"Yes. It depends on the precise location of the wounds, but yes."

And in this manner, Robert and the Medical Examiner worked their way through each of the eight victims, one at a time. Each victim had different kinds of wounds. "This indicates the indiscriminate method of swinging the machete or machetes," the witness explained.

The jury obviously found the testimony disturbing. The judge called a recess at one point to allow several jurors, who had tears in their eyes and looked sickened, to compose themselves. But the evidence had to be presented, and the jury had to hear it.

* * *

As the week wore on, the horror of the evidence never seemed to let up. There were police officers who had seen the scene of the murders. There was the second turncoat witness: the second killer who had agreed to turn state's evidence and testify, who told the jury directly that, yes, it was the Velnikov Bank that the killers had visited, where they received their pay, before the murders. Then, too, there were police officers who had conducted searches of the killers' homes and made the arrests of the men who had committed the murders.

Also, there were several less dramatic, but equally necessary witnesses. A pair of journalists told the jury about Rafael Castillo's career. An economist testified about Mr. Castillo's earnings during his lifetime and the earning potential he would have had if he had lived. The jury would have to assess damages, and lost earnings are a part of the damages, even if they are a less bloody part. The economist was needed.

Then, it was time to call a witness who would sound boring at first, but who had fascinating things to say: Martin Blankford, the forensic accountant.

* * *

"As an accountant," said the witness, "I can tell you this. Money laundering is easy, if the launderer is willing to commit the crime of money laundering. It's the cover-up that's hard. That is, the hard part is covering up the manipulations and hiding the money laundering."

It was late in the week. Robert Herrick had finally reached the point at which it made sense to call this crucial witness. Martin Blankford was about to tell the jury about money laundering—and about the Velnikov Bank's role in the drug trade done by the Cartel.

"Can you explain to us why that is so, Mr. Blankford? Why is the cover-up the hard part of money laundering?"

"If all you wanted to do was to launder money, and you weren't concerned about hiding it, you could put all of the illegal money into a friend's bank account and have him write a check to you for the same amount. But if the people you were trying to hide the transactions from, such as the Government, were to look at your friend's account, they would immediately see the money going in and going out. Your laundering would be useless, because it would be too easy to spot."

"So, is that why hiding the money laundering is hard?"

"Yes, indeed. You have to look at it from the point of view of the money launderer, who usually has a strong incentive to commit the crime." Martin Blankford smiled. Like most accountants, he loved to solve a mystery, and he liked to talk about bank accounts.

Earlier, Robert had gotten the witness to tell the jury about his professional qualifications. Mr. Blankford had a bachelor's degree in accounting from the University of Texas. He also had an "MBA," a Master's of Business Administration, from The Wharton School at the University of Pennsylvania. He'd spent ten years working at Coopers & Lybrand, which he explained was one of the big accounting firms—which were then called the "Big Eight." Many firms in the Big Eight, he explained with a smile, "didn't do very well in making money for their own accounts," and now the accounting firms were only the "Big Four." When he had left Coopers & Lybrand, Blankford had formed a partnership with another accountant and created what he affectionately called "my own accounting shop." Today, it had twenty-five accountants and nearly a hundred employees.

Martin Blankford had done work for the CIA, the FBI, and private firms like Exxon, Xerox, and Boeing, just to name a few.

"But the largest number of our clients are just people—individuals—who have tax problems or need accounting services done."

"Mr. Blankford, what is meant by the term 'forensic accounting'? And what does 'auditing' mean?"

"Forensic accounting means reconstructing transactions of the past. It means that we look at records of how money was handled and explain what they all mean. Auditing is the process of examining the actual assets, to see whether they match up with the books and records. There is a certain amount of similarity in the two, because both of them involve detective work."

He smiled at the jury. "Not detective work like Sherlock Holmes does, with a magnifying glass and fingerprints, but with records of how money was handled. Those can give you clues just like the clues that the famous Mr. Holmes uses."

"And in your capacity as a forensic accountant, did you have occasion to examine certain records of the Velnikov Bank?"

"Yes. We never did get all of the records that we wanted, but we got enough."

"Did you have enough information to make conclusions about the path of money that went through the Velnikov Bank?"

"Yes, sir."

"Did it involve money laundering?"

Jimmy looked as though he was going to object. But if he did, the judge was likely to overrule his objection, and the question and answer would only seem more important. He sat back, again, in his chair.

"Yes, sir. It involved a lot of money laundering."

"How could you tell?"

"We received records from the accounts of more than a thousand depositors. What the records showed was that the depositors handed in money in multiple thousands of dollars at a time, in cash. That means that the money was handled in hundred dollar bills, which are often used in the drug trade. The federal government requires reports of cash being handled in amounts of over ten thousand dollars, and always, the amounts were less than the amounts that require reporting to the federal government."

The accountant faced the jury. "So, these depositors were very, very unusual. And another thing. They each began their depositing at the Bank in multiple thousands, rather than building up the amounts."

"For normal customers depositing cash, you would expect uneven amounts, in dollars and cents?"

"Of course. The daily deposited amount from a legitimate restaurant, or dress shop, or other business that receives cash—well, the amounts may be 'four thousand, two hundred, eighty-nine dollars and sixty three cents,' or something like that. It's usually not going to be exact multiples of hundred dollar bills."

"And you wouldn't expect a given customer to start depositing amounts of eight thousand or more, without depositing a lesser amount earlier?"

"Exactly. Merchants usually build their businesses."

"And Mr. Blankford, did you come across what is called 'layering'? Please explain what that is."

"Layering means that money is passed from one business to another in short periods for no obvious reason, and some of the businesses may be empty shells, with nothing but a name. And yes, there were layers upon layers in the Bank's transfers, and the layers ultimately tied into the Cartel."

The testimony of Martin Blankford went on for several hours. He described not only the deposits, but also the payments and loans that were made. The payments, too, were in multiples of hundreds, and also in cash. Loans were made to various depositors that were paid from the accounts of those depositors. There were large numbers of transfers of money between these strange depositors. And then the same amount of money, or a nearly similar amount, would be withdrawn.

"Do you have a chart that shows the money flow, that you have put together?" Robert asked at one point.

"Yes," said the witness, and he projected the chart onto the motion picture screen that the courtroom provided. The diagram showed the deposits, transfers, withdrawals, and loans in a way that made them easy to follow.

"Now, is there any possibility that the Bank, and its officers, could have avoided knowing that the Bank was being used to launder money?"

"No possibility whatsoever."

"Why would you say that?"

"These kinds of transactions, first of all, are unusual, and anyone in the banking business would know that they are suspicious. And the truth is, no one can look at this pattern and not see how odd it is. Furthermore, the Bank was a direct participant in this process, in the layering. The money laundering could not have gone on without the Bank's active participation."

"Would you say that this was a well-hidden money laundering scheme?"

"No. It's not particularly well hidden. It's about somewhere in the middle. It's not one of the best hidden that I've ever seen. That's for sure. And surprisingly, it's not one of the least skillfully done that I've seen, but it's unusual, for this amount of money."

Robert felt a sense of satisfaction as he said, "I pass the witness."

* * *

"Would you say that the Bank's money laundering was hidden in the shadows?," Francel asked.

"Shadows? . . . I suppose so."

"And this secret, shadow defendant was essential to the drug business?"

"Oh, yes."

"This Bank was closer to the place where the murders happened than the Cartel?"

"Yes."

And with that, Francel said, "I pass the witness."

* * *

Jimmy Coleman's cross examination was brief. But very effective.

"Mr. Blankford, you've seen cases of banks being used to launder money without the bankers realizing it, haven't you?"

"Yes, of course."

"In fact, that's much more common, isn't it, than bankers doing it?"

"Yes."

"In other words, the typical pattern is for criminals to use a bank to launder money when the bank is completely clueless that money laundering is going on?"

"I suppose so."

"And in this case, the amounts involved in each transaction may have been large for an individual, but they were tiny compared to the size of the Velnikov Bank, weren't they?"

"I don't know. Finding out the size of the Bank wasn't part of my assignment for this case."

Jimmy made a visible show of shaking his head at that. And Robert was disappointed to notice that several jurors frowned, and some shook their heads, too.

"Now, the bankers in this Bank didn't have your fancy diagram in front of them, did they? They didn't have a diagram that showed the money in and the money out?"

"Nobody had this diagram until I put it together for this case."

"Mr. Blankford, it would be like focusing on a needle in a haystack, for a banker with the Velnikov Bank to focus on a given single one of these transactions that you've identified. Wouldn't it?"

"Well, I don't know whether I'd describe it exactly that way."

"Judge, I don't have any more use for this witness." Jimmy waved his hand in a dismissive gesture as he stood to address the court, with all of the jurors watching him closely. And by now, Robert had the same sickened lump in his stomach that he had been feeling all through this trial.

Then, suddenly, the week ended. Robert and Tom spent all of Friday night getting ready for what was to come.

38
THE LOCKDOWN

Monday morning came all too soon. The rest of the weekend wasn't enough to plan the upcoming week of trial, and Robert knew it.

As he looked out of his armored M-Rap verhicle when it approached the curb at the Federal Building, he couldn't see anything suspicious. There were people walking quickly past the building on the way to work. There was a woman in a threadbare shawl together with a young boy, probably heading for the Social Security department inside the Federal Building, or for one of the immigration offices. There were three soldiers in uniforms that Robert didn't recognize. All of them wore camouflage and military berets. Soldiers were frequently here at the Federal Building as color guards, to carry flags. Idly, Robert wondered what kind of ceremony these particular men were going to perform.

According to plan, his guards exited the armored car first. Then, also according to plan, Robert sprinted to a half-opened door held by one of the United States Marshals.

Immediately, a fusillade of automatic arms fire followed close behind him. Intended to kill him, he realized, and fired by footsoldiers of the Cartel—the same group that had tried earlier to kill Chipmunk, and then Robert.

"Oh, I see," he thought to himself. "So that's what those men in the camouflage uniforms were up to. No wonder I didn't recognize the insignia."

But he thought it quickly, while he ran through the metal detector inside the lobby and hit the floor behind it. On second thought, he said to himself, I'd better get up the elevator. He rushed toward the one that was open, and unfortunately, the open elevator was all the way at the end of the hall. "Is anything ever easy?" he said, half out loud.

At the same time, the Marshals drew their weapons. One man pulled an Uzi from his jacket, and another one extracted a weapon that Robert did not know. Civilians on the sidewalk outside were scattering, and ducking, and hitting the ground—or rather the concrete. Quickly, the armored car guards were behind their vehicle, covered by it; but they possessed only handguns.

It happened so quickly that no one was able to describe all of it, later, and investigators from the FBI reported a vast confusion of different stories. But what was certain was that one of the attackers, who was seen from inside though the fortified, more-than-bulletproof glass as he ran forward, made the mistake of opening the courthouse door and spraying a clip of bullets across it. The Marshals responded as soon as the man touched his trigger. A wall of automatic fire, in a concentrated burst, hit the open door from the Marshals' station. The man dressed in camouflage fell in a heap.

The other two fake soldiers ran.

Robert shook his head as the elevator crawled upward and took him toward the eighth floor. During his ride up, somewhere in the building, officers looking at surveillance monitors locked down the entire building. As he emerged, Robert realized that he was the last one to ride an elevator, because people trying to access the other elevators were vainly pushing buttons, over and over, frustrated by their lack of knowledge about what was happening.

As he entered the courtroom, Robert greeted the judge. "Good morning, your honor."

"Good morning, Mr. Herrick." There was Jimmy Coleman, next to his entourage, who nodded in his direction. None of them knew what had happened, but everyone knew that something had happened. Robert told them about it, quickly, in a short version. "And the building is locked down, I believe," he said as an afterthought.

"Not an ideal situation if you are a juror," said Judge Raines. "This courtroom is unlocked, because it's supposed to be open. But the jury room is like any other space in this courthouse, except that it is more securely locked. It cannot be opened from inside. The jurors have to sound the buzzer to get out. But I think it's locked, now, by an automatic lock that none of us have access to."

The bailiff shouted to the jurors from outside the deliberation room, keeping a loud voice because of the soundproofing that surrounded the jurors' enclave. The soundproofing was there for a good reason, of course, but on an occasion like this, it was inconvenient. The lawyers and judge all heard the bailiff's loud voice, which was a source of some strange amusement to them, because during a lockdown, unfunny events can seem funnier than they are. "There's . . . some . . . sort . . . of emergency," the bailiff yelled, "and . . . you'll . . . have . . . to stay . . . in . . . there."

It took three hours for the United States Marshal Service to inspect every room in the building and pronounce it clear. The jurors finally emerged, looking shell-shocked and stir-crazy. The judge gave everyone an hour. "Then, we're going to resume this trial."

An hour later, though, the judge relented. "Everyone's shaken up. I can see that. Let's take the day off and start again in the morning."

* * *

Meanwhile, El Jefe escaped from jail, and his escape was an elaborately planned event.

His lawyer brought him an emetic containing ipecac and sodium carbonate, which made him both vomit and foam at the mouth. "Quickly," the lawyer shouted. "I think someone has poisoned him."

The guards were on the telephone, immediately. They had no time to think. "The ambulance is on its way, Señor Gonzales-Huerta. Hang in there. Hang in there!"

The dispatcher at the ambulance service had been bribed to select a particular ambulance, with a particular driver. The driver had also been bribed. Both were expecting the call. The driver gunned his engine, just as he would have in a real ambulance ride, and the paramedics in the back stayed in touch with the hospital. They talked to a physician who was the hospital's chief resident, and they learned about El Jefe's supposed "symptoms."

The ambulance made its way through the walls and into the courtyard. A pair of guards carried El Jefe with a canvas stretcher. The ambulance attendants jacked up their mechanical stretcher, and together with the guards, they counted, "one . . . two . . . three!" as they edged the sickened man onto the pad. They wheeled him to the rear of the waiting ambulance, held the stretcher up, jacked down the undercarriage, and pushed El Jefe in.

With the patient inside, the driver threaded his way out through the gate and onto the streets. The stricken Cartel leader lay still and pretended to have trouble breathing.

Unbeknownst to the attendants inside, however, the driver did not take El Jefe to the hospital. Instead, he wound his way through a predetermined route of city streets, with lights flashing and siren blasting.

Finally, at an empty parking lot in front of a closed flea market, he stopped.

Silently, twelve men stood there in the parking lot, in a loose crowd. They opened the ambulance doors. The paramedics looked surprised, which was not surprising. They had been attending El Jefe, who, also surprisingly, had entirely normal vital signs. And now, El Jefe sat up and looked at the open back door of the ambulance. The members of the Balamarcas Cartel quickly boosted him down. They told the paramedics to run. The paramedics ran very fast.

"I thought you gentlemen were never going to get me out," said El Jefe. His men greeted him warmly.

They did not mistreat the ambulance driver or make him run. That wouldn't do, because the driver had performed his part correctly. There would be future occasions for bribing other people, and the Cartel would want them to be willing to follow through.

* * *

When Tuesday morning came, Robert hustled out of his armored car with unaccustomed speed. But he got inside without incident and reached the eighth floor.

Today was the day for the last of his witnesses. A police officer who had made the scene of the killings and who had taken the video that showed the bodies. The monitors, once again, were set up in the usual places in the courtroom. The officer walked to the witness stand, raised his hand to swear to tell the whole truth, and gave his name to the jury.

"You are the officer who made the videotape of the crime scene at the Castillo home?"

"Yes, sir. Unfortunately. It was the worst scene I've ever witnessed."

"And to your understanding, is the videotape the jury is about to see a correct representation of the scene?"

"Yes, sir. I just turned the camera on and recorded what I saw. As I understand it, this is that tape, uncut and uncensored."

"Your honor, we are ready to show the jury Exhibit Number 131, which is the videotape of the Castillo home after the murders in this case. And we now offer Exhibit 131 into evidence."

"Mr. Coleman, any objection?"

Jimmy winked at Jennifer Lowenstein, sitting next to him. This was the video, they both remembered, that had had the paradoxical effect of making viewers in the focus group *less* likely to believe that the Bank had participated in the murders. Not more likely, but *less* likely. Probably, the images on the screen were so ghastly that it seemed unlikely that a bank would do something of this kind. Jimmy hoped the jurors would have the same hidden bias, although they wouldn't do a psychological analysis of their own unconscious reasons or even recognize the irony in their reactions.

He smiled. "No objection, your honor."

With surprise, Robert pushed the button on the remote.

The videotape began, as it had on television, with a view of the front door of the building. It moved forward, into the hallway, and turned to the left, where it showed Rafael Castillo, lifeless and bloody. Robert let the tape proceed, without commentary, except that he asked the witness to identify each of the dead. The jurors were visibly disturbed by what they saw. When the tape reached the body of little Jonathan Castillo, two years old and bloody and lifeless, most of the jurors had watery eyes or outright tears.

Finally, the video came to an end. And there was a pause while everyone in the courtroom took a moment to recover.

Robert's voice was quiet when he announced, "Your honor, the plaintiffs rest."

39

A DIRTY TRICK

Jimmy Coleman made a big show of offering into evidence the cooperation agreement between Francel and Robert. At the same time, he angrily shouted, "Francel Williams can't be believed about anything, because he's bought and paid for, and he's agreed to help the plaintiffs instead of his own clients, the other defendants." He glared at the plaintiffs' lawyers.

And then, he surprised everyone.

He called the Bank President to the witness stand. "The defense calls Mr. Chola Velnikov to the witness stand," he announced with great fanfare. "The Founder and President of the Velnikov Bank."

The man in the purple pinstriped suit, with his purple shirt and orange shoes shining in the courtroom lights, made his way to the witness stand in a slow, majestic meander. He sat down and favored the jurors with a gleaming smile that was full of cold, white veneers.

His time on the witness stand, however, was brief. It lasted but a moment.

With the Bank President comfortably seated, Jimmy pretended to think. To consider. To weigh his options. His forehead had frown lines, and he rubbed his hands over his eyes.

But his show of thinking was only a show, because he had already planned what he intended to ask this witness. Which was . . . nothing.

"On second thought," Jimmy said slowly. "On . . . second thought. . . ."

He stopped and froze. He stared at Chola Velnikov.

By now, everyone in the courtroom was staring back at Jimmy. The judge looked disgusted. The jurors looked puzzled, and also, intrigued.

"On second thought. . . ." And again, Jimmy paused, deep in thought.

"On second thought, Mr. Velnikov, come back here. Step down from that witness stand. We don't need to offer your testimony."

The jurors stared as Jimmy paused yet again—and then went on. "Come back down here, Mr. Velnikov. We don't need to offer any testimony. The plaintiffs haven't offered any testimony that matters. We don't need to put on a defense."

Jimmy made a big show of shaking his head.

"Come down from the witness stand, Mr. Velnikov. The plaintiffs haven't proved their case against the Bank at all."

The Bank President looked toward the jury and offered another gleaming smile. Slowly, deliberately, with every eye in the courtroom now focused on him, Chola Velnikov obeyed his lawyer. He stood. Slowly, deliberately, he stepped down from the witness stand. And with his purple shirt and orange shoes again shining strangely in the courtroom lights, he walked to the back of the courtroom and out into the hall.

Jimmy paused for a moment. For dramatic effect.

And then he said, "Your honor, the defense rests."

"You are resting your case without calling any witnesses?" The judge's voice was incredulous.

The jury stared, as one, at Jimmy.

The judge's question invited Jimmy to say it again: "The plaintiffs haven't proved anything. Not anything at all. That's why the defense rests."

It took a moment, now, for the judge to react. The courtroom was silent. Finally, the judge looked up. With his anger just under the surface, Judge Raines spoke calmly, but it was obvious that he was forcing himself to speak calmly.

"Mr. Bailiff, please take the jury out."

* * *

By now, the judge was visibly angry.

"Mr. Coleman, you may have fooled the jury. But you've fooled no one else with that cheap dirty trick."

Jimmy was the picture of hurt innocence. "Your honor, nothing . . . I . . . did . . . was a . . . cheap . . . trick."

"Mr. Coleman, It is obvious that when you called Mr. Velnikov to the witness stand, you had no intention to offer any testimony from him. You just planned to make a show that is outside the evidence. And it meant that you were able to make an extra final argument during the evidence presentation, which was completely improper."

"Your honor, I called Mr. Velnikov with the intention of asking him questions. I did not know that I was going to decide that it was best to call him back, until . . . the moment I did it."

Jimmy looked friendly and angelic, or at least as angelic as his naturally reptilian appearance would allow. "Your honor, I looked over at Mr. Herrick and saw that he was ready to cross-examine Mr. Velnikov in a brutal manner. I could tell it. I could sense that Mr. Herrick was going to give no quarter when his turn came to cross-examine Mr. Velnikov. And I hadn't asked Mr. Velnikov anything at that point, and I decided not to, right then."

The judge stared at Jimmy for a moment. It was . . . possible that his explanation was true. The judge sat, stared, and thought.

A sensible judge tries to avoid getting into side controversies. To avoid hearings that are unrelated to the issues in the lawsuit before him. They waste time, compromise the judge's impartiality, and are difficult to resolve accurately. Trying to impose a penalty on Jimmy—an instruction to the jury that this conduct was illegal and improper and should be considered as evidence of the Bank's guilt, or even a monetary fine extracted from Jimmy personally—would require a complicated set of separate hearings. And delay the trial.

Finally, Judge Raines thought of an alternative that might be acceptable.

"I am considering instructing the jury to disregard this episode," he said slowly. "Mr. Herrick, do you request this kind of instruction?"

"Reluctantly, your honor, the plaintiffs would request that there be no instruction to disregard." Robert, by now, was shaking his head. "It would only call attention to Mr. Coleman's behavior, and the behavior of Mr. Velnikov, and it might highlight the whole thing in the jurors' minds."

"That's true." The judge did not know what to do, and he was casting about. "Well, maybe the appearance of Mr. Velnikov on the witness stand enables you, Mr. Herrick, to cross-examine Mr. Velnikov. He's claimed the Fifth Amendment, but maybe this shenanigan means he's given up the Fifth Amendment. He's waived the right to remain silent. . . . Maybe."

"Again, reluctantly, your honor, I would not want that opportunity. In the first place, Mr. Velnikov didn't break his silence. Mr. Coleman engineered this ploy, probably on purpose, so that Mr. Velnikov never actually said anything. And it's risky to do that. Although your honor may be right, and it may be that he's given up the right to claim the Fifth Amendment, still . . . a court of appeals might disagree. I've tried a clean case in this trial, and I'd rather not build in any events that Mr. Coleman can claim as errors on appeal, so as to ask an appeals court to reverse. And besides, we've never had the opportunity to take Mr. Velnikov's deposition. I have no idea what he might say. In fact, I was about to object on the ground that Mr. Velnikov was an improper witness who could not permissibly testify."

"You're . . . right about all of that, . . . of course." The judge was more puzzled than angry, by now.

He finally decided what to do. "We will have what we call the 'charge conference' this afternoon. I will hear proposals and arguments about what I should tell the jury: how to instruct them in the court's charge. And tomorrow, we will have final arguments."

Judge Raines dismissed the lawyers and stepped down from the bench.

As they left the courtroom, Tom Kennedy got over his shock for long enough to sound philosophical. "Sometimes there's nothing you can do when someone else does something that's dead wrong. Even someone who's as dead wrong as Jimmy Coleman, and even when everyone sees he's wrong. It's like what that poet said: . . . *'This is the way the world ends. . . . Not with a bang, but a whimper.' . . .*"

Tom's face contorted. "And just now, all the judge could do was whimper."

* * *

El Jefe sat comfortably in his elegant drawing room. He wore his customary camouflage clothes and his Gucci shoes, and behind him, his collection of rare pistols sat on their ornate shelves. The hillside below him was burned and blackened from the Mexican army's assault, but the house was intact. It was good to have escaped.

But he knew he would need to move away from here. The army would know where to find him. He would have to leave soon. But for now, it was comforting to be out of jail and in familiar surroundings.

And he was wondering where he should go next. Where he wanted to go next.

"If you want the job done right," El Jefe said to his second in command, "you may have to do it yourself. Nobody's killed those maggots in the United States that I ordered killed. . . . I think I'll do it myself. I think I'll go to the United States."

"But *Jefe!* You want to go to the United States, yourself? Just to remove someone? To remove this investigator? Or to kill that lawyer? *Yourself?*"

"I've got to leave here. They will be looking for me. And no one would expect me to go to the United States."

"But my *Jefe,* it is . . . too risky."

"Texas is nice this time of year."

"But . . . *Jefe!*"

"I'm just kidding. Just kidding!" El Jefe laughed. "It's just a joke. Keep up your sense of humor, my Lieutenant." And El Jefe threw his head back and laughed harder. "No, I'm not silly enough to go visit the United States. They may call me El Más Loco, and it may be true, but I'm only crazy, not stupid."

"Oh. You had me falling for the joke."

El Jefe was happy to be back here at Colina del Pescador. At his home; on his mountain. He was feeling playful. He laughed some more. "Keep your sense of humor, my man."

But then he grew a serious look. "Still, I know that I've got to leave here. I may have to move around. And keep moving for a while, in fact."

"Yes, *Jefe.*"

"Everybody's got to be somewhere. And I've got to be somewhere other than here. Yes, I'm going away. I just need to decide where." And El Jefe smiled, because traveling was not going to be boring, and it was a new adventure.

40

FINAL ARGUMENTS

Everyone in Judge Raines's courtroom stood as the jurors marched in. The judge paused. And then he said, slowly, "Mr. Herrick, your opening argument for the plaintiffs?"

And Robert responded, "Ready, your honor."

He faced the eight men and women who would decide his case. He was wearing his friendliest suit of clothes—light blue, with a red-and-blue striped tie—as he smiled and said, "Good morning, ladies and gentlemen of the jury!"

"Good morning!" came the response. Good.

"On behalf of Patrick and Anna, I want to thank you for your jury service here. I'm sure it's taken away from important activities you otherwise would have planned. I have seen how carefully you've listened. You are performing a part of democracy that only free people can perform."

It was standard verbiage for a beginning argument: thanking the jurors. In another setting, it might have sounded insincere. But in the solemn atmosphere of a courtroom, it rang true with the jurors, as Robert had known it would. A couple of them nodded with appreciation.

"Ladies and Gentlemen, Judge Raines has given you a set of instructions. And questions. He read them to you earlier, a while ago, and you will have a written copy when you retire to deliberate. These instructions are the law, and we all have to follow them, including you and me."

He paused. Then: "The questions that you have to answer, basically, fall into four groups. First, you have to say whether The Velnikov Bank acted intentionally to cause these eight murders. The answer should be yes. Then, second, you will be asked to answer, separately, whether the Bank was also negligent, in causing these deaths. Remember, 'negligence' is just a big word for carelessness, and the answer again should be yes, because of course, the Bank was much more than careless, since it caused these deaths intentionally.

"Third, the judge asks you what percentage of the total negligence this Bank is responsible for, out of the negligence of all of the defendants. The answer is that the Bank is the biggest of the careless defendants. It even paid the blood money to hire the killers, right here in this city. The fourth question is, what is the amount of the damages suffered by the plaintiffs, Patrick and Anna? And the judge tells you that the law requires you to measure the damages in money.

"At one level, the answer is that no one could ever have enough dollars to compensate another person for this kind of loss. But damages measured in money is all that the law can do, and the judge tells you to measure the damages this way. It's the law. The minimum amount that you should answer with, is a hundred million dollars, as we've been telling you throughout this trial. And you should award twice that amount, or two hundred million dollars, against the Velnikov Bank as punitive damages"—and here Robert's face contorted, and his voice rose—"so that no Bank like this one ever launders money and kills people, ever again."

People often think that jury argument by lawyers should be eloquent, complicated, and full of fancy words. The opposite is true: the argument should use simple words. Robert had prepared this argument to be easily understood.

"Now," he said, "ladies and gentlemen of the jury, let me cover each of those four groups of answers in a little more detail. Let me put the flesh on the bones of this outline."

By now, he hoped he had reached the jurors who were the most straightforward thinkers: the ones who might not want to follow the finer points. And next, for those who wrestled with details, he went over the law in the judge's charge. Explaining the legal definition of the word "intent," which is a seemingly simple, but actually complex, concept. Explaining the words in the judge's charge about negligence. Explaining every part of the measure of damages: lost earnings, medical and funeral expenses, and most of all, pain and suffering. And he showed the jury how the evidence supported the answers he had told the jurors about.

The end of his argument was simple. "Ladies and gentlemen, Patrick and Anna's plea to you is a plea for simple justice. They ask you not to turn away their plea. I know that you will find their cause to be right."

With that, Robert nodded and smiled at the jurors. And then sat down. He was satisfied with how it had sounded.

"Thank you, Mr. Herrick," said Judge Raines. "Let's take a recess so that the court reporter can get organized again." And everyone stood as the jury, and then the judge, exited the courtroom.

Robert found Tom in a conference room, explaining strategy to their clients. "Robert's finish, which you just heard, followed the conventional advice to a plaintiff's lawyer. As the plaintiff, you get two final arguments. You open the arguments. And you deliver a second argument, your final argument, after the defense argument."

"The defense lawyer is sandwiched in between," Robert continued. "He gets one argument, after the plaintiff opens, and before the plaintiff delivers the rebuttal argument—our closing. And so, the plaintiff shouldn't shoot off all of his emotional guns in the opening. That would allow the defendant to answer them all."

Tom took in from there. "Instead, the plaintiff ends the opening argument with a few short, unemotional phrases, asking for a just result. That's what Robert did. And the plaintiff reserves the emotional argument, our argument based on society's values, for the closing argument. That's when we will deliver our most vigorous denunciation of the defendant. That is the last word, insulated from attacks by the defense lawyer, and it becomes the argument that stays with the jurors as they go into the jury deliberation room."

Or at least, Robert thought, that's what we hope will happen. But Jimmy Coleman would have his turn after the recess. In just a few minutes.

* * *

Jimmy started by thanking the jurors, just as Robert had done. But he was more enthusiastic and friendly. "He's acting like an overgrown Teddy Bear," Tom whispered. "All smiley-faced and nice. It's an act, of course, but the jurors seem to like it."

But the niceness disappeared when Jimmy disagreed with every point Robert had made. "These murders were not an intentional act by the Bank! And the Bank wasn't negligent. And the only people who have any percentage of fault in this case are the man known as El Jefe, the Balamarcas Cartel, and the three killers who went to the Castillo home!"

He sounded like tractor wheels on gravel when he shouted, "And then: Mr. Herrick claims a hundred million dollars? Imagine that Patrick Castillo invested that amount in municipal bonds. It would earn many millions a year, tax free. The plaintiffs are trying to get rich off this tragedy."

Jimmy snorted. "The proper answer is, 'zero.' The amount of damages that the Bank owes is *zero!*"

But Jimmy's voice reached its scratchy loudest when he grabbed the cooperation agreement that Robert and Francel had signed. And he waved it around in the jurors' faces. "You can't trust a single thing these people have told you! Francel Williams is bought and paid for by this cooperation agreement. And Robert Herrick had to resort to an agreement with . . . admitted *murderers*, in order to make his case!"

Jimmy threw the cooperation agreement down on the table. "This agreement deserves to be thrown out. And the entire case deserves to be thrown out!"

It was an over-the-top argument. It was too sensational. But it also was one of the most effective moments in the entire trial, Robert realized. The jurors were staring, mesmerized by Jimmy's argument. Robert thought to himself: . . . Jimmy has just won the case.

As Jimmy sat down, Robert stood up to address the jury for the last time. His heart was in his throat.

* * *

"Ladies and gentlemen of the jury," Robert said slowly, "Jimmy Coleman has just ignored the evidence. And the law. He might as well have been in show business. There wasn't much substance to what he said."

He pointed at the Bank's vice presidents, who were sitting next to Jimmy. "Let's remember the testimony. El Jefe talked to the Bank about killing Castillo. To the Bank President. El Jefe's second-in-command told you that. Two of the killers, the ones who went to the Bank, told you how they got paid by the Bank. Of course the Bank did it intentionally.

"And in addition, the Bank was negligent. Remember: negligence just means carelessness. The Bank laundered money, millions of dollars, for the Cartel. And it paid the killers. It paid them, right after its President talked to the Bank President about killing Castillo.

"And remember: the accountant, Mr. Blankford, testified that the bank was the biggest defendant at fault in this case. It hid in the shadows. It did what it did right here, in this very city. It was essential to the Cartel's business. And Professor Cuevas, the expert on drug gangs, said the same thing. You should answer that the Bank was responsible for ninety per-cent—*ninety percent*—of the negligence in this case.

"Next, I heard Mr. Coleman making fun of the damages. He says that that Patrick and Anna have zero as damages. He must not have seen the same pictures, and the same video, that I did. Ladies and gentlemen, a hundred million dollars is a minimal figure for the terrorism sent to the Castillo home by this Bank. And there should be two hundred million as punitive damages, too."

He paused and looked at the jurors. They, of course, were staring back at him. "How do we measure damages in a case like this, with human loss and suffering so horrific? You might say, there's no amount that would do it. But that's a cop-out, because the law says that damages in dollars are how it must be measured. So, here's a way to think about it that might help. Imagine: what if there were a pill, a magical kind of medicine, that all eight people could take to avoid their pain and suffering as they died? To resume their lives, and become producing, lively people again? If little Jonathan Castillo could reach his full age and realize his potential? And if Patrick and Anna could reverse their loss? What if there were a pill like that?

"And here's the real question. If money were no object, what amount do you suppose that Rafael Castillo would pay for that pill? What would Patrick and Anna pay to buy a pill like that? And to put everything back, the way it was?"

He paused again. He showed the pictures of the dead, eight in a row, on easels, and then, one by one, he replaced each picture with a photograph of that person in death. An image of each murder victim, taken from frames of the video. He announced the name of each one. It was a standard plaintiff's argument that some lawyers call "The Roll Call of the Dead," but familiar or not, it was particularly fitting in this case.

There were tears in some of the jurors' eyes, after the last pictures, from seeing the images of Jonathan Castillo. Now Robert's voice was forceful and loud. "A hundred million dollars is a low figure! And so is two hundred in punitive damages. How much should a person, who has enough money, pay for the pill that makes the damages go away? Mr. Coleman is wrong!"

The moment had come. The moment when he could say it; the moment when he could ask the jurors for justice.

"I need your help. To right this wrong, I need your help." If a lawyer asks the jury for this kind of "help" too early, he is in danger of losing everything. Suddenly Robert's voice had become much quieter, little more than a whisper, but it was heard clearly throughout the courtroom. "I need your help, members of the jury, to make sure that the Bank doesn't get away with it. And I need your help to make sure that another Bank doesn't get tempted to do what this one did.

"In a moment, I will sit down. It will be up to you. Say to yourself, each of you: 'I have a chance. Me. Juror. I have a chance!' It all depends on you. As the lawyer for Patrick and Anna, I can do my job, but it doesn't mean anything without you. You. The Juror. The witnesses can risk everything to tell you the facts, and the judge can do his job. It doesn't mean anything without you."

Now, he lifted his voice a little. "You have a chance to do justice. Say to yourself, 'I have a chance. Me. Juror.' You are the last link in our system of justice. I ask you, I implore you . . . I *BEG* you . . . for a just verdict. One that holds the Bank responsible."

And he sat down, heavily.

* * *

Even the judge was shell-shocked. It took a moment before he said, "Ladies and gentlemen, you will now retire to deliberate upon your verdict."

"Good job, Robert." Tom winked at him.

Robert stared at the departing jurors. They didn't look at Patrick and Anna. They passed by Jimmy and his entourage, and they looked, instead, at the Bank's vice presidents. That was a bad sign. "I'm afraid," he whispered. ". . . I'm afraid . . . that from what I see . . . that the job I did . . . just wasn't enough."

41
THE VERDICT

Here is no sound that is more raw and exciting—or more scary—
than the buzzer that sounds from inside a jury deliberation room
to signal that there is a verdict.

In the case of *Castillo v. The Velnikov Bank*, it took three days for the
buzzer to sound. Three agonizing days for the lawyers who were sweating
out the jury. As the eight men and women filed into the jury box, Robert
and Tom both knew that this length of time was a bad sign for them. If the
jurors were going to return a verdict for the plaintiff, the buzzer would
have sounded quickly.

In what seemed like slow motion, the bailiff took the verdict sheets
from the juror who held them: the juror once known as "the foreman," but
now, in a less sexist world, called the "presiding juror." And the bailiff
handed them, slowly, to the judge. In what seemed like even slower motion, the judge studied the verdict, in dead silence. And studied it some
more. With this number of separate questions, understanding the jury's
answers took time. It seemed to Robert that the judge was even studying
the edges of the paper that held the precious words; he was moving that
slowly.

Finally, the judge spoke.

"Question 1 asks the jury, *'Do you find that The Velnikov Bank acted
intentionally to cause the death of the Castillo family?'*

"To which, the jury answered. . . ." The judge paused. Robert held his
breath.

"To which the jury answered . . . *'No.'* "

It was the end of the line, Robert thought. How could the jury have
said No? How could these eight people, who did not seem exceptionally

foolish or naïve, make such a mistake? Of course the Bank had acted intentionally. But the jury had said . . . that it hadn't. "No."

Across the courtroom, Jimmy Coleman pumped his fist in the air. And grinned. To Robert, it was obscene to see Jimmy celebrating this way.

But the judge was only beginning to read the verdict.

"Question 2 asks the jury, *'Do you find that the negligence of any of the following, if any, proximately caused the deaths of the Castillo family?'*"

Again, the judge paused. Maddeningly, for Robert.

"To which, the jury answered by naming each of the defendants as negligently causing the deaths. The Velnikov Bank was negligent and caused it. So did Alejandro Carlos Gonzales-Huerta, known as El Jefe; and the Balamarcas Cartel; and each of the three other defendants—the ones who entered the Castillo home."

Robert dared to hope. The jury had not found intent to kill on the bank's part. But the Bank was negligent? And so were all of the other defendants? How could the jurors have arrived at this conclusion? How could they . . . with so much evidence saying, proving, shouting, that . . . the Bank had acted intentionally?

But . . . he thought . . . juries do the unexplainable.

The judge read on. "Question 3 asks the jury to assign percentages of fault to each of the defendants. And the jury answered. . . ."

The judge paused again. Robert's hands were both balled into fists, and his stomach was trying to jump out of his skin.

"*The Velnikov Bank,*" the judge read slowly, ". . . *Fifty percent.* The rest of the defendants, all together . . . *fifty percent.*"

Patrick Castillo and Tom Kennedy both whispered the question at once: "What on earth does *that* mean?" Robert's mind was empty. The jury had found the Bank fifty percent negligent. What *did* it mean? What?

But the judge was still reading. "Question 4 asks, *'What sum of money, if paid now in cash, would compensate the plaintiffs for their damages?'*"

And the judge stopped there, before reading on. ". . . To which the jury answered, *'One hundred million dollars.'*"

By now, Jimmy Coleman was much less cheerful. Robert wanted to shout out the number. But he was content to whisper, almost silently, "*One . . . hundred . . . million . . . dollars!*"

The judge read on, still. "The punitive damages question . . . the question asking the jurors what amount of punitive damages, if any, the jury would award, is next.

"To which the jury answered, *'Two hundred million dollars.'*"

By now, Robert was trying to figure out what it all meant. He and Tom had studied it all carefully, beforehand—all of the possibilities. But in the snapping, violent state of their minds at the moment, all of their memory of that study was blank.

Judge Raines, like everyone else, was exhausted. He sat back in his big chair. And he said, ". . . Wow."

* * *

Figuring out percentages of damages owed, based on percentages of negligence found by a jury, is known to attorneys as "comparative fault." It is one of the most complicated and paradoxical areas of the law. And now, sitting in a conference room with their clients, Robert and Tom were still slow-witted about the meaning of the verdict. About the comparative fault questions.

"So," said Patrick. "What does it all mean?"

"I think . . . it means that we won," said Robert. "I . . . think."

"I always thought that a verdict meant that the jury decided who won. How can it be so confusing?"

"No. That's not the way it's done. Instead, the jury answers questions. And sometimes, nobody knows exactly what it means. Including the jurors."

Tom finally spoke. He was holding a memorandum from an associate of the firm, a long memorandum, that explained various possibilities about the verdict. Robert remembered asking for this research. What if the Bank were found to have acted intentionally? That would produce one kind of judgment. What if the Bank was negligent, but the jury said that only half or less of the fault was the Bank's? That would produce a different result. And so forth.

"I think," said Tom slowly, ". . . it means that we get a judgment for half the damages found by the jury. In other words, . . . fifty million dollars."

"Fifty million?" Patrick asked.

"It's what I think happens. We'll have to . . . look at it . . . in a less hurried moment, back at the office. But I think . . . fifty million dollars. We've won fifty million . . . dollars."

"Then," said Tom, "there's the punitive damage amount. But that's even more complicated. But anyway . . . at least fifty million. I think."

Patrick's face screwed up, in pain for a moment. Thinking about his family, Robert realized. From his nephew, little Jonathan Castillo, to his parents. But then, he relaxed. And spoke slowly.

"I think . . . I think, that . . . fifty million dollars . . . that's a victory."

* * *

Hundreds of miles to the south, the pilot was landing El Jefe's Learjet 45 XR at the Manuel Cresencio Rejon International Airport in Mérida, Mexico. In the center of the Yucatán Peninsula.

"You have a limousine ready to pick us up, don't you?" he asked his Lieutenant.

"Nothing but the finest," said the Lieutenant. "I know you, *Jefe*."

Their legs were stiff from the flight. Three hours, all the way from El Jefe's airstrip near Colina del Pescador. A driver from the Alfaro Limousine Company was there to greet them.

"A Cadillac limousine, señor," said the driver. "I know you wanted either the Mercedes or the Cadillac, and this one actually is the nicer of the two. Welcome to Yucatán!"

"Yucatán is a good place to start again," El Jefe said to his Lieutenant. "Reluctantly, I will sell the property at Colina del Pescador. And how we will handle the money, that will be a challenge, because I no longer wish to use Velnikov's Bank. Yucatan is a good place for us to re-establish our operations because it is one of the few places in Mexico where there is no other strong cartel. We can relocate here."

"And it has excellent transshipment points, whether by land, or sea, or air," agreed the Lieutenant. "It is at the southern end of our country, next to Guatemala and Belize. Quiet and easy to get around."

They did not know that the controllers in the tower had suspected their identity from remarks about the flight while they were in the air. And from their takeoff point. And the controllers had notified the local *policía*. Who did not have confidence about who or what they might be up against if they tried to arrest El Jefe. And so *la policía*, in turn, had called the army.

From the highest commanders down to the lowest enlisted soldier, the entire army knew about El Jefe. A company of the Mexican army was on the way, traveling at double time.

But this was not all of the bad news that was coming to El Jefe and his *Lugarteniente*. They were outside the airport perimeter by now and heading toward *la playa*, the beach, where El Jefe planned to wait for a few months in welcome anonymity, when suddenly, from nowhere, an enormous force collided with their limousine, on the side where El Jefe was sitting.

A teenager in a stolen Corvette, pilfered from the same area near *la playa* where they were headed, had just T-boned El Jefe's ride, while running a stop light. It was just a random collision with a teenage thief, joyriding in that low-slung car and traveling way too fast.

The teenager apparently wasn't hurt. He disappeared faster than anyone else could get out of the limousine. The only way that they knew he was a teenager was from a glimpse of his disappearing backside, together with the fact that he must have been a teenager to have stolen this car and driven it this way.

When the ambulance came, the paramedics couldn't extricate El Jefe, at first. They had to open the limousine through the opposite door, and they found the injured man wound up in the upholstery in an odd pattern. Finally, they just ripped him free, because he was bleeding too fast to stay alive if they didn't get him inside the ambulance quickly.

And with a wailing siren, El Jefe began his trip to the Hospital named after General Augustín O'Horan, in the center of Mérida.

42
THE BANK'S OFFER

We know to expect that Jimmy will file a Motion to Disregard the Verdict," said Tom Kennedy. "With all kinds of claims about the worthlessness of the witnesses."

"Maybe not," Robert answered. "The *Wall Street Journal* says that the Bank is having severe solvency problems. There's concern about a run on the Bank, which might be caused by our verdict. The verdict we won seems to threaten the solvency of the Bank. Depositors are scared that the Bank is going to go belly up, and creditors are demanding to be paid without extending anything. That usually puts pressure on a defendant to come to the table and settle, quickly."

"Well, that would be good news. I guess we can hope for that."

The afternoon was cloudy, with a gray canopy where the sky should have been. Hundreds of tiny cars, forty stories down, crept along the freeways, and the vivid green that bordered Buffalo Bayou stretched westward until it disappeared into the mist.

Suddenly, Donna DeCarlo's voice came through the intercom. "Robert, your favorite opponent is calling you. It's Jimmy Coleman."

"Speak of the devil," said Tom.

"Well, yes, literally." Robert pushed the button. "Hello, Jimmy. What can we do for you?"

The scratchy voice sounded unusually friendly. Even conciliatory. "Robert, the Bank is willing to talk to you about settling this case. And getting rid of it. We'd give up the possibility of appeal and give up filing any motions to attack the verdict."

Robert was wary, but he tried to sound friendly too. "Well, it's always my habit to try to settle every case, if it can be done. Even after the verdict. But it depends on what you've got in mind, Jimmy."

"My client is willing to pay half of the judgment that would be entered against it for actual damages. Half of fifty million. Without the punitive damages, of course. It would come to twenty-five million."

"Ahhh . . . well . . . I'll convey your offer to my clients. But I don't know that I'd recommend it to them. They won a hard-fought verdict. And Jimmy, you know that it's a whole different proposition, trying to settle a case after the verdict has come in."

"Of course." Jimmy's grating voice was agreeable. "That's why I'm negotiating! But we've got a lot of grounds for appeal. And that's only the beginning of the reasons you should accept my offer. I'll spell them out."

"I'm listening. I'm all ears, as the saying goes."

"Several things. First, you may not be aware of this, but that crazy turncoat witness, that José Luis Leyva, has retracted his story. I'm informed of this by reliable sources within the Government. That means the Bank has a pretty good claim for a new trial based on newly discovered evidence."

"Newly discovered evidence is a hard argument to win. And besides, the judge knows that that witness went back and forth."

"Here's an even better argument. The Bank can't pay the judgment that is likely to be entered on your verdict. That verdict is going to mean that the Bank won't be able to pay its debts."

"I've heard rumors to that effect. Tell me what you know about it."

"The Bank is facing demands from every supplier to be paid in cash. Creditors all know about this verdict, and they think the Bank won't be able to pay them back. And the Bank is frozen out of the interbank lending market, which is any bank's life blood. Robert, if you insist on trying to get the judge to enter a judgment, and if we appeal that judgment, the Bank is going to become insolvent. And you'll get nothing."

At that, Robert was silent.

"The Feds will come in and take the Bank over. The FDIC—the Federal Deposit Insurance Company—will swoop down out of the sky. And you know what happens then. The Feds will be interested in doing everything possible to protect the Bank's depositors. To protect those little people who have accounts with the Bank, holding their life savings. The depositors will come first, before any other kind of debt. The depositors will have priority in getting paid, over any plaintiffs that have big claims for punitive damages. The punitive damages don't cover any kind of loss, and they'll be the first thing that's thrown out. The next thing that will be thrown out is your fifty million in actual damages, because the Feds will be fighting to protect the depositors."

Again, Robert was silent.

"It's going to be public soon, and we'll be past the point where anything can be done to prevent a collapse, unless you and I can come to an agreement." Jimmy's voice rose a little, and it rasped like sandpaper. "I'm trying to save the Bank from complete destruction, and that's all I'm trying to do. I'm trying to save the Bank, even more than I'm trying to reduce your damages."

"Well, Jimmy . . . we . . . we would need to inspect the books of the Bank. We'd have to verify what you're saying to us." Robert's head was spinning at the news.

"We'll show them to you. We'll show you whatever you wanted to see. But remember, it's a situation that changes day by day. We're facing an oncoming collision between efforts to keep the Bank afloat and demands from the creditors it depends on. If you want to look at books, it had better be today. The situation will be worse tomorrow."

And Robert knew that it was true. "Yes, that's the way Banks die."

"All right," he said finally. "I'll talk to my clients."

* * *

El Jefe's lawyer finally arrived from the airstrip near Colina del Pescador, flying in on El Jefe's Learjet. "*Jefe,* my condolences on your accident."

Two well-armed men in camouflage uniforms stood inside the hospital room. "We need to confer in private," the lawyer told them. He had obtained clearance for this.

"What is this rope thing that ties your leg cast to the ceiling?" the lawyer asked.

"My right leg is shattered in what they call a multiple compound fracture. It has to be stretched."

"And what else?"

"I've lost part of my spleen. Fractured right arm. Fractured hand. Kidney damage." El Jefe did not sound as fierce or indifferent as he had sounded in times past.

The lawyer was hesitant to give El Jefe the news he had come to give. "The Government wants you in court, immediately. For extradition proceedings. I will try to delay it as long as possible. But Jefe, a judge in Mexico City has ordered you to be brought before him at the very moment when you are able to travel. The extradition warrant is already with the court, of course. The judge knows that you are injured, and he knows you have to have an elaborate apparatus around you. He doesn't understand all of the details, but he's apparently aware that there's something like this rope that ties your leg to the ceiling."

The lawyer coughed. "But your injuries won't help us to avoid the extradition proceedings. The President has ordered up means of transportation that will allow you to be transported in a similar apparatus, so that you can be moved without harm. Moved to the court, in Mexico City. . . . I . . . I am sorry, Jefe."

El Jefe was silent. He just looked away, toward the window. Which was covered with sheet metal. He was in jail, within the hospital.

"Jefe, the Government wants to hold these extradition proceedings immediately. I don't have to tell you what the outcome is going to be. There's going to be an extradition order. The judge will condition it on the United States giving up the death penalty, but that's all we can hope for. We can appeal, but the Government will expedite the appeal."

"Well, . . . let's delay it."

"Jefe, it is impossible. Your escape from the state jail, in the ambulance, was brilliantly executed. We all lifted a glass in your honor, after you pulled that off. But the Government was not amused. The Government was embarrassed. It was an international incident. The United States ambassador asked whether it was true: 'A fugitive who was subject to the most serious terrorist-related charges in the United States gets away from a Mexican jail because the Mexican authorities carry him out to his escape vehicle, which is a fake ambulance?' The Government wants to save face, now."

El Jefe was quiet. Pain medicine—from oxycontin at times to synthetic opiates of various kinds—had quieted him, and now, the situation quieted him too. He looked away, toward the window that wasn't there. Finally, he spoke, barely above a whisper.

"Lawyer, show some value. Show that there's something you can do. Something you can accomplish. Delay it. . . . Delay it as long as you can."

43
HERE WE GO AGAIN

I t was another brilliant sunny day. Robert sat at his big mahogany desk, with Tom in front of him. Fluffy clouds floated in a bright blue sky, and the huge oriental carpet below the desk reflected the sun with its many shapes and colors. Beneath the greenhouse-style windows, a mass of geraniums bloomed, as always, in shades of red, pink, and white.

"I really tried." There was resignation in Robert's voice. "I tried over and over to persuade Patrick and Anna to settle this case so that they could recover something, rather than recovering zero. Now it's too late, even if they wanted to. The opportunity is gone. The Bank is gone."

"Twenty-five million dollars." Tom sounded equally dismal. "Who would want to give that up?"

"Well, evidently, Patrick and Anna want to give it up. They wouldn't settle, even after they understood that if they didn't, the Bank wouldn't be able to pay them anything. They sat here and said, 'Well, let the Velnikov Bank go out of business.' And they said, 'That's what we want, anyway.'"

"And now, I guess they've gotten what they want."

"Yep. The Feds have descended on the Bank like an army of Saracens. And the Bank is already shut down. Completely. You know the pattern, Tom."

"Yes, of course. We both know. First, the Feds will find a bigger bank to take over the assets of this Bank. To buy them. For less than its ongoing value, or less than the value if the Bank were salvageable. Then, the bigger bank will reopen this Bank, but under a new name. And the whole thing will be organized so that the takeover protects the people with accounts at the Bank. The depositors."

"Which will mean, of course, that we won't collect any of our damages for Patrick and Anna. The judgment will be a worthless sheet of paper."

"Patrick and Anna get zero, and that, in turn, means that this law firm gets zero. There's an attorney's fee of zero, even though we tried the case and won it. Won it big, in fact."

"Well, look at the bright side." Robert was philosophical. "For once, Jimmy Coleman told us the truth. What he said would happen to the Bank has turned out to be one hundred percent accurate."

Suddenly, the intercom buzzed, and Donna DeCarlo's voice came into the room. "Robert, the red-headed Cuban is on the phone. Your beautiful wife."

"Hi, Maria." Robert's voice was morose.

She almost said it to him: Mother Serena was right. He had seemed to win. But he had lost. The psychic had known what would happen and had told her the truth.

But she could never say it to Robert. He would go ballistic, hearing that she had told him to settle on the basis of an occultist's advice.

So she said something else. "I heard what happened to your case. I'm so sorry for you. A zero result is hard to take, especially after the way you fought. Especially a zero result, after you've won."

"That's right."

"Well, here's some good news, or at least some better news. The Mexican authorities have extradited Alejandro Carlos Gonzales-Huerta. The head of the Cartel; the one known as El Jefe. He's arriving today on a C-17 Globemaster, and he's probably in the airspace of the good old USA by now."

"Yes, that's a good thing. What will happen next?"

"El Jefe now is in the custody of the Department of Justice. They have dozens of potential charges to file against him, including all of the murders in your lawsuit. El Jefe is going to die in a maximum-security prison."

"You won't get to try El Jefe on state murder charges, through the D.A.'s office?"

"The mud-wrestling begins, now. The State of Texas versus the Federal Government. We can fight the Feds over the right to try El Jefe, but the Department of Justice will probably win that battle. We can try him afterward for the murders, of course, but we probably won't, because the Feds will already have convicted him of murder. Plus a lot of other crimes."

"Well, maybe that's best."

"And here's some more news," Maria said flatly. "Two of the hands-on killers, the ones who went to the Castillo home, have pled guilty. Baldassaro, the one who drove the car, will get life in prison. The other guy, who went into the house and helped with the murders, will get life without the possibility of parole."

"Okay. . . . Good." Robert spoke tonelessly.

"And the third guy—the worst one, the ringleader—that guy's about to go to trial. The other two will testify against him."

"That one is facing the death penalty."

"Yes."

"He should be facing the death penalty. After seeing those eight bodies, killed with machetes, including the baby. . . . I'd say that that's the only just verdict."

"Yes. But . . . there's still one more loose end to tell you about. A case of injustice, and you're not going to like it, Robert, any more than I do."

"What's that?"

"As you know, the Special Crimes Bureau has been investigating the Velnikov Bank's officers. They've been heavy into investigating them—for money laundering, bank fraud, and drug trafficking. They're just about to ask the grand jury for an indictment. And the biggest target of the investigation is . . . well, I bet you can guess."

"Chola Velnikov? The purple-and-orange guy?"

"Yes. He's their next target defendant. But here's the problem. Chola Velnikov has disappeared. Vanished. The last thing heard about his travels was that he boarded a flight to Moscow a couple of days ago."

"To . . . Russia?" Robert was dumfounded.

"Chola Velnikov speaks Russian. We think he might have dual citizenship: both American and Russian. It's vague, and the Russians won't tell us. But he's probably there in Russia. Somewhere."

"Great. We try a big case, and we win it, but then, our clients decide on a course of action so that they get zero. And the attorney's fees are zero too. And now, I'm hearing that the really bad guy is a fugitive."

"And possibly a successful fugitive. My guess is that Velnikov has gotten away completely. The Russians haven't ever been cooperative about extradition, and here, the fugitive is a Russian citizen charged with complicated, hard-to-prove banking crimes."

"So this is the way it ends."

"Robert, listen." Maria sounded desperate. "I want you to take me on a serious vacation. I need a vacation. And you need a vacation."

Her exasperation increased. "I want us to go away for a month, at least. To . . . to . . . Italy. I want us to rent a villa near Florence. In the olive oil and wine country, in Tuscany."

"Well," Robert said slowly, "that may be difficult for a little while."

There was a silence. It was Tom who finally broke it. "Maria, what Robert's trying to say is, we signed up a new case this morning. A big case. Bigger than the Velnikov Bank case."

"And there are some things we need to do right away." Robert immediately was upbeat. Even excited.

"Robert . . . vacation . . . we need. . . ."

"This is a good case," Robert said happily. "The kind of case we all went to law school to handle."

"You've . . . got . . . another huge case . . . already?" By now, her exasperation had become incredulity.

"Well . . . ahhhhh . . . yes. . . . But this one is a really good case."

Another silence. Until finally, Maria spoke. Her voice was as resigned as Robert's had been at the beginning of the conversation.

"Here . . . we go . . . again," she said softly.

Postscript

I've tried to write this book so that the lawyering is real. So that the lawyers do what lawyers really do, and so that the legal issues are true to life. That's been my objective in all of my books.

In a democracy, especially one that uses juries, ordinary citizens need to understand the law. But the trouble is, most Americans get their information about the justice system from fiction. And the fiction that they read doesn't show the law the way it is. It ranges from television foolishness to the novels of John Grisham. These are not very good sources for understanding how the law works.

Take Grisham's biggest early book, *The Firm*. That was a well-constructed novel, no question: an excellent novel in terms of what makes a novel. But it was not about lawyers. For example, if you left this particular "Firm," the partners would have you killed. I've known some firms where the work would kill you if you stayed there, but I've never known a firm where you'd be killed if you left. And that's not the only transmogrification of the legal system in *The Firm*. With the kinds of weird ideas that come from a book like that, people have little chance of using the democracy to make sure the justice system is working right. I get a kick out of reading Grisham sometimes myself. He's been phenomenally successful, of course, and again, *The Firm* is a fine novel; it's just that no one can learn about the legal system from it.

At the same time, all fiction requires a degree of distortion. Many tasks in the law, just like many tasks anywhere, are boring, but the objective of a novel isn't to be boring. Instead, it's to be interesting and readable. And so, good fiction requires compression of events and characters, which means that it has to depart from reality to some degree. I've tried to depart less than other books, but there always are some fictional unrealities.

And so, in all of my books, I've included a postscript, like this one, to point out what is real and what is not.

* * *

First of all, this story features Jimmy Coleman as the bad guy from the big law firm. The public seems to believe that small-firm lawyers are more likely to be ethical than big-firm lawyers. I don't think so, myself. In my experience, big-firm lawyers are just as good people as small-firm lawyers, and they are no more likely to pull dirty tricks than lawyers in little firms. In fact, it's somewhat the opposite. What I've seen is that the most unreliable lawyers tend to be in small firms or in solo practices. I guess the reason is, to be an acceptable player in a big firm, you have to make an adequate effort to play by the rules.

But in deference to the general public attitude, I've made Jimmy Coleman a bad guy. And his minions accept him as a bad guy. It's one of my concessions to the demands of fiction. I've never known anyone who was as entirely sleazy as Jimmy is, although I've seen most of his tricks and I've seen (a very few) lawyers who came close. Jimmy's evil persona is a type of dramatic compression, to give this story a serviceable villain.

Another misconception, I think, is the apparent belief of the public that big-firm lawyers have huge advantages over smaller-firm lawyers. The genuine mega-case, involving billions of dollars, millions of documents, and hundreds of witnesses, does require a big firm, or at least a medium-sized firm with backup from other firms and from by-the-job contract lawyers. But the case in this book is not that kind of case, and a big firm would not have an advantage. In the final analysis, a big firm is just a group of lawyers who staff a case according to its requirements. A big firm is really just a shifting group of smaller firms under one roof. In fact, I think a small firm may have an advantage in some kinds of cases, and sometimes, experienced lawyers leave big firms to start boutique practices. They think they'll be able to practice at a higher level of quality by setting up a smaller firm. My local newspaper carried a story on the day that these words were written, telling about my former student Don Looper's decision to leave Looper, Reed and McGraw, which is a big firm and a fine one, to start his own new firm. It will be a much smaller firm, doing the kind and quality of work that Don wants to do, with people he wants to have lunch with.

Along that line, many members of the public have low regard for prosecutors and high regard for lawyers who defend people accused of crime. I've done both, and I don't agree with that view. Assistant district attorneys are people who went to the same law schools as other lawyers, and they have concerns about guilt and innocence that parallel public attitudes. At the same time, the public sometimes assumes that defense lawyers have a hard time defending clients they know are guilty. Not so, because unfortunately, most of their clients are guilty, and there wouldn't be anyone to defend the majority of the accused population if defense lawyers had a rule against guilty clients—even clients guilty of horrible crimes. Instead, the hardest cases for criminal defense lawyers involve clients they believe are innocent. The pressure is disproportionate, then.

At the same time, it should surprise nobody when a defense lawyer argues to a jury a theory that he doesn't believe at all, himself—and makes it sound as though he believes it. That's what we, the public, tell them to do, through our system! And we hope that the result will be the conviction of most of those who are provably guilty, and the acquittal of as close to all of the innocent as is humanly possible. Our system does better at this than people sometimes suppose, if you take into account only people who have been detected, apprehended, and charged. Detection and proof-gathering are the most uncertain parts of the system.

I'm not sure about the damage amounts that are negotiated, won, and lost in this book. We've had lots of so-called "tort reform" legislation, which supporters believe is good but detractors think is "deform" rather than reform. These changes have reduced the recoverable damages in personal injury and death cases. Amounts like a hundred million dollars may sound dramatic, but they would be huge amounts for a negligence recovery, even in a multiple-person death case. They could happen, conceivably, and so they are fair to write about in fiction, although I don't think these damage amounts are typical.

* * *

The Motion to Dismiss that Jimmy argues against Robert is realistic in most ways. In recent years, the Supreme Court has made dismissals easier to get in a federal courts by adding to the required information that a plaintiff has to include in the original suit papers. But my story makes a minor departure from reality, because under the Federal Rules, the arguments can only involve the facts that are claimed in the plaintiff's suit papers. My story has the lawyers arguing about all of the known facts, in general, rather than arguing the claims in the plaintiff's suit (in the "complaint").

If you adjust to thinking of Jimmy's argument as claiming that the facts asserted in the complaint are not enough, and are too "speculative," then the scene is close to reality. But even my law students have great difficulty in absorbing the legal standard for a Motion to Dismiss. You have to be able to distinguish between the facts that actually happened, many of which are unknown to the plaintiff at the beginning of the suit, and the facts stated in the plaintiff's complaint, which reflect the lawyer's imperfect knowledge. I didn't try to convert this scene into a law-school-type effort for the reader, and so the scene is not quite right—but it's close.

The deposition questions are realistic. Depositions are a device by which lawyers question witnesses under oath, including the other side's witnesses, and find out what the facts in the lawsuit are, in detail. The idea is that this kind of "discovery," as it is called, leads to better trials. I often have my doubts, because sometimes it appears that all that discovery produces is just more expense. But that's our system (which is the most expensive in the world). Lawyers can also ask written questions and demand documents, and these kinds of discovery are even more expensive.

My story shows the strategy of trying to shield one's own witnesses from having their depositions taken by the other side. This strategy is used sometimes, and so is answering incompletely and withholding key documents. I've also seen a few lawyers use Jimmy's tactic of objecting to every question, and it can be effective at preventing the opposing lawyer from getting information. It can also produce confusing answers and make the deposition hard to use at trial. It's a dubious trick, but it's hard to prevent. And it works sometimes.

One method of insulating a witness from deposition, which is shown in this book, is to have the witness plead the Fifth Amendment. I've seen that done a surprising number of times. It makes sense, because the guiltiest civil defendants can be guilty of crimes too, and they're entitled to plead the Fifth. The tactic makes a mess for the plaintiff's lawyer because there is no uniform way of handling it in civil cases, as there is in the criminal courts. The guilty defendant wants to have his lawyer depose everybody on the plaintiff's side, assert the privilege against self-incrimination himself to avoid being deposed, and then sandbag the plaintiff by testifying at trial, so as to know everything about the adversary but spring his story as a surprise on an unknowing plaintiff. That situation is depicted in this case, and so is a tactic I've seen a few times: the defense lawyer pretends to call the defendant as a witness, but then feigns a sudden realization that "the plaintiffs haven't proved their case." Then, the defense lawyer pronounces, with conviction, "So come back down from the witness stand, Mr. Defendant! We don't need you to testify after all, because the other side doesn't have any evidence."

One of the hardest scenes to write was the one where Robert meets with Francel Williams and makes a "deal" with the "other defendants."

Readers did not seem to realize, at first, that different parties in a lawsuit with seemingly antagonistic interests often have important interests in common, and in this situation, they may make agreements to cooperate in front of the jury. In this case, Robert's interest is in persuading the jury to find that the Bank is the party most at fault. Robert would be trying to do that in the trial, anyway. If he succeeds only in getting the jury to say that the Bank is, say, ten percent (10%) at fault, he will recover from the Bank only ten percent of the damages the jury finds. A bigger percentage of fault on the Bank leads to a bigger recovery for Robert's clients. And the other defendants have the same interest. It would benefit El Jefe, the Cartel, and the at-the-scene killers to have the biggest possible percentage of fault put on the Bank. So Robert and Francel have the same objective, here, in spite of being on opposite sides.

But an agreement between Robert and Francel matters less to the other defendants, since it is likely that they will never pay anything anyway. And so Francel gets Robert to throw in a sweetener: a low limit on the entire amount of damages that any of these parties will ever be expected to pay, if they are held liable, and if they ever can pay. The "other defendants" don't care much about the civil suit, of course, because they have bigger problems, but the judge has appointed Francel to represent them, and so he tries to represent them.

Agreements like this are not unusual. I know lawyers who believe that it is practically malpractice to fail to try to "make a deal" with parties on the other side. Of course, when a defense lawyer like Francel argues to the jury along with Robert that the plaintiff's damages are enormous and should be paid by the target defendant, the picture is potentially misleading. The parties are required to disclose an agreement of this kind, so that the jurors can be told about it (as Jimmy tells them, in this story), but there's still a strategic effect from having a defense lawyer argue that the plaintiff is right.

The phrase, "the target defendant," is well known to trial lawyers. A plaintiff's lawyer may sue a handful of defendants instead of just one, or may sue a dozen, or scores of them. But usually, there is one defendant—or there are a few of them—whom the plaintiff's lawyer concentrates upon. Sometimes, the target defendant is the one who is most provably guilty, but sometimes, the biggest factor is the solvency of the target defendant. An old joke says that if Adolf Hitler and his mistress Eva Braun were defendants in a case, and Adolf was penniless, a plaintiff's lawyer would blame only the solvent one: Eva Braun, even if she had almost nothing to do with any wrongdoing. And that's true even if there's much less evidence against Eva. In this story, there is evidence against the Bank too, but its solvency figures into Robert's motivation. It has to, if he is going to represent his clients competently.

The scenes involving jury selection, opening statements, presentation of evidence, and jury arguments are true to life, although they show a shortened view of each step. The jury selection and arguments might consume a day, or multiple days, in a case like this. But the shortened scenes here are examples of dramatic compression: a concession to the needs of telling a good story.

The court's instructions and verdict questions to the jury are mostly realistic, although they are simplified from the technical wording that would be used in a real case in my state. In many courts, the jury does not decide who wins. The jury answers factual questions, such as whose negligence caused the occurrence, what percentages of fault are attributable to each party, and what the amounts of different kinds of damages are. The jury answers these questions about the ultimate, controlling factual issues, and then, the judge is the one who grants judgment. The jury may not know who has won.

In fact, it's often complicated, even for the lawyers, to figure out who has won or how much, especially when the jury assigns different percentages of fault to different defendants. In my state, Texas, a defendant who is found only fifty percent (50%) at fault owes only fifty percent of the total damages suffered by the plaintiff, but a defendant who is assigned more than fifty percent—say, fifty-one percent (51%)—owes the entire amount of damages: one hundred percent. And so, in this case, when the jury assigned only fifty percent of the fault to the Bank, it cut the damages owed by the Bank to only fifty percent of the total damages, or fifty million, instead of one hundred million. The plaintiffs would just have to realize that they'd lost half of the damages they had suffered, since the other defendants could not pay it even if there is a judgment against them. A juror typically will not know the law about this.

The insolvency of the Bank in my story is realistic too. Banks go out of business all the time, and the FDIC—the Federal Deposit Insurance Corporation—swoops down, gets a federal judge to shut the bank down, and sells the assets to another bank, which is able to protect the depositors. Since the creation of the FDIC, bank deposits have been insured. The insurance limit these days is $250,000, which covers most depositors, and the new bank is chosen so that it will protect even larger deposits. In recent years, no depositor has lost money because of an insured bank failure, and depositors' confidence tends to prevent a panic or "run on the bank."

And by the way, settlement of a case can occur at any time, including after the verdict. There were negotiations after the verdict in this story. I've settled cases during the appeal process. It's not uncommon for a case to be settled even after the United States Supreme Court has agreed to hear it, and for the Court to declare that the case has become "moot." Then, it is removed from the Supreme Court's docket without a decision.

* * *

People have asked me about the verdict in which the jury found that the Bank did not act "intentionally." How could the jury have found anything other than that the Bank *did* act intentionally, they ask, since the Bank laundered money and the Bank President talked to El Jefe about the killings in advance? There are two answers.

First, and most probably, the jury might have compromised. There were a few people who didn't think that the Bank was even negligent. How on earth could they think that, you might ask? Well, all kinds of people think all kinds of ways. Sometimes some people discount the testimony of anyone who is himself a criminal, is in custody, or has made an agreement with prosecutors. And some people are just plain irrational. I've heard about jurors who have had a hard time accepting the idea that the oral testimony of witnesses they've heard was "evidence." This kind of thinking drives other jurors crazy, of course. Sometimes, then, the result is an agreement among jurors to give a little up to each side of this argument.

Second, the legal concept of "intent" is not as simple as it sounds. I don't want to make this postscript a treatise, so let me just say that the jurors get definitions of terms like this and sometimes the definitions are hard to apply to real facts in real cases.

* * *

About the psychic in this story: obviously, I don't believe she has supernatural powers. The method that these masters of the occult use, instead, is to gather information from answers to their questions and from the subject's appearance, and to ask further questions or make pronouncements by using that information. The devices described in this story are, indeed, from handbooks that tell aspiring psychics how to do it. A "Barnum Statement" appears to the customer to be an amazing insight but actually is carefully disguised to hide the fact that it applies to almost anyone. It is a standard tactic. So is the "Rainbow Statement," which artfully covers two or more opposite possibilities and therefore impresses the customer with its "rightness."

I've never consulted a psychic, but I know people who have, of course. Usually, it's just for fun. There's no harm in that, and it keeps psychics in business, so that our economy is closer to full employment. Then, there are people—like Maria, here—who believe the stuff. Sometimes, a psychic can provide useful information, not from the spirits, but from intuitions about the customer, which most psychics are good at making. For instance, the psychic may see that the customer is pompous and may advise a little more humility. Or the psychic may infer that the customer is too timid about a particular life choice, and she may suggest a greater boldness. Maybe this kind of thing can even be helpful. Or, maybe it can get people to do harmful things (such as giving thousands of dollars to the psychic).

* * *

The role of the Balamarcas Drug Cartel in this story is, unfortunately, also realistic. El Jefe, whose official name in this book is Alejandro Carlos Gonzales-Huerta, bears some resemblance to Miguel Angel Trevino-Morales, a notorious drug kingpin who was captured on a dirt road near Nuevo Laredo in 2013. A helicopter from the Mexican Navy forced Miguel Angel's vehicle to pull over, and Mexican marines surrounded him and his bodyguard. He had been the head of the Los Zetas Cartel and was known, after the custom of that Cartel, as "Z-40." After that, cartel watchers predicted that leadership of the Zetas would pass to his brother, Omar, but that the command structure would be weakened. The power vacuum would lead to a franchise structure, like what is described in this story after the capture of El Jefe. And that, it was thought, would lead to less violence.

Z-40's reign was a rampage of horrifying violence. George Grayson is a professor at the College of William and Mary and the counterpart in real life of the New York expert whom I invented here (Professor Cuevas). Professor Grayson teaches Latin American politics and is a scholar of drug gangs. He has written a book about the Zetas. As Professor Grayson put it, Z-40 was "the most sadistic drug capo in Mexico. He delights in inflicting torture and pain. He deserves to be in the lowest rungs of Hell." By now, the professor says, most of Los Zeta's leaders are either dead or behind bars, and that may weaken the Zetas. But they are still around. Recently, my local newspaper carried a story about the impending trial of an accused Zeta assassin who murdered a cooperating witness right here in the United States, in Houston. (His lawyers have a simple story: "He wasn't there." It's not their job to help prove his guilt, even if he is in fact a Zeta and even if there's a ton of evidence saying that he did it.)

My description of Mexico's determination to eradicate drug violence is accurate, I think, although there will be a great deal of pain during the time it takes to accomplish that. Mexican President Enrique Peña Nieto was elected in 2012 on a platform that included reducing Mexico's orgy of drug violence. The arrest of Z-40 was an important victory in this war. It was precipitated by a tip to the Navy. Z-40's car carried $2 million in cash, eight rifles, and 500 rounds of ammunition. He was also accompanied, naturally, by an accountant, because after all, a drug lord needs up-to-date information about how well his finances are hidden. The newspaper photograph of this drug emperor shows a well-dressed man who could have stepped out of the pages of *GQ Magazine*, although he wore an open-collar shirt resembling a military uniform. My description of El Jefe is imaginary, especially his Gucci loafers, but the idea of a drug lord as a sharp dresser might fit some of them.

Z-40 was the subject of extradition requests by the United States, just as El Jefe is in my story. A grand jury in the United States had indicted him for a slew of crimes, including murders on both sides of the border, drug trafficking, kidnapping, and of course, money laundering. The Justice Department had advertised a $5 million reward for his capture. And Z-40 is not unique. U.S. citizens need to be aware of the drug violence on this side of the border that originates from Mexico.

Incidentally, I made up the names of the cartels. There isn't a Balamarcas Cartel or an Escondidas Cartel. They're fictionalized, like the names of El Jefe. The locations of the events in Mexico include some real places but are jumbled and aren't in any particular Mexican states. Hermosillo isn't where Durango is, for example, and those places involve different drug gangs.

* * *

The institutions described here of the NSA, the National Security Agency of the United States, are mostly real, as is NSA's capacity to listen in to conversations among Mexican drug dealers. The methods are constantly changing, however, and I don't know that any description will fit tomorrow. Also, I don't know that El Jefe's conversations would be heard simultaneously by a ship, an aircraft and a satellite, but the basic picture is accurate. Actually, three listening posts are not required. Two properly positioned signal acquisitions are enough, although they may require so-called "spherical trigonometry" instead of flat or "Cartesian" mathematics. I haven't been able to verify the location of the collecting point—whether it is the Roaring Creek Station, as I wrote. I imagine that the NSA keeps details confidential. In any event, the system's ability to track a source is amazing, and so are its methods of collecting, deciphering, and translating the contents.

James Bamford, author of *The Shadow Factory* (2008), wrote that the NSA installation at Fort Meade is a "secret city." The "Ninth Floor" is indeed where the top brass are housed. Site M has a computing capacity that defies imagination, just as my story describes. But one potential problem with my story is that El Jefe might have known about the NSA's capabilities. After NSA leaker Edward Snowden despicably published classified NSA information and alerted the enemies of the United States to our intelligence methods, newspapers reported that Latin Americans did not learn anything, because they already knew. One headline said, "Latin America Aware That U.S. Listening In." But what was El Jefe to do? He couldn't avoid the telephone, and he thought his encryption was fine. Like most people, he didn't understand it.

I found that some readers were surprised by the warrant process that the NSA has to go through to read the contents of some kinds of messages. The "FISA Court," with FISA referring to the Foreign Intelligence Surveillance Act, issues warrants. Its operations and its rulings are mostly secret, which has troubled some people. Historically, the NSA has examined "metadata" within the United States—data that do not include the contents of conversations, but that tell only which phone numbers are connected to which other numbers—and NSA personnel cannot legally listen to conversations involving these domestic telephone numbers without warrants from the FISA court. The metadata help to supply the information that supports these warrants. Honestly, I do not know what is required in the case of a conversation within a foreign nation such as Mexico, and I suspect it is difficult to find out exactly what the NSA does to listen to that; but apparently, less is required than what is needed to listen to U.S. conversations. Recently, the German government protested when it found out that the United States had tapped the telephone of the German Chancellor. I doubt that the same kind of warrant is always required for foreign-to-foreign conversations.

Incidentally, people who make broad claims about privacy are heavily critical of the NSA's practices. These criticisms have influenced the top of our Government, and the requirements that the NSA must follow are in flux. They may always be. Foreign conversations are a separate issue. The incident with the German Chancellor shows that it's a sensitive problem, but then again, every major foreign government listens to other foreign governments. I don't think we have a good way of stopping them, and we might not want the United States to be the only one that is disadvantaged internationally by forbidding itself to do it.

* * *

The military maneuvers that are described here, when the Mexican army attacks El Jefe's mountain, are well known. The basic handbook of battle strategy was written in the 1800's by a Prussian tactician named Carl von Clausewitz, and his ideas are still studied today by armies across the world. The tactic called a "flanking maneuver" in my book was a von Clausewitz favorite. One of its best known uses was during the Civil War in the Battle of Chancellorsville, where Robert E. Lee, the Confederate commander, faced Union forces under General Hooker that outnumbered his army by two to one. Lee agreed with his brilliant tactician, Stonewall Jackson, to set up a "fixing force" consisting of enough troops to keep the Union Army convinced that the enemy was in front of them. Meanwhile, Jackson would take his division around to the side (the flank) of the Union ranks and attack from there.

How many troops, Lee wanted to know? "My whole command," was Stonewall's laconic reply. In this manner, the Confederates under Jackson used a concentrated force (another of von Clausewitz's prescriptions) to overwhelm the Union soldiers at a weak point, and from there, they drove to the Union "center of gravity" (which von Clausewitz also described). Unfortunately for the Confederacy, Stonewall Jackson was killed at Chancellorsville by friendly fire—accidental fire from his own troops. Some people believe that the South would have had a chance to win the war had Jackson survived, although I'd say this is doubtful.

The tactics of combat, in von Clausewitz's day and in the present, are unavoidably contradictory. The simpler plan is best, because battle creates massive confusion. In von Clausewitz's elegant phrase, the "fog of war" is ever-present, and it means that complicated plans are likely to fail. The tactics of the Mexican army in my story are more complicated than a simple assault, and this is a disadvantage. But the element of surprise is supremely important, and my description shows the Mexican army surprising El Jefe's forces with a flanking maneuver—in spite of the self-generated confusion that must have resulted from its air-and-ground, divided-forces attack, and in spite of the knowledge El Jefe gained through intelligence. The Israelis are the best in the world at this sort of thing. Acting under conditions of extreme complexity (and therefore confusion), the Israelis have overcome larger forces by surprise, time and time again.

Incidentally, although strategies of war are not usual subjects of study in American education, citizens should know about these things. Just as we need to understand the American political system so that we can vote sensibly, we should have enough basic knowledge to influence decisions about the use of our military forces.

* * *

About the methods of money laundering that are featured in my story: frankly, I don't think it would work well to use a large number of individuals who have nothing, either as borrowers or as depositors. The idea of "layering"—shifting money from one corporation or entity to another—is a part of money laundering, yes, but that's about the only part of the money laundering in this story that is true. My objective is not to describe the techniques to would-be financial detectives, and it isn't to help money launderers, for sure.

* * *

One major truth in my story is that lawyers prefer to settle lawsuits if they can get fair settlement value. And they would say that it is not only what they prefer, but that it is also what they usually think is best for their clients. The lawyers on each side try to handicap lawsuits in the same way that bettors handicap horse races, and they negotiate toward settlements that reflect their expectations about outcomes in potential suits—what statisticians call their "mathematical expectancies." One factor driving this approach is that the cost of litigation is enormous. Often, it is prohibitive in amount, so that the loss from trying a case is bigger than the difference between settlement possibilities and the elusive ideal of complete victory.

Law professors have extensively analyzed the outcomes of trial versus settlement. They describe the phenomenon of the "vanishing trial." Recent figures show that only 1.5 percent of civil cases are resolved by juries in federal courts. One of the law journal articles is entitled "Don't Try," because that is the way in which the American judicial system is trending. The authors say that in most cases, there is a clear winner and a clear loser in a trial. Usually, the loser has mistakenly believed too strongly in his or her case. Settlement is the rational norm, and trials are anomalies that result from erroneous decisions.

And in personal injury and death cases, the loser is most often . . . the plaintiff. Defendants win most of the contested trials that accuse defendants of negligence. The reason is obscure, but I think it is that plaintiffs are ordinary people who have no experience with the realities of the justice system, and who are irrationally hopeful because of the fiction they have read and because of the near-universal reverence Americans have for juries. They think, "I know I am right; I am deserving," and they are bolstered in their belief by contemplating their injuries. But defendants are often larger, more sophisticated entities that have more knowledge of the justice system, because these kinds of well-heeled businesses are the ones who have the money that makes them target defendants in the first place. In my story, Robert's clients refuse to settle—and end up with nothing. That is a frequent outcome from insistence on a trial. Robert was right to advise them as he did, although the clients are the ones who get to decide.

In courtroom fiction, a settlement doesn't produce a fraction of the drama that a trial does. And so, in fiction, a trial has to be chosen as the moral pathway, the high road, even when settlement seems more attractive, to make a readable story. In this way, lawyer fiction tends to create a misleading picture of a trial as more proper, more right, and more moral than settlement. I don't think that's true at all, in real life. My story ends in a trial too, because that's needed for readable fiction, but I try, throughout my novels, to show that Robert Herrick doesn't think trials are any nobler than settlement, and in fact, he believes that it is foolish to refuse to settle when you are offered fair settlement value. Trials are not more moral, in that case.

Many people are of two minds about this. The vanishing trial is a terrible thing, they think. Jury trials are an important part of American justice. It is distressing to see them decline to near-nothingness. But most knowledgeable people also would prefer never to have to have a jury decide something that is important to them. Well-informed people tend to vote with their feet, avoid trials, and settle if they can, even though they revere the idea of the jury.

And this is Robert Herrick's view as well.

— David Crump
Houston, Texas

Visit us at *www.qpbooks.com.*

www.ingramcontent.com/pod-product-compliance
Lightning Source LLC
Chambersburg PA
CBHW051635260626
47170CB00004B/1191